**Kate Hardy** has been a
toddler. When she isn't
theatre, live music, ballet a
husband, student children and their spaniel in Norwich. You can contact her via her website: katehardy.com

**Melissa Senate** has written many novels for Mills & Boon and other publishers, including her debut, *See Jane Date*, which was made into a TV movie. She also wrote seven books for Mills & Boon True Love under the pen name Meg Maxwell. Her novels have been published in over twenty-five countries. Melissa lives on the coast of Maine with her teenage son; their rescue shepherd mix, Flash; and a lap cat named Cleo. For more information, please visit her website, melissasenate.com

Discover more at millsandboon.co.uk

# SURPRISE HEIR FOR THE PRINCESS

### KATE HARDY

# WYOMING MATCHMAKER

### MELISSA SENATE

MILLS & BOON

First Published in Great Britain 2021
by Mills & Boon, an imprint of HarperCollins*Publishers* Ltd
1 London Bridge Street, London, SE1 9GF

www.harpercollins.co.uk

HarperCollins*Publishers*
1st Floor, Watermarque Building,
Ringsend Road, Dublin 4, Ireland

*Surprise Heir for the Princess* © 2021 Pamela Brooks
*Wyoming Matchmaker* © 2021 Melissa Senate

ISBN: 978-0-263-29955-7

0321

MIX
Paper from
responsible sources
FSC™ C007454

This book is produced from independently certified FSC™
paper to ensure responsible forest management.

For more information visit: www.harpercollins.co.uk/green

Printed and bound in Spain
by CPI, Barcelona

# SURPRISE HEIR FOR THE PRINCESS

## KATE HARDY

For Gerard, with all my love.

# CHAPTER ONE

THE VIEW FROM the ferry was almost enough to persuade Liam to give up portraits for landscape photography. A milky turquoise sea reflecting the deep red ball of the setting sun, a sky that looked almost airbrushed from hazy blue at the horizon to deep peach at the top, and the sun itself starting to dip behind the silhouetted island of San Rocello. He'd never seen anything so gorgeous.

But he wasn't here on holiday; he was here to take the official photographs of Princess Vittoria di Sarda, before her grandfather stepped down and she took over as the ruler of the little Mediterranean kingdom.

Although Liam's discussions with the king's private secretary had gone some way to reassuring him that he'd been chosen on the merit of his work, the commission still felt a bit like nepotism. The princess's younger sister Isabella happened to be his own little sister Saoirse's best friend, and he knew that Izzy had suggested him to her grandfather for the job.

He took a deep breath. This flutter of nerves was absolutely ridiculous. He'd photographed plenty of people for upmarket magazines and Sunday supplements, including A-list celebrities and high-ranking politicians. Some of his work hung in the National Portrait Gallery in London. And he'd honed his social skills during his apprenticeship, so he was comfortable mixing at any level of society.

But this was the first time he'd been commissioned to take a royal portrait.

And he had a fine line to walk. The private secretary had explained that the king wanted a formal portrait of the future queen. Izzy had scoffed. 'Nonno will want you to take something stuffy, with Rina dolled up in a posh frock, dripping in jewels and wearing a sash.'

'That's pretty standard stuff for a princess,' Liam had pointed out.

'And it's about a century out of date,' Izzy had grumbled. 'I hate the way the palace stifles her. The world needs to see the woman behind the tiara.'

*The woman behind the tiara.*

All the press photographs and the paparazzi snaps Liam had seen of Vittoria di Sarda showed a cool, collected and businesslike woman. Perfectly groomed, always with a faint smile. Not quite Mona Lisa, but heading that way. She certainly wasn't a scatty ball of energy, like her little sister; looking at Izzy, seeing her laugh in his kitchen with his sister and munching toast, anyone would think that she was just another art student rather than a princess. Vittoria, on the other hand, looked every inch a royal.

The portrait her grandfather wanted would work perfectly well. Vittoria traditionally wore her dark hair in a classic and slightly old-fashioned style that reminded Liam of Grace Kelly; she had a gorgeous bone structure, and arresting violet eyes that reminded him of a young Elizabeth Taylor. She could definitely carry off the traditional pose with posh frock, diamonds and royal regalia.

But Izzy had also shown him some selfies from her

phone, just to prove her own description. 'See? She looks like sunshine when she smiles.'

Vittoria di Sarda looked much softer in those candid snaps. Sweeter. She glowed. She didn't look like the woman who was about to start running a country; she looked approachable and warm.

He shook himself.

He shouldn't be thinking along those lines. Apart from the fact that he'd never get involved with a client, he'd learned the hard way that careers and relationships didn't mix. He'd already done the raising a family bit, when he was eighteen and Saoirse was twelve; although he'd never regretted his decision to walk away from his place at university to get a job and look after his little sister, ensuring she wasn't taken into care, his girlfriends had resented the time he'd spent with his sister. Some of them had taken the 'it's not you, it's me' tack when they'd dumped him, but the more honest ones had said they didn't want to settle down and raise a young teenager when they weren't much older than that themselves. They'd wanted to go out to parties and have fun, not stay at home. The fact that Saoirse was his only living relative and really important to him had just passed them by.

Later on, when Saoirse was older and didn't need him so much, his girlfriends had resented the time he spent on his career. Time spent travelling, or on a shoot, or in his darkroom, or working on a digital image. They couldn't see the tiny differences on an image that he could, and got fed up hanging around waiting for him.

Liam was tired of being torn in two and made to feel guilty, so he'd kept all his relationships casual over the last few years. He wanted to focus on his career, on his goal: of becoming the best portrait photographer of his generation.

And maybe, just maybe, Vittoria di Sarda would be the one to help him get there.

Vittoria finished reading her dossier.

Liam MacCarthy, photographer and older brother of her little sister Izzy's best friend. A man who'd turned down a place at university after their mother had been killed, who'd brought up his sister and who still lived with her in London. A nice guy, according to both Izzy and Pietro, Izzy's bodyguard; it seemed he'd taken Izzy under his wing, too, over the last three years. A man whose actions showed he believed in family and duty, just like hers.

But this commission to take her official portrait wasn't nepotism. He was good at his job. Seriously good. His work featured in upmarket magazines and Sunday supplements, and he already had work hanging in the National Portrait Gallery in London. He'd take the kind of portrait her grandfather wanted, and do it well.

Even so, Vittoria wasn't looking forward to the sitting. Over the last year, she'd felt more and more stifled at the palace. She was prepared to become queen—since her father's untimely death in a yachting accident when she was eleven, she'd been pretty much in training to step up to the throne—but her mother and grandmother were pressuring her to make a dynastic marriage before her coronation.

Once, she'd dreamed of marrying for love. Rufus, the fellow student she'd fallen head over heels for during their MBA year, seemed to feel the same way about her; and he'd loved her for herself, not because she was

Princess Vittoria di Sarda of San Rocello. She'd thought he was going to ask her to marry him. Until he'd actually met her family and realised that their life together would be lived on the equivalent of a floodlit stage; Rufus had backed away, saying that he loved her, but he really couldn't handle the royal lifestyle.

It had taught Vittoria that love wasn't compatible with duty. But she still couldn't quite bring herself to agree to get engaged to José, the son of a Spanish duke that her mother and grandmother had lined up as an eligible suitor. They'd met a few times socially and had absolutely nothing in common. But time—and suitable men—were both running out. She had to make a decision. Sooner, rather than later, with her grandfather wanting to step down at the end of the year.

If only she could escape for a few days to clear her head. Somewhere she could think things through without any pressure…

The next morning, Liam headed for the Palazzo Reale in the centre of the capital. The palace was a huge Renaissance-era building, built from pale cream stone; its tall windows were flanked with louvred shutters, painted the same cream as the stone. The imposing entrance had marble steps leading up to huge bronze doors.

Liam re-read the instructions in the email from the Private Secretary, Matteo Battaglia; he went over to the security checkpoint to introduce himself, then went through the security procedure before being escorted to the Private Secretary's office by one of the guards.

'Delighted to meet you, Mr MacCarthy.' The Private Secretary shook his hand.

'*Buongiorno*. Delighted to meet you, too, Signor Battaglia,' Liam responded.

Signor Battiglia gave him an approving smile and took him through to the king's office.

Liam remembered what Izzy had told him when he'd asked how he should address her family. It was the same as for the English royal family; he should call her grandfather 'Your Majesty' and Vittoria 'Your Royal Highness' the first time, and then 'sir' or 'ma'am'.

He waited politely for the king to speak.

'Good morning, Mr MacCarthy.' King Vittorio held out his hand for Liam to shake.

'*Buongiorno, Vostro Maestà.* Thank you for inviting me here.'

The royal visage was completely impassive and Liam didn't have a clue what was going through the king's head. 'Princess Isabella speaks highly of you.'

'That's good to know, sir.' All this formality made the neck of Liam's shirt feel tight; Liam rarely wore a suit at work, but today was definitely a suit and tie day. What he really wanted to do was to get his camera out and start work.

There was a slight twinkle in King Vittorio's eye when he added, 'Though Izzy also says your coffee is atrocious.'

It broke the ice and Liam laughed, relaxing for the first time since he'd walked into the palace. 'I'm afraid my barista skills aren't quite up to my darkroom skills, sir.'

'So you'll be using traditional film rather than digital?'

Liam was pleased that the king was aware of the difference. 'A mixture, sir,' he said. 'I use a digital camera a lot of the time, but I like analogue. There's something special about developing a print.'

'Indeed.' King Vittorio inclined his head. 'I liked the photographs you took for that article on Shakespearean actors. Quite remarkable how you dressed them all in plain black and yet they still looked like the characters of their most famous roles.'

And that was enough to finally convince Liam that he'd been given the job on merit and not just because of his little sister's friendship with Izzy. The king had actually seen his work and liked it. 'Thank you, sir. I asked them to declaim their favourite speeches and took the shots as they talked. I think a face should always tell the story in a portrait.'

The king made a noncommittal noise. 'Let's take you to Vittoria. She's waiting for us in the Throne Room. Walk with me,' he added imperiously.

Didn't protocol mean that you had to walk behind a king? Liam wondered. But the king had said to walk *with* him. Perhaps he could compromise by being half a step behind.

Liam hauled his tripod and camera over his shoulder and walked through the corridor with the king. The place was amazing and, although he specialised in portraits, there were plenty of little details that made him itch to photograph them. The black and white marble floors, the full-length windows hung with voile curtains, the silk wall hangings. And he'd just bet there was a suite of rooms with a classic enfilade, where the doors between each room were so perfectly aligned that you could see every doorway from one end of the suite. He could just imagine taking a series of portraits of the princess, one in every doorway...

Then they walked into the Throne Room. The red carpet was so thick that Liam literally sank into it with every step. The walls were hung with red damask silk; the high ceilings were painted in cream and gold, and Venetian gilt and glass chandeliers hung down, glittering. On one wall there was an oil painting of King

Vittorio, next to portraits of various others that Liam assumed were former kings; all were set in heavy, ornate gold frames. There was a white marble fireplace with a mirror above it reflecting the chandeliers, and on the mantelshelf sat an ornate ormolu clock flanked by matching candelabra.

It was all very traditional, and a portrait taken here would send out a very strong message.

There were two thrones in red velvet on a raised dais at the far end of the room. Sitting on one of the thrones, reading, was a young woman.

Vittoria di Sarda.

'Vittoria, may I introduce Liam MacCarthy, photographer? Mr MacCarthy, this is my granddaughter, Princess Vittoria,' King Vittorio said.

She closed her book, setting it down on the throne next to her, and stood up.

The press photographs and even Izzy's snaps hadn't done her any justice.

Vittoria di Sarda was absolutely stunning.

You could drown in the depths of those violet eyes.

Liam opened his mouth and found himself silenced. Not good. He wanted her to see him as he was: a professional, not some tongue-tied bumbler.

He'd met lots of beautiful women in his working life, and dated several equally beautiful women in his private life, but none of them had made his pulse race like this.

'I'm delighted to meet you, *Vostra Altezza Reale*,' he said, just about managing to string the words together. Thank God Izzy and her bodyguard Pietro had spent the last week schooling his Italian pronunciation and teaching him important phrases. Otherwise he might have accidentally called her a festering slug or something equally terrible instead of 'Your Royal Highness'.

'My sister's said a lot about you, Mr MacCarthy,' she said, offering him her hand to shake.

His skin tingled where hers touched his, and he didn't know what to say.

This was crazy. He wasn't a talker, as such, but he was always good with his clients, conversing just enough to put them at their ease. If he carried on like this, the portrait he ended up with would be even worse than the stuffy waxwork Izzy was worried he might end up taking.

He dragged himself together with an effort. 'Thank you for sparing the time to see me, ma'am.'

'You could hardly take my portrait without me actually being here,' she pointed out.

Was she teasing him or irritated by him? He couldn't tell. That beautiful face was inscrutable.

Best to play it safe and be businesslike. 'With your permission, ma'am, I'll set up my equipment.' At her nod, he did so in silence, but he kept glancing at her. She was dressed perfectly for the formal, old-fashioned portrait that Vittorio had requested, in a white haute couture gown teamed with a midnight-blue velvet cloak, a sash and a royal badge. Her hair was styled very simply, and she wore a tiara with matching earrings, necklace and bracelet.

Dripping in diamonds.

Was that what people wanted from a modern princess? Wealth, haughtiness and an air of distance? Or did they want something warmer, a view of a woman who had something in common with them?

Liam itched to take a different set of photographs from the one he'd been commissioned to do. To remove the sash and the diamonds, replace them with single pearl earrings and a single-strand pearl necklace, and end up with a softer and sexier look—like Beaton's 1954 portrait of Elizabeth Taylor or Karsh's gorgeous 1956 portrait of Grace Kelly.

Maybe he could talk her into letting him take a second set of portraits. Especially as he'd promised to take one for Izzy.

Though he wanted to take one for himself, too. He wanted to see the woman behind the tiara. The woman she kept hidden. The woman whose smile was like sunshine.

'I'll leave you to it,' King Vittorio said.

'Thank you, sir.'

'Give my love to my granddaughter when you're back in London.'

'Of course, sir.'

Liam waited until the king had left. Vittoria, while she was waiting for him to finish setting up, had her nose back in her book. He couldn't resist a quick snap.

The sound of the shutter alerted her, and she stared at him. 'Why did you do that?'

'Testing for white balance, ma'am,' he fibbed.

'I won't insult you, Mr MacCarthy, by saying that I hope none of the photographs you take today appear anywhere without the prior approval of the palace press office,' she said coolly.

She really *was* a royal, he thought. An ice princess. But he'd like to see more of the woman he thought she might be behind that image. The sister Izzy had described—the woman who'd been sitting lost in a book. That moment had reminded him of his sister, when she was small: how Saoirse had always lost herself in a book, like her favourite fairy tale princess Belle.

Was that who Vittoria was, behind the tiara?

'Of course, ma'am.' Wanting to reassure her, he added, 'The contract I signed stipulated that all negatives and original files will be the property of the House of di Sarda, to use as you wish, and I'll be credited with the images.'

'Good. Then let's get this over with.'

Interesting, he thought. As a woman who was destined to be a queen, she must surely have grown up very used to having her photograph taken. He couldn't help wondering: did she, like Izzy, want a different portrait from the one her grandfather had commissioned?

He looked at her. 'Once we've taken the official portraits, ma'am, would you allow me to take a portrait for Izzy? I mean, Princess Isabella,' he corrected himself swiftly. He didn't have the same easy, familiar relationship with this woman that he did with her sister, so he needed to be more formal in the way he referred to Izzy.

She tipped her head very slightly to one side, and his pulse went up another notch as he realised how beautiful her mouth was. *Kissable.* He really had to get a grip.

'What does Izzy want?' Princess Vittoria asked, surprising him with a lapse into informality.

He was taking a risk, but he caught her fleeting expression and it gave him the courage to be honest. 'Something that makes you—and I quote—not look like a stuffed waxwork.'

She laughed, and for the first time he saw a glimpse of the sister Izzy adored. At that moment he knew that *this* was the woman he wanted to photograph, not the official Princess.

'That sounds like Izzy.' She paused. 'Your little sister's best friend.'

He inclined his head. 'I'm sure your security team

has a dossier on me.' What did surprise him was that she might have bothered to read it.

She inclined her head. 'Let me see. Aged thirty. Never married. Didn't go to university—but you finished your A levels while looking after your sister, and then you took an apprenticeship.'

He shrugged. 'University wasn't an option. It's irrelevant.' But he knew just as much about her, thanks to some research on the internet and a conversation or two with her sister. 'Did you enjoy studying in London— economics for your first degree and then for your MBA?'

*'Toccato,'* she said. 'You clearly have a dossier on me.'

'I need to know my subjects before I take their portrait,' he said. 'The whole point of a portrait is to tell a story. To show the world who you really are.'

'Goodness. That's frightfully intimidating.'

He threw the ball back in her court. 'Only if you have something to hide.'

'Call me Dorianna Grey?'

There was an edge to her humour.

He couldn't work her out. They'd never met before. And yet the way he found himself instinctively responding to her... *My dear Lady Disdain.* Except Vittoria was a few rungs higher up the social scale than a lady.

He looked into those stunning violet eyes and, for a second, he couldn't breathe. And then, shockingly, he realised how much he wanted to kiss her. To feel her mouth against his. To coax a response from her. To kiss her until they were both dizzy.

That desire was completely inappropriate, for a multitude of reasons. Vittoria di Sarda was his client, and he never mixed business with pleasure. She was the sister of his little sister's best friend, which made her pretty much off limits; because when it got messy—and it *would* get messy—that would make life difficult for Saoirse. And Vittoria was from a completely different world, one where he didn't belong.

*Focus,* he reminded himself.

This was business.

'Izzy loves you,' he said.

'And Saoirse loves you.'

He liked the fact that she pronounced his sister's name properly. *Sur-sha.* 'She's a good kid.'

Vittoria raised an eyebrow. 'You could have gone to university.'

Not to Edinburgh, where he'd planned to study. They'd lost their mum five months before his A levels, in a car accident; how could he uproot Saoirse and drag her off to a city where she knew nobody and where he'd be too busy studying to spend enough time with her to help her settle in properly? Becoming a teenager was hard enough; he'd wanted to keep things as stable for her as he could, which meant she needed to stay at the home and school she knew. 'I have a diploma and plenty of professional experience. A degree wouldn't have added anything.'

'You put your duty before your own needs,' she said softly.

His duty to look after Saoirse. There hadn't been anyone else to do it; their father had died when Saoirse was small and their grandparents had either been very elderly and needing care themselves or had passed away.

But it hadn't just been duty, and he wanted Vittoria to know that. He'd never seen Saoirse as a burden and he never would. 'My sister isn't my duty,' he said, equally softly. 'She's my *family.*'

Again, there was a fleeting expression in her eyes before the royal mask came back. But it was there for long enough for him to see it and recognise it as wistfulness.

So was Izzy right? Was Vittoria suppressing herself for the sake of duty? Because she loved her family?

Not that it was any of his business.

'What else is in your dossier?' she asked.

'That you're a patron of several charities.' Izzy hadn't been clear about whether Vittoria had chosen them herself or whether their grandfather had chosen them.

And then there was the duty aspect. 'That you lost your dad when you were young—' like him '—so you're next in line to the throne and your coronation will be at Christmas,' he added.

'Nonno wishes to stand down,' she said.

'And how do you feel, becoming the Queen of San Rocello at the age of twenty-eight?'

'That,' she said, 'is irrelevant.'

Echoing his own answer to her. And that told him everything: like him, she'd chosen duty before her own desires. And she'd made that choice for the love of her family.

Though he did need to know how she felt. It would affect the portrait.

Maybe he could try a different tack. But what?

Not her love life. Although the paparazzi had photographed her with several eligible men over the years, she didn't appear to have a partner. Though Izzy had muttered something dark about their mother, their grandmother and an arranged marriage.

Could someone royal marry for love? Or did they have to marry someone politically suitable?

Not that *that* was any of his business, either.

'What were you reading?' he asked instead.

She raised an eyebrow. 'What do you think I was reading?'

This felt like a test. Fiction, non-fiction, poetry, a play? He had no idea what she liked reading, but he definitely had the impression that words were important to her. 'If you were Izzy, it'd be something frothy. If you were Saoirse, it'd be something political. If you were me...' He looked her straight in the eye. 'Words, words, words,' he quoted softly.

She laughed. 'So which of us is Polonius?'

He was pleased she'd picked up the reference. 'Neither, I hope. Though he did have a point about being true to yourself.'

'Is that why you take portraits?'

'People interest me,' he said.

'And you read Shakespeare? Or was *Hamlet* your A level text?'

'The dossier again?' he asked.

'Photography, English Literature, History and History of Art.' She ticked off his subjects on her fingers.

'Economics, Maths and History,' he countered. Subjects perfect for a future queen: a background in tradition, with modern business sensibilities. 'Mine were pretty much your opposite, though obviously there's a bit of science in photography—physics and chemistry.'

*Chemistry.*

That was a stupid word to use. Because it made him think of a different sort of chemistry. The one that made him notice the exact curve of her mouth, the length of her eyelashes, the tilt of her nose.

*Focus,* he reminded himself again. 'Would you prefer your official photographer to have a degree?'

'No. I was wondering if you minded. Four top-grade A levels—you could've had your pick of any university.'

He'd be honest with her. 'I minded a bit when I was eighteen,' he said. 'But Saoirse was more important to me. Twelve isn't a great age to move to a different school, let alone a different city. I still ended up with the career I wanted; the apprenticeship meant I learned my trade hands-on instead of in a lecture room. And my old photography tutor lent me books and invited Saoirse and me over for dinner once a month so I could talk theory with her and discuss composition, while Saoirse did the usual teenage girl things with her daughters. I owe her a lot.'

'The woman you dedicated your first award to.'

He nodded. And not just because of the tuition. Patty had helped him convince the authorities that he was perfectly capable of looking after Saoirse. Luckily his mum had already taught him how to cook a few simple dishes, so he'd be able to look after himself as a student. His mum had owned the house outright since his dad's death; and the proceeds of her life insurance meant that he and Saoirse could pay the bills until he was earning a decent salary and could support them both. 'And if she could see me now, she'd be cross that I was chatting about myself instead of focusing on my subject.'

'Very diplomatically put,' she said. 'I can see why Izzy likes you.'

'I like Izzy. And she's safe with me.'

'I already knew that,' she said.

'Because of the dossier?'

'Because Pietro likes you,' she corrected.

She'd discussed him with her sister's security detail?

And then he realised. This was what her life must be like. A series of dossiers, learning about people so you could be politically discreet. Knowing that everything you did, everything you said, would be analysed, and not always correctly. Living your life in the public eye, twenty-four-seven.

Which was exactly why King Vittorio had asked for a traditional portrait, Liam realised. To put across the message that the public face of the monarchy might change, but the monarchy itself would go on.

Why hadn't Izzy told her that Liam MacCarthy was gorgeous?

Tall, with dark hair he'd clearly tried to tame today in deference to his royal clients, cornflower-blue eyes and fair skin. And the most beautiful mouth...

She shook herself. Ridiculous. Liam MacCarthy was here to take her portrait, that was all.

Nothing could possibly happen between them. They were from different worlds and she'd learned from Rufus that getting involved with someone not from her own background led to heartbreak.

She ought to just let him get on with this. Let him take the portrait her grandfather wanted, then leave.

But he was the first man in years who'd made her feel a spark. Who'd fenced with her, responded to teasing.

She'd liked his quick wit. The way he'd quoted Shakespeare at her and picked up her veiled references—unlike José, who'd simply looked blank and turned the conversation back to cars.

Liam MacCarthy intrigued her.

Which was exactly why she should be on her utmost regal dignity with him. She couldn't afford to react to him as a man.

'Where do you want me?' The words slipped out before she could stop them.

Oh, no. That sounded like flirting. 'To sit for the

portrait, I mean,' she added swiftly. 'Unless you'd prefer me to stand.'

He gave her an assessing look, and heat curled up through her, from the bottom of her feet to the top of her head. 'If you don't mind, ma'am, I'd like to take a range of shots.'

Back to the formal 'ma'am'.

Of course he wouldn't call her Rina, the way her sister did—short for Vittorina, her family pet name. He wouldn't even call her Vittoria. To him, she was Your Royal Highness or ma'am.

Sometimes, protocol really grated on her; yet, at the same time as it made her feel boxed in, she recognised that it protected her.

He directed her to sit, to stand, to change position. He changed the lighting and worked almost in silence. Vittoria felt herself growing more and more twitchy, then her impatience finally burst out. 'Do all your sittings take this long?'

'That depends, ma'am, on my subject.'

She met his gaze; he masked it quickly, but for a moment she was sure she could see the same heat in his eyes that she felt pulsing through her.

'The sitting goes more quickly for both of us if my subject talks to me,' he said. 'Like the ones I did of the Shakespearean actors. They declaimed their favourite speeches from their favourite roles.'

Sometimes it felt as if she were playing a role. But she didn't have any new speeches. 'So is this where I tell you all about San Rocello, its exports and its history?'

'You could—but that's the economist in you talking.' He paused. 'Tell me what you love doing. Tell me about your passion.'

*Passion.* Something else she had to suppress. A

queen couldn't be passionate. A queen needed to be diplomatic and sensible. A royal first and a woman second.

Looking at his mouth, she could imagine it moving
in passion, and she had to suppress the sudden shiver
of desire.

Things weren't meant to be this way, and it tipped
her off balance. It also made her cross with herself.
She'd been trained to react with dignity and calm. A
queen-in-waiting. But something about him made her
react to him as a woman—something deep and prime-
val and which she didn't really understand. She wasn't
sure whether it scared her more or excited her.

What did she say?

She glanced round the room.

Thankfully someone had put a silver bowl of roses on
a low table and she seized on them gratefully. 'Roses,'
she said. 'They're my passion.'

'Sadly, it's slightly too early in the year for roses,
or I'd suggest a few shots by the roses I assume are in
the palace gardens,' he said. 'But you can tell me about
your favourite rose. Describe its colour, its scent, the
touch of its petals.'

His voice was husky and incredibly sensual, and her
mind was translating his words into something else
entirely.

Please don't let the heat she could feel in her cheeks
actually be visible.

'Ma'am?'

'Call me Vittoria.' The words came out before she
could stop them.

'Vittoria,' he said softly.

And, oh, she could imagine him saying that as he
drew her into his arms for a kiss…

She shook herself. 'I was lying about the roses.'

'Would I be right in guessing books are your passion?'

Yes, and she didn't get anywhere near enough time to read. Which made her feel even more trapped and frustrated—but she didn't want him to guess that. It was private. Something she needed to keep to herself. She shrugged. 'You saw me reading when you came here.'

'And the palace has a library?'

'Yes, of course.'

'Show me, Vittoria.'

It wasn't so much a command as a request. A temptation. She didn't dare move.

'When Saoirse was small,' he said, 'her favourite story was *Beauty and the Beast*. She loved the film, too, and she used to sing the soundtrack all the time. Mum and I took her to see the stage show for her birthday when she was seven. I remember, it was a matinee. Not the sort of thing your average thirteen-year-old boy would put up with, but I went because I knew it'd make my mum and my sister happy. She loved every second, and she loved it even more when we went for dinner afterwards and the waitress lowered the lights and came out carrying an ice-cream with a fountain candle. The whole restaurant sang "Happy Birthday" to her.'

The yearning in his eyes as he shared the memory made Vittoria's heart crack a little.

'That was a bright spot. And I used to tease her that she should have been called Belle.' His eyes met hers. 'And I have a feeling that might be who you really are. The princess who loves stories. The princess whose dream is a castle filled with books.'

He was the first person she'd ever met who'd seen that.

So, instead of ignoring his request, she nodded and beckoned to him to follow her.

# CHAPTER TWO

THE SECOND THEY were in the palace library, Liam's face lit up. 'What a fabulous room. This is perfect. This is where I want to take a photograph of you for Izzy. But you'll need to lose the diamonds.'

'Lose the diamonds?'

He sighed. 'All right. I'll take one with the diamonds, for your grandfather. But do you have a maid or something who can bring you pearls instead?'

'Pearls?' And now Vittoria knew she sounded stupid. As if she were parroting his words.

He took his phone from his pocket and drew up a photograph. 'Like this,' he said.

The subject of the portrait was instantly recognisable. 'Princess Grace of Monaco.'

'It's by Yousuf Karsh. One of the two photographers whose work I admire the most,' he said. 'The simplicity means people focus on the subject, not the trapping. And what I want is you without the diamonds, with a book in your hand, sitting on that window seat. Then I want you to read me your favourite poem.'

No more 'ma'am', she thought. He'd forgotten the protocol completely, to the point where he was bossing her about and telling her what to do. But this was Liam MacCarthy all fired up, seeing a vision he wanted to capture behind his lens. Was this what drove him? She found his purpose and focus irresistible.

'Take the portrait for Nonno, first,' she said, 'while someone fetches the jewellery you want me to wear.' She went to have a quiet word with the footman who waited at the doorway, then followed Liam's directions and posed for a portrait that he deemed suitable for her grandfather.

There was a discreet cough and the footman placed the jewels Liam had asked for on a low table.

'Thank you,' she said. In her view, the staff weren't the invisible servants they might have been a hundred years before. She'd been brought up knowing that their staff did their job so she could do hers, and without them life would be a lot less smooth. They deserved her respect as well as their salary.

'That's perfect. *Grazie,*' Liam added.

She liked the fact that he'd thanked her staff, and she liked it even more that he'd bothered to do it in their own language. This was a man who didn't take things for granted, then. She knew from the dossier that his flat in Chelsea was worth a lot of money, but she now also knew he'd worked for it.

'Do you need help with your jewellery, ma'am?' he asked.

She raised an eyebrow. 'This is the twenty-first century, not two hundred years ago. Princesses are perfectly capable of dressing themselves.'

Amusement glittered in those gorgeous eyes. 'To be fair, two hundred years ago, with all those tiny buttons down the back of a dress, princesses would've needed someone to help them.'

'And how would you know about…? Oh.' It dawned on her. 'You did a photo shoot.'

He inclined his head. 'Plus, Saoirse did a module

on the history of fashion, and part of the assessment included being involved in an exhibition of Regency clothing at the V&A.'

Which obviously he'd taken an interest in, and probably attended. She liked that.

But the idea of him taking off her jewellery made her feel flustered. It was too intimate. 'I can manage,' she said, taking off the tiara and putting it on the table next to the pearls. Her earrings and necklace were next. She replaced them with the simple pearl studs and single string of pearls. And how ridiculous that her hands were shaking slightly. Why on earth was she imagining him lifting her hair away from her nape and pressing a kiss on the skin he uncovered, before fastening the pearls round her neck? Crazy. She *never* had thoughts like this, particularly about someone she'd only just met.

'Is this what you had in mind?' Worse still, her voice was slightly quavery. She really hoped he hadn't noticed.

He stepped back, narrowing his eyes, and assessed her.

She thought—hoped—it was a professional gaze.

'Take off the cloak, the sash and the badge,' he said.

Her dress would be more than acceptable at any society event; it was shoulderless, but perfectly demure. She'd be exposing far more skin if she wore a swimsuit. So why did it make her feel as if she was undressing for him when she took off the cloak, sash and badge?

'And your shoes,' he said. 'I'd like you to sit on the window seat. Draw your feet up and look out of the window.'

She did so. Despite the fact there was a footman in the room with them—and if anyone walked in, they'd simply see a photographer working with his subject—this felt incredibly intimate. As if they were alone. Nobody but the two of them in the whole world. Everyone and everything else just dropped away; she was only aware of Liam. His nearness. The way he looked at her. His mouth. His breathing.

And it was the first time in so long that she'd felt *herself* at the palace. Unfettered. Unstifled. Just Vittoria.

She'd already worked out that, as a portrait photographer, Liam tended to see a little more deeply and pick up more cues than the average person. Would he see that this was the real her, not the princess? And, if so, what would he do about it?

'One more prop,' he said, and took a book from the nearest shelf.

It was a slim volume in red Morocco binding, tooled with gold.

And how incredible that he'd chosen a book at random that she would have picked, given the choice: a copy of Shakespeare's sonnets.

Liam asked her to change position on the window seat several more times, then frowned. 'No. I know what's wrong.' He stepped forward. 'May I?'

She didn't have a clue what he intended, but now he was really up close and personal. His eyes were stunning, and his pupils were so huge that she couldn't see his irises. Was that because of the lower level of light in the room? Or did he feel that same crazy attraction that made her pulse skip?

He stretched one hand towards her and she held her breath for a second.

He mussed her hair slightly; his fingers accidentally brushed her skin and made her feel as if she were burning.

She could feel her lips parting. Could see the expression in his eyes change as he looked at her mouth. Could see his own lips parting.

For a heartbeat, everything stopped; it felt as if it was just the two of them, the sunlight filtering through the window and dancing across their skin. It would be so easy to cross that tiny distance between them. All she had to do was stretch up, very slightly, and kiss him...

Then he coughed and stepped away. 'Ma'am.'

Vittoria felt the colour rush into her cheeks, along with shame. For pity's sake. Liam MacCarthy was here to do a job, and that was all. She'd probably never see him again. He wasn't a man she should let herself moon over, particularly as she wasn't in a position to let herself moon over anyone.

'Read to me,' he said, his voice husky, and a frisson went down her spine.

Shakespeare's sonnets. She didn't need to open the book, because she knew her favourite one by heart; but she hoped that holding the book would act as enough of a barrier—so he'd see her as a queen-to-be, not the girl who dreamed of reading in a castle full of books. Because she knew Liam MacCarthy wasn't the Prince who'd build her a library and she had to put her duty first.

'"My mistress' eyes are nothing like the sun..."'

The beauty of the poem took over and she lost herself in the words, gazing out of the window.

She reached the bit that always amused her. '"I grant I never saw a goddess go; My mistress, when she walks, treads on the ground."'

And then a soft, husky voice took up the final couplet: '"And yet, by heaven, I think my love as rare As any she belied with false compare."'

She hadn't noticed that he'd walked back to her, right up close. She found herself gazing at him, rapt. Those beautiful words, in that beautiful soft Irish accent, held her spellbound.

He reached towards her, and she knew he was going to brush the pad of his thumb along her lower lip. A prelude to a kiss. This time, he wouldn't hold back. This time...

The clock on the mantelpiece chimed the quarter hour, and he drew his hand back.

'Thank you, ma'am, for your patience and co-operation.'

How stupid was he?

Liam was aghast at how he'd nearly made a complete mess of this—you never, ever, crossed the line between a professional relationship and a personal one. Especially when your subject was the granddaughter of a king. A woman who was about to become the queen of her Mediterranean realm.

He started to pack up his camera gear in silence, not trusting his mouth to come out with the wrong words and *really* drop him in it.

'Good afternoon, Mr MacCarthy,' she said, and he hated the way that the gorgeous, soft, sunshiny woman he'd almost kissed had turned back so quickly into the dignified, starchy princess he'd first met. Izzy had said her sister was stifled by the palace, and he could see that for himself. There was a huge difference between the almost shy girl in the library and this formal, regal woman who was very much in control of herself.

'Ma'am,' he said, giving her a clumsy half-bow.

'Give my regards to Princess Isabella when you see her next.'

Then she swept out of the room, where the temperature felt as if it had just dropped twenty degrees. The footman lingered until Liam had finished packing up his camera gear, then escorted him back to Matteo Battaglia's office.

'I trust all went well, Mr MacCarthy?' Signor Battaglia asked.

'I think so,' Liam said. 'Obviously I need to do some post-production work on the digital files and develop the negatives, but I'll take digital copies of the prints and give you an encrypted link to a gallery on my website so King Vittorio can choose which ones he'd like me to make finished prints of, then I'll courier the negatives and final prints to you in a couple of days. You have my details if you need to get in touch in the meantime.'

'Of course. I'll look forward to hearing from you.'

Liam was pretty sure that he wasn't supposed to ask to say goodbye to the king or to Vittoria. What was the protocol? Meeting Vittoria di Sarda had driven way too much out of his head. 'Please thank His Majesty and Her Royal Highness for their co-operation,' he said instead, and shook the Private Secretary's hand.

Then he brooded all the way back to his hotel, where he collected his travel baggage, settled his bill and checked out. He brooded all the way on the ferry back to mainland Italy. He brooded all the way on the plane back to England and then the train and the Tube back to Chelsea. Thankfully Saoirse was out somewhere, so he brooded all the way to his darkroom; and he especially brooded when he developed the negatives.

The shots in the Throne Room were good. But the ones he'd taken for Izzy... Well, that wasn't true. He hadn't taken most of them for her. He'd taken them for *himself*. And they were spectacular. The best pictures he'd ever taken in his life. That last one, when he hadn't been able to resist finishing the sonnet for Vittoria, and she'd looked all dazed and sweet, and he'd been right on the cusp of kissing her...

God, he was an idiot.

No way would a princess even have a fling with him, let alone anything else.

And that last picture wasn't going to be seen by anyone except himself.

He'd hung the 'processing—do not disturb' sign on the door of his darkroom, so Saoirse wouldn't disturb him when she came in. He had enough time to finish developing the negatives as well as doing the postproduction work on the digital files. Focusing on the technical side of things meant his emotions were perfectly buried by the time he emerged.

He followed his nose—takeaway pizza, he was sure—to find Saoirse, Izzy and Pietro in the kitchen.

'Hey, there.' Saoirse greeted him with a hug. 'Did you have a good trip?'

Not quite how he'd phrase it, but he didn't want her to worry. 'Fine. And thanks for leaving me to my darkroom whenever you got in.'

'Of course. I know better than to risk ruining undeveloped negatives or a pile of new photographic paper. You drilled into me years ago that even a couple of seconds of light from the screen of a mobile phone would wreck things.' She smiled at him. 'Help yourself to pizza.'

'Thanks. Your grandfather sends his love, Izzy,' he said.

'He obviously liked you,' Izzy said with a grin. 'Did Rina give you a message for me?'

'She sends her r—love, too,' Liam said, but Izzy had already noticed the slip.

'What did she really say?' Izzy demanded.

He grimaced. 'Give my regards to Princess Isabella when you see her next.'

Izzy whistled. 'You clearly upset her.'

He wasn't going to tell her what he'd done. Instead, he made a noncommittal noise.

'Actually, it probably wasn't you.' Izzy pulled a face. 'Mamma's got it into her head that Rina needs to marry before she becomes queen. She says there has to be a royal marriage and then the coronation.'

Liam damped down his instant reaction. Of course it would be an arranged marriage. Vittoria di Sarda would have to get married for political reasons. Even if she didn't, marriage to a commoner would hardly go down well with her people, would it?

And why was he even thinking about marriage and Vittoria, anyway? He didn't want to get married to *any-one*, let alone a woman he'd only met once. He'd been let down by too many girlfriends who expected his un-divided attention. Maybe he'd just never managed to pick Ms Right, who'd understand that his family and his career were both important to him; but he was tired of feeling torn between his love life, his career and his family.

'An arranged marriage?' Saoirse looked shocked.

'Because she's going to be queen.' Izzy folded her arms. 'And the man Mamma's suggested—he'd suffo-cate her. He's dull and all he cares about is money and fast cars.'

So her husband wouldn't see the beautiful princess sitting on the window seat and dreaming. He'd see the haughty woman in the Throne Room.

'Mamma had probably been on at her all morning about it and she'd had enough, and she took it out on you. I hope you didn't take it to heart if she did the Scary Winter Queen act on you.' Isabella sighed. 'Though I suppose that means Nonno got his stuffed waxwork.'

No way was he showing Izzy all the shots he'd taken, but he could soften it a bit for her. 'I took some shots in the Throne Room, as requested by your grandfather.'

He smiled. 'And I asked your sister if I could take some in the library.'

'You really did take some for me?' Izzy beamed. 'Thank you. I'll make you coffee for the whole of the next week, for that.'

Liam couldn't hold back a smile. Izzy was irrepressible.

'So when do I get to see the shots?' Izzy asked.

'After your grandfather's approved them.'

Izzy rolled her eyes. 'This is my sister we're talking about.'

'And your grandfather is my client,' he reminded her, 'so he gets to see them first. If he chooses to share them with you, that's his decision. It's not mine to make.' Izzy's face fell, and he took pity on her. 'Here. These are the ones I took for you.' He handed her the prints.

She and Saoirse pored over them together in silence.

'Liam, I always knew you were good, but that's *stunning*,' Saoirse said at last. 'I think these are the best pictures you've ever taken.'

No, they weren't. But the evidence of *that* was staying private.

'I don't think I've ever seen such a beautiful picture of Rina.' Izzy fished out her favourite. 'In her happy place, too. She loves that library. And I…' Izzy swallowed hard. 'That's… Thank you. I'm not going to worry about the other pictures, now. Even though the pose might be stuffy, I know you won't have made her a waxwork. That's my sis—' She gulped the rest of the word off.

Saoirse hugged her. 'Iz. Now isn't the time to get homesick and be miserable. We have exams in a month.'

'I know. It's just… I *miss* her, Sursh. And it's my birthday next week.' She bit her lip. 'I know it's not special, like my twenty-first—' like Saoirse, Izzy had taken a couple of gap years before deciding on her university course '—but it still doesn't feel right not to spend the day with any of my family.'

Liam thought he must've gone temporarily insane, because the words came out before he could stop them. 'Why don't you see if your sister can juggle her schedule and come to London? Even if it's just for one day. And even if she can't, I'll cook you a birthday dinner and Saoirse will make you a birthday cake. We think of you as family,' he added gruffly.

'Liam, you're brilliant. Thank you.' Izzy hugged him. 'And you're family. You're the big brother I never had.'

'That's all sorted, then.' He wriggled out of the hug. 'I have work to do. See you later, girls.'

Liam didn't hear anything from the girls later in the week about Vittoria coming to see Izzy, so he assumed the schedule-juggling didn't work out. He also assumed that Izzy and Saoirse would want to go out with their friends on Izzy's birthday, so he arranged for Izzy to have dinner with them on the Monday night, the day before her birthday.

He marinaded chicken mini fillets in lemon juice before wrapping them in prosciutto and sage, prepped new potatoes for roasting, and asparagus and Cavalo Nero for steaming. He bought some of the first English strawberries along with shortbread thins and some clotted cream for pudding. Saoirse had made an incredibly rich chocolate cake and sprayed it with edible gold paint, and Liam had bought a cake fountain to top it. Saoirse had decorated their kitchen with birthday-themed bunting, and there was Prosecco chilling in the fridge.

Half an hour before Izzy was due to arrive, Saoirse came into the kitchen where Liam was sorting out last minute details, holding her mobile phone. 'You know you made extra chicken so Pietro could eat with us and you could have some cold for dinner tomorrow?'

'Uh-huh.'

'Could dinner stretch to two extra guests?'

All he'd have to do was prep some more veg. 'Yes. Why?'

'Vittoria's managed to come to London, after all. It's all been a bit last minute. Izzy doesn't want to dump us, because she knows you've gone to a lot of trouble to make a fuss of her. And she's worrying about asking you if her sister and her security detail can come for dinner, too, because she thinks she's being entitled.'

Vittoria di Sarda.

Here, in his flat.

Liam's heart skipped a beat.

'Tell Izzy it's fine,' he said, trying to sound as casual as he could.

He was glad that he had to spend time prepping more veg and re-laying the table, because that stopped him having time to think about Vittoria being here. Which was ridiculous in itself. He knew perfectly well that she wasn't coming here to see him; she was in London to see her sister. All he was doing was hosting dinner.

But he still remembered how Vittoria had looked in the library, in that moment when he'd almost kissed her, and anticipation prickled down his spine. How would it be when he saw her again? Would she be the formal queen-to-be or would her softer side come out because her little sister was here?

Half an hour later, the flat intercom buzzed, and Saoirse let their guests in.

Izzy came in and hugged Liam before introducing her sister and Giorgio, Vittoria's security detail.

Even though this was a relaxed dinner with her sister, Vittoria was wearing formal business dress—a navy dress with a matching jacket that Liam recognised from his studio work as haute couture, teamed with high-heeled court shoes and a little clutch bag. Her hair and make-up were immaculate; and her jewellery was minimal, diamond earrings and a simple pendant necklace.

She looked every inch a princess.

'*Benvenuto nelle nostre casa, Vostre Altezza Reale,*' Liam said with a small half-bow.

'Thank you, Mr MacCarthy,' she said, her voice equally formal.

Right. So it was definitely the princess rather than the girl in the library who was his guest. He'd make sure he behaved accordingly.

Izzy rolled her eyes. 'For pity's sake, you two. Stop being so stuffy. I know you've met on official palace business, but tonight *isn't* palace business, so let me introduce you properly. Rina, this is Liam, who's the nearest I'm going to get to a big brother. Liam, this is my big sister, Rina.' She gave both of them a steely look. 'Surely you get fed up to the back teeth of the formality at home, Rina? And as for you, Liam—' She shook her head in apparent despair. 'Don't treat my sister like some visiting dignitary.'

'Strictly speaking,' he pointed out, 'that's what she is.'

'She's my sister. Tonight's a sort of family dinner,' Izzy protested. 'And it's *my* birthday—'

'So you can act like a princess if you want to,' Liam teased.

She cuffed him. 'For that, I'm not letting Rina give you what she brought you.'

'Ah, now. Manners, young lady. We should always bring our host a gift when we're invited somewhere.'

Liam gave Vittoria a sidelong look. The love for her

sister in her eyes and her teasing expression were both vivid, and he itched to photograph her.

'Thank you for having us to dinner—may I call you Liam?' she asked. 'Izzy's right. Tonight isn't the night for formality.'

'Of course.' The way she spoke his given name made a shiver run down his spine.

'Good. And thank you especially for letting us come at such short notice,' Vittoria continued. 'It's not much of a gift, but we brought wine; and Izzy says you like cooking.'

'I do.'

She handed him a bottle of olive oil. 'This is from San Rocello. Extra-virgin, first pressing.'

Was she giving him an economist's spiel, or was she talking as someone who liked food and would spend time in the kitchen if she could? Izzy made great coffee, but always burned toast because she was too scatty to pay attention. But in that one photographic sitting he'd worked out that Vittoria paid attention to detail…

Then Liam made the mistake of looking into those amazing eyes. '*Grazie*, ma—' He stopped himself. She'd practically given him permission to use her first name. 'Thank you, Vittoria.'

For a moment, everyone else in the room was forgotten: his sister, hers, Pietro and Giorgio. It was just the two of them. A heartbeat. Two. He almost reached out to take her hand…

And then he shook himself. 'May I offer you a drink? Dinner will be ready in ten minutes.'

He sorted out the drinks, seated everyone at the table and served dinner.

'Our grandfather was very pleased with the portraits you sent him,' Vittoria said.

'Good.' Which meant they would be used; and it was quite likely that one of them would end up in the National Portrait Gallery.

'And Izzy sent me the ones you took for her.'

His eyes met hers. Did she wonder what had happened to the photograph from that more private moment? Maybe he'd show her. But not now. 'Did you like them?' he asked instead.

'You're very talented,' she said.

Which wasn't the same as saying that she liked them. It was a diplomat's reply.

'Liam's really good,' Saoirse said.

'And dinner's getting cold,' he pointed out, hoping it would change the subject.

Everyone ate with gusto, to his relief. After everyone had finished pudding, he brought the birthday cake over to the table and lit the fountain candle, then they all sang 'Happy Birthday' to Izzy—himself and Saoirse in English, and Vittoria, Pietro and Giorgio switching to the Italian. *'Tanti auguri a te...'*

When the cake fountain had finished, Izzy closed her eyes to make a wish, then started cutting the cake.

'I'll make coffee to go with the cake,' Liam suggested.

'No! Anyone but *you* on coffee duty,' Izzy begged.

'My coffee isn't that bad,' Liam protested.

'Yes, it is. You microwave it when it gets cold. Your coffee is awful,' Saoirse agreed.

'*Really* awful. I'll make it,' Pietro said, and proceeded to sort it out.

'Don't be offended,' Vittoria said. 'Nobody's good at everything—and the chicken was quite delicious.'

Liam could tell she'd been well schooled in diplomacy. *Nobody's good at everything...* He wondered what she might not be good at, then pushed the thought away; it was none of his business.

'Happy birthday, piccola,' Vittoria said, and raised her glass of Prosecco in a toast to her little sister.

Izzy beamed. 'I'm so glad you're here, Rina. I didn't think you'd have time to see me, so I was thinking about skiving off and coming home for a couple of days.'

'Which isn't a good idea, so close to your exams. And of course I'd make time for you. I always will. You're my little sister and I love you.'

Vittoria couldn't help glancing at Liam; she could see in his face that he understood exactly where she was coming from. It was the same for him.

'I just wish Mamma wasn't putting all this pressure on you to get married,' Izzy said, frowning. 'It's utterly ridiculous. Why on earth do you have to get married before you become queen? This is the twenty-first century, not the sixteenth.'

'It's just how it is,' Vittoria said gently. Though she, too, wished she didn't have to get married. She knew it was her duty, and she'd do what was expected of her; but she wanted enough time to get to know her future partner and grow to at least respect him, if not fall in love with him, before they married.

What she'd seen of José so far didn't fill her with much hope. All they had in common was a royal background. He adored fast cars and sport, which bored her; and she liked exploring gardens and nature, which bored him.

'There's so much pressure on you,' Izzy continued. 'Once you get married and become queen, you'll lose the little freedom you have now. When was the last time you had some time to yourself?'

Vittoria thought about it and couldn't remember.

She'd clearly taken too long to answer, because Izzy pounced. 'Exactly. The palace suffocates you, Rina.'

Vittoria was going to deny it, but she knew her sister would call her on it. 'It's just how it is,' she said again.

'Why don't you take some time for yourself now?'

'Now?'

'While you're in London.' Izzy brightened. 'Like a modern-day *Roman Holiday*.'

Vittoria groaned. Her sister was a huge Audrey Hepburn fan, so Vittoria had ended up seeing the film a gazillion times. 'It's a lovely film, *piccola*, but it's of its time. Back in the nineteen-fifties, someone might notice a princess—but then they'd have to go and find a phone before they could tell the press about it, so the princess would have time to escape. Nowadays, almost everyone has a mobile phone, so they'd snap a picture or take a video, and it would be round the world in three seconds flat.' Which was why she had to be in strict control of every single second of every single day, making sure that the paparazzi never saw her frowning or bored or cross. She had an image to uphold.

'If you looked like you do right now,' Liam said, 'that's true. But if you didn't…'

That got her attention. She looked at him—and oh, those cornflower-blue eyes felt as if they could see into her soul.

'What are you saying?'

'Dress differently and change your hair. People might give you a second glance and think that you look a bit like Princess Vittoria—but then they'd see what you were wearing, realise that a princess wouldn't scruff around in chain store jeans and canvas shoes because she always wears a haute couture dress or suit and designer heels, and they'd move on. Leaving you in peace.'

*Anonymity.*

Given how much her mother was pressuring her right now, Vittoria really wanted a respite; it was why she'd carved time she didn't really have out of her schedule to come to London and see her sister, to grab a few little moments of joy to see the person she loved most in the world.

And now she was being offered a couple of days where she could be herself instead of a queen-in-waiting. Just a little time out before she stepped back into her real world.

'It'd be really easy to change your hair,' Izzy said.

'I can't cut it or dye it,' Vittoria warned.

'You don't need to,' Saoirse said. 'Remember what my brother does for a living. And he's done a few fashion shoots so he knows loads of people who work in wardrobe departments—people who can get you a wig. Something that'll suit your skin colouring but won't attract notice: say, mid-brown hair in a chin-length bob,' she added thoughtfully.

'You could borrow some clothes from me, or from Sursh,' Izzy added. 'We're all about the same size.'

'And you'll need contact lenses, because your gorgeous eyes are a giveaway,' Saoirse said. 'Brown eyes. They'll go with your colouring, too, and they're practically invisible.'

'Hang on, guys. Princess Vittoria can't just do things on a whim. She has a schedule,' Liam said.

Vittoria exchanged a glance with him. It seemed he understood her life. Then again, he also worked to a schedule and had the pressure of other people's deadlines—something their sisters were both yet to really experience.

Did he ever feel stifled by his job? Or, when he'd shouldered the responsibility of bringing up his sister at the age of eighteen, had he felt trapped at the same time as loving her dearly? Because, right now, that was exactly how she felt: she loved her grandfather dearly and she would never shy away from her duty, but she needed some space. Just a little time for herself. Time where she could blend into the crowd, be just another one of the billions of people on the planet.

'You're meant to be on *our* side, Liam,' Izzy said, putting her hands on her hips and giving him a hard stare. 'You know someone who can sort out a wig and contact lenses by tomorrow morning, right?'

'Yes.'

'Well, then. Ring them. And you call Matteo Battaglia, Rina. Tell him you've got the worst period in the world so you need a couple of days off, and then you can have your *Roman Holiday*. Except, obviously, not in Rome,' Izzy added with a smile. 'It'd be a London holiday.'

Vittoria shook her head. 'The press already know I'm staying in your apartment. They'll look for me.'

'Then stay somewhere else.'

Vittoria rolled her eyes. 'I can hardly book somewhere incognito. No, Izzy, it's a lovely thought, and thank you so much—but it's completely unworkable.'

Liam knew he shouldn't really be encouraging the girls. But he'd seen that moment of longing in Vittoria's eyes, just before she masked it. He knew how it felt to shoulder greater responsibility than was normal for someone of your age and, while not resenting it, occasionally wanting to escape it and have some time for yourself.

He'd been lucky. Patty, his old tutor, had helped him out. Maybe it was time to pay it forward and give someone else a break. He could make this happen for Vittoria. Give her a respite, just a couple of days to step outside her royal bubble.

And neither of the security details had spoken up to say it was a ridiculous idea, so maybe Izzy's scheme wasn't quite so crazy after all.

'You could stay here, if you wish to stay in London. Or I can book you a suite somewhere, so there isn't a paper trail back to you.'

Vittoria turned to look at him, her face full of questions.

And that made him push it that little bit further. 'I also have a bolthole. A cottage by the sea. I was going there anyway this week to do some planning, so you're very welcome to join me. There's nothing like the sea to clear your head.'

'A cottage by the sea...'

'It has three bedrooms.' She didn't need to know that he used one of them as his darkroom. 'One for you, one for Giorgio—' he glanced at the bodyguard, who looked approving '—and one for me, so I can drive you there and maybe show you round the area if you'd like to explore, or stay out of your way if you just want time to yourself.'

A few days by the sea. Time for herself—something she wanted so very badly. It was so tempting.

This was only the second time she'd met Liam. Going to his cottage meant entrusting herself to a near-stranger. A man she found distractingly attractive. Which meant this was a bad idea.

On the other hand, he was clearly close to Izzy and

treated her as part of his family. Izzy obviously trusted him, or she wouldn't have spoken so frankly in front of him. She already knew that Pietro approved of him—and the security detail would have raised any concerns with her grandfather before letting Izzy spend time in Liam's company.

Which meant he was safe.

So did she go with him, take those few days to re-charge herself properly? Or did she do what she was supposed to and go back to the palace?

The sensible side of her knew that she should put her duties first. That wanting a break was self-indulgent—no, more than that, it was *selfish*.

But the part of her she usually kept hidden—the woman Liam had seemed to notice when he'd taken those photographs in the library—wanted to do it.

'Do it, Rina,' Izzy urged.

Vittoria looked at her sister and then back at Liam. 'If you're sure it's no trouble?'

He met her gaze. 'It would be my pleasure.'

There was nothing leering or anything that made her feel uncomfortable in his face. Just fellow feeling—as if he understood what it was like to feel constricted. And that decided her. 'Thank you. I'll talk to Matteo Battaglia.'

'Brilliant.' Izzy hugged her. 'This is going to change your life.'

## CHAPTER THREE

AT A QUARTER to ten the next morning, Vittoria was ready to go. Izzy and Saoirse had both raided their wardrobes and lent her the kind of clothing that wouldn't attract a second glance: faded jeans, plain T-shirts and floral canvas pumps.

Liam had called in a couple of favours the previous evening and organised some people to come to Izzy's flat first thing, ostensibly as suppliers for a student art project, but in reality to sort out contact lenses and a wig for Vittoria's disguise. She knew they'd be discreet, because they were used to working with celebrity clients and keeping things private. She'd chosen brown contact lenses, on Saoirse's advice, and a mid-brown wig that looked natural with her skin tone.

The woman who stared back at her from the mirror wasn't the princess in haute couture and diamonds; she looked like any other professional woman in her late twenties who was getting away from the office for a few days.

'You look great. Normal,' Izzy said.

'Thank you.' Though Vittoria didn't feel normal. She felt strange. Borrowed clothes, borrowed hair and eyes… Didn't they say be careful what you wished for, in case you got it? She'd wanted anonymity. Now she had it. And it wasn't quite what she'd expected. It felt odd.

'I feel a bit bad, deserting you on your birthday,' she said.

Izzy laughed. 'This is the best birthday present ever. Knowing that you're actually going to unwind, for once. Anyway, you already celebrated with me last night.'

'I guess. As long are you're sure.'

Saoirse's phone beeped. 'That's Liam. He's waiting outside for you,' she said.

Izzy hugged her sister. 'We won't come down with you, in case the press twig who you are. Have fun and let me know when you're there safely.'

'I will.' Vittoria hugged her back. 'Thank you. Both of you.'

'We've hardly done anything. We just made a few suggestions and lent you some clothes. It's Liam who's actually sprung you from the public eye,' Izzy said.

And that was something Vittoria hadn't allowed herself to think about, because it was even more worrying. Spending a few days with the first man in years who'd made her feel something. Particularly as he wasn't from her background. Hadn't she learned anything from her experience with Rufus? Royal life was a lot to handle for people who hadn't been brought up in it. She couldn't afford to get emotionally involved with someone else who decided he didn't want that kind of life and would back away from her after she'd lost her heart to him.

She'd almost forgotten herself and kissed Liam in the palace library. In front of the footman, because right at that moment she hadn't been aware of anyone else in the room apart from Liam MacCarthy. What might happen in a little cottage by the sea? When Giorgio was in his room, and she and Liam were alone? She trusted Liam, but she wasn't entirely sure she trusted herself.

Was this all a mistake? Was she just being self-indulgent and pathetic, wanting a breather from her responsibilities? Should she say that she'd changed her mind? But everyone had gone to so much trouble to help her that it would feel churlish.

Her nerves grew as she followed Giorgio down the stairs from Izzy's flat.

'Liam's is the grey car, second on the right,' Giorgio said.

Well, of course Liam would have been in contact with her security detail and kept him informed about everything. Giorgio's presence and protection was about the only reason why her grandfather wouldn't be too angry with her when he found out about this—an escapade that would be instantly forgiven had it been Izzy, but the heir to the throne was expected to be much more sensible.

Again, she considered chickening out and going back to her real life.

But she'd felt so constrained, lately. So tired of being told what her duties were, and how she had to get married for the sake of the monarchy. She'd been longing to escape for *months*. Besides, this wasn't running away from her responsibilities for ever: she was simply stealing a couple of days by the sea. Days where she could just be *herself*.

There were a couple of photographers milling about outside. They'd clearly been tipped off that Princess Vittoria had come to visit her little sister; but Giorgio was good at making himself invisible, and the changes to her own appearance meant that none of them gave her a second glance as she slid into the passenger seat of Liam's car.

She was very fortunate that Liam wasn't the sort of man to insist on driving a bright red Ferrari or something similarly eye-catching. An anonymous grey car—even if it did seem to be top of the range—meant that they wouldn't have to run the gauntlet of the press.

'Thank you, Mr MacCarthy,' she said as she fastened her seatbelt.

He pushed his dark glasses up into his hair and looked at her. 'I thought we'd agreed on first-name terms? Actually, thinking about that, if I call you Vittoria it might make people put two and two together.'

'So I get a borrowed name as well as borrowed clothes?' This was a step too far.

'No. It needs to be something you'll recognise and react to. We could anglicise your name and shorten it slightly.' He smiled. 'Vicky.'

'Izzy calls me "Rina".'

'The press might pick up on that.'

'Oh.' She didn't have an answer to that. 'OK, I guess I'd better be "Vicky", then.'

'Feel free to change the music, Vicky,' he said with a smile, gesturing to the car's sound system.

'It's fine,' she said, and kept silent while he drove them out of London, guessing that he might want to concentrate on where they were going.

Once they were on the motorway heading north out of London towards East Anglia, he said, 'Let me know if you need a comfort break or want to stop for a drink.'

'Thank you.'

Funny, she had a whole stock of conversational openings designed to put people at their ease. But right now, she couldn't remember a single one of them; instead, when she opened her mouth, she found herself saying, 'So what's the village like?'

'It's a traditional fishing village—a harbour, lots of little fishermen's cottages and a wide sandy beach after the dunes.' He smiled. 'If you want a sneak preview, have a look on my website. The beach is the third one on the landscape gallery.'

There was a wide strip of sand that looked golden in the sunlight, darkening as it neared the edge of the sea; a froth of white showed the waves lapping onto the shore, and the sea graduated from turquoise in the shallows through to almost navy at the horizon. The sky was filled with storm clouds, deep and dramatic grey. 'That's gorgeous.'

'It was a lucky shot,' he said. 'The sun lit up the sand from behind me, and it was the perfect contrast to the sky. Sometimes you just happen to be in the right place at the right time.' He paused. 'So, is there anything particular you'd like to do in your few days of escape?'

'I don't know,' she said. It had been so long since she'd had a real choice in what she did, she wasn't sure where to start. 'What sort of thing do you normally do?'

'Walk, work and think,' he said. 'Though I've lent the cottage to my best friend and his family in the past. I spent some time here with them last summer, so the order of the day was making sandcastles on the beach. We went out on a boat trip to see the seals, and we've gone hunting for shells and fossils.' He gave her a sidelong look. 'What do you normally do at the beach?'

She couldn't remember the last time she'd been to the beach just for fun. It was always something to do with conservation, heritage or tourism. 'I don't usually have time to go to the beach.'

'This is your *Roman Holiday*, Vittoria,' he said gently. 'You can do whatever you want.'

She'd got exactly what she'd wished for.

And, now there were no boundaries, it was faintly scary.

She was so used to working with royal protocols; but here, there were no protocols. She wasn't quite sure what to say or do. She and Liam barely knew each other; they didn't have a shared history or shared references.

Or maybe she was overthinking this. Maybe they *did* have a shared frame of reference—he'd been a parent to his little sister at the age of eighteen, and she was about to become queen at the age of twenty-eight. So many responsibilities at such a young age; maybe he'd guessed that she was struggling and he was helping her because he'd been there, too.

This was a step outside her usual life. Something to refresh and revitalise her, to help her cope with the parts of the palace that she found stifling.

An adventure.

So she should just stop worrying and enjoy it.

It took them three hours to get there, but finally Liam parked in the driveway of a pretty flint and brick cottage. 'My neighbour who keeps an eye on the place when nobody's here promised to pick up some milk, bread and a few bits from the deli,' he said, opening the door and ushering her into the kitchen.

There was a deep red flagstone floor; the walls were painted pale blue and the cupboards were cream. There was an old-fashioned butler's sink underneath the window and a range cooker nearby. The room was large enough to have a scrubbed pine table and chairs at one end; it looked very much like a family room. Normal. Everyday. All the things she didn't usually have.

It didn't take long to view the rest of the house. Next was the living room, with a wood-burning stove, comfortable sofas, and stripped oak floorboards with a patterned red rug in the centre. A steep staircase led to the next floor, which had two rooms—one was a darkroom and one had a double bed—plus a bathroom. There was a second flight of stairs which led to another bedroom which had a wide double bed, a view of the sea and an en-suite shower room.

This was exactly where she could imagine having a bolthole.

'It's a lovely house,' she said. But there was one thing bothering her. He'd said there were three bedrooms. She'd only seen two.

'Choose whichever bedroom you'd like,' Liam said.

She really would have to say something now. 'But there are only two.'

'One of them doubles as my darkroom. I'll sleep there on the sofa bed.'

She shook her head. 'I can't ask you to do that.'

'It's what I normally do if I have friends staying,' he said. 'It's fine.'

'Then, if you're sure, I'd like the room on the top floor, please.' She'd loved it at first sight: it was light and airy.

'Good choice,' Liam said. 'The view first thing is gorgeous. I'll leave you to freshen up while I sort out lunch.'

'I'll bring everything in from the car,' Giorgio said, and Liam handed over his car keys with a smile of thanks.

Her surroundings were much simpler than what she

was used to, but utterly charming. The whole place had a feeling of warmth—a feeling of *family*. Like rare days at the palace when her mother and grandmother had gone to see friends, and she could walk around the gardens with her grandfather, as she'd once done with her father, have a simple lunch with him and forget the weight of her future crown. Or when Izzy was home and she managed to get time off, so they could both curl up on the window seat in her room and talk…

Giorgio brought up her bags; she thanked him, called Izzy to let her know they'd arrived and the cottage was lovely, unpacked, then freshened up and went downstairs.

Liam had laid the table in the kitchen with salad, fresh bread, cheese, ham and what looked like dressed crab.

'It's all local produce,' he said. 'Even the coffee's roasted by the local deli.'

'And I didn't let him make the coffee, so it's safe to drink,' Giorgio said with a grin.

Vittoria noticed that her bodyguard had already become friendly with Liam, to the point where they were comfortable teasing each other. It was a good thing; but it was also unsettling, because she wasn't sure what her own relationship was with Liam. They were acquaintances—she knew he was close to her sister—and she thought they could easily become friends. She liked him instinctively. But he was also a man who made her feel things she couldn't afford to feel, and she needed to get herself back under control. Fast.

'This all looks delicious—thank you,' she said. 'But I don't expect you to wait on me, and I'll do the washing up.'

He raised an eyebrow.

Did he *really* think she was that spoiled and privileged? That stung. 'Yes, I do know how to wash up. I fended for myself when I was a student,' she said coolly.

'I apologise. I didn't mean to assume that you were helpless.'

But he clearly had made that assumption. 'And I can cook,' she said. 'I like cooking; I just don't get the chance to do it much.'

'Then if you'd like to cook while you're here, do it,' he said.

And that took all her defensiveness away.

This man had been kind enough to help give her a couple of days of freedom from the pressure of always being on show in her normal life; yet she'd snapped at him. 'Sorry. I didn't mean to be snippy with you.'

'It's fine,' he said.

She really hoped that wasn't pity in his eyes.

'So what would you like to do after lunch?' he asked.

'Could we go for a walk on the beach, then pick up some shopping for dinner?'

'Sure—unless you'd rather eat fish and chips on the quayside tonight,' he said. 'Your choice.'

Like a tourist. Eating fish and chips from the wrapper, with their feet dangling over the edge of the quay. And nobody would see the princess: she'd be just like everyone else.

And it was her choice. She didn't have to think what would be best politically; she could do whatever she wanted, just for the sheer joy of it.

'There are plenty of options,' he said. 'We could have fish and chips tonight, or go to the pub, or one of us can cook dinner. If you want to go exploring somewhere, we can eat on the way home. Whatever you like.'

How long had it been since she'd been able to choose?

'I think I'd like fish and chips tonight,' she said. 'But I'm still doing the washing up after lunch.'

'Fine. Then I'll dry,' he said.

There was something fragile about Vittoria di Sarda, beneath her cool royal exterior, Liam thought. Although she was a princess, she didn't behave as if she was entitled—unlike some of his past girlfriends, who'd demanded more than he'd been prepared to give.

Not that he should be thinking about her in terms of being a girlfriend. He could list half a dozen reasons off the top of his head why getting involved with her would be a bad idea—for them both. She was his guest. He ought to leave it at that.

After lunch, they headed for the beach, with Giorgio strolling a few paces behind them, looking like any other tourist checking his phone but in reality finely tuned to any situation that could become difficult for the princess. Liam had already had a long chat with Vittoria's security detail, the previous evening, briefing him about the area and any potential risks. Given that the English royal family had houses only a few miles away, Giorgio was relatively relaxed.

In the first part of the beach they reached, there were small children playing with buckets and spades, and Liam noticed Vittoria looking wistfully at them.

'Didn't you do that sort of thing when you were small?' he asked.

'It feels like a very long time ago, now,' she said. She frowned. 'You're a couple of years older than me. Doesn't it feel like a long time ago to you?'

'No, because I still build sandcastles with my god-daughters—my best friend Olly's girls,' he said. 'And sometimes Olly and I get a bit competitive and see who can build the most ornate castle.'

'Men,' she said, rolling her eyes.

How weird it was, Liam thought, that even though she didn't look the same—she didn't even have the same eye colour, thanks to the contact lenses she was using—she still made his heart skip a beat. The more time he spent with her, the more he liked her. The more attractive he found her. The more he wanted to be with her.

But she was off limits. He really needed to keep remembering that.

He took his shoes off so he could walk along the edge of the sea; she did the same, dangling the canvas shoes by their laces as she walked along.

'I can't remember the last time I walked barefoot on a beach, with the waves washing over my toes,' she said.

'The beach is a good place. The sound of the sea can drive all the worries from your head,' he said.

'Is this what you do when you're out of sorts?'

'Pretty much,' he said. 'I'll come here with my camera, listen to the waves and the birds, and take a few shots to ground me again.' He looked at her. 'Given that you live on an island, I'm surprised you don't walk on the beach more often. Don't you have a special royal beach?'

'No—as you already know from your visit, the palace is in the capital. Although there's a port, there isn't a beach you can walk on.' She shrugged. 'There's always the garden.'

'Or the library.'

Again, her gaze met his and it sent a frisson of desire down his spine. He could still see the woman he'd photographed on the window seat, her face all soft in the diffused light. The woman he'd almost kissed. The woman he was tempted to kiss right now: but he held himself back.

'Why do you take portraits rather than landscapes?' she asked.

'Partly for commercial reasons—I get more commissions for portraits than I would for landscapes—and partly because I like the challenge of showing someone's character through an image,' he answered honestly.

'But you take landscapes when you're out of sorts. Is that your dream, to be a landscape photographer?'

'No. I want to be one of the greatest portrait photographers of my generation,' he said.

'*Nonno* was impressed with the photographs you took. I saw them, too: they're good.' She looked him straight in the eye again. 'But he only showed me a single one from the library. Where I was still wearing royal regalia.'

'Because the others weren't the ones he commissioned. Izzy asked me to take a photograph for her—and I took several.'

Her eyes narrowed slightly. 'But you took more than the ones she showed me.'

'When you were quoting Shakespeare,' he said. 'There's one—' He stopped.

'Can I see it?'

'It's not going to be used anywhere. You have my word on that.'

She was silent.

'Vittoria,' he said softly. 'I keep my promises.'

'I imagine you do, Mr MacCarthy.'

She'd gone all cold and regal on him. Which he probably deserved.

'Nobody else has seen it. Not even Izzy.'

She inclined her head. 'However, given that it's of me, I think I have a right to see it.'

She had a point. He sighed. 'All right. Give me a moment.' He checked the signal, then logged in to his cloud-based storage. Then he fished out a single picture. The one he'd taken when he'd finished the sonnet for her. Without comment, he handed her his phone.

She stared at the portrait.

And he could see the colours changing in her face as she looked at it—first pale, then a deep blush.

'Oh,' she said, her voice all soft and breathy.

'It's the best picture I've ever taken,' he said. 'Without question. It's a career-changing shot.' He waited a beat before adding, 'And I'm not intending to publish it.' Because that moment was too private. It revealed almost as much about the photographer as it did about his subject: and he hoped she hadn't worked that out for herself.

'I…' Her eyes were wide. 'I don't know what to say.'

'Then don't say anything. Just keep walking along the beach,' he said, and held out his hand for his phone.

She looked at the portrait once more, then gave his phone back.

'Thank you,' he said, logging out of his storage space and then stuffing the phone back in his pocket.

They walked on without speaking. As they walked on the sand and the sound of the sea worked its usual magic on him, he found the silence between them slide from being awkward to being relaxed.

Vittoria was completely stunned by that photograph. It felt as if Liam had captured the inner her, the one she had to mask when she was a queen-in-waiting. The woman who dreamed, who looked up at the stars and wondered at the universe.

She'd never really felt before that someone understood her and saw who she was inside, even Rufus. Certainly not José, the man that her mother was pressuring her to accept as her husband and future consort. He was handsome and had been brought up in royal circles; but he didn't make her heart beat faster and she hadn't felt an emotional connection to him.

Though she knew her duty and she'd do what was expected of her: marry a suitable man and produce the next heir to the throne.

All she needed was a little time to steel herself for that duty.

Her hand brushed against Liam's as they walked, and it felt as if she'd been galvanised.

Why was she so aware of him?

She'd never reacted like this to anyone before. Not the couple of boyfriends she'd had in her late teens, and not Rufus.

Vittoria had promised herself that she'd never make the mistake she made with Rufus again. She'd marry someone who'd grown up in the same sort of world that she had and could deal with all the media intrusion. Maybe it was a little too much to ask that she could fall in love with him, first.

Liam took her hand, squeezed it and let it go.

She looked at him, shocked. 'Why did you do that?'

'Because right then you looked really sad,' he said softly, 'and I'm not sure if I'm allowed to give you a hug.'

'How do you mean, allowed?'

'Protocol.'

So, even though this was meant to be her time out

of being a princess, there were still the same boundaries. She frowned. 'Do you hug Izzy?'

'I have done, in the past. Purely in a brotherly way,' he added, 'when she's had a rubbish day and needed the equivalent of a big brother to tell her that everything would work out just fine.'

It was the sort of thing she would've done, had he been the prince and Saoirse had been the one to need a hug. And in the short time she'd known Liam she'd started to realise that he saw the world in much the same way that she did. Pragmatic, practical, doing what needed to be done without a fuss. Of course he would've hugged Izzy when she needed it.

Then she found herself wondering what it would be like if Liam hugged her... Except she didn't want a hug from him in a brotherly way.

For pity's sake.

This was meant to be a respite, not time to have a wild fling with her little sister's best friend's brother.

But now the idea was firmly lodged in her head and she couldn't get it out.

She let her hand brush deliberately against his a couple of times; the touch sent a frisson of desire through her. But she noticed that he didn't take the hint and didn't hold her hand. It made her feel like an embarrassed teenager trying desperately to get the boy she liked to notice her, and being turned down.

She thought about it.

He'd said just now that the hand-squeeze had been all about comfort; but she remembered the look in his eyes in the palace library, when he'd whispered Shakespeare to her and she'd thought he was going to kiss her. Comfort? No. She rather thought it had been something else. The same thing that was making her feel so antsy. Longing. Need. *Desire.*

So what was holding him back now? And how could she take that barrier away?

She shook herself. This wasn't sensible. And she was sensible, businesslike Princess Vittoria, who was simply pretending to be carefree tourist Vicky. She needed to remember that.

Even though she had to try really hard to suppress that prickling awareness—and didn't succeed completely—Liam MacCarthy was easy to be with. The silence between them as they walked along the beach, watching dogs racing around, was companionable rather than awkward. He was giving her space, and she appreciated that.

Then a large black Labrador rushed over, so intent on playing chase with another dog that he banged into her, nearly knocking her over.

Liam caught her and stopped her from falling, holding her close to him.

She could feel the warmth of his skin through his T-shirt, and it made her tingle all over.

'Are you OK?' he asked.

She nodded, not trusting herself to speak because she knew her voice would come out all wobbly: a wobbliness that had nothing to do with the near-accident and everything to do with the fact that he was holding her.

'I'm so sorry,' the dog's owner called, 'I'm afraid the boys get a bit carried away as soon as their paws hit the sand. The little one's ten months old and has no sense whatsoever. Are you all right?'

'No harm done,' Liam called back.

'Thank you for catching me,' she said when she finally trusted herself to speak.

'You're welcome.'

And was it her imagination, or was there something in his blue eyes—that same awareness she had towards him?

By the time they walked back to the harbour, a queue was forming outside the chip shop.

'Why don't you wait here with Giorgio while I wait in line?' Liam suggested.

'I need to give you the mon—' she began, and he shook his head.

'Buying fish and chips for three isn't going to bankrupt me. It's fine. Cod and chips all right with you, Vicky?'

She knew she should give in gracefully. 'Thank you.'

'Giorgio?' Liam checked.

'Yes, please,' the bodyguard said.

'Great. Find somewhere to sit, and I'll come and find you with dinner.'

Vittoria sat down on the low harbour wall next to Giorgio and waited for Liam's return. The view across the salt marshes was amazing; there were a few boats moored up on the harbour, and the long sea wall stretched out towards the beach. Couples and families were sitting on the harbour wall, too, eating fish and chips; the children all seemed to be fascinated by the gulls, who stalked up and down the quayside, gimlet-eyed, waiting for someone to drop a chip so they could swoop in and grab it.

Nobody paid her the slightest bit of attention.

How good it felt to be able to merge into the crowd. To be just a normal person. Not to have to school her expression and mask her thoughts all the time.

'OK?' Giorgio asked softly.

She nodded.

'He's one of the good guys,' Giorgio said. 'I'm glad you agreed to Izzy's plan.'

'Nonno's not going to be pleased, when he finds out,' she said, wrinkling her nose.

'He'll be fine. He'll understand.'

She knew what her security detail wasn't saying. The ones who'd make a fuss about the situation were her mother and her grandmother: the ones who were pressuring her to agree on terms with José and organise the official engagement.

'Put it all out of your head. You can deal with it later. Just enjoy having time off—time for *you*,' Giorgio advised.

He'd been her security detail for nearly ten years, since she'd gone to London as an undergraduate; she knew his words of advice were meant kindly. And it was good advice. 'I will,' she said. Except it was much easier said than done.

They sat just enjoying the view and chatting about nothing in particular until Liam returned with three boxes of hot cod and chips. 'I hope it's OK, but I added salt and vinegar to all of them, because that's the best way to enjoy fish and chips,' he said, handing them each a box, a wooden fork and a paper napkin. 'And I played safe with drinks and bought us each a bottle of still water.'

'Lovely. Thank you so much,' she said.

'My pleasure.' His smile made her heart feel as if it had just done a backflip.

Summer, sunshine and the sea. Along with his nearness, it was a heady combination.

Not wanting to say anything else in case she started sounding like a starry-eyed teenager, Vittoria concentrated on the food. The chips were perfect: hot, crispy

with the tang of salt and vinegar. The fish was beauti-
fully fresh, the batter light, and she could see exactly
why the queue outside the shop was so long.

When they'd finished, Giorgio bought them all a
whippy ice-cream with a flake.

Just like all the other tourists.

*She blended in.*

And she enjoyed lingering on the quayside, laughing
and chatting and people-watching, without the worry
that someone was going to spot Princess Vittoria of
San Rocello in the middle of it all and turn the whole
thing into a media scrum. The pressure, the weight that
seemed permanently between her shoulders and made
her head ache most nights, started to ease.

By the time they got back to the cottage, it was beginning to get chilly.

'Are you tired?' Liam asked. 'Or would you like to
walk back over to the dunes and watch the stars come
out?'

'I think I'd like that,' she said. 'But let me grab Izzy's
fleece, first.'

'Sure.'

'I'll stay here,' Giorgio said. 'I trust Liam to keep
you safe, but you know what to do if there's a problem.'

She nodded. 'The panic button.'

By the time she'd come downstairs, Liam had sorted
out two thermal mugs of hot chocolate and a blanket to
sit on, which he stuffed into a tote bag and slung over
his shoulder. They walked out to the dunes where he
spread the blanket out and handed her a mug after she'd
sat down. She could see the first stars appearing, and
a narrow crescent moon hung above them, reflecting
on the surface of the sea. The swish of the waves on
the shore and the sound of birdsong were all they could

hear. It was utterly magical. Though it was also cold, and neither the hot drink nor Izzy's fleece was quite enough to keep her warm. Liam must have noticed her shiver, because he shrugged off his jacket and put it round her shoulders.

'Won't you be cold?' she protested, feeling guilty.

'I'm fine.' He paused. 'Though if you want to lean against me, we could share some body heat.'

Every nerve-end prickled.

Was this Liam's way of saying he wanted to hold her? Would he kiss her? Vittoria could hardly breathe. All she'd have to do was turn slightly, tip her face up to his…

Or was he doing this in a completely platonic way, just being kind to the older sister of his little sister's best friend?

She was unsure about the situation—or about what she wanted it to be.

Move closer, or stay distant?

# CHAPTER FOUR

THAT HAD BEEN a really stupid move, Liam thought.

What had he been thinking, asking Vittoria to move closer, to share their body heat?

He sounded like a teenager on his first date. Awkward, socially inept, and cringe-makingly embarrassing.

When his sister found out—which she would, when Vittoria told Izzy and Izzy told Saoirse—she'd kill him.

But then he felt the sand shift under the blanket as Vittoria shuffled slightly closer to him.

And it just seemed natural to slide his arm round her shoulders. Gently. Lightly.

She slid her arm round his waist, and for a second he couldn't breathe.

They were from different worlds. Of course this was never going to work out between them. He shouldn't even start something he knew they couldn't finish. A fling was out of the question. Someone in Vittoria's position couldn't just have a mad fling.

But he really, really wanted her. He couldn't remember the last time he'd wanted someone so much.

But then he made another mistake: he stole a glance at her.

She was looking up at him, her face sweet and guileless in the moonlight.

He forgot who she was, where they were. All he could see was a woman next to him in the moonlight, lifting her face to his for a kiss. The woman he'd wanted to kiss on the window seat of her library, all soft and sweet and taking his breath away. The woman who was right here in his arms.

It was impossible to resist.

He lowered his head until his lips brushed hers. Once. Twice. His mouth tingled where it touched hers. She tasted of hot chocolate and salty sea air and something sweet that was just her, and he wanted more.

Then she slid her free hand round his neck; the arm she'd wrapped round his waist drew him closer. And Liam was completely lost; nothing existed except kissing Vittoria. It felt as if he'd waited his whole life for this moment, where her mouth was claiming his and she was holding him as tightly as he was holding her.

There was a shout from further down the beach which jolted him back to the present. In one horrible moment, he realised where he was. Who he was kissing. And why he shouldn't be doing anything of the sort.

He broke away from her. 'I'm sorry. I shouldn't have...'

Colour slashed across her cheekbones. 'It's OK. We'll just pretend it didn't happen.'

Yeah, right. He had a feeling he'd be lying awake tonight until stupid o'clock, thinking about her and that kiss.

But he went along with it. 'Sure.' He didn't dare look her in the eye. 'We probably ought to go back.'

He got to his feet, waited for her to stand up, then sorted out the blanket and travel mugs.

'Don't you want your jacket?' she asked.

'No, it's fine. I'll be warm enough walking.'

This time, the silence between them as they walked back to the cottage was awkward. He didn't know how to fix it. Why had he been so stupid and given in to the urge to kiss her?

The worst thing was, now he knew what it felt like to kiss her, he wanted to do it all over again. And he knew he shouldn't.

Back in the kitchen, Giorgio was reading the newspaper at the table with a mug of coffee beside him. He looked up as they walked in. 'Did you have a good walk?'

'Yes. But all this sea air has made me sleepy,' Vittoria said, and smothered a yawn that Liam was pretty sure was fake. 'I hope you'll excuse me.'

'Of course. Sleep well,' Giorgio said with a fond smile.

Liam didn't quite want to leave it like this. They still had another couple of days here, and he wanted them to be good ones, not filled with awkwardness because of his stupid mistake. 'I meant to say, earlier—the weather's meant to be good, so perhaps you'd like to go to see the seals tomorrow? There's a huge colony of common and grey seals a bit further round the coast, at Blakeney Point. It's quite a popular sight.'

'I remember—you said you'd gone last year with your best friend and his family.' She spread her hands. 'If it's OK with Giorgio, that'd be nice.'

Liam looked at the security detail. 'Risk assessment time?'

'Risk assessment time,' Giorgio agreed.

'We'll talk it over,' Liam said. 'If Giorgio's happy, I'll book tickets online and we'll go after breakfast tomorrow.' He had to suppress the sudden vision of waking in Vittoria's arms, because that definitely wasn't going to happen.

That kiss on the beach had been a mistake, and it wasn't going to be repeated—no matter how much he wanted it to.

'See you tomorrow,' she said, and left the kitchen.

Back in her room, Vittoria took off the wig and removed the contact lenses before showering and changing into a pair of pyjamas covered in sunflowers. The design was so very Izzy, and she felt a sharp pang, missing her little sister.

Izzy, too, had been instrumental in Vittoria's escape.

Today had been so very different from the kind of days she usually spent. No pressure, no having to be diplomatic—except for the moment when Liam had shown her the final photograph he'd taken in the library, and she'd had to mask her instant reaction. She'd looked as if she was about to be kissed, her expression all soft and dreamy and her lips parted. She hadn't looked like a princess; she'd looked like a woman dreaming of her lover.

Or a woman wondering what it would be like if a man she'd only just met kissed her.

She'd wondered.

And now she knew.

She'd been kissed in passion before. Kissed tentatively. Kissed by the man she'd thought she loved.

But nothing had felt like Liam MacCarthy's mouth against hers. Once definitely wasn't enough.

What was she going to do?

She'd told Liam and Giorgio that she wanted an early night. She'd fibbed that the sea air had made her sleepy; considering that she lived on an island and was very used to sea air, it had been a very stupid comment and they would both have known she was lying. Lying to herself, too, because she had a feeling she was going to spend most of the night awake, thinking about Liam MacCarthy and remembering the touch of his lips. Wishing she could kiss him all over again.

But she had a duty to fulfil. OK, she wasn't officially dating José, but she knew their families were trying to negotiate terms for a marriage. She couldn't afford to let herself fall for someone she definitely couldn't have, so she needed to keep Liam MacCarthy at a distance. No matter how much she wished that things could be different.

On Wednesday morning, there was a knock on Vittoria's door.

'Yes?' she called, sitting up in bed and pulling the duvet respectably round her.

The door opened a crack and she heard Giorgio's voice. 'Liam's booked the tickets for the seal trip. We need to leave in three-quarters of an hour.'

'OK. I'll be ready,' she said. With the wig and the contact lenses, she didn't need to worry about her hair or make-up. Even though she'd learned to be quick and flawless with cosmetics, it was nice to be able to choose *not* to wear any make-up without worrying what the press would say and what kind of spin there would be on the story—most probably about the princess looking ill, and then the suggestion that being queen would be too much for her.

'Liam's making bacon sandwiches,' Giorgio added, 'and I'm making coffee.'

'Wonderful. Give me fifteen minutes.'

Ten minutes later, she went downstairs in jeans, a T-shirt and the floral canvas shoes.

'Morning, Vicky.' Liam greeted her cheerfully, as if that kiss last night had never happened and neither had the awkwardness.

Even though she hadn't been able to stop thinking about that kiss, now wasn't the time or the place to discuss it. So she followed his lead. 'Morning, Liam.'

He slid a plate in front of her with a bacon sandwich cut neatly into triangles. 'Help yourself to ketchup or brown sauce.'

She smiled. 'I'll leave mine unadulterated, thanks. This looks lovely.' She tried to imagine José making her breakfast in their private apartment, and failed dismally. Whereas she could easily imagine Liam making waffles with maple syrup, or cooking eggs Florentine, or toasting cinnamon bagels.

Tough.

Liam wasn't going to be part of her future. She'd just have to find a way to fall in love with José.

But Vittoria's resolution failed miserably later that morning, when Liam had driven them further down the coast to catch the boat. He'd insisted on her wearing sunscreen plus Izzy's sunhat—a white floppy bucket hat covered in roses—and Giorgio helped her into the boat. Somehow she ended up sitting between him and Liam, and when the last people got onto the boat they all had to move up a little. Vittoria was very aware of the press of Liam's thigh against hers. He stretched one arm out behind her, to give her a little more room, and rested his other hand on the edge of the boat. It would be so easy to move in closer to him. Though she intended to keep a tight control of her feelings and stay exactly where she was, with just enough distance between them.

They listened to the skipper going through the safety briefing. The boat was sailing smoothly and she'd got herself back under control when they hit a rough patch of water, the boat rocked unexpectedly, and she ended up practically falling into Liam. His arm tightened round her, keeping her safe; except she noticed that when they were sailing smoothly again he didn't move his arm away.

Should she move?

Stupid question. Of course she should.

But she didn't want to. And this was her sort-of *Roman Holiday*, her stolen time away. So it didn't count, did it?

She stayed right where she was, in the protective circle of his arm, enjoying his nearness.

The boat's skipper was telling them all about the area and what they were going to see, though Vittoria was so aware of Liam's proximity that she found it hard to concentrate.

They drew nearer to the spit of land in the distance. A blue building with white windows, a semi-circular roof and an observation tower came into view, and the skipper told them that it used to be the lifeboat shed but was now the visitor centre. There were lots of seabirds flying about; the skipper taught them the differences between the varieties of gulls and told them what to look out for.

As they moved further along the shingle and sand spit, the seals came into view, basking in the sun; many of them turned their faces to look at the boat, as if they were as intrigued by the occupants as the passengers were with them. One or two raised a flipper, as if waving. They had such pretty faces, with those huge dark eyes, smiling mouth and long whiskers; Vittoria's heart melted.

One or two of the seals shuffled off the sand, moving surprisingly fast; once in the water they immediately changed from slightly ungainly creatures to agile swimmers, ducking beneath the waves and popping up again to look at the boats.

'Don't crowd to the starboard side of the boat,' the skipper warned. 'You'll all get the same opportunities to take photographs, because we'll be returning the same way and the port side will get the better view on the way back.'

People on the starboard side of the boat, closest to the seals, were snapping photos.

Liam surprised her by taking his phone from his pocket. 'Budge up, Giorgio—we'll take a selfie to send to Izzy,' he said, keeping his voice low so he didn't ruin the commentary for the other passengers.

'You use a *phone* camera?' she asked, keeping her own voice low. 'When you're... A professional photographer?'

He smiled. 'The best camera is always the one that's to hand. Sure, a phone doesn't have the same flexibility as an SLR, but I'm never going to be snobby about it.' He took a couple of shots. 'You can choose which one you want to send her later.'

'Thanks.' She took some pictures of the seals on her phone and reviewed them.

The disappointment must've shown on her face, because he said softly, 'What's wrong?'

She shrugged. 'I wanted to capture the expressions on the seals' faces. These are a bit too far away.'

He took a camera from his pocket, checked one of the settings and handed it to her. 'Try this.'

He was offering her his camera? But this was what

he did for a living. Wasn't this an expensive, precious piece of kit? 'But isn't it—?' she began.

'It's a digital compact camera,' he said. 'It's old and battered and very reliable. It's the one I keep in my pocket if I'm not going somewhere specifically to shoot something. I also use it when I'm checking out the background for a shoot. I've set it on auto mode, so you don't have to spend time focusing the shot.' He showed her how to use the zoom.

'Thank you. Though it's a bit intimidating, taking photographs next to a professional.'

He shook his head. 'Ignore what I do for a living. Take the shot that pleases you. There are rules that can help you take better compositions, yes; but we can go through those another time, if you want to. For now, just keep it simple, use the zoom if you want close-ups, and look at the details that interest you. I'll send you the pictures over Wi-Fi when we get back.'

'Thank you.'

Finally she got the pictures she wanted. Her hand touched his when she gave the camera back to him, sending a surge of awareness through her, and she was glad of the sunglasses that meant he couldn't read her feelings in her eyes. Though his glasses meant that she couldn't read his feelings, either.

Princess Vittoria di Sarda was cool, confident and collected. She'd been trained for years not to let any situation throw her. The woman sitting on a boat full of tourists, with borrowed clothes and a borrowed name, didn't feel in the slightest bit cool or collected. She felt like a teenager with a crush on a friend's big brother. And it threw her completely.

Liam didn't slide his arm round her on the journey home, and she wasn't sure if that was more of a relief or a disappointment. It was definitely a mixture of the two. Relief, because it gave her the space to get her thoughts collected again; disappointment, because she liked his nearness.

She focused on the skipper's commentary all the way back to the harbour, and Giorgio was the one who held her hand to steady her while she climbed off the boat and back onto the quayside.

They had a simple lunch in a little pub with the most amazing sea views, then Liam drove them further round the coast to another beach. 'I'm guessing that looking in tide pools and beach-combing for fossils isn't part of your everyday life.'

'No. It's not something I ever really remember doing,' she admitted.

He glanced at her canvas shoes. 'They should be fine. You're sensible enough to realise the rocks will be a bit slippery and be careful where you put your feet.'

Vittoria thoroughly enjoyed looking in the tide pools, spotting crabs, anemones, limpets and starfish. She took a few shots on her phone for Izzy.

On the way back to the car, they beach-combed for fossils.

'So what kind of fossils are we looking for?' she asked.

'Sponges and coral. Or a belemnite.'

'What's that?'

'Apparently it was a bit like a squid but had a hard skeleton. Look for an amber stone that looks a bit like a bullet casing, and is about the length of your thumb.'

They continued looking, and Vittoria bent to pick up a cylinder-shaped stone. 'Do you think this is a belemnite?' she asked, handing it to him. Her fingers tingled when her skin touched his.

'Definitely.' He smiled at her and dropped it back into her palm. 'Well spotted.'

Again, at the brief touch of his skin, she felt that weird tingling. 'There are three or four others here,' she said. 'But someone else might enjoy finding them, so I'm not going to take more than one.'

His smile was full of approval and made her feel warm all over.

They called into a supermarket on the way back to the cottage to buy the makings of dinner. Liam insisted on taking the basket before they got to the checkout.

'This isn't fair. You paid for dinner last night.'

'We don't want a paper trail leading back to you, re-member,' he said softly. 'And if I was in London I'd be buying groceries. So this is pretty much the same thing.'

She couldn't argue with him. But she could send him a thank-you gift once she was back in San Ro-cello. A first edition of his favourite book, perhaps, or a piece of art. He'd given her time to herself. And that was priceless.

Back at the cottage, Vittoria shooed Liam and Giorgio into the enclosed back garden while she cooked dinner.

'The princess is nothing like her sister, is she?' Liam said. 'So quiet and controlled. I guess it goes with her job.'

The security detail nodded. 'It will be good for her to have this break. She never takes time off.'

'Does she really have to marry whoever her family says she has to marry?'

Giorgio shrugged.

'What a waste,' Liam said softly. 'She deserves someone who understands her, makes some space around her and makes her feel special.'

Giorgio's raised eyebrow spoke volumes.

'Don't worry. I know I can't be that man. I don't have blue blood and her family would never accept me,' Liam said. 'I'm not going to do anything inappropriate.' He really hoped the security detail didn't have a clue about that kiss last night. 'And I won't do anything to hurt her.'

'Good,' Giorgio said. 'Technically, she's my boss, but she feels like my little sister.'

'I have a little sister,' Liam reminded Giorgio, 'so I know exactly where you're coming from. You want to wrap them in cotton wool and save them from the harshest bits of the world. Though that isn't healthy, either. They need to learn to fly. And sometimes it's hard to find the middle way.'

'Very true,' Giorgio said.

'So what's he like? The guy her family want her to marry?'

Giorgio shrugged. 'It's not my place to judge.'

'OK. If she really was your little sister, would you be happy for her to marry him?'

'I'd want my little sister to marry someone who loved her for herself,' Giorgio said diplomatically. 'But the princess lives in a different world. One where people have expectations of her. Where everyone watches everything she says and does.'

A world where Liam knew he'd never fit in. And he heeded the warning. He wouldn't do anything to make Vittoria's life harder. 'I'll go grab us a drink from the fridge,' he said.

When he went into the kitchen, Vittoria was humming along to a pop song on the radio, making gnocchi. She seemed completely unaware of Liam's presence as he watched her; and she looked so cute, so relaxed, that he couldn't resist taking a couple of snaps on his phone.

A portrait of a princess; a portrait of her relaxing, doing something she enjoyed.

That was the thing missing from the formal portraits he'd taken, he realised. Happiness. In the formal ones, she'd been shouldering a weight. Here, she was free.

He wasn't going to break the moment for her; he quietly got two cans of drink from the fridge and went back into the garden.

Vittoria had already made the pesto while the potatoes were boiling. She enjoyed the task of making the gnocchi: sieving the cooked potatoes, cutting the flour in with a blunt knife and then kneading the dough with her hands. She'd forgotten how relaxing it could be, shaping the dough into the little balls and then flipping it along the tines of a fork to get the traditional ridges on one side and a thumbprint on the other.

When she'd cooked dinner as a student, it had been fun rather than a chore—a kind of balance to studying hard.

When had life stopped being fun?

She would never shirk her duty, but these stolen days had shown her that she needed a little more balance in her life.

Once she'd made the gnocchi, she sliced strawberries and set them to steep in balsamic vinegar and black pepper; then she sliced up mozzarella, plum tomatoes and avocado and arranged them on three plates and decorated them with a tiny drizzle of pesto. Funny how such a simple thing could make her feel so good.

She laid the table, then called Liam and Giorgio in from the garden.

They were both appreciative of the meal.

'It wasn't exactly difficult. The first course and pudding were really just assembly jobs,' she pointed out.

'But you made the pesto and gnocchi yourself. You could've just bought some ready-made from the chiller cabinet at the supermarket,' Liam said. 'And this is the best pesto I've ever tasted. Really fresh and zingy.'

The compliment warmed her all the way through. Particularly because it was specific, so it felt genuine rather than flattery. 'Thank you.'

'So what's the plan for tomorrow?' Giorgio asked.

'If it's dry we could go and look for bluebells,' Liam said. 'There are some bits of really ancient woodland here, and there's nothing more gorgeous than a bluebell carpet. The best time to visit is mid-morning, when you get all this soft, dappled light.'

'It sounds as if you've done a shoot in a bluebell wood before,' Vittoria said.

'I have. And among snowdrops, and in a poppy field.' He paused. 'You'd look spectacular in a poppy field. Very Monet.'

Was he seeing her with an artist's eye, or a man's?

She damped the thought down. They'd agreed that yesterday's kiss should be forgotten. The problem was, she couldn't forget it. It kept sliding back into her head, and even thinking about it made her mouth tingle.

Liam and Giorgio insisted on doing the washing up, and Giorgio made coffee.

'I'll sort out those photos for you,' Liam said, and downloaded the photographs from his phone and camera to his laptop at the kitchen table. 'Feel free to have a look,' he said when he'd finished. 'Let me know which ones you'd like, and I'll forward them to you.'

Their selfies on the boat with Giorgio looked as if they were just like all the other holidaymakers having fun. Vittoria chose one, plus the ones she'd taken of the seals, and he sent them to her phone.

Part of her wanted to ask for a copy of the portrait he'd taken in the palace library—that last, very private shot. But she knew she'd only brood over it, and it was pointless wishing for something she couldn't have. 'Thanks for sorting this out for me,' she said instead, and set out to compose a bright text to Izzy to go with the photographs.

# CHAPTER FIVE

ON THURSDAY MORNING, Liam drove them to a bluebell wood.

'I've never seen a bluebell carpet in real life. Not even when I lived in London,' Vittoria said as he parked the car.

'Really? There are loads of bluebells in Richmond Park and Highgate Woods. They were my mum's favourite flower. We used to go and see them every spring.' He smiled. 'After Mum died, I used to take Saoirse to see them and then we'd go for hot chocolate afterwards.'

'A way of remembering your mum?' she guessed.

He nodded. 'I wanted Saoirse to be able to remember her. And I thought a sight and a smell might help anchor it for her, as it does for me.'

It was a bit like the way Vittoria remembered walking with her dad through the palace rose garden and thought of him every time she smelled roses. Maybe she should share that with Izzy, to help her to remember their dad. 'I guess I was too busy studying and trying to learn some diplomatic duties to look for bluebells,' she said.

He frowned. 'Don't you have bluebells in San Rocello—or mainland Italy?'

'We have *giacinto di bosco*, yes, but they're not quite the same as English bluebells.'

He nodded. 'Dad taught me that English bluebells had narrower bells than European ones, and only on one side of the stem.'

It was the first time Liam had talked about his father to Vittoria, though she remembered him saying that his father had died when Saoirse was very small and he wasn't quite in double figures.

'Your father liked flowers?' she asked.

'He was a horticulturalist. He worked at Kew,' Liam explained.

'So you know a lot about plants?'

'Not that much,' he said, 'but we had an amazing garden at our old house. Mum kept it up after Dad died—he'd planted it so there would be colour all year round. Obviously at my flat now there's only the patio, and it's not fair to expect Saoirse to spend a lot of time on the plants if I'm away, so I just have stuff in pots that don't need a lot of attention. Though it's a shame. I want to keep Dad's memory alive, too.'

'Do you miss him?' The question was out before she could stop it.

'Yes. I guess you must feel the same about your dad. Wishing he could see you all grown up, wondering if you've grown into the person he thought you'd be. If he'd approve of your choices, your actions.'

She looked at him. 'Obviously I didn't know your dad—but I'm beginning to know you, and I think any parent would be proud to have a son like you. Someone who cares, who's made a huge difference to his little sister's life.'

There was a slash of colour in his cheeks. 'Thank you. And I think any dad would be proud of the woman I'm getting to know—someone who thinks, who notices details. Someone who's going to make a fair and balanced ruler.'

She inclined her head in acknowledgement. 'Thank you. Though I wasn't fishing for a compliment.'

'I didn't think you were. I wasn't, either. But it's hard growing up without a parent.' For a moment, his expression was bleak.

On impulse, she took his hand and squeezed it. 'Harder for you—at least I still have my mother. Even if she does drive me a bit crazy.'

'Mum used to wrap us both in cotton wool after Dad died,' Liam said. 'It was only when one of her friends had a quiet word with her about smothering us that she made an effort to be—well, more relaxed.'

Her own mother was definitely overprotective, Vittoria thought. Though she didn't have friends who would nudge her to be less smothering; if anything, Vittoria's grandmother encouraged her to be overprotective of both her daughters and the monarchy.

Then she realised she was still holding Liam's hand. Not the best idea, she reminded herself. 'My dad liked flowers, too,' she said, gently disentangling her fingers from his. 'I used to love walking in the palace rose garden with him. I still walk there, sometimes, because it makes me feel close to him.'

'I get that,' he said softly. 'And it's not just the sight, is it? It's the scent. The best rose garden I've ever seen is up on the north-east coast at Alnwick. I did a photo shoot there for a Sunday supplement and it was like breathing roses as you walked round. The scent was unbelievable.'

And then he stopped. 'Here's your bluebell carpet,' he said softly.

She hadn't really been paying attention to their surroundings as they walked; she'd been focused on him.

And there it was. A haze of blue underneath the trees in the dappled sunlight, as far as the eye could see. The scent in the air was delicate, a kind of green floral. Vittoria closed her eyes for a moment to breathe it in, and knew this scent would always remind her of a late spring English morning—a morning spent with Liam.

They walked in silence; she was spellbound by the sheer beauty of the flowers, and took several snaps on her phone. Liam had his compact camera in his pocket and persuaded her to sit on a fallen tree and pose for pictures. 'I'm taking these for Izzy,' he said, and was very precise in his instructions for each pose.

Again, she saw the artist at work—and she liked what she saw. He was focused, intense, and she loved the sheer energy as he paced about, looked at her, changed his own position anywhere from being on tiptoe to squatting down, directed her to move her position or her head a little bit to get the precise angle he wanted, then took another shot.

He made her laugh when he asked her for what he called the classic female shots—one with her arms raised and her eyes closed and her head tilted back as if looking at the sky between the treetops; one with her holding one hand out towards him; one with her leaning against a tree trunk. It was surprisingly fun; she hadn't expected to enjoy this so much.

'Can I take a picture of you?' she asked, when he'd finished.

He looked slightly surprised, then nodded and handed over the camera. 'Sure.'

'So I assume there are rules for portrait photography?'

He smiled. 'A few. Though you don't always have to

stick to the rules. You can break them—but it's better if you know *why* you're breaking them.'

He wasn't just talking about photography, was he? Her pulse leapt. 'Uh-huh,' she said, trying to sound calm and collected. Except she didn't feel calm or collected. She wanted him to kiss her again. And that wasn't fair.

With an effort, she said, 'Tell me the rules.' And then maybe she'd remember her personal rules, too.

'OK. With women, it's all about the curves; with men, it's about angles, so you're looking for a V shape with broad shoulders and a narrow waist. You're looking for a strong jaw, the eyes slightly squinting, and his head tilted away from the camera—but not too far, or he'll look arrogant and aggressive.'

She'd never thought about that before.

'Do you want me to face you full on or look away?' he asked.

'What's the best one?'

'That's your choice, because you're the one taking the portrait and telling the story,' he said. 'But even if it's face-on, you'd want your subject to turn very slightly so the nose is off-centre. That gives more shape and definition to the face.'

Liam had a beautiful nose. A beautiful face, she thought. And a mouth she desperately wanted to run her forefinger along and kiss again. She damped down the feelings. Not here, not now. 'Turn your face slightly to the left,' she directed, and he did so.

Funny, seeing him through the lens made her look at him differently. Made her focus on the little details. Everything from the cornflower-blue of his eyes, to the length of his eyelashes, to the tiny grooves at the corners of his mouth which told her he smiled often.

'Next, decide what kind of light you want. It's up to

you whether you want to use a flash, but consider that if the light source is from the same angle as the camera it'll flatten my features, because there aren't any shadows.'

She liked the way he explained things so clearly.

'Keep the composition simple. And check the background.' He smiled. 'In a forest, you don't want a tree trunk growing out of your subject's head or a branch growing out of an ear.'

'Got it.' She looked at the screen on the back of the camera. 'Right now, there's a tree growing out of your head. So I ask you to move, right?'

'Yes. And if I'm not looking straight at the camera, don't crop in too tightly. It's a better composition if you have some "lead room"—that's the space in a photo, between the subject and the edges of the picture. You need that to be in front of me, in the same direction as I'm looking. If the space is behind me, it makes your audience frustrated because there's all this empty space doing nothing, and they want to know what I'm looking at.'

'But if there's empty space in front of you, they still won't actually know what you're looking at,' she pointed out.

'True, but it means *I'm* the focus of the photograph—not, say, my ear,' he explained.

He talked her through a few more of the rules, and she took several shots in between each one, making him change his pose accordingly. Each picture was better than the previous one, because he'd taught her a little more. And it surprised her to realise that she was feeling more confident in her own abilities—more grounded. Not just in the skills he'd taught her this morning, but everything; he'd made her focus on her ability to see things, to plan and make decisions. Things that applied to more than taking a photograph.

Right at that moment, she felt strong: capable of doing anything. Because he was beside her? Or was he simply bringing out something that was already there? She'd been following so many rules for so long, she wasn't entirely sure. Maybe his own confidence in his skills—a confidence she found compelling—was rubbing off on her.

'So the poses you made me do… Are there male equivalents?'

'Yes. Though any pose can be gender-swapped. It depends on what you want to say with the picture,' he said. 'If I assume the pose, you tell me whether you need me to move, and if so how.'

And she loved every second of it. Seeing him put his right hand up to his chin, his thumb to the side and his index finger across his lips as if he was telling her this was a secret, a glint of mischief in his eyes. Standing almost side-on with his arms folded. Turning up the collar on his jacket, one hand on each lapel. Taking off his jacket and holding it over his shoulder with one finger, the other hand casually in his pocket. Leaning against a tree, with the leg closest to her bent up and his foot against the trunk.

It showed how strong his thighs were. And all of a sudden, she couldn't breathe. She could imagine him in a very different pose. On a hot summer night, when she'd woken and left their bed to get a cool drink… Naked, face down on a wide bed, with a sheet carelessly thrown across his lower body and showing how strong his back was, how perfect his musculature.

Heat prickled all the way through her.

'Done?' he asked.

Her mouth felt as if it had stuck to the roof of her mouth. Was this how he saw his models? Was this how he'd seen *her* when he'd asked her to pose for him?

'Vittoria? Are you OK?' There was a note of concern in his voice which snagged her attention away from the images in her head.

'Yes. Sorry. Wool-gathering.' She really hoped her thoughts hadn't shown in her face.

'Can I see the shots?'

She nodded mutely and gave his camera back.

He switched it to playback mode and scrolled through the shots. 'I can definitely see progress,' he said. 'You pay attention and you pick things up quickly. San Rocello's going to be lucky to have you in charge.'

The compliment warmed her all the way through. Particularly because she could tell it was sincere. She was used to people flattering her in the hope that she would give them influence or a business deal, but Liam didn't want anything from her.

But, oh, she was going to have to get those other images out of her head.

Because it couldn't happen. It couldn't last. And a fling with him—even if a future queen could abandon caution to the wind and have a mad fling—wouldn't be enough for her.

They strolled back to the car park, chatting easily, and he drove them further round the coast. They stopped to pick up sandwiches and takeaway coffee from a deli-café—he'd brought reusable mugs from the cottage—and then headed along a walkway at the edge of a pine forest.

'This one's gorgeous. It's been used as a film set quite a few times,' he said.

There were no beach huts here, and no cliffs. Just pine trees, a wide expanse of sand and an area that seemed to be covered in tiny flowers.

'It's a saltwater lagoon,' he said. 'When the tide comes in, it's covered.'

They walked along the beach together, with Giorgio as always giving them enough space to talk privately yet staying near enough to be there immediately if he was needed.

'I've been thinking. You said earlier you want to be best portrait photographer of your generation, but aren't you that already?' she asked.

'I have a good reputation,' he said, 'but I think you can always learn more in your chosen field and do better. And I'm not where I want to be, yet.'

'So you're driven.'

'Yes,' he said, 'but I'm the one who makes the decisions on who's doing the driving.' He looked at her, his blue eyes thoughtful. 'You're just as driven as I am—but is being queen what you'd choose?'

'That's irrelevant,' she said. 'I always knew I'd be the queen some day because I'm the oldest child. If my father had lived, I would've taken over from him instead of from my grandfather.' Though she would've had more of a breathing space before the coronation. Right now, the end of the year felt very close indeed. Her last summer of freedom wasn't stretching out before her; it was going to vanish in the blink of an eye.

'If you weren't a princess—if you could do anything in the world—what would you do?' he asked.

'I don't honestly know,' she said. Because she deliberately hadn't let herself think about it. What was the point of wondering, when your path in life was already mapped out for you?

'I guess you never had the freedom to choose,' he said softly.

'No.' It hadn't mattered before, and she couldn't let it matter now. 'You didn't exactly have much freedom of choice, either,' she pointed out.

'True, but I don't think I missed out—maybe I missed out on having a social life at university, but since Saoirse turned eighteen I've been able to pretty much please myself with what I do and where I go. I know she won't do anything stupid like have a party and invite the kind of people who'd trash the flat.' He shrugged. 'I guess we both had to grow up fast.'

Vittoria rather thought he meant the two of them, rather than himself and his sister. 'It must've been tough, though, being a parent figure when you were so young yourself.'

'I had people I could ask for advice if I needed it. Patty, my old photography tutor, was so kind,' he said. 'But I guess I was lucky. Saoirse was in with a good crowd. It could've been much tougher.' He wrinkled his nose. 'My sister will always have a home with me, whenever she needs it. Just as I'm guessing you'd always find space for Izzy.'

'Yes. Of course I would.'

'But it's kind of put me off the idea of being a parent in the future. Been there, done that—I'll never regret putting her first, ever, but...' He blew out a breath. 'In the early days, every girlfriend I had seemed to end up resenting her. Probably my fault for picking the wrong kind of girl; they wanted to go to parties, and they got fed up when I couldn't find a babysitter.'

'She doesn't need a babysitter now.'

'No—but my career takes me away a lot. I have to go where my subject is. I can't expect them to come to me.'

'Why not?'

He smiled. 'Well, you were my last subject. Where would you say was the most appropriate place for the shoot—some random location in London, or the palace?'

'Point taken. But surely your girlfriends don't

mind you travelling? Surely they like the chance to go with you?'

'It's not the travelling. It's the fact that my career comes first. If they came with me, I wouldn't be able to go and do touristy stuff with them because I'd be going there to work, not for a holiday. And I'm tired of being asked to choose,' he said. 'My family or my girlfriend; my career or my girlfriend.' He shrugged. 'Right now, I'm happily single—and I plan to stay that way. I want the freedom to follow my dream, to be the best photographer I can be. And if that means giving up on relationships, that's fine by me.'

He'd made his position very, very clear; he was single, and planning to stay that way.

Not that it was any of her business. And not that she was in a position to start a relationship with someone her family would definitely disapprove of. She knew her grandfather had liked Liam—but that was purely as an artist and a businessman. A potential partner for his eldest granddaughter was a very different matter. Plus, she'd learned from Rufus that having a non-royal background was the biggest hurdle to any relationship with a commoner. If anyone could overcome it, she thought Liam might be that man; from what she'd seen of him, he was bright, he paid attention to the small things, and he understood the struggle of responsibility. But he'd just made it clear he wasn't interested in a relationship.

This *Roman Holiday* thing was turning out to be a double-edged sword. On the one hand, it had given her a breathing space she'd desperately needed; on the other, it had given her space to dream of things that just weren't going to be possible in her real life. Right now, she actually dreaded going back. She didn't want to follow all the old rules any more. She wanted to make new rules, ones that might move life at the palace onto a more modern footing. But was she strong enough to do that on her own?

She concentrated on looking for pretty shells and walking at the edge of the sea.

Today was the last day.

Tomorrow she'd be going back to the real world. To the airport. To San Rocello. She wouldn't be Vicky the tourist, walking barefoot on a beach, any more; she'd be Princess Vittoria, wearing the perfect business suit and high heels. And the weight that had lightened on her first day here settled right back in the centre of her shoulders.

She didn't say much for the rest of the afternoon; and Liam, clearly realising that she didn't want to talk, didn't push her. She managed to make small talk during dinner at a local foodie pub, chatting about how delicious the locally made goat's cheese was, and the seafood risotto. Things that didn't really matter.

And then they were back at the cottage, where Giorgio pleaded a headache and a need for an early night.

Was that what she should do? Borrow a book from the shelves in the living room and have an early night, too?

But Liam said quietly, 'It's your last night. It's a nice evening; come and sit in the garden with a glass of wine.'

The wine was crisp, dry and perfectly chilled. Liam had put cushions on two wrought-iron chairs, and they sat side by side, looking up at the stars.

'Penny for them?' he asked.

She had intended to be polite and not admit to what was really going on in her head, but something in his eyes made her tell the truth. 'I've enjoyed my time here. It's really helped recharge me. Izzy's right about the palace making me feel stifled. But I know I have to go back to San Rocello.' And do her duty. Which she'd already shirked for four whole days.

Either she'd spoken aloud or he was seriously good at working out what people were thinking, because he asked, 'Do you really have to get married to this guy your family's chosen for you?'

'José?' She sighed. 'Probably. Or someone like him.'

'I understand that you have to marry someone from a royal background,' he said, 'but can't you choose him yourself?'

'Sometimes I wonder—' She stopped and screwed up her nose. 'Forget I said that.'

He looked at her. 'Sometimes it helps to think out loud and bounce ideas off people.'

If she talked to anyone about this, it should be Izzy. But she hadn't wanted to burden her sister, especially so close to Izzy's Finals.

'If it helps,' he said, 'I promise it won't go any further than me.'

She thought about it. Given how much time Izzy had spent at his flat over the last three years, he would know a lot about her sister's life. If he'd wanted to sell a story to the press, he'd had plenty of opportunities, and he definitely had the contacts. But he'd done nothing of the kind.

She could trust him.

If she chose.

'I feel disloyal even thinking this,' she said. 'I know what my family expects from me. I'm going to be queen. I need to marry, produce an heir and a spare, and bring up those children so they'll be able to do their own duty well, when it's their time. And of course I'll do my duty, just as my father would've done if he'd still been alive— just as my grandfather has done.'

'But would it be different if your dad hadn't died?' he asked. 'Obviously you'd still eventually be queen, but would you have been able to choose your own husband?'

'I don't know,' she admitted. 'I think maybe my dad would've wanted me to find someone I loved—someone who loved me.'

'So who's putting the pressure on you to marry someone you don't love? Your grandfather?'

She shook her head. 'My mum and my grandmother. Nonna's very traditional—and I think when my dad died my mum found it hard to cope. She's pretty much followed my grandmother's lead in everything since then, wrapping me up in cotton wool and...' She shook her head. 'I love my mother. But sometimes I wish she'd lighten up. I wish she'd find another partner—not because it would take the pressure off me, but because I worry that she's lonely.'

Liam took her hand and squeezed it. 'As lonely as *you* are?'

'If so much as a single word of this gets back to Izzy, you're toast,' she warned, scowling at him.

'It won't,' he reassured her. 'Not because I'm scared of you, but because I know how you feel. I try not to let Saoirse know if I'm out of sorts about something, too.'

'Thank you.' She sighed. 'Being at the palace can be a bit isolating. I've got my mum, and my grandparents, and that's it. My local friends have all moved away, my uni friends are scattered across the globe, and—oh, this is turning into such a pity party.' She grimaced. 'And that's not who I am.'

'Of course it isn't. You're bright, you're independent, and you're about to shoulder a really heavy responsibility. I mean, don't most monarchs accede the throne when they're fifty or so?' he asked.

'I guess.'

'It's a lot of pressure. And I agree with you: it's not a good idea to get married to someone you don't love and who doesn't love you. You're going to have enough on your plate. Talk to your grandfather. Tell him you need more time to find the right partner. Tell them you'd like to choose your own husband. You're going to be queen, so surely you get to make some of the rules?'

'And if they all say no?'

'Negotiate,' he said. 'To do a job well, you need to be happy in that job. And you're not going to be happy shackled to someone who doesn't understand you. As the queen, you need a consort you can rely on. Someone you can talk to. Someone with a bit of common sense. Someone who understands your heart.'

She inclined her head. 'Sadly, consorts don't quite come to order.' She looked up at the stars in the sky. 'Do you ever wonder if there's more?'

'To the universe? Maybe. You?'

'I…' She pushed the longing back down. 'No.'

'Or did you mean more than life in a goldfish bowl?' he asked gently.

How could he see through her like that? Was her public mask slipping? Would other people see it, too? Or was it because Liam had a connection with her that he could tell what was going on in her head?

'What you asked me among the bluebells this morning—if I could do anything I wanted, what would it be? I've been thinking about it all day and I still don't have an answer.'

He didn't push her.

And finally, she admitted, 'Sometimes I'm not sure who I am, deep down.'

'When I take a portrait,' he said, 'it shows me who

someone is. I get them to talk to me. Tell me their hopes, their dreams. Sometimes it's obvious they're not telling me what they really feel, so I ask questions from completely left field. Stupid things, like those internet quizzes Saoirse and Izzy love about what sort of cookie you are. Or I ask them to read something, or tell me a joke—and then, once they open up to me, I can take a portrait of who they are.'

She remembered her own photo shoot with him. 'You asked me to read you my favourite poem.'

He inclined his head. 'Shakespeare's *Sonnet 130*. And that told me a lot about you. Vittoria, I know you have a duty, but it doesn't make sense to marry someone you don't love.'

She had no choice. She had to marry someone who understood protocol and the demands of a royal lifestyle. Love on its own wasn't enough, or Rufus wouldn't have backed away from her.

Liam took his phone from his pocket and tapped into a website.

'These are the photographs I took for your grandfather. Your official portrait,' he said. 'Look at her from the outside. Pretend this is a stranger, not you. Can you see what I see? A woman who's proud of the traditions she comes from. A princess. Someone cool, calm and collected. Reliable in a crisis. Prepared to do the best for her people.'

Where was he going with this?

'Unofficially…' He showed her the photographs he'd taken when she hadn't even been aware of him using his phone: of her on the beach, of her making the gnocchi. When she'd been relaxed. When she'd felt happy.

'And this.' The photographs they'd taken in the bluebell wood that morning, when she'd been laughing and smiling and intrigued by him. When she'd done the poses she'd thought at the time were a bit ridiculous, but had gone along with them because she could see he was having fun, and she'd enjoyed it too.

'Maybe I'm presuming things, but as a photographer I'm used to looking past the trappings and seeing who someone really is. I think these photographs show the real you,' he said, 'the one that people don't see. A woman who's usually reserved, but here you're the woman behind the tiara. Laughing. Open. Beautiful. Izzy says you're like sunshine when you smile. And you are.'

She'd never heard her little sister say that about her, and it brought a lump to her throat.

And then he flicked over to the photograph he'd taken of her in the library.

'*This* is you,' he said, his voice cracking. 'The you I saw. The you I kissed on the beach. The you I wanted to kiss among the bluebells this morning, when you were pretending to be me and bossing me about.' He paused. 'The you I want to kiss now, even though I know it's unfair of me because you have to go back to San Rocello and you have duties to fulfil. The you I want to kiss now, even though I'm not looking for a relationship—and even if I was, I know there isn't a snowflake's chance in hell of things working out between us.'

She knew he was right.

She could be sensible Princess Vittoria, agree with him there wasn't a hope for them, and walk away.

Or she could be herself. The woman who wanted him to kiss her. Who wanted to kiss him back. Who wanted more.

Just for tonight...

She'd never felt such a strong compulsion before.

Longing. It wasn't just about sex—though there was definitely desire there—it was about *connection*.

Tentatively, she stretched out a hand and stroked his cheek.

He slid his hand over hers, then turned his head so he could drop a kiss into her palm. Then he gently drew her hand away and kissed her in the garden under the stars, his mouth warm and sweet and enticing.

This time, they had birdsong rather than the swish of the waves for background noise.

This time, there wasn't anyone to interrupt them with an ill-timed shout.

It was just the two of them, the stars and the nightingales. It felt as if rainbows were filling her head, and she'd never wanted anyone as much as she'd wanted this man.

She broke the kiss. 'Liam.'

He sighed. 'Vittoria. I'm sorry. I know I overstepped the line.'

'No. I wanted you to kiss me.' She took a deep breath, thinking about the moment in the bluebell wood when she'd had that vision of him naked and in her bed. When desire had been so strong, it had stopped up her words. 'I want more than kissing. I want you.'

His cornflower-blue eyes were almost indigo. 'I want you, too. But we can't do this. It's going to hurt too many people.'

She shook her head. 'There's nobody to hurt. I'm single. You are, too.'

'But your family's arranging a marriage.'

To someone she didn't love. Someone who didn't make her pulse beat a tattoo, the way it was beating right now. And maybe Liam had given her enough to think about tonight. Maybe she didn't have to marry someone so fast. Maybe she could take her time and choose her consort wisely.

She took a deep breath. 'I'll do my duty, when the time comes. But this is now. Time for me. My *Roman Holiday*, as Izzy calls it. You, me, no strings.' A fling she knew a queen-to-be couldn't have; but Liam had said earlier that you could break the rules, as long as you knew why.

She knew why she wanted to break the rules tonight.

She wanted him.

Wanted him more than she'd ever wanted anyone in her life.

He brushed his mouth against hers. 'Just so you know, I don't sleep around.'

'Neither do I.' She took another deep breath. 'But I can't get you out of my head, Liam. I haven't been able to stop thinking about you since that moment in the library. I thought you were going to kiss me, then.'

'I almost did,' he admitted.

'I wish you had.'

He shook his head. 'I never mix work and my personal life. And that photo shoot was work.'

'That last picture in the library wasn't,' she said. 'You didn't take that for my grandfather, or even for Izzy, or she would've shown me.'

'No. I admit, I took it for me. Because you're captivating,' he said. 'You're the most beautiful woman I've ever met, but it's not just the way you look. It's *you*. The way you make me feel. I can't stop thinking about you, either. But we don't have a future. I have my career to think of and you have your duty. I'd never fit into your world, and you can't fit into mine. I wouldn't ask you to choose between me and your duty because it wouldn't be fair.'

'I know.' She sighed. 'And I wish things were different.'

'So do I. But they're not. We need to be sensible.'

She stared at him. 'How can I be sensible when you're still touching me?'

Before he could pull his hand away from her cheek, she twisted her head to the side, just as he'd done to her, and pressed a kiss into his palm.

He sucked in a breath. 'What do we do about this, Vittoria?'

She was glad he hadn't called her by that ridiculous borrowed name. He saw her for who she was. Vittoria. Not the princess, but the woman. She looked him straight in the eye. 'We might not be able to have for ever—but we can have tonight. A moment out of time.'

There was a deep slash of colour across his cheeks as he thought about what she'd just said and clearly came to the right conclusion.

'Do you have a condom?' she asked.

He inclined his head.

'Then what I want,' she said, just in case it wasn't clear enough, 'is to spend tonight with you. To make love with you. To wake in your arms.'

'And Giorgio?'

'He wouldn't come into my room. He'd knock and maybe talk to me through my door, but he wouldn't come in—not unless he had reason to think I was in danger.' In a way, she was in danger. In danger of losing her heart to Liam. When she was with him, she didn't feel stifled under the weight of duty. She was herself.

But she'd made the terms of this clear. It was just for tonight. A moment out of their real lives, for both of them. One night with no future. And, even though it scared her that doing this might mean that no man would ever match up to him and she'd have to settle for second best, that was still better than never being with him at all.

'Your room?' he asked softly.

'That's actually your room, isn't it?'

'Yes.' He stole a kiss. 'Are you telling me you were thinking about that? About me sleeping in your bed?'

She felt the colour flood into her cheeks. 'Yes.'

He stole another kiss. 'I did the same.'

'And I thought of you, this morning,' she whispered. 'I imagined taking a photograph of you asleep. In my bed. Face down, with a sheet thrown casually over you, and your back…' Her mouth dried.

'I don't do nudes, even arty ones,' he said. 'But that's how I'd want to photograph you, too. Your hair loose and tumbled over my pillow, a sheet drawn up with one hand, looking all shy and adorable.'

'Take me to bed, Liam,' she said.

He didn't need a second urging, though he did pause long enough in the kitchen to kiss her and then to lock the back door. 'Because, once I'm in bed with you,' he said, his voice low and husky, 'I don't want to have to leave until the morning.'

'That works for me.'

And a delicious shiver of excitement rippled down her spine when he picked her up in the living room and carried her up two flights of stairs to her room.

'Caveman,' she teased.

'Better believe it,' he teased back, and held her close as he set her back on her feet, leaving her in no doubt about how much he wanted her.

And then he kissed her again, and she stopped thinking about anything at all.

# CHAPTER SIX

THE NEXT MORNING, Vittoria was woken by the dawn light filtering through the curtains, even though they were lined. She lay on her side in the wide bed, with Liam curled protectively round her, his arm wrapped round her and drawing her close to his body.

He'd been a gentle but intense lover, exploring and discovering where she liked being kissed or touched, what made her catch her breath with desire.

Last night had been a revelation.

Nobody, even Rufus, had ever made her feel like this.

But she knew Liam was right. This thing between them didn't stand a chance of working out. Her background was what had made Rufus break up with her all those years ago. If you weren't from that kind of background, life in a royal family would be tough to cope with. Even if you were used to fame and dealing with the media in a different arena, it wasn't the same as living in a goldfish bowl. Plus, Liam had explicitly told her that he wasn't looking for a relationship. His career came first.

She lay there for a few precious minutes, savouring the feel of his skin against hers and wishing things could be different. That there was a way for them to be together. But, whatever way she looked at it, she couldn't find a solution.

Eventually she felt him stir and draw her closer. His breathing changed, signalling to her that he'd woken. When his lips grazed her shoulder, she turned round to face him.

He kissed the tip of her nose. 'Good morning.'

'Good morning.' And it was more than good, waking in his arms.

'I need to go back to my own room,' he said.

Before Giorgio realised what had happened. Yeah. She knew. 'I wish…' Though it was pointless saying it out loud; it would only make her feel miserable, because things *couldn't* be different.

'Me, too.' He kissed her one last time. 'You know your favourite poem? Just for the record, my mistress' eyes are nothing like the sun. They're this amazing, *amazing* blue. Until yesterday, I would've said violet blue—but, actually, they're the shade of a newly unfurled English bluebell. I really wish I'd asked you to remove those contact lenses yesterday, so I could've taken a proper shot to showcase your eyes.'

The compliment made her feel warm all over. Nobody had ever said something like that to her. Liam saw her with an artist's eye—the woman, not the princess. And she loved the fact he actually quoted poetry. Particularly as he knew her favourite poem; again, it made her feel that he understood what made her tick.

It was on the tip of her tongue to suggest they went back to London this morning via the bluebell wood, but she knew it would be a mistake. Yesterday was yesterday. Last night was last night. A one-off. Never to be repeated.

He twirled one unruly curl round his finger. 'And this. I knew you'd look cute with your hair all messy in the morning.' He grinned. 'Shakespeare's black wires, I think.'

This was goodbye. So she let herself twine her fingers through his hair. 'You look cute and messy this morning, too. And your eyes are the same blue as cornflowers.' She stroked his cheek. 'I'd be worried if *this* was a damask red rose, though.'

'Hard-drinking photographer, face pasty white from a nocturnal partying lifestyle and starting to get broken veins in my face from all the alcohol,' he said.

Which made her laugh. From what she'd seen, Liam MacCarthy worked hard rather than drank hard. He didn't give her the impression that he was a party animal—if anything, she rather thought he'd find them dull—and during this week he'd been up early rather than staying awake all night and sleeping all day. 'Yeah.'

'Coral.' He rubbed the pad of his thumb along her lower lip. 'I always thought that was an orangey colour. Your mouth is more rose-coloured. By which I mean pink.'

She really didn't want the day to start. She definitely didn't want him to leave her bed.

But she had a plane to catch, and he had a life to get back to.

Dragging out their parting would only make both of them miserable. Better to cut it short now.

'I'm not very good at goodbyes,' she said.

'Me, neither.' He paused. 'So let's say goodbye now. When I drop you off at Izzy's place—as Vicky—I won't see you again before you leave for San Rocello.'

'I know.' And how that made her ache.

'You and me—it can't work. Not in the real world. You have responsibilities and I have my career.' His eyes were filled with regret.

'I know.' She took a deep breath. 'We probably won't

see each other again.' They moved in different worlds. And anyway, she'd hate having to be a polite stranger with him, pretending that last night had never happened. It was pointless trying to cling on to something that didn't have a foundation, something that would just make them both miserable.

'The last few days—they were a moment out of time for both of us,' he agreed. 'Don't worry. I won't sell you out to the press.'

She stroked his face. 'I already knew that. I just wish…'

'…it could be different. So do I,' he said softly. 'But we both have to be sensible.'

Sometimes sex just wasn't enough. Right now, she wanted to remember the feel of Liam holding her, the shape of his body round hers, the touch of his skin. She held him tightly, without speaking. And he was holding her just as tightly, so she was pretty sure he felt the same way. Both of them wanting what they couldn't have, and neither of them able to see a solution that worked for both of them. She couldn't give up her job, and she knew it would break his heart to give up his. There was no middle ground, no compromise.

Finally, he kissed the top of her head. 'I'll see you downstairs for breakfast,' he said softly.

She knew she ought to say something witty. Make a joke. Even though right at the moment it felt as if her heart was cracking. 'Just as long as Giorgio's the one in charge of making the coffee,' she said lightly.

'Yes, ma'am.'

She knew he was teasing, but his words also put the official distance back between Princess Vittoria di Sarda of San Rocello and Liam MacCarthy. The royal and the commoner. The photographer and his subject.

After he'd gone she showered, changed into her borrowed wig and clothes and the contact lenses, packed, and stripped the bedding.

She kept everything light over a breakfast of toast, local lemon curd and coffee; Liam drove them back to London and dropped her and Giorgio at Izzy's flat. There were no photographers around to notice her, so her disguise wasn't really needed. But she damped down her longing for more time with Liam and enjoyed spending the rest of her time in London making a fuss of her little sister.

Once at Izzy's flat, she asked Giorgio to go to a bookshop for her to buy a copy of the new biography of Karsh. She wrote a brief message inside the flyleaf.

*Liam. Thank you for everything. Vittoria.*

She posted it on the way to the airport, and she was sitting on the plane back to San Rocello when she checked her email. There was one from Liam, sending her a link to his website and giving her an access code.

The web page made it very clear that this was a private portfolio, one which you could only log into if you had the access code. She typed in the code he'd given her, and as soon as she opened the gallery she realised that Liam had sent her all the photographs from her time with him in Norfolk—the ones he'd taken of her, and the ones she'd taken of him—as well as that very private one he'd taken of her in the palace library.

This felt like a message. Maybe she was just presuming things, but it felt as if this was his way of confirming to her what he'd promised earlier: that what had happened between them would stay private. The photographs, the closeness, the things she'd told him.

And the fact he'd sent her that private photograph told her that she could trust him.

She studied the photographs carefully. He was right; she did look carefree and happy. But the camera had also picked up something else, something she really hoped he hadn't seen for himself: that she'd lost her heart to him. Because the look on her face was definitely the look of someone in love. She looked all starry-eyed, even behind those ridiculous contact lenses. If she was honest with herself, that was exactly how she felt about him. She liked him as a person—his dependability, his strength, the way he noticed things. Physically, he made her heart beat faster just with a look or a smile. But it was more than simple liking or physical attraction. During those few days at the coast she'd fallen in love with him.

What was she going to do?

She and Liam had already agreed that things simply couldn't work out between them. They didn't have a future.

But she really couldn't accept an arranged marriage with José: a man she didn't love now and didn't think she ever would.

She knew she was expected to get married, for the sake of her duty—if nothing else, she needed to produce an heir—but she remembered what Liam had said about her needing a consort she could rely on. Someone she could talk to, who understood her. He'd advised her to talk to her family, explain that she needed more time. Negotiate.

To negotiate well, you needed to be clear on all your facts. She was going to approach this in the same way as she did all her other royal duties: with care and consideration. So she spent the rest of the flight reading San

Rocello's constitution very closely, rather than moon-ing over photos of Liam MacCarthy.

By the time the plane touched down, she was smil-ing, armed with the facts she needed: certain clauses in the constitution were very explicit about the fact that the king or queen didn't have to be married before he or she could accede the throne.

And this gave her the confidence to stand up to the pressure.

Liam made another print of a photograph from the blue-bell woods shoot, this time making a really tight crop.

Vittoria di Sarda was beautiful.

Beyond beautiful.

Even with the wrong hair and the wrong eyes, she captivated him. It was in the curve of her mouth, the tiny laughter lines beginning to fan out from the cor-ners of her eyes, the way she tilted her head.

And how he wished he'd taken some shots of her, this morning. When he'd been teasing her with her favou-rite poem, and she'd laughed up at him from the pillow.

The only images he had from that were in his mind's eye, and it wasn't enough. How long would it be before the images faded, before he forgot the feel of her skin against his and the scent of her hair?

He never usually let himself get that close to his girlfriends. Balancing his family and his job was hard enough; he'd found adding a relationship and all its de-mands into the mix led to feeling guilty that he wasn't focusing well enough on any area of his life.

And now he'd fallen for a woman who was com-pletely out of his reach. He'd fallen for the woman with her cool, calm, collected carapace. He'd fallen even harder for the woman beneath that carapace: the woman who'd asked for an on-the-fly photography lesson and cheekily taken his portrait, the woman who'd walked barefoot at the edge of the sea with him.

The woman who'd kissed him underneath the stars.

*'A rose by any other name would smell as sweet...'*

The words bounced into his head. Forget the name. Vittoria was still a princess and always would be. But roses... He wanted to photograph her in a rose garden. He wanted to kiss her in a rose garden. He wanted to scatter rose petals on the crisp white sheets of a wide, wide bed and make love with her by the light of the moon.

And how weird was it that his aim of being the best portrait photographer of his generation suddenly felt so empty and pointless? The images weren't enough for him any more. He wanted something else: he wanted Vittoria. In his arms. Always.

'It's not going to happen,' he told himself out loud. 'So just snap out of it and get on with your work.'

'What do you mean, you're not going to marry José?' Princess Maria demanded, looking aghast at her eldest daughter.

'Exactly what I said, Mamma.' One good thing about learning to look composed in public, no matter how you felt inside, was that you could do it just as successfully in your private life. So Vittoria sipped her coffee casually, making it look as if she didn't have a care in the world. Inwardly, she was a churning mess.

'You know you have to get married before you accede the throne,' Queen Giulia, her grandmother, added.

'Mamma, Nonna—I love you both dearly and I respect you,' Vittoria said quietly, 'but in this case I can't do what you ask of me. I don't want to marry someone I barely know and who has nothing in common with me

other than his background. I want the time and space
to choose who I marry, rather than rushing in. And I've
read the constitution. Very thoroughly. There isn't actually a legal requirement for the monarch to be married.'

Maria's mouth tightened. 'I don't care what the constitution says. It's like Nonna says. Our people expect
their ruler to be settled. So you need to get married and
*show* them you're settled.'

'Mamma, they already know I'm settled. I'm not the
sort to spend my life partying and gadding about. I've
taken on more and more duties from Nonno every year,
representing our country on numerous occasions, and
I've done the job well.'

'But you need an heir,' Maria said.

'And a spare. I know. But there isn't a legal requirement for me to marry before I become queen, and it
would be so much more sensible not to rush things.
We need to find the right consort for the country—
and for me.'

'I think there's more to this than meets the eye,'
Maria said darkly. 'This secret getaway of yours—did
you meet up with Rufus again? Is *that* what all this is
about?'

'No. I haven't seen Rufus in years.' Looking back
now, Vittoria was pretty sure that her mother and grandmother had tried to show Rufus that he'd never fit in
to the palace. No wonder he'd backed away. It would
take someone much stronger than Rufus to stand up to
her family.

'Is there someone else?' Giulia asked.

*Yes.* Liam's face flashed into her head. Liam, in her
bed, that last morning, teasing her with Shakespeare
and then kissing her until they were both dizzy. 'No.'
And it was the truth: Liam had made it very clear that he

couldn't and wouldn't offer her for ever. She'd fallen for a man who was out of reach, so effectively there wasn't someone else. 'I'm simply saying that I'm ready to be queen but I'm not rushing into marriage. I want time to get to know my future husband and fall in love with him before I get married.'

Maria's mouth thinned. 'Marriages aren't about love.'

'I disagree. Marriage should be all about love,' Vittoria said.

'I know you loved Rufus, and he loved you—but he wouldn't have been able to cope with life as your consort,' Maria said, this time a little more gently. 'You need someone who's been brought up with this background, someone who won't buckle under the pressure. It's not an easy thing to do.'

'I need more than that,' Vittoria said. 'I need someone who loves me for me. Who sees me for who I am, underneath all the trappings of royalty.'

*Someone like Liam MacCarthy.*

'It doesn't happen like that for people like us,' Giulia said.

Vittoria looked at her grandmother, shocked. 'Are you saying you don't love Nonno?'

'Of course I love your grandfather. But I had to learn to love him,' Giulia said.

'Just as I learned to love your father, and just as you will learn to love José,' Maria added.

'With respect, Mamma and Nonna, I disagree. I know traditions are important to you both, but traditions should underpin a monarchy, not lock it into the past.' Vittoria lifted her chin. 'Society changes, and a monarchy needs to change with its people, so it stays relevant. I want our country to be at the forefront, not seen by the rest of the world as a place that can't move on.'

Her mother and grandmother frowned, but at least neither of them was trying to shout her down. This time, perhaps, they were listening to what she said.

'I worry about you, Rina.' The use of the pet name alerted Vittoria. 'I was so worried when I found out you'd taken this ridiculous secret break.'

Worry. That was the crux of it, Vittoria knew. Her father had died in a sailing accident—and Maria was clearly panicking that something might befall her eldest daughter in the same way. It was why she wrapped both her daughters in a suffocating mix of cotton wool and tradition.

'Mamma, I didn't take any reckless risks. I stayed well away from the edges of cliffs, and I didn't swim out of my depth or anywhere near a riptide. No water-skiing, no paragliding, nothing to worry about at all. I was perfectly safe. Giorgio was with me.' Something suddenly occurred to her. The last thing she wanted was for her security detail to get into trouble. 'It was my idea, so don't blame him, Mamma. He did his job perfectly, keeping me safe. And Nonno was fine about it.' Which was true. After a slightly uncomfortable interview, King Vittorio had come round to his granddaughter's point of view.

'I know you think we wrap you in cotton wool,' Maria said. 'But we lost Francesco.'

'We couldn't bear losing you, too,' Giulia added. 'It was bad enough when you went to study in London. Every time we turned on the news and heard about an accident or a fire or some terrible thing happening, we worried.'

'And when nobody knew where you were, these last few days... We were frantic,' Maria said.

'Izzy knew,' Vittoria said gently. 'And I'm pretty sure Giorgio would have called Nonno if he thought I was taking too much of a risk.' She took a deep breath. 'I know you both love me—as I love you—and I understand that you worry about me. But I need to *live*. I can't be a good ruler if I feel stifled all the time. This isn't about disrespecting you, but we need to find a better compromise. One where you worry less and I breathe more.'

'So you refuse to marry José,' Maria said.

'I do,' Vittoria confirmed. 'Becoming queen will be hard. I need you both on my side, not fighting against me.'

'We just don't want you to make a mistake,' Giulia said. 'Rufus was a mistake.'

'Maybe if we'd supported him better, taught him how to deal with the royal lifestyle, it could have worked,' Vittoria said. 'I can't change the past. But I'm saying no to José. I will discuss it with you—of course I will, because you're both important to me—but at the end of the day I need someone I can feel comfortable with. Someone I can trust.' Someone like Liam—though she knew that was too much to wish for. 'And, while you're thinking about that, I'll go and get some more coffee from the kitchen.'

'You're going to be the queen at the end of the year,' Maria said. 'The queen doesn't go to the kitchen on an errand.'

'Actually, Mamma, I think the queen *should* go to the kitchen on an errand, from time to time. The castle doesn't run itself. I have a responsibility to the staff here—to make sure they're properly supported in their jobs. Which I can't do if I don't have a clue what's going on or who any of them are, or what they do. A good leader understands a business from the bottom up—and nowadays a monarchy is equivalent to a business.' She lifted her chin. 'I'm not going to be a figurehead queen. I did my MBA in London, remember. I understand the

challenges a business faces, and I've always intended
to be a working queen. One who listens to her subjects
and does her best for her people and her country.'

Maria was clearly about to say something, but Giulia
placed a hand on her arm. 'Our girl has a point, Maria.
And we've always taught her to respect our staff—we
cannot function well as a monarchy without them. Understanding what they do will deepen Rina's understanding of our people.'

Maria looked at her. 'You're not a little girl any more,
Rina. You've grown up.'

Vittoria hadn't been a little girl for a long, long time.
But it was good that her mother had finally noticed.
'I'll always be your daughter, Mamma,' she said gently.
'But, yes, I'm old enough to make my own decisions.
Good ones. Ones I've thought through.'

Giulia's eyes filled with tears. 'Your father would
have been so proud of you.'

'I hope so. And I hope I'll make you both proud of
me, too. You've both taught me so much,' Vittoria said.
'But, please, call off the negotiations with José's family. It isn't fair to either of us.'

Maria and Giulia looked at her for a long, long moment.

Then Maria nodded. 'All right. We'll do it your way.'

Vittoria hugged them. 'Thank you for trusting me,'
she said. 'And in future I'll try not to worry you.'

'And we,' Giulia said, 'will try not to make you feel
so smothered.'

'Thanks.' Liam took the parcel from the postman. He
hadn't ordered anything online, and he wasn't expecting
anything. The address on the front was in handwriting
he didn't recognise. Frowning, he looked at the back.

There was a London postcode, but the surname didn't mean anything to him.

Still puzzled, he opened it to discover a hardback biography of his favourite photographer. There was nothing else in the parcel; he opened the flyleaf, and then he saw the inscription.

*Liam. Thank you for everything. Vittoria.*

It was a book he'd been meaning to order for himself. She must've remembered him saying how much he admired Karsh. Typical Vittoria, having perfect manners and sending her host a thank-you gift.

But in those six words there was definite finality.

She'd used someone else's surname when posting the book—he assumed either Giorgio or Pietro.

But it would be rude not to thank her for the gift, he told himself, ignoring the fact that part of him was jumping at the chance to contact her again.

He emailed her.

Thank you for the book. I'd been meaning to order a copy. Liam.

The reply came later in the day. Short, polite, but not inviting further conversation.

You're very welcome. Vittoria.

Time to leave it, he thought, and buried himself back into work.

'What's this in aid of?' Liam asked a few days later, eyeing the excellent coffee and wholemeal chicken salad sandwich that Saoirse had brought him, along with an apple.

'I'm just making sure you eat something nutritious. You've skipped dinner three times in the last week, so either you're forgetting to eat because you're so busy, or you're stuffing your face with fast food because you're hungry and it's quick. Even if you scoff junk for the rest of today, I'll know that, if you've eaten this, you'll have had two of your five portions a day. And that's probably better than any other day this week.'

Bless her. She was trying to look after him, the way he'd looked after her for years. He gave her a hug. 'Love you, Sursh.'

'Love you, too. But I really am worried about you, Liam. You're working crazy hours, even by your standards.' She pulled back slightly. 'Can you delegate anything to me, or maybe hire an assistant?'

'No.'

'Why not?'

Telling her the truth would mean admitting that he was trying to keep himself too busy to think about Vittoria. 'I'm fine. You know what my job's like, all peaks and troughs. I had a few days off recently, and now I'm making up for it.'

Her eyes narrowed. 'Did something happen while you were away?'

*Yes. I fell in love with your best friend's sister and I don't know what to do about it, so I'm burying myself in work.* 'No,' he fibbed.

She didn't look as if she believed him. 'You always take a gazillion pics when you go to Norfolk. You haven't shown me a single photograph, this time.'

He'd taken photographs. He just didn't want to show her, because they were a dead giveaway and he wanted to protect Vittoria as well as himself. The princess all dreamy in the bluebells; the princess relaxing by the sea and unbending into a woman he wanted so much it was like a visceral ache. 'I was busy showing Izzy's sister round.' *And falling in love with her.* He pushed the thought away. He couldn't afford to fall in love with her. They didn't—couldn't—have a future.

'Vittoria's been acting weirdly, too. She's been really quiet with Izzy. And she tells Izzy *everything.*'

Liam knew that wasn't strictly true. Vittoria obviously hadn't told Izzy about their near-kiss at the palace, or Izzy would've told Saoirse. And Vittoria definitely wouldn't have told Izzy about their stolen night together. She'd also sworn him to secrecy about how lonely and isolated she felt at the palace, asking him to keep it from Izzy—to protect her little sister from the knowledge. But she'd shared it with *him*… 'She's probably just busy, catching up on all the stuff she didn't do when she had those unplanned days off over here.'

'I suppose so.' Saoirse shook her head. 'Something doesn't feel quite right, but I can't put my finger on it.'

Liam had no intention of explaining it to her. 'I honestly think you're worrying over nothing. But thank you for the sandwich.'

After his sister had left, he leaned back thoughtfully in his chair. So Vittoria was acting weirdly and being quiet with her sister. That was exactly the way Saoirse was complaining that he was behaving. So what did that mean? Was she missing him as much as he was missing her? Did she lie awake at night, wondering if there was some kind of middle way where she'd get to do her regal stuff, he'd get to follow his career dreams, and they could be together?

He had no idea.

They'd said it was goodbye. They both knew there was no point in dragging things out, trying to cling on to some form of friendship. Even when she'd sent him the book and he'd thanked her for it, there had been a tacit agreement that it was over.

But maybe it wasn't.

Maybe it was time to open up a conversation and find out how she felt.

And he was shocked to feel a weird flicker somewhere around the region of his ribcage. He couldn't quite put a name to it, but he thought it might be hope.

Talking without words.

It was what he did for a living: telling a story through a picture.

Maybe this was the way forward.

Later that day, he searched through his digital archive and fished out a shot of a rose that he'd taken during a shoot in a garden.

A single red rose.

How would the future Queen of San Rocello interpret his message? And, more importantly, was he fooling himself—or would she reply?

A picture of a rose. Without comment. There was definitely meaning in this, Vittoria knew. Liam wasn't the sort of man who'd send something at random. It was deliberate. A red rose. Was Liam referring to what she'd told him about walking in the palace gardens when the roses were in bloom, and feeling close to her dad? Was this his way of telling her he missed her?

She definitely missed him. In odd little moments during the day, when she found herself looking at the photographs she'd taken of him, and wished she was back under the stars with him. Or when she woke in the middle of the night and her bed felt much too wide, and she wished she was back in that little room overlooking the sea. It wasn't just loneliness; it was *his* company she missed. Waking in his arms and talking, as they had on that last morning. With him, she could be herself. And she missed that, too.

She closed her eyes, and for a mad moment she could imagine him brushing her lips with a rosebud, until her mouth parted and he dipped his head to kiss her...

Oh, for pity's sake. This mooning around had to stop. She needed to be *sensible*.

OK, so she'd managed to talk her mother and her grandmother round on the subject of her arranged marriage, but that didn't mean that she could have a future with Liam.

Then again, he'd sent her the photograph.

Was he expecting a reply? Hoping for a reply? Waiting to see what she did next?

Why hadn't he sent her a proper message? Traditionally, a red rose meant true love, so was this his declaration?

And what should she say to him?

She shook herself. Ridiculous. She'd been training for her role for so long. She knew exactly what to do and say in almost every situation, and she was bright enough to work out what to do in situations that were new to her.

Except this one. Because she couldn't think straight where Liam MacCarthy was concerned.

He'd sent her a picture without a comment. So perhaps she should do the same.

She'd picked up a shell from the beach on that last day. She fished it out of the drawer where she'd stored it, took a snap of it on her phone, and sent it to him without a single word of explanation.

* * *

A seashell?

What on earth did Vittoria mean by a seashell? Liam wondered.

He remembered that she'd picked one up from the beach on their last afternoon together. After he'd told her that he wasn't looking for a relationship. Had she sent him a picture of the shell to remind him of that conversation? Or was it a reminder of their first evening on the beach near the dunes, when they'd watched the stars come out and he'd kissed her? Or maybe it was a warning, a reminder of that last morning, when they'd woken together in the room with the view of the sea and agreed that this was goodbye.

He drummed his fingers on his desk as he thought about it. The longer he dwelt on it, the less he could work out what it meant.

It was his own fault. He'd been the one to start this, sending her a picture without a caption. A picture was meant to be worth a thousand words. This seashell was the equivalent of two single-spaced A4 pages of text. Was he reading things into the picture that weren't there? What was she trying to say to him?

And what did he want to reply?

The obvious thing to do would be to send a photograph of a bluebell. But flowers, he knew, had meanings. Everyone knew what a red rose meant, but what about bluebells? He needed to be sure that he wasn't sending her the wrong message. Checking online told him that the bluebell was a legally protected flower in England—who knew what she'd make of that?—and that in the language of flowers it was a symbol of constancy and everlasting love.

Two flowers in a row, expressing love. Wooing her

with flower photographs. Wooing her, when he knew it couldn't possibly work out between them. The princess and the photographer. They were worlds and worlds apart. This was insanity.

But he couldn't get Vittoria out of his head. He thought about her all the time. And he had a nasty feeling that this weird feeling, the one he couldn't pin down, might just be the 'everlasting love' signified by a bluebell.

And he really didn't know what to do about *that*.

Knowing it wasn't a sensible idea, he sent the photograph to her.

Bluebells?

Vittoria stared at the picture.

It was an English bluebell, with narrow bells down one side of the stem only. Liam was definitely reminding her of their conversation that last morning. When he'd told her he wished he'd asked her to take out the brown contact lenses in the woods, because her eyes were the same colour as the bluebells.

Were they the same colour as bluebells?

She left her desk and headed for the bathroom, where she stared at herself in the mirror.

Eyes the colour of bluebells…

She and Liam hadn't spoken since he'd dropped her at Izzy's flat. They'd agreed that it was over. Neither of them had messaged the other—except for his email to her with the access code for his website, the brief exchange when he'd thanked her for the book, and now the photographs.

What was he telling her, this time?

And what should she reply?

She went back to her desk and logged in to the private gallery on his website. Then she zoomed in on one of the photographs she'd taken of him in the bluebell wood.

He'd said that a portrait showed you who someone was.

He'd also said that these were pretty much stock male portrait poses.

And here he was, his right hand up so it almost cupped his chin, his thumb to the side and his index finger across his slightly pouted lips.

Almost as if he were saying, 'Shh.' Telling her what she was seeing was secret.

There was a glint in his eye. Like a mischievous little boy?

Or was that glint something else? His feelings, something he didn't want to tell and wanted to keep secret?

She zoomed in on his eyes. Beautiful eyes: with long, long lashes and tiny crinkles at the corner. Were they telling her his feelings for her?

He had a beautiful mouth, too. And when she remembered how that mouth had made her feel, she went hot all over.

She wanted to wake up in his arms again. Wanted him there with her, teasing her and laughing with her and making love with her.

But even if he felt the same—even if he was prepared to change his career plans to fit in with her life—would it be fair to ask him to do that? To be with her, Liam would need to move from London to San Rocello. Away from his sister, away from his work, away from the home he'd built over the years.

She'd be asking him to give up so much.

Just like his old girlfriends who'd resented him

spending his time with Saoirse or building his career. Although Vittoria didn't want to be the be-all and end-all of his life—for her, too, family was important, and she wanted him to be able to follow his ambitions—her role as queen would have to come first. There wasn't a middle way, however she looked at it.

Even if she did let him come to her, even if he was willing to give up everything she asked him to—was she making the same mistake again? Would he, like Rufus, realise the royal life wasn't for him and back away?

Maybe it was better to say nothing. To bury her hopes intact, instead of having them crushed. To leave it as a might-have-been. Instead of acting on the temptation to reply, to find a picture of a cornflower and send it to him to continue the flirting by flowers, she went back to reading the report she'd been working on before his message arrived.

No reply.

Maybe she was busy, Liam told himself.

But three more days without a reply told him that either Vittoria didn't want to play this game any more, or she didn't like whatever she'd read into his last message.

It was what they'd agreed anyway that night. A one-off. Not to be repeated.

He'd been stupid to wish it could be otherwise.

# CHAPTER SEVEN

VITTORIA WOKE, FEELING NAUSEOUS.

She must've eaten something at the reception last night that had disagreed with her.

But sipping cold water didn't help with the nausea, which seemed to come in waves. The idea of coffee— which she loved—made her feel worse. Even the smell of it was disgusting, and she left her mug untouched.

She felt dreadful all morning. Maybe she was going down with some kind of bug. Or maybe she was going to get poetic justice for the fib she'd told to the private secretary about having the period from hell, to get those few sneaky days away, and she really *was* going to have the period from h—

She went cold.

*Period.*

Hers were regular practically to the hour.

And it should have started yesterday morning.

She dragged in a breath. She was being ridiculous. There were dozens of reasons why her period might be late, or why she might miss one altogether. Besides, that one night she'd spent with Liam, they'd been sensible. They'd used condoms.

A little voice in her head reminded her that the only

one hundred per cent guaranteed form of contraception was abstinence.

The risk of a condom failing to protect her was tiny. So tiny as to be almost negligible.

But even a tiny risk was still an actual risk.

And a missed period plus feeling sick added up to something that scared her so much, her skin felt too tight.

Vittoria was out of sorts all day. She wanted to go out and buy a pregnancy test so she could prove to herself that she was being ridiculous and of course she wasn't pregnant. But there was no way she could purchase a pregnancy test herself. Someone would notice what she was buying, someone might tell the press—and, with modern technology making the rumour mill work globally twenty-four-seven, all sorts of stories would be flying round the world within seconds. Speculation as to whether Princess Vittoria was pregnant, who the father might be, and why she'd kept the relationship secret from her family and her friends…

But she also didn't want to put that kind of burden on any of her staff. Swearing them to secrecy and asking them to go and buy a pregnancy test for her really wouldn't be fair.

If she went to the palace doctor, her mother or her grandparents would know about it; they'd worry and start asking questions. And no way could she confide in her mother or her grandmother. Apart from the fact that she knew how disappointed they'd be, they'd only just agreed to stop smothering her in cotton wool. This news would definitely wreck the new relationship she was trying to forge with them. If she couldn't be trusted not to get accidentally pregnant, how could she be trusted to choose her own consort?

Vittoria had never felt more isolated in her life. With only a small family, and her close friends not even living in the same country—she couldn't remember when they'd last managed to get together—there was nobody she could turn to.

Buying a test online and having it delivered wasn't an option, because all the palace post was screened.

The more she thought about it, the more panicky she felt.

She still hadn't found a solution by the evening. And when her mobile phone rang with a video call and she saw Izzy's name flash up on screen, she nearly didn't answer—she didn't want her sister to see her in such a state. But just ignoring the call and pretending to be busy wasn't fair to Izzy. Her sister's last exam had been that morning and she wanted to congratulate her.

Forcing herself to sound bright, Vittoria answered the call. 'Hey, it's my favourite sister. How are you?'

'Brilliant. Free from exams for ever!'

'Congratulations, that's great. I assume you're going out tonight to celebrate the end of Finals?'

'Sursh and I are going out for champagne,' Izzy said.

And how pathetic was it that Vittoria found herself wondering where Liam was, or if he'd be buying the girls celebratory champagne?

'Rina? Are you OK?'

'Yes, of course,' she lied. For pity's sake. Where was her impassive royal face when she needed it?

'You don't look it,' Izzy said. 'You looked worried sick. Is it Nonno?'

'No, he's fine,' Vittoria hastened to reassure her.

'Then what's wrong?'

To her horror, Vittoria felt a tear slide down her cheek. And, of course, Izzy noticed it.

'You're crying. Is it Mamma? Have she and Nonna changed their minds and they're trying to make you marry José?'

'No.' Vittoria closed her eyes. 'Iz, I might…' The words stuck in her throat.

'Right. I'm getting the next flight over,' Izzy said. 'Or the overnight train, if there isn't a flight.'

'No! It's…' Vittoria forced herself to breathe. 'I just… I might be pregnant.'

'*Pregnant?* How?'

'Shh. You know how this stuff works.'

'I mean who?'

'Are you alone?' Vittoria asked, panic coursing through her as a nasty thought hit her. If Saoirse was there and overheard any of this, and she told her brother…

'Sursh has just gone home to change.'

Thank God. 'You can't tell *anyone* about this. Anyone at all. Promise me.'

'I promise.' Izzy frowned. 'Have you done a test?'

'Not yet.' And she desperately wanted to. She needed to know for sure. 'But I can't go and buy one myself. I can't see the doctor without Mamma finding out and worrying. You know the post is checked so I can't buy one online, and I can't put that kind of burden on any of the staff.'

'That's easily sorted. I'll get one,' Izzy said, 'and I'll bring it to you.'

'That's ridiculous. I can't ask you to do that.'

'You're in a muddle and you need someone to lean on,' Izzy said. 'Which would be me. You've always been there for me. Let me be there for you, Rina.'

'But you've got Finals celebrations with your friends.'

'What's more important? A party, or the person I love most in the whole world?'

And now Vittoria really was crying. Even though her sister was hundreds of miles away, right at that moment she didn't feel alone. 'You can't get here tonight. There isn't a commercial flight and I can't send a private plane over.' Not without a lot of explanations she wasn't ready to give. 'Go to your party.'

'Then I'll get it tomorrow and bring it,' Izzy said, undaunted.

'Love you, Iz.'

'Love you, too. Now, stop panicking. You might not even be pregnant. It might be stress making you late,' Izzy said. 'How late are you?'

'A day. Which I know sounds utterly ridiculous, but I'm regular to the hour, Iz. I always have been.'

Izzy was clearly counting backwards in her head, because she said, 'So if you are pregnant, it happened while you were in Engl— Oh, my God. Are you telling me it's Liam's?'

Adrenalin coursed through her veins. 'Iz, you promised not to say anything to anyone.'

'And I won't. But, if you *are* pregnant, you need to talk to him,' Izzy warned.

'I know,' Vittoria said miserably. It wasn't a conversation she wanted to have.

'You did use protection, didn't you?'

'Of course we did.' She dragged in a breath. 'But obviously something went wrong.'

'Oh, Rina. Look, it's going to be OK,' Izzy said, 'and I'll get the first flight home tomorrow. We'll sort it out.'

Vittoria thought wryly that her little sister sounded very much like her. Except this time, it would be her scatty little sister rescuing her, not the other way round.

'Try to get some rest,' Izzy said, for all the world as if she were the elder sister. 'I'm not going to say a word to anyone. And I love you. Whatever the result is, whatever you decide, I've got your back.'

That love and protectiveness only made Vittoria want to cry even more.

'Don't worry. It's going to be fine,' Izzy said. 'I love you.'

Somehow Vittoria got through the rest of the evening, along with a morning where she couldn't face her morning coffee and panicked even more. And then Izzy was there, breezing into the palace and smothering everyone in hugs. 'Just a fleeting visit—a bit of post-exams homesickness,' she explained to their mother and grandparents. And, as soon as she could, she swept Vittoria up to her room. 'I need a proper catch-up with my big sister,' she announced.

As soon as the door to Vittoria's suite was closed, Izzy hugged her. 'All righty. Time to pee on a stick.'

'How did you get the test?' Vittoria asked. If Izzy had asked Saoirse to buy it, and Saoirse had made the connection…

'I asked Pietro to get it,' Izzy said. 'And he won't be telling. He doesn't know who it's for, just that it's not for me.'

'Thank you.' It felt as if half a ton of rocks had fallen from her shoulders.

Izzy handed over the little box. 'So how long has this thing between you and Liam gone on? Since your official photograph?'

Vittoria shook her head. 'There was a point in the photo shoot where I thought he was going to kiss me—when he took those pictures for you. And then he took another shot. A more private one.'

'Can I see?'

Considering how much her sister had already done for her, it would be churlish to say no. Vittoria logged into the private portfolio, then handed over her phone. 'Look for yourself. I need to do that test.'

Pregnant or not pregnant?

She peed on the stick and waited, her breath shallow; her heart felt as if it was beating so loudly that the whole palace could hear.

Time seemed to drag. For pity's sake, how long was two minutes?

But finally there was a blue line to tell her that the test was working. She stared at the other window, willing it to stay blank.

If it was blank, meaning she wasn't pregnant, then she had time to think about what she wanted to do. Time to think about how she felt.

If there was a second line…then everything would change. What then? Was San Rocello progressive enough to accept the idea that their new queen would be a single mum? She rather thought not.

What other options were there?

Termination was the obvious one. She'd never judge another woman for taking that option—everyone's circumstances were different, and you had to make your own decision based on your personal circumstances. But it wasn't the option she wanted for herself.

Liam had a right to know about the baby; but he'd already told her that he didn't want to bring up a family because he'd done that already with Saoirse. So she was pretty sure that, although he was attracted to her and he'd do his best to support her, he wouldn't actually want to make a family with her.

Which brought her back to being a single mum.

If she wasn't the queen-in-waiting, nobody would bat an eyelid about her pregnancy or the baby.

But, in her situation, it would be a political minefield.

How on earth would she tell her family? They'd be devastated.

She realised then that she was staring unseeing at the stick, not focusing on the little window. She blinked and narrowed her eyes at it.

There was a second blue line. A strong one.

Underlining that she'd taken a risk, been reckless, and lost.

And then she was promptly sick, retching until her stomach was empty and her face was clammy.

Once she'd washed her face and hands and disposed of the test stick, she headed back out to Izzy.

Her sister took one look at her and wrapped her arms round her. 'Oh, Rina.'

'Positive,' Vittoria whispered.

'It's very early days. Four or five weeks since the start of your last period,' Izzy said thoughtfully. 'OK. The important thing here is what *you* want to do.'

'Mamma and Nonna—they'll be so disappointed in me. So angry.'

'We'll deal with that later. Right now, we need to focus on you.' Izzy blew out a breath. 'Are you going to tell Liam?'

Vittoria nodded. 'He has a right to know. And, I guess, to be part of the decision.'

'But he doesn't have the right to pressure you into anything you don't want to do,' Izzy warned.

'You know him.' Ironically, probably better than Vittoria did. 'He's not like that.'

'So tell me exactly how things are between you,' Izzy said. 'I looked at all the pictures in that file. The ones he took of you, where you're all starry-eyed and blossoming, and the ones you took of him, where he looks as if he can't take his eyes off you.'

'We didn't set out to have a fling. He was just being kind, giving me a bit of space—I don't know, maybe paying it forward because someone gave him a break when he was struggling. Except I was so aware of him, Iz. And when he kissed me under the stars, that first night at the cottage, it felt like a hundred rainbows blooming in my head, and I forgot everything else in the world. We didn't go to bed together that night—but we grew closer. And that last night, we…' She spread her hands. 'It just felt right. And waking up with him, the next day.' Even thinking about it made her miss him.

'Does he know how you feel about him?'

'You know him, Iz. You know he's observant, because of what he does for a living. And you just said I look starry-eyed in those photographs. He must've seen it, too.'

'OK. I'll ask the hard question. Do you know how he feels about you?'

'No.' How could she be so clueless? She was meant to be taking over the running of a country, and right now she was making a total mess of her own life.

Izzy hugged her. 'I can see in your face that you're beating yourself up. Don't. If it helps, since I've known Liam, there hasn't been anyone special in his life. He dates, but not very seriously. He's really focused on his work—even more than you are.' She paused. 'I don't think he takes people to his cottage, either, except for his best friend. So that has to count for something.'

When had her little sister grown up and become so wise? Or was Vittoria as guilty as her mother and grandmother of treating Izzy as if she was much younger than she really was?

'We agreed it can't work. He's got his career and I'm going to be queen. And he's not from our world, Iz. It's a lot to cope with if you haven't been brought up in it.'

'If the guy really loves you, he'll make it work. He'll learn whatever skills he needs so he can deal with life at the palace,' Izzy said. 'Just because Rufus couldn't do it, it doesn't mean that Liam can't.'

'He was very clear about the fact he doesn't want a relationship. He's already done the parenting thing with Saoirse—though he was clear about the fact he didn't regret that, either,' Vittoria added swiftly. 'But he wants to focus on his career.'

'Do you think your news might change his mind?' Izzy asked.

'I don't know. But I don't want him to feel he's under any obligation,' Vittoria said.

'So what you're saying is that you want him to be with you and the baby, but only because he wants to be there?' Izzy asked gently.

'I want someone who sees me for who I am and loves me for that. Not someone who has to learn to love me because I'm going to be the queen and he's going to be my consort.'

'Anything else is second-best—and you're worth more than that,' Izzy said. 'Have you talked since you've been back at the palace?'

Vittoria wrinkled her nose. 'Not exactly.'

'Why not?'

'There wasn't any point. It was a fling. It's over.'

'But?' Izzy asked gently.

'He did send me an email with the password to the

private gallery, and two photographs. A red rose, first, and then a bluebell.'

'A red rose and a bluebell? What's that supposed to mean?' Izzy asked.

'I don't know. I sent him a picture of a seashell.'

Izzy shook her head. 'Oh, my God. You're as bad as each other. Just talk to each other and stop playing games. It sounds to me as if you've both made all these big speeches about not having a future together, and you've both painted yourself into a corner, and neither of you knows what to say now. I bet you're both waiting for the other to make the next move. Stop letting pride or whatever get in the way. Go and see him. Talk. Be honest.'

'What if he doesn't feel the same way?'

'Then we'll deal with it. I've got your back. If he doesn't love you, though, he's an idiot and he doesn't deserve you.'

The indignant look on her sister's face made Vittoria smile. 'I love you, Iz. Thank you.'

But, all the same, she worried.

How was Liam going to react? She didn't have a clue. She didn't really know him that well. Those moments of connection between them in England had taken her breath away; but would they be enough to sustain a relationship, especially one that would be lived out in the very public world of the San Rocello royal family?

There was only one way to find out.

She definitely wasn't going to tell him the news by text, by phone or even by video call. This was something that needed to be said face to face. She needed to see his reaction, to know how he really felt.

It took Vittoria a while to find the right words—until after Izzy had gone back to London—but she kept her text simple.

Need to talk to you about something face to face.
Where/when are you available in the next week?

And now the ball was in his court.

Need to talk to you about something face to face.
Where/when are you available in the next week?

Liam looked at the text and frowned.

What did Vittoria need to talk to him about? And why did it have to be face to face? Had someone found out about their fling and it was going to cause a scandal? But neither of them was dating anyone else, and he knew she'd decided to stand up to her family about the arranged marriage issue. So, even if their fling had been leaked, he couldn't see what the problem was.

He texted back.

Is everything all right?

Of course. Is there a window in your diary?

She sounded cool, calm, collected and extremely businesslike.

Not the woman behind the tiara who'd melted into his arms. Not the woman whose smile was like sunshine. Not the woman whose eyes reminded him of spring bluebells.

A window in his diary, indeed. Anyone would think this was a business meeting. Though, if it was—if she wanted him to take some other portraits—surely she would've given him an idea about the brief?

Which meant this had to be personal. And it stung that she was being so formal with him. They'd spent the night together, woken in each other's arms. Had it really meant so little to her? OK, they'd agreed to regard it as a fling and they'd said goodbye. But he'd wondered if there was a way of finding a compromise. Surely it hadn't been completely one-sided?

He thought about it some more.

He hadn't heard anything through Saoirse or Izzy, both of whom were planning to go up to Edinburgh tomorrow to see an art exhibition. He hadn't seen any rumours in the news.

So what exactly did the future Queen of San Rocello want with him?

There was only one way to find out. He checked his diary.

Have location shoots in London Mon/Wed/Fri. Planned dark room sessions Tuesday and Thursday. Can work round those.

Tuesday works for me. I'll book a meeting room at a hotel and let you know the venue.

This definitely sounded like business; he'd been deluding himself that it might be personal. There hadn't been a hint of warmth in her texts. No kiss used as punctuation at the end of a message. No more flirting by photograph—she still hadn't replied to his bluebell. The soft, sweet, slightly shy woman he'd spent time with on the coast had turned back into an efficient machine. The Winter Queen.

And that hurt.

Well, he could be a machine, too.

Meeting room good for me. Let me know location and time.

He didn't add a kiss to soften the message or make it less impersonal.

But he was out of sorts for the rest of the day. Brooding. Wondering what she wanted from him—and whether he was prepared to deal with the formal princess, rather than the woman he'd escaped to the seaside with.

And on Tuesday he'd find out what she wanted.

# CHAPTER EIGHT

A BUSINESS MEETING.

What did you wear to a business meeting with a princess? Liam wondered.

He'd worn a suit to the palace when he'd gone to shoot Vittoria's official portrait; he'd worn faded jeans when he'd taken her to the beach and kissed her. Neither extreme felt right for this. And Vittoria still hadn't given him a clue what this was about, even though he'd asked her explicitly if there was a brief or anything in particular he needed to bring to the meeting. Subtle questioning of Izzy hadn't given him any more information.

So maybe he'd simply go as his professional self. The confident and competent portrait photographer whose outfit on a shoot made him practically invisible. Black designer jeans, a silky black long-sleeved top, black shoes. And he took his laptop and compact camera with him, just in case.

The hotel she'd chosen was near a Tube station. He left himself extra time to get there, in case of delays, but everything ran on schedule. There was a big difference between arriving a couple of minutes early for a meeting in order not to waste any time, and turning up so early that you appeared desperate and hampered yourself in any negotiations. So he found the nearest coffee shop, bought a double espresso, set an alarm on his phone to make sure he didn't lose track of time and end up being late, and settled down in a corner to work on some post-production stuff on his laptop.

When his phone vibrated to warn him it was time to leave, he made his way to the hotel where the receptionist gave him directions to the meeting room. He rapped on the door and walked in. It was an anonymous room with cream-coloured walls, a corporate blue carpet, a rectangular oak table with eight executive office chairs, and a large screen which was obviously for use with a laptop and presentation software.

Vittoria was sitting at the head of the table with a glass of water in front of her, Giorgio to one side. His heart actually skipped a beat at seeing her again.

'Thank you for coming, Mr MacCarthy.' Her voice and her expression were both inscrutable.

She could honestly be this formal, this cool with him, after the night they'd shared together? After waking up with him, with her expression all soft and sensual?

The pleasure he'd felt at seeing her drained away, and his skin suddenly felt too tight. OK, so maybe it had been unrealistic to expect her to fall into his arms—they'd agreed that night was a one-off. But he had expected some warmth from her. He didn't understand why she was freezing him out. Why was he even here?

'You're welcome, *Vostra Altezza Reale*.' He used the formal phrase deliberately, pushing back at the woman who was clearly in full regal mode. *Your Royal Highness.*

'May I order you some coffee? Something cold?'

The coldest thing in the room, he thought, was Vittoria herself. Polite and utterly inscrutable. And he still didn't know why she'd asked him to meet her. 'I'm fine, thank you, ma'am.'

She gave a small signal to Giorgio, who left the room.

This was starting to feel a little surreal. Why would she ask her security detail to give them privacy? She trusted Giorgio literally with her life; surely it wouldn't matter if he heard any confidential business matters?

'What did you want to discuss?' he asked. And why had she been so insistent on this meeting being face to face?

'How are you?' she asked, not answering his question.

Frustrated. Churned up. Feeling as if something was about to drop on his head from a great height. So, instead of giving her an anodyne answer and asking an equally polite but meaningless question, he took the direct route. 'Right now I'm very much in the dark about why you wanted to see me. Isn't this something that we could've talked about over the phone or a video call?'

'No.'

Then he noticed how pale she looked, and frowned. She'd asked him how he was, but he hadn't asked her how she was. And, although her make-up was flawless and someone who barely knew her would just think she was being regal, on closer inspection he thought she looked tense. Upset. And it took the fight out of him, because now all he wanted to do was hold her close. Protect her. Tell her that whatever was wrong, he'd be by her side and he'd help her get through whatever it was. 'Are you all right, Vittoria?' he asked gently, completely forgetting protocol.

'I...' She dragged in a breath. 'Sit down, Liam. Please.'

Now he was worried.

Was she ill? Seriously ill? *Terminally* ill?

Was she going to ask him and Saoirse to help her prepare Izzy for some terrible news?

He sat down and forced himself to breathe. And he waited for her to fill the silence—to tell him what she wanted.

Seeing Liam again made Vittoria's heart do a backflip. He was dressed as a professional photographer, all in black so it would make him practically invisible at a shoot and he could blend into any background.

Except he was far from being invisible to her. She was acutely aware of him.

Those beautiful eyes.

That gorgeous mouth.

The hands that had held her close, cherished her.

And now she was going to have to tell him her news. She still had no idea how he'd react, though in her head she'd gone over every possible reaction he might have and worked out how to respond. Shock. Anger. Dismay.

The only reaction she hadn't bothered to think about was delight, because she already knew he wasn't going to be delighted about this. If you'd made it perfectly clear that you didn't want to settle down and have a family, then obviously you weren't going to be too thrilled at the idea of becoming a parent.

'I wanted to tell you in person,' she said, 'because I think you have the right to know.' She took a deep breath. 'I'm pregnant.'

What?

Liam stared at her in shock, trying to process what she'd just told him.

It was the last thing he'd expected to hear.

Pregnant?

She couldn't possibly be.

'You're pregnant,' he said, just to check that he'd heard her correctly.

She said nothing, simply inclined her head. And he couldn't see Vittoria behind her mask. All he could see was the princess, coolly telling him that they'd accidentally made a baby when they'd spent that night together.

He certainly didn't think it was anyone else's baby. But he still couldn't quite get his head round this. 'We were careful. We used condoms.'

'There's always a tiny, tiny chance that contraception won't work.' She spread her hands. 'Unfortunately, we were that chance.'

He shook his head, trying to clear it. He'd resisted every girlfriend who wanted him to settle down and raise a family; the way he saw it, he'd already done that with Saoirse. Now was the time when he'd wanted to focus on his career. He was clear about his goals and he knew how to get there. He was putting the work in.

But Vittoria was pregnant.

With his baby.

And *that* changed everything.

He could be selfish. Walk away. Stick to his original plans and focus on his career.

But if he did that, he'd lose his self-respect.

Which meant there was only one choice.

He was about to open his mouth and ask her if she was sure, if she'd done a pregnancy test—but of course Vittoria di Sarda would've done a test. She wouldn't be sitting here if the test hadn't been positive.

Now he thought he understood why she'd asked Giorgio for privacy. Not to protect her, but to protect *him* when she delivered news that she knew would shock him to the core.

She was pregnant.

With his baby.

The words repeated over and over in his head.

What did he do now? What did he say? Did she want to keep the baby? Did she want him to bring the baby up with her?

*I wanted to tell you in person because I think you have the right to know.*

That didn't give him a clue about her feelings or what she wanted. Was she telling him that this was a royal baby so, although he had the right to know of the baby's existence, she didn't plan to acknowledge him as the father? Or was she being proud, expecting him to reject her and being cool with him so she could protect her heart?

He had no idea.

And what did he want?

He'd worked hard to build his career, from the very lowest rung. He wouldn't be able to fit that round supporting Vittoria in her royal duties; he'd have to give it up. Move away from London, away from his sister. And that was assuming her family would even accept him as her partner, which he doubted very much. Vittoria's mother and grandmother wanted her to marry the son of a Spanish duke, so it was pretty obvious how they'd react to the idea of her settling down with someone without a single drop of blue blood in his veins.

He didn't have a clue what to say.

All he knew was that Vittoria was pregnant with his baby.

And that he'd never, ever shirk his responsibilities.

'Obviously I'll do the right thing,' he said. 'I'll stand by you.'

\* \* \*

Breathe. Don't cry. Don't let the hormones take over, Vittoria warned herself.

She knew that Liam didn't want to settle down and bring up a family. He'd told her why, that night when they'd talked under the stars. The night they'd really connected. *The night they'd made the baby.* Over the last few days, since she'd tried to work out how he'd react, she'd expected him to walk away.

Though it wasn't until he'd spoken that Vittoria realised what she'd wanted him to say. Deep down, she'd wanted him to tell her that he'd changed his mind about having a family—that he loved her, that he wanted to bring up their baby with her. Make a family with her.

What he'd actually said was that he'd do the right thing. That he'd stand by her.

That, if anything, was worse than the arranged marriage her mother and grandmother had been planning before she'd met Liam. Because it meant his decision to stay with her was all about duty and nothing to do with love.

He'd been here before, parenting his younger sister; and he'd been very clear that he'd walked away from university and his own chances because he'd loved his sister. He found Vittoria physically attractive—the baby, she thought wryly, was proof of that—but he didn't love her.

And that was the deciding factor.

She wouldn't settle for anything less than love. So she'd give him what he'd said he wanted. Freedom to pursue his career.

'There's no need to "stand by me", as you put it. It's the twenty-first century,' she said crisply. 'I'm perfectly capable of raising this baby alone. I have the resources.' Not that money could ever take the place of love, but she wouldn't be struggling financially and could afford to pay for the kind of nanny who'd bring joy into a child's life while Vittoria was working. Izzy would stand by her. And eventually her mother and her grandparents would come around.

And she'd do it all without Liam beside her.

Hurt that Liam clearly saw her and the baby only as a duty, she hit back in the only way she knew how. With coolness. 'You don't need to be involved in the slightest.'

'You don't need to be involved in the slightest.'

The words felt like a physical blow.

Was Vittoria saying she didn't want Liam to be involved? That she didn't think he was good enough to be the father of a prince or princess?

Together, they'd created a life. They had responsibilities—to each other and to their child. Did she really think he'd walk away from that? Did she really believe he was that selfish?

Well, she could think again. No way was his child going to be brought up by a string of nannies in a distant corner of the palace where they wouldn't be seen or heard by the royal family, the way he was pretty sure Vittoria had been brought up. His child would be loved—the way he and Saoirse had been loved, during the few years they'd had their parents.

He folded his arms. 'I'm sure we can come to some kind of custody arrangement.'

She looked shocked, then. 'You want custody of the baby?'

'This baby's mine as well as yours,' he pointed out. 'I didn't dump my sister in a boarding school because it would've been more convenient for me to do so, and I'm certainly not planning to do that with my child. So I suggest our child spends weekdays with me in London, and weekends and some school holidays with you. I'm sure any lawyer would agree with me, because clearly you'll have royal duties to fulfil—which means you won't be around for much of the time.'

'You want custody,' she repeated, as if she couldn't quite believe what he'd said.

'I want to be there when my child grows up. I remember having two parents, but I also remember what it was like growing up with a single parent. And I have experience of rearing children, because I've acted as a parent to my little sister.'

'I know you gave up university for Saoirse.' Vittoria dragged in a breath. 'But you said you didn't want to get involved with anyone, that you didn't want to settle down and start a family, because you wanted to focus on your career.'

'Which is correct. But I'm at a place in my career,' he said, 'where I don't have to chase after people. I can set the parameters. So I'll accept appointments for shoots only when my child is at school.'

'What if a shoot overruns?'

That was an easy one. 'They won't. The contracts will have the kind of penalty clauses that'll make even the most difficult of clients stick rigidly to the schedule.'

'What if the shoot's abroad?'

He shrugged. 'Either I'll turn the job down, or I'll reschedule it for a time when my child is staying with you.'

'You'd give up your career for the baby.'

'I'd work around my baby,' he corrected. 'Which makes it the best of both worlds. It means my baby has a dad and will know he or she is dearly loved; and meanwhile my career carries on as I planned.'

She frowned. 'But you said you didn't want responsibilities.'

'That was then. The situation's different now. Like it or not, we made a baby. And that's a game-changer.'

Where had this hard, cold stranger come from? There wasn't a hint of a smile in those cornflower-blue eyes. Where was the man who'd told her that her smile was like sunshine, the man who'd carried her up two flights of stairs to her bed?

And why did he keep calling the baby *his* child? The baby was *theirs*. And she was the one who was carrying the baby, not him.

'Do you have a problem with that?' he enquired.

Yes. She had a lot of problems with it.

And he hadn't even asked her how she was feeling— if she'd got morning sickness, if she was bone-deep tired all the time, if her feet were puffy or if maybe she wanted a hug because she was tearful and struggling to deal with the hormones.

Nothing.

Obviously she'd just been a fling to him. Casual. Meaningless.

And all that business of quoting poetry at her, at making her laugh in the bluebells and holding her close on the beach, kissing her under the stars—it had been mere flirtation to him. Just sex. Nothing deeper.

What a fool she'd been.

Particularly as he'd even told her straight out that he didn't do relationships. He'd been honest with her. She'd been very stupid to think her news might change his mind.

Well, it *had* changed his mind.

Just not in the way she'd expected. It seemed that now he wanted the baby—but he didn't want her.

And that hurt.

That *really* hurt.

She'd thought he understood her. That they'd had a connection. But she'd been oh, so wrong.

He hadn't suggested trying to bring the baby up together. Because he didn't love her? Or because it was the same situation as Rufus all over again—that he didn't want to be constrained by the restrictions of a royal lifestyle?

She'd never thought of herself as a coward, but she couldn't bring herself to ask him if they could work this out together. She didn't want him to see her as his duty. She wanted to be loved. And she couldn't see a single sign of love in the man facing her across the table.

A queen never shows her feelings, she reminded herself. Cool, calm, collected. That was the order of the day.

'I'll give the palace lawyer your details. Perhaps you can put her in touch with your lawyer and they can come up with a workable solution between them,' she said, standing up and pushing her chair back. 'I don't think there's anything left to say. Goodbye, Mr MacCarthy.' She just about resisted a sarcastic, 'Have a nice day.'

And she walked out of the meeting room with her chin held high, every inch the princess. Because she wasn't going to give Liam MacCarthy the satisfaction of crying her eyes out and begging him to love her and their baby, so he could reject her all over again.

Liam stayed where he was as the door closed behind her, feeling as if he'd just been squashed by a steamroller.

What the hell had just happened?

Two weeks ago, he'd spent a few days in a secluded cottage near the beach with a woman who'd made his heart beat faster: a woman who was out of his reach, but he'd wanted her anyway. The more he'd got to know her, the more he'd liked her and the more he'd found himself falling in love with her. To the point where he'd broken some of his own rules and carried her to bed on that last night.

They were from different worlds. He knew that. She had responsibilities she couldn't walk away from—well, technically she could walk away, but he knew she loved Izzy and wouldn't dump those responsibilities on her sister. And he didn't come from a world where you needed a bodyguard, or where the world was watching you all the time, waiting for you to put a single foot wrong. But he'd hoped that maybe they'd find a way to bridge that gap—that they'd find a way together. He'd started flirting with her by photographs, and he'd been delighted when she'd flirted back. It had given him hope that they might just have a chance of working things out between them.

But then she'd closed off. He'd assumed her silence meant she'd thought about it and changed her mind.

And now she'd summoned him for a royal audience. There was no other way to describe what this meeting had just been.

According to her, he had the right to the knowledge that she was expecting his baby, but he didn't need to be involved with the child in the slightest. She'd suggested that his lawyer should get in touch with hers to come up with a workable solution.

It made him so angry that he wanted to punch something.

This was a *baby* they were talking about, not a piece of property.

If she was going to take that kind of attitude, why hadn't she just communicated through her lawyer in the first place? Or delegated the task to the palace secretary? Why had she asked him to meet her face to face?

He had no idea. But she'd made it clear she didn't want him. That night under the stars, she'd told him she wanted a partner who loved her—a partner she loved back.

Obviously, she hadn't meant him. That flare of desire between them had been just that: desire. Sexual attraction. Nothing that involved deeper emotions. He'd been stupid to hope otherwise.

If she'd wanted him, she would've said so. Or at least shown some warmth. But she'd been every inch the unapproachable queen-to-be. She wanted to communicate with him only through their lawyers.

And he was shocked to realise how much that hurt.

Vittoria was expecting his baby. They could have made a family—something he knew they both missed. And for a second he could almost see their child at the beach, building a sandcastle: a little girl with her mother's smile and amazing eyes, and his own unruly hair. Vittoria herself, barefoot and smiling at the scene, her knees drawn up and her hands clasped loosely by her ankles. A dog next to her, with his chin resting on her feet. Himself, capturing the joy of the moment with his camera, and then going over to his wife and kissing her…

He blinked the vision away. Stupid. It wasn't going to happen like that. And how utterly ironic that he'd only realised what he really wanted when it was completely out of his reach.

'Where to now, ma'am?' Giorgio asked.

'The airport,' Vittoria said.

'I'll have the car brought round,' he said. 'Do you need anything while we wait?'

Yes. She needed Liam. But he'd made it clear he didn't want her. 'I'm fine, thank you.'

She didn't say a word on the drive back to the airport. She just about remembered to thank the driver—being a royal meant having good manners, not being rude and entitled and taking things for granted.

To her relief, the private flight meant using a different entrance to the airport and an extremely quick boarding time. Although their flight time couldn't be moved, being on the plane was much better than being stuck waiting in the airport. One step closer to home.

'Rina.' Giorgio almost never used her pet name, but right at that moment he took her hand and was looking concerned, almost like a big brother. 'I might be speaking out of turn, but is there anything I can do?'

'Thanks, but I'm fine,' she fibbed.

'No, you're not,' he said softly. 'I've known you for more than a decade.'

She knew what he was being too tactful to say. The last time she'd been this upset was when Rufus had walked out on her. For a moment, she considered confiding in her security detail—but it wouldn't be fair to burden him.

'OK. I'm not fine,' she admitted, 'but I will be.' She'd have to be fine. There was no other choice.

Their country might not approve of her being a single mum, but they'd all have to make the best of it. And she'd have to learn to stop yearning for something she couldn't have. Stop wishing for love. Maybe her mother and grandmother were right after all; for a royal, an arranged marriage was the only workable option. This whole thing with Liam had underlined that a relationship with someone not from a royal background would only end in tears.

# CHAPTER NINE

WITH HIS SISTER in Edinburgh, it meant Liam didn't have to put on an act and pretend nothing was wrong. He could just go straight into his darkroom and bury himself in work—because at least if he did something where he had to concentrate, he wouldn't have the headspace to think about Vittoria. Vittoria and their baby.

At least, that was the theory. In practice, he couldn't concentrate, and even developing some simple prints appeared to be beyond him. Everything he touched went wrong and he had to repeat everything.

Eventually, there was a tight band of tension across his eyes, and he had to acknowledge defeat. But when he went downstairs to make himself some coffee, he could hear chattering—and he could smell pizza.

He walked into the kitchen. 'I thought you weren't due back for a couple of days?' he said to Saoirse.

'I wasn't. But it seems I have a job interview in a couple of days, so we came home early.' She walked over to him and hugged him. 'Are you OK?'

'Yes.' The lie was automatic. He glanced at Izzy. Did she know about the baby? Did Saoirse? Did they know Vittoria had come to London today, so that was the real reason why they'd come back early?

Probably not, he thought, or one of them would've said something by now.

This was a mess. Fighting with Vittoria wasn't making either of them happy, and it would hurt their sisters, too.

He didn't even know where to start unpicking this and making it right. Maybe he needed to sleep on it.

'So, what's this interview?' he asked.

'It's at the V&A—in the department where I worked on that exhibition.'

She'd loved that, he remembered. To the point where she'd added more textile modules into her degree. 'And the interview's in a couple of days? They're not giving you much notice.'

'The notification was in my spam box,' she said. 'Luckily I had to check something else and found it. So I'm home early to give me some time to do the prep.'

'Well, it's good to have you home. I missed you.' And he meant it. Though he was glad she hadn't been there when he'd come back from that meeting with Vittoria, feeling bruised and rejected and utterly miserable. 'When do you plan to go back to San Rocello, Izzy? Or are you staying in London for a bit?' It was like picking at a scab, and he only just stopped himself asking her when she'd last seen her sister or when she was going to see her again. Whether she could maybe make Vittoria see sense...

'I'm staying in London for a bit,' she said. 'While I was away, I was offered an internship with a design agency.'

'And your family's OK about it?'

She nodded. 'I talked to Rina about it. Being her, she asked me all kinds of awkward questions—to make sure

I was doing the right thing for me. She's scary when she's in Winter Queen mode.'

Something like he'd seen today. 'Uh-huh,' he said.

'She doesn't mean it when she's being all cold.'

Didn't she? 'How do you know?' The question came out before he could stop it.

'When I was younger, sometimes I thought she was freezing me out—and later I realised she was doing it to protect me,' Izzy explained. 'There was this one time, when I was fifteen, and I desperately wanted her to take me to this party because I knew this guy in her set, a guy I really fancied, was going. She flatly refused and went all Winter Queen on me. Every time I knew he was going to be somewhere she was going, I asked her to take me. She always refused and froze me out when I tried to discuss it with her. I resented it for months. But about a year later I heard a rumour about him. It seemed he wasn't very good at understanding the word no. Rina knew I liked him, but she also knew I was too young to listen to her warning me off him— that I'd probably think I could change him—so instead she froze me out. She refused to take me to any social events with her, so I wouldn't be anywhere near him and risk being alone with him. She did it to protect me.'

Freezing Izzy to protect her...

Vittoria had frozen him, this afternoon. Completely.

And that still hurt. He turned the subject back to art, until Izzy left for her own flat and Saoirse had gone to run herself a bath.

And then, when he was alone, he let himself think about it.

Vittoria had frozen him out after he'd sent the bluebell picture.

Was there something about bluebells that might have upset her?

He couldn't think of anything. So what, then? Had she not known how to reply?

He couldn't work it out.

But he did know she'd planned to talk to her family about the arranged marriage. And there was the fact that she was pregnant. Did any of her family know about the baby? Or was he the first person she'd told?

He thought about it some more. Was she freezing him out to protect him, the way she'd frozen out Izzy to protect her? Did she have to marry the Spanish duke's son, after all?

No. That didn't feel right.

He was missing something—like when you cropped a photograph in the wrong place. What was in the gap?

He flicked through the photographs in his private portfolio and found the one of Vittoria in the library: the bookworm, the woman who lit up around words. Another of her at the beach, when she'd been looking for fossils and beachcombing without a care in the world. Another, in the bluebell wood.

And then there was the portrait that was only in his head: the woman who'd woken in his arms.

All of those pictures were warm.

None of them—not even the formal ones he'd taken for the palace—was like the woman he'd faced today. The scary Winter Queen.

Had today been an act?

He'd taken her words at face value, and he'd been hurt and angry. But had he misunderstood?

He thought about it.

Vittoria was facing a dilemma that countless women had faced before her: an unplanned pregnancy. It was the twenty-first century and attitudes towards single parenthood had changed—unless you were a royal. The new queen being a single mum would cause a massive scandal in San Rocello.

What choices did she have?

The obvious one was a termination. But she'd made it clear that she planned to keep the baby.

And she wouldn't step down from taking over from her grandfather, because she'd spent years in training to be queen. And Liam knew she felt the same way about her little sister as he did about his: a fierce, protective love. She'd never just dump her responsibilities on her little sister and expect Izzy to take over as the queen. Apart from the fact that Izzy had never had the training, Izzy wanted a career in art. Vittoria would support her.

She'd love the baby, too. Her 'resources' weren't just financial. Of course she'd want her child to have a different upbringing from her own—one where the baby felt loved and valued for him or herself, not just because this child was next in line to the throne.

And she'd been well aware that if Liam was her partner, he'd have to give up his career and the life he'd worked so hard to make for himself. So had she pushed him away so he didn't have to choose between the career he wanted and the family he'd said he didn't want? Had she given him what she thought he wanted—what he'd told her he wanted?

But now he realised that wasn't what he wanted. At all.

He wanted her. He wanted their baby. He wanted to make a family with her.

And he needed to tell her.

The only thing was, if he phoned her he had the

strongest feeling she'd let his call go to voicemail and push him to talk to her solely through their lawyers.

Izzy had been her normal self with him today, which he didn't think would be the case if she knew about the baby and what a mess he'd made of seeing her sister today. It wasn't his place to break the news to her, so he couldn't ask for her help in setting up a meeting with Vittoria.

But there was one person who might be able to help.

He grabbed his phone and dialled the number.

'Mr MacCarthy?'

'Yes. Mr…' Liam realised then that he didn't actually know Giorgio's surname. 'Giorgio. I'm so sorry to disturb you, but I need your help.'

'Really?' Giorgio drawled. 'I don't think there's anything I can do to help you.'

'Please don't hang up,' Liam said swiftly. 'Please just give me three minutes of your time. I know you're close to the princess and you told me you think of her as your little sister—and right now you probably want to punch me.'

'There is that,' Giorgio agreed, his voice very cool.

'I've been an idiot. I'm assuming you know the full situation?'

Giorgio was silent. Which told Liam nothing.

OK. He'd try to do this without mentioning the baby, then, just in case Vittoria's bodyguard didn't know. 'I'm firmly in the wrong,' he said. 'I should have dug deeper and been more honest—with myself as well as with Her Royal Highness.' He took a deep breath. 'I need to talk to her. Face to face, and in private—well, obviously if she wants you there then I'd be guided by her wishes.'

'Then why don't you call her?'

'Because I pushed her too far this morning and I

don't think she'll answer my call. I think she expects my lawyer to be in touch with hers.'

'Then I don't see how I can help.'

'You care about her,' Liam said. 'And you knew this Rufus guy.'

'Yes.'

'I'm not Rufus. I nearly let her down the way he did—but I've realised now I was listening to the words coming out of her mouth instead of what she was really saying.'

'Why are you asking me to help and not Princess Isabella?' Giorgio asked.

'Because I don't know how much Izzy knows— actually, I don't know how much *you* know,' Liam admitted. 'I don't want to make things difficult between Izzy and my sister. I'm trying to find a way that causes least hurt to everyone.'

'That's fair.'

'So can you help me, please? If I get on the first plane tomorrow to San Rocello, could you persuade the princess to meet me? Say, twenty minutes?'

'Twenty minutes is a long time.'

'If I haven't fixed things by then, you can punch me. Hard as you like,' Liam said.

There was the ghost of a smile in Giorgio's voice as he said, 'I rather think the princess can do that for herself.'

'She probably could,' Liam said dryly. 'She wouldn't need to do it physically.'

'All right. Come to the palace, and I'll tell Matteo Battaglia to expect you. Let me know your arrival time.'

'Thank you, Giorgio. I really appreciate it.'

'Don't hurt her again,' Giorgio said.

'I won't. Just so you know, I hurt her through stupidity, not because I meant to,' Liam said. 'I'd never hurt her intentionally.' He paused. 'One more thing. Can the meeting be in her father's rose garden?'

'That,' Giorgio said, 'convinces me more than anything else you've said.'

'Thank you,' Liam said. 'I won't let her down again.'

The second he ended the call, he went online to book the first possible flight to San Rocello. To his relief, there was one seat left on an early flight in the morning. He booked it and texted the details to Giorgio.

The following morning, Liam felt ridiculously nervous. This was the most important meeting of his life. If he got it wrong…

But his shoes were clean, his shirt was pressed and his tie was tied properly. Just what he could remember his mum telling him to do on what he'd once thought was the most important meeting of his life, his interview at Edinburgh university.

'Wish me luck now, Mum,' he whispered. 'Because I really, really need it.'

He propped a note for Saoirse against the kettle, to tell her he was out all day at a meeting, then drove to the airport.

Having no luggage and the minimum carry-on meant that check-in and security clearance were swift. Giorgio had sent him a text confirming that the meeting was set up in the rose garden. Liam settled into his seat on the aeroplane and tried to put himself into Vittoria's shoes. Was she as mixed up over this as he was? Hurt, angry, afraid?

But he couldn't second-guess her. All he could do was be honest with her. Listen to her—and listen properly, this time. Tell her how he really felt.

She was the queen-to-be. Fair, impartial, believing

in justice. So he knew she'd listen to him. He just hoped she wanted the same thing he did.

Although everything ran on time, the journey seemed to take for ever—plane, ferry, taxi—but at last he was outside the palace. The last time he'd gone through the palace security measures it had been to take some photographs, which were an important move in his career. This time, the stakes were so much higher.

The Private Secretary took him through to the palace gardens, where Giorgio was waiting.

'Thank you for arranging this, Giorgio,' Liam said.

'Don't let her down,' was all the bodyguard said, and took him through to the rose garden.

Vittoria was sitting on a wrought iron seat under a bower of roses, reading. Every bit of her exuded calm; but when Liam was close enough to see her eyes, he could tell that she was as nervous about this as he was.

'Thank you for agreeing to see me,' he said.

She inclined her head in acknowledgement.

Giorgio said something in rapid Italian which Liam couldn't follow, then walked over to the end of the garden. They were still in his line of sight, but had the privacy to speak frankly.

'First off,' Liam said, 'I apologise. I was an idiot. I was listening to what was coming out of your mouth instead of listening to what you were really saying.'

'Uh-huh.' She wasn't giving a millimetre; right now, Liam knew that he was talking to the Winter Queen.

How was he going to get through to her?

'Secondly,' he said, 'are you all right?'

'I'm fine,' she said. 'Why did you come here today?'

*To tell you I love you and I want to make a family with you.*

But if he told her that, he had a feeling she'd throw

it back in his face. She was still being formal with him, and he needed her to feel comfortable enough to open up to him again. So he'd make the concessions.

'To listen,' he said instead. 'To understand.'

Her eyes narrowed. 'We said it all yesterday. There's nothing else to listen to and nothing else to understand. I'm pregnant and you're fighting me for custody.'

'Let's rewind a bit,' he said. 'I think the conversation we had yesterday went very, very wrong for both of us. So let's go back a couple of weeks.'

She frowned. 'A couple of weeks?'

'Yes.' To something he hadn't quite understood at the time, but he'd done some research since. 'You and Izzy called it your *Roman Holiday*,' he said, 'so I'm assuming you know the film?'

She looked surprised, but nodded.

'I didn't—so I looked it up. And it wasn't a *Roman Holiday*,' he said quietly. 'Yes, on a superficial level, there are similarities. The princess in the film spends time as a commoner, and so did you. But that's as far as it goes. This isn't the nineteen-fifties, and Giorgio was with us when we went to the cottage by the sea. I never had any intention of writing a story about you for the press. I didn't have a fight with anyone, you didn't rescue me from a river, and I didn't bring you back to San Rocello.'

She said nothing.

'The kiss happened.' He paused. 'In the film, they don't spend the night together. But we did.' He took a deep breath. 'I woke with you in my arms. It was perfect.'

She said nothing, but at least she wasn't disagreeing. And the faint colour in her cheeks gave him hope.

'And, that night, we made a baby.'

'But you gave me all the photos from my time with you. Just like in the film.'

'No, I gave you *access* to them,' he corrected. 'I still have the originals—and maybe one day I might publish them.' Before the look of horror in her eyes bloomed any further, he said swiftly, 'Though, if I do, firstly it will only be with your full permission, and secondly you get to choose which ones we publish. And, going back to the film, there's another really important difference. I'm the photographer, not the journalist.' He waited until she met his gaze, before finishing quietly, 'I'm not the one who walks away.'

'You said you didn't want to raise a family,' she reminded him, 'because you've already done that with Saoirse. You said you wanted to concentrate on your career.'

'I know what I told you, and it's exactly how I thought I felt,' he said. 'But you're expecting our baby, and that changes everything.'

For a moment she wasn't the Winter Queen any more; she was the woman whose smile was like sunshine. Even though her mouth wasn't smiling, her eyes were. Just enough to give him hope.

'But, just so we're clear, I'm not here because of the baby.'

Her face shuttered. 'You said you'd stand by me. Do the right thing.'

'You'd only just told me you were pregnant,' he said, 'and I wasn't thinking straight. It was a knee-jerk reaction. And then you told me I didn't need to be involved—so I think we hurt each other. But I'm sorry I hurt you.'

'I'm sorry, too,' she said.

'I'm not going to fight you for custody. I don't want

to hurt you. Ever. I should have told you how much I missed you, when you left to come back to San Rocello. That's why I sent you the picture of a rose.'

'A picture's worth a thousand words—but I didn't really know what you were trying to tell me.'

'I think most people have the same idea what a single red rose means,' he said dryly. 'But it wasn't just that. It was all the other stuff that goes with a rose for me. Your favourite poem. Our conversation, that last morning. What you told me about missing your dad. It's why I wanted to meet you here—in a place that I know has happy memories for you, a place that means *family* to you.' He looked at her. 'And you sent me a photo of a seashell. What did that mean?'

'I picked it up on the beach. I wanted you to think about the beach, where you kissed me for the first time.' She looked straight at him. 'And where we walked together, the day we made the baby.'

Was she telling him she loved him?

He still wasn't sure.

But those memories made him feel warm all over.

'And then you sent me a photo of a bluebell,' she said.

'Because it was the colour of your eyes,' he said. 'And the carpet of the woods where I taught you how to take a good portrait.' He looked at her. 'Did you look up its meaning?'

'No.'

'You should have done,' he said softly. But that was where their flirting by photographs had ended.

'What does it mean?' she asked.

'Everlasting love. Constancy,' he said, and waited for that to sink in. 'And then,' he said, 'you ghosted me. Did you change your mind about me?'

She shook her head. 'I didn't know what to say. I remembered you saying you thought my eyes were the same colour as bluebells, so I was going to send you a cornflower—that's the colour of *your* eyes. But then I looked up the meaning of a cornflower. Apparently, it's "delicacy and refinement". And that wasn't what I wanted to say.'

He laughed. 'I'm not delicate—or that refined. But you are.'

She shrugged. 'I didn't know what to say to you,' she said. 'I didn't know if you were just flirting with me or if you were serious. And then I had something to sort out for Nonno. And time just got away from me, and the longer it went on the harder it was to know what to say to you. In business, I know what I'm doing. When it comes to emotional stuff, I'm not so sure of myself. The last time I was in love, I thought Rufus loved me all the way back. But he didn't. He walked away.'

'I know,' Liam said softly. 'But I'm not Rufus, and I'm not walking away.'

'But you said you want to concentrate on your career.'

'I do,' he said. 'But I also want a family. I know I told you I didn't—at the time, I *thought* I didn't. But this baby has made me think about what I really want.' He paused. 'Izzy said you used to freeze her out to protect her. And I think that's what you did to me yesterday; you pushed me away, because you didn't want me to feel I had to choose between you and doing what I love.'

She stared at him, those beautiful bluebell eyes widening slightly.

'But the thing is,' he said, 'that's not quite what I want any more.' He paused. 'Ask me what I want, Vittoria.'

Her voice was cool, calm and collected, as was her expression; but he could see by the shallowness of her breathing that she felt anything but cool and calm and collected. 'What do you want, Liam?'

The fact she'd used his first name gave him hope.

'I want *you*,' he said softly. 'I want to be a family with you and our baby. Not because I feel it's my duty but because I want to be with you. Both of you. And not because you're a princess, because I couldn't care less about how much money you're worth or how far back you can trace your family tree. Titles, diamonds, castles—none of it matters. The important thing is love.'

Her eyes glittered with unshed tears. 'Are you saying that you love me?'

'Yes, I love you, Vittoria,' he said. 'And I want to marry you. I want to make a life with you. I want to wake up with you every morning and I want to go to sleep at night with you beside me. I want to teach our baby—our children, if we're lucky—how to build sandcastles. I want to teach them to count and to read and to grow roses and to take photographs. But I don't want just the fun parenting stuff. I want to be there when they wake in the night and need a cuddle, or when they're out of sorts and need someone to listen—whether they're tiny or a stroppy teen, or in years to come maybe when they're an adult with their own children. And I want to do it all with you. Because I love you.'

She swallowed hard. 'You mean that?'

'Yes. And I want you to be sure that I love you for yourself, Vittoria. As far as your family is concerned, I'm from the wrong background—I'm not the son of a royal. But I grew up knowing I was loved, and I brought up my little sister so she was secure and knew she was loved. I believe that's worth more than all the money and castles and power in the world.' His throat felt thick, but until she believed him, he was going to keep talking. 'The only thing that matters is love. I'll tell that to your grandparents and your mother. And I'll keep on telling them until they understand that I love you for your own sake, and that I'm prepared to learn whatever you need me to so I can support you and be your anchor when you become queen.'

'You love me.' Her voice was full of wonder.

'I love you,' he confirmed.

'You really, really love me.'

He coughed. 'This is where you're supposed to say it back. But only if you mean it.'

'I love you,' she said. 'And I mean that.' She took a deep breath. 'But is that enough?'

'It is for me. Isn't it enough for you?' he asked.

'Of course it is. But I come with complications. And it means you have to give things up. I don't want you to do that. You've worked so hard. I can't ask you to give up your career.'

'I won't be giving up my career,' he said. 'Mine's a little more flexible than yours. I'm at the stage where I can choose which jobs I accept. I put my career on hold for my sister, because I love her—and I'll put it on hold again whenever I need to for our baby. And for *you*.'

A tear rolled down her cheek, and he risked leaning over and wiping it away with the pad of his thumb.

'Don't cry. It's going to be fine. I love you, I'm here, and I'm not going anywhere. Well, I do have to go somewhere, just for a little while,' he corrected himself. 'Saoirse has an interview tomorrow. I want to be there to make her breakfast, calm her last-minute nerves and remind her that she knows her stuff, to just be herself in front of the interviewer and remember to breathe. I'm her only family, and I won't abandon her. But I'll always be there for you, too.'

* * *

Vittoria remembered him talking about the girlfriends who'd wanted him to put them first and ignore his little sister's needs. 'If she's got an interview, I'd expect you to be there—just as I'd want to support my own sister,' she said. 'I'll never try to make you feel guilty or tear you in two.'

'Thank you.'

'But,' she warned, 'being with me—it's not going to be easy. Being a royal means everyone watches you, every minute of every day, and judges you. You can't ever be grouchy or look tired, because people will speculate and spin stories. It's like living in a goldfish bowl. Rufus walked away rather than dealing with it.'

He looked grim. 'I'm making a supposition here, but I'm guessing that's one of the reasons why your mother wants you to marry someone who was born into it—someone who's been brought up coping with it and won't let you down.'

'It is,' she agreed.

'I'm not Rufus. And we need to learn how to manage the press,' he said. 'We'll make friends with them. Work with them. Instead of trying to be perfect, we will show them the human side of the palace. That you're like every other mum-to-be who has morning sickness. That I'm like every other dad who's grouchy after a broken night when I'm trying to hit a deadline. We'll let the press share our family, and then they'll protect us.'

She thought about it. 'Share our family.'

He nodded. 'Though this is all a bit of a moot point, because you haven't agreed to marry me yet.'

'You haven't actually asked me,' she pointed out.

'I will,' he said. 'And I also want to talk to your family.'

'You mean ask their permission?'

'Not so much permission,' he said, 'because you're not anyone's property, but I'd like their blessing. I want to be courteous and show them that I'm considering their feelings, too. I don't have a royal background, but they need to know that I'll love you and cherish you for the rest of my days—and I intend to stay right by your side, whatever happens.'

She could barely believe that he loved her and wanted to be by her side. Be a hands-on dad.

'I don't have a ring in my pocket, and I think Saoirse should have our mum's engagement ring, so I can't offer you that in the future, either.' He smiled. 'So I guess we're going to have to go shopping at some point.' He dropped to one knee. 'I kind of wanted to ask you in the palace library, where it all started. But then I saw you reading on this bench, and I know that this is the right place. I hope your dad's looking down right now and knows I'm asking you to marry me in the place that he loved most. I hope my dad's there with him, swapping plant stories. And my mum's making them both a mug of tea so they can skulk off into a greenhouse afterwards and potter about and talk about which parks are the best for taking toddlers to.'

She felt the tears filling her eyes. 'That's—that's a lovely picture.'

'And I have weddingy demands.'

She couldn't help smiling. 'Weddingy demands?'

'Absolutely. I want this to be a family wedding. Izzy and Sursh as our bridesmaids. Your grandfather walking you down the aisle. Your mum and your grandmother dabbing their eyes in the front row and sighing over what a fairy tale bride you make.'

'Works for me,' she said.

'Good.' He smiled up at her. 'Vittoria di Sarda, I fell in love with you on the day I first met you,' he said. 'And even when you had the wrong colour hair and the wrong colour eyes, and you were wearing clothes you wouldn't normally wear in a million years, I fell deeper in love with you every day. I'm not promising you perfection—there will be days when I'm grouchy with you and you're the Winter Queen with me, and you're going to criticise or choke on my coffee—but I promise to love you with all of my heart, all of my soul, all that I am. If your family gives us their blessing, will you marry me?'

'Yes,' she said, and kissed him.

# CHAPTER TEN

'So, DO I ask Matteo Battaglia to make me an appointment with your grandfather?' Liam asked.

'No. We're doing this as a team,' Vittoria said.

'If you come with me, it looks as if I'm hiding behind your skirts,' Liam pointed out. 'If I can't even face your grandfather on my own, how is he ever going to believe that I can cope with a royal lifestyle and a pack of paparazzi?'

She looked at him thoughtfully. 'You have a point. But Matteo can stonewall you and claim that Nonno's diary is full and you'll have to accept what he says at face value; whereas I also have access to Nonno's diary and I know where the gaps are.'

'In that case,' Liam said, 'I'll apologise to your grandfather's private secretary later for going behind his back and ask you to make an appointment for me.' He paused. 'Do you know when your mother and grandmother are free, too?'

'You're planning to face all of them at once?'

'That makes it sound as if it's going to be an ordeal,' Liam said.

She had to be honest. 'It might be.'

He shrugged. 'In the old days, weren't knights supposed to fight dragons to win the princess's hand? This is the modern equivalent.'

She raised an eyebrow. 'Really?'

He laughed. 'Except obviously you're not a chattel to be given away.'

'And there's the whole dragon-slaying thing,' she pointed out.

'All right, it was a stupid metaphor,' he said. 'I was trying to be too clever, and I failed.'

She kissed him lightly. 'I like the fact you can admit when you're wrong.'

'Let's rewind,' he said. 'I'd like to meet your family and ask for their blessing. Obviously, they'll have concerns, so I'd like the chance to talk to them, find out what worries them, and either reassure them or work towards reassuring them. And I know that sounds more like a business deal than planning a wedding,' he added swiftly, 'so I also want you to know that I love you and I'm going to do whatever it takes to make you happy.'

A man who thought things through. Who planned. Who did things sensibly—and who loved her and wasn't afraid to tell her. 'That,' she said, 'sounds like an excellent plan.'

'With goals. Specific, measurable, achievable, realistic—the only thing missing is "timed",' he said, smiling. 'And I think the timing is now. Provided they're free, of course.'

Three brief phone calls later—all conducted in rapid Italian Liam couldn't follow—Vittoria turned to him. 'Would you like to accompany me to the library? They'll meet us there.'

The library.

The place where it had all started. Where he'd seen

the woman behind the tiara. The woman he'd fallen in love with.

That had to be a good sign—right?

Vittoria signalled to Giorgio that all was well, and took Liam's hand.

Liam's stomach was tied in knots. This was the most important meeting of his life, and he had to get it right. He needed to convince Vittoria's family that he was the right partner for her—even though he was from the wrong background.

Right at that moment, it felt like every exam, his driving test, and every 'first day' of his life rolled into one. Knowing he needed to prove himself. Except with exams and his career, he'd known what he was doing. He'd been pretty sure of the results, because he'd put the work in and honed the skills he needed.

This was something he had no control over, and it was terrifying.

Silently, he walked beside her.

He only realised he was gripping her hand too tightly when she whispered, 'Liam, I kind of need some circulation in my fingers. Would you mind loosening your grip?'

'Sorry.' He dropped her hand. 'I didn't mean to hurt you.'

'It's fine.' She stole a swift kiss and laced her fingers very loosely between his again. 'It's kind of reassuring to know you're nervous.'

'How?'

'Because it means I'm that important to you,' she said. 'You're not taking any of this for granted.'

'No. But, whatever happens today, I love you and I'll be there for you and the baby. I'll make it work,' he promised.

She paused outside the door to the library. 'Ready?'

Not in a million years. 'Ready,' he confirmed.

'I love you,' she whispered, and stood back to let him open the door for her.

Vittoria's family were sitting on the comfortable sofas arranged in a semi-circle in the centre of the room—the king, the queen and the princess. Although the setting appeared to make it informal, Liam knew it wasn't informal in the slightest. It wasn't normal for a princess to ask the rest of the royal family to a meeting, and it wasn't normal to introduce a commoner at said meeting. Her family were astute enough to realise this was an interview. He was going to be the one doing most of the talking and answering their questions. And the seating was set up very much like an interview panel.

'Nonno, Nonna, Mamma—I'd like to introduce you to Liam MacCarthy,' Vittoria said. 'Liam, you have already met my grandfather, King Vittorio. This is my grandmother, Queen Giulia, and my mother, Princess Maria.'

Liam gave a formal bow. *'Vostro Maestà, Vostre Altezze Reale,'* he said.

Three inscrutable royal faces gazed back at him. And nobody asked him to take a seat. Maybe this was a test to show that he could cope with pressure. Well, he'd make sure he passed—because this was too important to fail. He couldn't and wouldn't let Vittoria down.

'We were very pleased with your official photographs of Vittoria, Mr MacCarthy,' the king said.

'Thank you, sir.' Liam smiled.

'And it was kind of you to host Vittoria in England,' Queen Giulia added.

The politeness oddly made him feel even more

nervous. Perhaps it would be better to think of this in terms of an assignment. He needed to get the pose right and the lighting right, and bring out the story behind the picture.

Except in this case he was the subject, and he had no control over the pose or the lighting.

'What brings you to San Rocello, Mr MacCarthy?' Princess Maria asked.

This was it. His moment. Liam glanced at Vittoria, who gave an almost imperceptible nod.

'I was hoping to speak to you all,' Liam said. 'Sir. Ma'am. Ma'am.'

Again, they had inscrutable expressions. No feedback. It was like working in a room with a difficult light source and without a light meter to help him get the balance right; he had to rely on his own instincts. Make sure that he was enough.

'I realise that this might come as a—' Shock? No, because that signalled bad news. For a moment, he wished he'd asked Vittoria to delay the meeting for long enough for him to work out a speech. Then again, even with preparation he might get it wrong. It was better to speak from the heart. Be honest. 'A surprise,' he continued, 'but I would like your blessing to marry Vittoria.'

'You want to marry Vittoria,' the king said. 'Perhaps you could explain why you think we would give you our blessing, Mr MacCarthy.'

'Because I love her, sir,' Liam said. 'I mean I love *Vittoria*—it has nothing to do with her being a princess, and everything to do with who she is.'

'So do we assume from this that you had some kind of affair during Vittoria's holiday?' the queen asked.

He wanted to squirm, but he faced her. 'That,' Liam said, 'makes our relationship sound tacky and flimsy.

Which it isn't. With respect, ma'am, I fell in love with your granddaughter the first day I met her.' He took a deep breath. 'When I took photographs for her sister in this very room.'

Silence.

He had no idea whether this was going well or badly. All he could do was press on. 'Obviously I'm not from a royal background, and I realise that might cause you some concern about my suitability. But I'd like to reassure you that I will always put Vittoria first. And that I love her.'

'I see,' Vittorio said. 'And you can support my granddaughter in the manner to which she has become accustomed?'

'Not quite,' Liam said. 'I'm not a prince. I can't shower her in priceless jewels, buy her a castle in every country, or employ dozens of staff. But I have a comfortable income, I have a good reputation in my industry, and I own a flat in Chelsea as well as the cottage by the sea. I have supported my family for years.' He met the king's gaze levelly. 'I'm aware that I'm not the kind of person you expected Vittoria to marry. I apologise for that, but I'm not ashamed of my background. My father was a horticulturalist at Kew Gardens, and my mother taught art. They were good people, kind and loving, and I hope I can bring that same goodness, kindness and love into our marriage.'

And oh, he dearly wanted what his parents had had. A marriage where they'd worked as a team and backed each other. Loved each other.

Vittoria's mother and grandmother exchanged a glance. Liam was horribly aware that his words were inadequate.

What would he worry about, in their shoes? What

had gone wrong with Rufus? Apparently the man had backed away because he couldn't handle the royal lifestyle. So Vittoria's family might worry that he would do the same. 'I know a royal life isn't an easy one, especially as it's lived very much in the public eye, and I'll probably make mistakes,' Liam said. 'But I hope that someone on your staff will point me in the right direction to help me learn whatever I need to know, so I can support Vittoria properly in her duties and not repeat my mistakes. Right now, my Italian's at a very basic level, but I intend to become fluent as quickly as possible. And I'm not afraid of hard work.'

'No. A man who put his own dreams aside to bring up his younger sister definitely isn't afraid of hard work,' Vittorio said.

The king had clearly either seen that dossier Vittoria had read before Liam took her portrait, or she'd briefed him.

'And how do you feel about all this, Vittoria?' the king asked.

'I love Liam,' she said simply. 'And he loves me. That's all I need to know.'

'I see,' he said, and turned to Liam. 'So, Mr MacCarthy. What if I don't give you my blessing to marry my granddaughter?'

Liam lifted his chin slightly and looked at the king. 'Family is important to both of us. With respect, sir, we intend to marry whether we have your blessing or not. But we'd both be happier if we had our family there to share the celebration and the love.'

'Celebration,' the king said thoughtfully. 'Should I assume you want a full state wedding?'

'I want,' Liam said, 'whatever will make Vittoria happy. Whether it's a simple and very private family ceremony, or whether it's a more elaborate celebration so her country can share in it. The type of wedding isn't important. What's important is that we're together. A team. And that our families are there.'

Was it his imagination, or was there a tiny glint of approval in the king's eyes?

OK. So they understood he loved Vittoria, he was prepared to work hard to make sure he fitted in to a royal lifestyle, and he intended to be constant. What else would a rich family be worried about? That he was a gold-digger who planned to steal the princess's heart, then dump her and take her to the cleaners, perhaps? 'I will instruct my family lawyer to arrange a prenup, to say that I am entitled to absolutely nothing if this marriage doesn't last,' Liam added. 'Though I do believe this marriage will last, because I love Vittoria and that's not going to change. Ever. I will love her—' and their baby, though he rather thought that particular piece of news needed to wait for a little bit longer '—with all my heart and soul, for the rest of my days.' He looked at them. 'Is there anything you're concerned about that I haven't addressed?'

'Being a consort isn't easy,' Giulia said. 'How do you propose to cope with that side of Vittoria's life?'

That was an easier question. 'As the queen of your country,' he said, 'Vittoria will have a lot to think about and a lot to worry about. My job as her consort, ma'am, will be to take some of that care from her. To be there when she needs me, but not wrapping her in cotton wool or crowding her. Supporting her. Holding her hand when she thinks the next step she needs to take will be too hard, and reminding her that she's an incredibly capable woman who can do absolutely anything she puts her mind to.'

'Well, young man,' Giulia said. 'It seems you understand what a consort's role is.'

'And I intend to do it well.' Liam took a deep breath. 'Of course you have concerns—just as I would about anyone who wanted to marry my sister. You love Vittoria and you want the best for her. The way I see it, Vittoria needs the support of someone who loves her. Someone who will listen to her worries, let her bounce ideas, ask questions to help clarify her thoughts, and help her to find a solution. She needs someone who will put her first, and that to me is worth more than any title or money I could bring to a marriage. I can't offer perfection, but I will love her with all my heart and soul—all that I am—for the rest of my days. And I'm prepared to do whatever it takes to make this work. I know you only have my word for it, but I hope that Princess Isabella can reassure you that I'm honourable. That I have integrity.'

'How do you know you love Vittoria, Mr MacCarthy?' Maria asked.

'Because my world's a better place with her in it, ma'am,' Liam said. 'And without her everything feels as if it's monochrome and underexposed. She's the one who brings the light in, for me.'

'You've known Vittoria for, what, a month? How do you know your feelings won't change?' Giulia asked.

Vittoria had told him that her mother and grandmother were overprotective. But he understood where they were coming from; they were asking the same kind of questions he'd want answered by anyone who wanted to marry Saoirse.

All he could do was speak from the heart. Tell them how he really felt.

'My feelings probably will change, ma'am,' he said.

'I love Vittoria for who she is now. But people aren't static and neither is love. People grow and change. But I think Vittoria and I are both old enough to realise how each other is likely to change in the years to come. And I know I'll love the woman she becomes.' He took a deep breath. 'I can stand here and declare my undying love for the next hour, but they're just words. You have no way of knowing that I mean them, and I can't say anything to prove how I feel about Vittoria. But I think I can show you.'

'How?' the king asked.

'May I show you the photograph I took, sir?' He gestured to his phone.

At the king's nod, Liam tapped in the password to his private portfolio and brought up the last picture he'd taken in the library.

'A good portrait will show you the person behind the image,' he said. 'And, looking back, I think this is the moment I fell in love with Vittoria. This is the woman behind the tiara. She's bright and capable, a little shy, and she loses herself in Shakespeare.'

The king studied the photograph, then handed the phone to the queen. She, too, examined it, then passed it to Vittoria's mother. And Maria gave a sharp intake of breath. 'My daughter,' she said softly. 'I've never seen you like that, Rina. You glow.'

'That's the woman I see,' Liam said, his voice equally soft. 'The woman I want to spend the rest of my days with. The woman I want to grow old with. The woman I want to have ch—' He stopped.

'Go on, Mr MacCarthy,' the queen said.

Liam glanced at Vittoria. Should this come from him or from her?

Or perhaps from both of them. He'd said they were a team. Now was their first chance to prove it.

'There is one more thing we need to tell you about,' he said quietly, and took her hand.

This was the turning point, Vittoria knew. The moment where her family would accept or reject Liam. And it was so, so important that they accepted him.

'One little thing,' Vittoria said. 'Nonno, Nonna, Mamma—or perhaps I should say Bisnonno, Bisnonna and Nonna.'

Just as she'd expected, her grandparents and her mother looked at her in utter shock.

'You're pregnant?' Maria asked finally. 'How pregnant?'

'It's very early days,' Vittoria said. 'I did the test a few days ago. I know Liam and I have done this completely the wrong way round—traditionally it should be marriage, then a coronation, and then a christening. I know we're disappointing you, and I'm sorry about that.'

'Is that why you want to marry my granddaughter, Mr MacCarthy?' the king asked. 'Because of the baby?'

'No. I want to marry your granddaughter because I love her,' Liam repeated. 'And, even though the baby isn't planned, he or she will be very much loved. I'm prepared to do my share of changing nappies and getting up in the night.' His voice thickened slightly as he said, 'I hope our baby will grow up with a grandmother and great-grandparents who love him or her as much as I know my parents would have loved a grandchild.'

Vittoria knew that was going to be hard for him, not being able to share his baby with his parents. Just as it would be for her, only being able to share memories and photographs of her father, rather than seeing him give her child a piggyback through his beloved rose garden. 'And my father,' she added softly.

'Francesco.' Maria blinked back tears. 'Your father loved babies, Rina. Yes, you're right. He would have loved being a Nonno. And I...' She shook her head. 'This wasn't what I expected to hear today.'

'I'm sorry I've disappointed you, Mamma,' Vittoria said. 'I know this isn't what you and Nonna wanted for me.'

'Maybe,' Maria said, 'we were wrong. Maybe love is more important than a shared background.' She looked at Liam. 'It's not going to be easy, but you seem to have both feet on the ground, Mr MacCarthy. Being practical and pragmatic... Those are important qualities in this world.'

'Love is the most important thing,' Liam said. 'It's easy for me to talk. But please don't judge me now, ma'am. I'd like you all to judge me in a year's time— when you'll have seen me prove my words every day. When you've seen me change nappies, bring Vittoria co—no, not coffee, because Izzy says my coffee's terrible, a cup of tea,' he corrected, making Vittoria smile. 'When you've seen me settle a teething baby, when you've seen me noticing that little pleat between her eyes that Vittoria has when she worries about something and I've persuaded her to talk to me so I can share her worries and reassure her. When you've seen me be there.'

'A year's time. When we'll have a baby's laughter in the palace again,' Giulia said. 'And, a year after that, pattering feet. It will be nice to have a child in the garden again.'

'A wedding, a christening and a coronation,' the king

said. He paused, and Vittoria felt the weight of every second. Would her grandfather understand how much she loved Liam? Would her family welcome him? Or was this going to end up rocking the monarchy to its foundations, maybe fracturing it beyond repair?

'Nonno, I hope you won't make me choose between love and duty. I want both,' Vittoria said. 'Liam completes me. With him, I can be myself. I know it's OK to be vulnerable and I know it's OK to lean on him. I trust him. I want to share my life with him. I want our children to grow up, secure that they're loved for themselves.'

The king said nothing, and this time Vittoria couldn't read his eyes. He was totally inscrutable.

'I will do whatever it takes to make this work,' Liam said. 'But the one thing I will not compromise on is my family. I love Vittoria, and I intend to support her. I'll learn whatever I need to. But the one thing I can do well is negotiate with the press. If we make friends with them, if we give them stories, they won't look for faults or gossip. They'll see a queen who understands her people because she shares the same worries that they do, and they'll celebrate her. A bride who worries that she'll trip on the carpet down the aisle, a mum who juggles a busy job with a baby who wakes at three in the morning, a woman who steps up to the top job and wants to do it well so she can lead by example and encourage others to be the best they can be. She isn't Rapunzel in her ivory tower or Sleeping Beauty waiting to be woken. Vittoria's part of the modern world, leading her country and making a difference.'

That was how he saw her? Vittoria wondered. It was a lot to live up to. Daunting.

Until she looked into Liam's eyes and saw the love

shining out at her. And that gave her the confidence to believe she really was the woman he saw.

'Vittoria,' Liam finished, 'will be the best queen ever. And I'll be with her, every step of the way.'

And finally, the king smiled. 'All right. You have my blessing, Mr MacCarthy. Liam.'

'Thank you, sir.'

'I think,' the king said, 'in the circumstances you'd better start calling me Nonno.' He rose to his feet, hugged Vittoria, and then shook Liam's hand. 'Congratulations. And welcome to our family.'

Vittoria's mother and grandmother hugged them both.

'And now,' Vittoria's mother said with a smile, 'we have a wedding and a christening to plan…'

# EPILOGUE

*A year later*

'So HOW DO I look?' Vittoria asked, standing in the doorway.

Liam looked at his wife and his heart skipped a beat. 'Breathtaking,' he said. He leant in to whisper in her ear, 'If it wasn't for the fact that your schedule's timed down practically to the second, I'd take you to our room and show you just how gorgeous you look.'

She grinned. 'Later. But I wasn't asking as your wife. How do I look in queenly terms?'

'Perfect,' Maria said, and deftly scooped the baby from Liam's arms. 'Francesca, come to Nonna. Your *babbo* has to get his camera out and take your *mamma's* official coronation photographs.' She kissed the baby, who gurgled and pulled her hair. 'Your father would be so proud of you, Vittoria. As am I.'

'She's beautiful, brave and clever. I think I'm beyond proud,' Liam said.

'Oh, you two.' But Vittoria was laughing.

They'd laughed a lot, this past year. At their wedding, when Liam had scooped her up and danced with her in the palace rose garden. On their honeymoon, when they'd escaped to Liam's little cottage by the sea and walked at the edge of the sea at sunset, kissing as the first stars came out—except, the second week, it turned out that the rest of the San Rocello royal family had rented a stately home nearby and insisted on joining in the celebrations. He'd taken a lot of photographs of the royal family since the day they'd accepted him as Vittoria's husband-to-be, but the ones he took that week were his favourites.

They'd laughed—and cried—when their daughter was born, and agreed that she should be called after both their fathers, Francesca Philippa. The good wishes sent by the people of San Rocello had been humbling in the extreme. Francesca's christening had been a day of national celebration.

And now it was Vittoria's coronation day.

His beautiful queen.

It would be a solemn occasion. But Liam intended it to be full of joy. And, later that night, he was going to enjoy taking off her crown and her gown and making love to the Queen of San Rocello for the very first time.

'What are you thinking?' Vittoria asked.

He grinned. 'Not in front of your mother.'

'She's busy singing to Francesca. She won't hear.'

He leaned over and whispered his thoughts in her ear, and his grin broadened when she blushed.

'That's my queen,' he said. 'I love you, Vittoria. *Ti amo. Per sempre.*'

\* \* \* \* \*

# WYOMING MATCHMAKER

MELISSA SENATE

## Chapter One

Detective Ford Dawson's latest case: a missing wedding gown. With one unexpected twist.

"So you came home from work and your dress was gone?" Ford asked Trudy Dunbar, the middle-aged woman sitting across from him on the sofa. He tried hard to keep from looking at the younger woman—the aforementioned twist—sitting beside the victim.

He'd taken note of the surname when Trudy had called the Bear Ridge Police Department to report the theft, but he hadn't expected her to be necessarily related to Danica Dunbar—or that Danica would be here with Trudy. Luckily for Ford, he had a solid poker face, which had helped to hide the jolt he'd felt at the sight of her. He could easily see the family resemblance between the two women, though Trudy was probably twenty-five years older, a few inches shorter, with straight blond hair cut to her chin.

Tears brimmed in Trudy's hazel eyes. "Well, I got home from work, changed into comfortable clothes and then took Bixby for a walk—that's my French bulldog."

At his name, the little black-and-white dog scampered over, jumped up on the sofa and settled beside Trudy.

"The dress was there when I left, hanging on a hook on the back of my bedroom door," Trudy added. "When I returned, it was gone."

"How long were you out?" he asked.

"About forty-five minutes. I take Bixby to the park every night at six thirty. It's our routine."

A routine someone had obviously noticed.

"My niece here bought me the dress as a wedding gift," Trudy said, looking at Danica with tear-filled eyes. "So I feel doubly terrible that it was stolen. I just brought it home yesterday."

"Don't you worry, Aunt Trudy," Danica said, squeezing the older woman's hand. "Ford—

Detective Dawson," she quickly corrected, "will get your gown back and before the wedding."

*And how could you possibly know that?* he wanted to snap. Two months ago, they'd shared an unforgettable night together before she'd left his bed at three in the morning like it was spewing hot lava—without explanation. He could be the worst detective in Wyoming for all she knew about him.

He wasn't—Ford was damned good at his job. But still. Danica hadn't had a chance to get to know him. So what had sent her running out of his life so fast? After a night that couldn't have gone any better—until it had come to a screeching halt. He was a seasoned detective and couldn't figure this out. It grated.

"Do you have any idea who might have taken the dress?" he asked, flipping a page in his notebook. This wasn't a typical burglary; nothing else had been taken or disturbed. He doubted someone randomly broke in, noticed the wedding gown hanging on the back of the bedroom door, and decided to make off with only it instead of the contents of Trudy's jewelry box, which according to Trudy included an untouched diamond tennis bracelet. Someone had targeted the gown itself.

Trudy took a sip of her coffee. "Well, my fiancé was dating three different women before we met, and they do all give me the stink-eye when they see me around." She shrugged. "Two of them marched up to Cole to yell at him when I was standing right next to him."

Hmm. A jealous ex? Could be.

"Do you know their names?" Ford asked.

Trudy shook her head. "You'd have to ask Cole, though I'm not sure he'd feel comfortable telling you. He probably wouldn't want to accuse anyone without proof. Cole is such a tenderhearted man."

A month ago, Ford might not have thought that a man dating four women at the same time could be described as tenderhearted. But such was the new normal in town, ever since almost one hundred single women of all ages had moved to Bear Ridge, ready to pair up with their soul mates. There'd been a severe shortage of single women— ten men to every woman—and it had started affecting more than just lonely bachelors. The few restaurants and bars had begun to fail. The one bridal shop closed. Young people were leaving in droves for Prairie City, a bigger, more bustling town a half hour away. Business at the Dawson Family Guest Ranch, which Ford co-owned with his five siblings, was booming since the majority of their guests were from out of town and state. But two good cowboys and a reliable cook in the cafeteria had quit, saying they were moving on since there was no nightlife anymore, no one to ask out. The one single cowgirl on staff, hounded for dates day and night, couldn't take it another second and quit. She'd moved to Prairie City.

That had led the new mayor and town council, which included Ford's sister, Daisy, to hatch a plan to bring single women to town to boost the economy and keep folks here. After a social media blitz about Bear Ridge's available and marriage-minded men—there'd been an accompanying photo of a wealthy rancher who looked a lot like one of the Marvel movie actors—the women had started coming to town in droves to meet their potential true loves. A free matchmaking service was provided, too.

Ford, who was looking to settle down, hadn't bothered signing up. Not after what had happened with Danica.

But dating was now the town pastime for singles. The bars and restaurants and parks and Main Street were full of couples, full of dates and even wedding ceremonies after whirlwind romances. At a speed dating event a few weeks ago that Ford had worked—there was always at least one fistfight at this kind of thing—the mayor had announced that dating was a numbers game and sometimes you had to kiss a lot of frogs to find your prince or princess. The singles had taken that to heart and you'd see the same man or woman with a new date every day until a match was made. But that didn't mean feelings didn't get hurt.

Love was serious business. Everyone knew that.

"I'm sorry about your gown, Ms. Dunbar, and I will do my best to get it back for you," Ford said to Trudy. "I'll be in touch the moment I have information for you." He took a final sip of his coffee and then stood. "Oh, when is the wedding?"

"In two weeks—on Saturday night," Danica said. She popped up. "I'll walk you out."

Interesting. Maybe he'd finally get his explanation for what happened back in February. But should he be thinking about that two months later? Harping on it? Completely down on dating when there were plenty of single women in Bear Ridge now?

"I sure hope Aunt Trudy doesn't leave town because of this," Danica whispered as she walked him out to the porch. "She moved here for a fresh start and now that she's found her second chance at love, this might taint it and send her and her fiancé packing."

He remembered Danica talking about her lack of family in town during their night together. Her parents had retired to Arizona and her one sibling lived far away, so she'd been alone here. Her aunt Trudy, one of her few remaining relatives, had been married to a man who hated small-town life, but they'd divorced recently and Trudy had finally come back to her hometown.

Ford had once felt the same as Trudy's ex. It had taken him a long time to realize it wasn't small-town life he had a problem with, but the particular small town of Bear Ridge. The minute Ford had graduated from high school, he'd fled. Leaving his five siblings behind hadn't been easy, but staying was out of the question back then. He'd moved to Casper, a small city hours away, and become a cop. But the life he'd built there had been missing something for a long time. It had taken him almost twenty years to come home.

Now he was the last single Dawson. One by one, his siblings had moved back to the Dawson Family Guest Ranch, where they'd all once said they'd never step foot again. And one by one, they'd met their matches in every context. Then there was him. The oldest, at thirty-five—and alone.

And now that Bear Ridge was full of single women, he was hung up on the one who'd walked away. Same old story.

He looked at Danica, beautiful in the glow of

the porch light, her long blond hair in a swirly tumble past her shoulders, her blue eyes full of so many different emotions he couldn't assess them all. He saw worry for her aunt. And clear nervousness about standing here with him. Yeah, he wasn't too comfortable either. From naked in his bed to awkward almost-strangers.

"I promise you I'll do my best to find the thief and the dress," he said. He couldn't promise it would be in one piece or that it wasn't in an alleyway Dumpster, covered in garbage. He'd seen the damage inflicted by scorned exes, and it was never pretty.

"I appreciate that," she said. "Especially given—" She clamped her mouth shut.

*Especially given what happened between us... how awkward this is...*

"No worries," he said.

But he didn't mean it. How was he supposed to move on from Danica when he didn't know what had gone wrong between them? They'd made love, fed each other whipped-cream-covered strawberries, then lay spooned and talked about everything and anything for hours. He'd been so relaxed with her against his chest, his arms wrapped around her. He'd been hopeful about the newfangled future he envisioned for himself. And then she'd crept off in the middle of the night, mumbling something about how this wasn't going to work, sorry, but she had to go. The next day he'd left her a voice mail: no response. He'd sent roses to her office, asking if they could talk. All he'd gotten back was a two-line text saying they just weren't a match, sorry.

He'd been so damned thrown for a loop that he'd considered asking his sister, whose favorite subject was relationships, what the hell could have gone wrong, but he couldn't bring himself to talk about it. He just grumbled around for a few weeks. And now he was once again close enough to Danica Dunbar to smell her intoxicating perfume.

"I'll be in touch with your aunt," he said, emphasizing the words *your aunt*.

She nodded and he booked down the stairs and into his squad car.

He'd spent all those weeks trying to forget her, and now he was right back into remembering.

Danica stayed out on the porch, needing to catch her breath and slow her heart rate. When her aunt had called the Bear Ridge Police Department about the burglary, Danica had figured there was only a small chance of Ford Dawson being the cop to show up. But, lately, the odds hadn't been in Danica's favor in any aspect of her life.

"He sure was a handsome one."

Danica turned around to find her aunt coming outside.

So handsome. Six feet two, rock-hard muscles, thick dark hair and the bluest eyes. The way he kissed… "Yeah, I guess," Danica said, trying for a neutral expression. "I'm sure he'll find your dress, Aunt Trudy. Ford is very dedicated to his job and this community."

Trudy narrowed her eyes. "Ford, huh? You clearly know him. I thought I sensed something in the air. You two have a history?"

Danica nodded and leaned against the porch railing. "Unfortunately, we…want different things," she said as memories of lying in his arms came flooding back. "I think I should just be on my own for a while. Till I figure myself out."

"You do what feels right," her aunt said, putting an arm around her.

That made Danica feel better. Though she wasn't sure what *was* right. After her marriage had fallen apart a year ago, she'd taken that entire time for herself, to regroup, to cry, to know who she was apart from her ex, a man she'd been with since middle school. Before the influx of single women, Danica had been asked out constantly. She'd finally started saying yes to the ones who seemed kind. She hadn't connected with anyone. Until Ford.

For a few beautiful hours back in February, she thought she'd found the man of her dreams in Ford Dawson. Kind. Honest. Open. Warm. Funny. Generous. So good-looking. Seriously sexy. And what a kisser. The moment she'd felt his lips against hers, she'd been a goner.

And then, as they lay together in bed, her back against his chest, his arms around her, he'd mentioned children, and anxiety had pushed the air out of her. He hoped for six, like his parents had had. At least four, for sure. Any combination.

Danica was thirty-one and had yet to feel maternal urges, that stirring her friends talked about. She loved children, particularly her goddaughter, her best friend Molly's one-year-old baby girl. But her ex-husband, who'd left her after ten years of marriage because she hadn't been ready to start a family, had told her he didn't think she'd ever be ready and she should just admit the truth—that she didn't want a child. Danica didn't think that was true. She'd always been able to see herself with a baby—way in the future. But the want, the maternal feelings, the baby fever, even during the early years of her marriage when she'd thought she was finally on her way to being happy, feeling safe and secure in the world, never happened.

She'd lost her marriage because of I'm-just-not-ready. And she hadn't been able to talk about it with anyone, not even her best friend. When Danica's ex had confessed to cheating on her, to having fallen for someone else, Molly had been newly pregnant, going through her own divorce, and Danica hadn't felt comfortable talking about her lack of baby fever. Recently Danica had finally told Molly that she wasn't sure she wanted kids, and her friend's theory made her feel better about not being ready.

According to Molly, Danica's ex-husband was the typical golden boy who liked trophies, which Danica always had been to him until she wouldn't give him what he wanted next: a child. So he'd left her. Molly truly believed that Danica had married him more because it had been expected and was safe than because there was any great love between them. She thought that when Danica did fall in love, as an adult woman with experience behind her, she just might feel those first maternal urges.

Maybe to all of it. Maybe not. There was nothing wrong with not wanting children.

But there was something wrong with starting

a relationship with a man who'd made it crystal clear he wanted *six* kids.

So she'd made excuses and fled the house that she herself had found for Ford as his real estate agent. He'd had a housewarming party earlier that day, and she hadn't left until three in the morning.

"Well, I'm gonna head upstairs and pack," Trudy said. "Good thing I only rented this Airbnb till the end of the month."

Danica nodded, turning to head back into the cute little house. Many married residents and retirees had listed their homes on the vacation rental websites and were raking it in while taking long-awaited vacations, the singles having long filled up the few inns in town and the motels just outside of town. She'd invited Trudy to stay with her, but her aunt had wanted her own space and somewhere to "canoodle" with her dates. Not feeling comfortable staying in the rental anymore, Trudy was moving in with her fiancé and both the bride and groom were excited for the jumpstart on their lives together.

"Ga-ba!"

Danica turned at the sweet little voice. Across the street, a toddler was walking between a young man and woman, each holding a hand. Every few steps, they'd swing her forward, giggles bursting.

Danica smiled, waiting for that feeling to come over her. The *I want that*. It didn't.

"Ooh, Danica! Danica!"

Danica looked across the street to see the mayor of Bear Ridge waving at her and rushing toward her. What was this about?

"I'm hoping you can help me," Pauline Abbott said, pushing her square silver glasses up on her nose. "I'm fresh out of a meeting and it seems the team working on a round of matchmaking applications was doing a terrible job. You know everyone in town, Danica. And since you're not dating, would you help?"

Danica was about to wonder how the mayor knew so much about her personal life, and then remembered that Pauline had been sitting at the next table in Grill 307 yesterday when Danica had been having lunch with Molly and grumbled, "Ugh, I'm not dating anymore, that's it. Mr. Right will just have to drop out of the sky."

That was basically how Molly had ended up with her own dream man. She'd pretty much just had to wait until Zeke Dawson, one of Ford's brothers, got over himself, and once he did, he realized the woman he'd been looking for was right there all along. Molly, his administrative assistant, and now a partner in business and life.

"It's not done by computer and algorithms?" Danica asked.

"Goodness, no," Pauline said. "Matching ticked boxes isn't going to bring people together. Oh, whoop-de-do, they both like horses and walking along the beach at sunset." She let out one of her famous snorts. "Our system takes a bit longer, but our matchmakers can pair people based on real compatibility—what they actually say they want in a partner."

Makes sense, Danica thought. "What do I need to do?" she asked. "Seems like a lot of responsibility. A lot to get wrong. Like the predecessor did."

Pauline waved a hand. "Oh, you'll do wonders. You're in the business of bringing people and houses together. It's the same concept, only it's people and people. You just match folks up with what they're really looking for. Someone says they want three bedrooms and two baths, you don't show them two-bedrooms-and-one-bath properties, right?"

"Right," Danica agreed. Huh. "I suppose I could give it a go." Maybe she'd find a great guy whose paternal urges weren't stirring past the age of thirty, either.

"You're a peach!" Mayor Abbott said, handing Danica the forms. "There are about fifty-some-odd here. Our motto at Bear Ridge Matchmaking Central—a lid for every pot. Of course, not everyone in this group will be a match, but there's more where this came from every day as singles put themselves back in after bad dates. We do have a good success rate, though."

That had to be true, based on all the handholding going on in town, plus Danica's own aunt. Even Danica's neighbor three houses down, a sweet widower with four very yippy but cute dogs, had found love with a woman with two huge Irish wolfhounds and two cats. They were going to make it work.

The mayor zipped back across to her car and drove off.

Danica stared at the pile of wants and hopes and dreams in her hand. How wonderful would it be to bring people together, bring love into their lives, even if she had to be alone.

## Chapter Two

Ford had a half hour left on his shift, so he headed over to Cole Harmon's house, not too far from the center of town. Cole was an accountant with an office on Main Street, and from the little Ford knew about him, Trudy Dunbar's fiancé was a solid citizen. He found the man outside, constructing a flower box in the front yard in the sun's last light, two border collies lying on the porch steps.

As Ford exited his squad car in the driveway, Cole walked over. "What a mess. But, as I told Trudy, I have no idea who would have taken her dress." He shook his head. "Could it really have been one of the women I was dating?"

"Well, it's somewhere to start," Ford said.

Cole let out a sigh, and Ford got it. Cole didn't want to name names when there was no proof his exes had anything to do with theft. "I went out with Samantha Withers four times."

Samantha Withers. A blond woman in her early fifties who managed the garden center came to mind. Ford had been back in Bear Ridge only a few months, but he tended to know who was who.

Ford jotted that down in his notebook. He'd use his phone's Notes app, but the old-fashioned method made it clear what he was doing, and that tended to put people at ease. People at ease talked more, opened up. "You broke up with her?"

Cole nodded. "I was very casually dating three women when I got matched with Trudy. We met and that was it. I knew she was the one in fifteen minutes. I called all three women the next day and told them I enjoyed getting to know them but I'd met the woman I was gonna marry."

Huh. "You said that?"

"I did. I was that sure. And I was right. Getting married in two weeks."

Had Ford felt that way about Danica? In the past, his mind never went to marriage; he'd been pushing away serious relationships and commitments from the get-go. But now that he did want to find his other half and have children, now that he was actually ready, a different feeling had come over Ford as he'd held Danica in his arms and they'd talked while eating those strawberries. It had been the absence of that familiar tightness in his chest, in his throat, when he'd get too close with a woman he was seeing. The warmth and contentment and ease when he'd been with Danica had settled in his chest instead. Maybe *that* was knowing? Very likely it was just the first step. But a step Ford was glad to finally be taking, even if he'd gotten his heart handed back to him.

"How'd Samantha take the breakup?" he asked.

"Not well. She ranted in my ear and told me I led her on and that she never would have gone to Horizon Point with me if she'd thought I was going to end things a couple days later."

Horizon Point was a famed overlook in Bear Ridge with a gorgeous view of the mountains and the Bear Ridge River. Lots of engagements happened there. And two murders, both so-called "crimes of passion," an old-fashioned phrase that had always bothered Ford. However, the murders were decades old and sixty-two years apart.

"And the next lady?" Ford asked.

"CeCe Womax. When I called her to tell her I'd met The One, she demanded to know who it was, if she was younger, and then yelled at me for a good minute and said I was a 'class-A jerk' and that she hoped *I* got dumped." CeCe's name didn't ring a bell. She was likely a newcomer.

Ford jotted all that down. "And the third?"

"Brianne Johnson. She was just quiet for a moment and then said, 'well, isn't that nice' and wished me well. That was it. So I doubt it was her."

Except sometimes the quiet ones made the loudest moves in secret. Brianne had her own dog-training/grooming business. He knew this because he'd once taken his brothers' dogs to her. Ford had been dog sitting, and both Dude and River had rolled in something disgusting. When a simple bath didn't get rid of the stink, he'd taken them to Brianne, who'd fit him in right away and returned them slightly lavender-scented.

The culprit could be any of them or none of them. He'd devote tomorrow morning to talking to each one. Ford had a few other cases going, but he wanted to get back Trudy's dress—if it was in one piece—as soon as humanly possible.

"Find your better half, yet?" Cole asked.

"Nah. I haven't been as lucky as you."

"You'll find her," Cole said with the assurance of a man in love.

Ford had to get the ridiculous notion out of his

head that he had *already* found her. For whatever reason, his very brief relationship with Danica Dunbar hadn't worked out, and he needed to let it go.

Danica sat at her kitchen table, a cup of coffee to her left and the pile of matchmaking requests in front of her. There were fifty-four forms, half men, half women. Each form had either been uploaded online and printed or turned in at the drop box at the town hall and included a max of three photos, a short "who I am and what I'm looking for" section and the usual boxes for age range and how important things such as political agreement and religious affiliation were. Danica read through the first one, from Kelly McDougal, forty-two, divorced, two teens in high school… *hoping to connect with a man who isn't looking for a mother or a maid. I'm a middle school teacher with a lot on my plate.*

Danica looked hard at Kelly's photo, trying to get a feel for her. She had a great combo of warmth and grit stamped on her face, curiosity and intelligence in her pretty hazel eyes. *Okay, Kelly, let's see who might be for you in this group.* Danica took another sip of her coffee and scanned the forms. Ooh, here was a good-looking forty-four-year-old, also divorced, a mortgage broker… *am not interested in dating single mothers*. Next! Forty-seven-year-old Thomas was a comptroller for the county, looking for a "traditionally minded woman who enjoys catering to her man." Danica's mother was that woman, and she and her husband had been mostly happily married for thirty-five years. Unfortunately, Danica's mother hadn't been supportive of her when she and her ex had been breaking up and had even said, *Well, can you blame him for wanting a wife who wants a child? I mean, really, Danica. Sometimes I don't think I'll ever understand you.*

That had hurt. Bad. Because Danica wasn't too sure she understood herself, either.

She took another long sip of her coffee to clear her head and get back to finding love for Kelly. But the doorbell rang, and Danica had a feeling it might be the mayor, back with an armful of new matchmaking requests.

It wasn't the mayor. It was Danica's older sister, Candace, with a baby in a pink-and-white car seat. Candace looked exactly as she had the last time Danica had seen her two years ago—tall and slim, long straight blond hair past her shoulders, the same blue eyes as her own. Candace's features were a bit sharper than Danica's. They were just a year apart, but they'd never been close, not even as children.

"Candace? This is a surprise—a very happy one," Danica said, her gaze going from her sister to the baby. Candace had called to let Danica know she was pregnant and then again when she'd had the baby, but she'd refused all offers of help or for Danica to come visit. Candace had moved to Los Angeles when she was eighteen and always claimed to be busy or going on auditions for commercials or walk-on roles in soaps. She hadn't had much success, and Danica had always heard the disappointment in Candace's voice the few times she'd actually answered the call.

Her sister's eyes got misty—and Candace Dunbar wasn't a crier. "Can I stay with you for a while? Till I get settled?"

Danica felt her heart actually soar. "Wait—you mean you're moving here?" She opened the door wide. "Come on in."

Candace stepped inside and closed the door. "It just didn't happen for me in LA. I barely have any savings left. And I have to think about Brandy," she said, caressing the beautiful baby girl's wispy blond curls. "She's five months old."

"She's absolutely precious," Danica said, marveling at the tiny creature. Her niece. Her dear sister's child, no matter how distant Candace had always been. "And of course you can stay with me. Did you know Aunt Trudy moved to Bear Ridge, too? She's engaged."

Candace's eyes widened. "Really? That's great. Last I heard she was getting divorced." She bit her lip. "I've been a terrible sister and niece. Wrapped up in my own world and problems. But I'd like to change that."

Danica grabbed her sister into a hug. "Let's start right now."

Candace smiled and gave Danica another hug. "I'm so relieved you're being so welcoming."

"Always, Candace," Danica said.

Her sister gave her another hug, which felt so good. "And I'll admit, an old friend sent me a link to a story about the call for single women and all the great available men in town. I've had one bad relationship after another in LA. I'm done with bad boys and Peter Pans. I want someone I can rely on. Someone who'll be a father to Brandy."

"Who *is* her father?"

Candace grimaced. "Someone who claims he's not, that he supposedly was told he can't have kids." Her eyes got teary again, and she blinked hard. "I've accepted that. I'm now ready for a fresh start. I just hope I don't make the same mistakes here."

"Well, sounds to me like you know what you want, Candace. I think you're gonna be just fine."

Her sister smiled. Brandy let out a little cry. "She's late for her nap. I have her bassinet in the SUV."

"This place has three bedrooms, and it's just me," Danica said, leading the way to the living room. "So you can take the big guest room and we can turn the smaller one into a nursery for Brandy."

Again Danica just stared at her little niece, marveling over how lovely and wondrous she was. A tiny being with her entire life ahead of her, the world to experience. She felt her heart truly give a little leap. *Because you're my niece? Because maybe we have a chance to be close, after all?*

Danica's friend Molly had said a time or two that she had a feeling Danica's lack of maternal urges were rooted in how distant her family was. Her parents weren't cold, exactly, but they weren't loving either. They were prickly and judgmental and tended to keep to themselves.

"Have you heard from Mom and Dad?" Danica asked.

"They sent me a generous check when Brandy

was born and they said they booked a flight to come see her, but they canceled, of course. This or that came up. I can't even remember the excuse."

"Well, like you said, fresh start. For you, me, Brandy and Aunt Trudy."

"I'm glad she found her guy," Candace said. "Trudy deserves to be happy after all she's been through." She looked at Danica. "You, too," Candace added warily, as if she was getting too personal with a sister she barely knew anymore.

"Me, too, is right," Danica said with a nod. "I've been trying, but it's not easy out there. In fact, I have a side job—volunteer—as one of the town's matchmakers. Let's go put Brandy down for her nap, and then you can fill out a form for yourself. I'll see if there are any matches for you in the stack I have."

"I just want nice. Dependable. Someone I can really count on to say what he means and mean what he says. You know?"

"I know. The last guy I dated was very up-front about what he wanted. It just didn't align," she added wistfully.

Candace nodded. "Sorry. Well, you'll find someone for yourself in that stack, too."

She wasn't looking anymore. And it wasn't like anyone could match up to Ford Dawson.

*Chapter Three*

All three of Cole Harmon's exes had alibis for the time frame of the theft of Trudy Dunbar's dress. Ford had had to tread carefully with how he'd approached each potential suspect. In the morning, after he'd fortified himself with two cups of coffee at the BRPD, he'd gone over to the home of Samantha Withers—the one who'd ranted in Cole's ear and complained about going to Horizon Point with him the night before he broke up with her—and said he was investigating a wedding dress stolen from Trudy Dunbar's home. He waited. Surprise had crossed Samantha's face, then she'd smirked. "Serves her right," Samantha had said as they'd stood in the foyer of her condo. "That's what that multi-timer Cole gets. Someone got mad enough to steal his fiancée's wedding gown. Ha, wait till my friends get a load of this." She'd let out a snort.

Ford had been a detective long enough to know that Samantha Withers wasn't his perp. Thieves were a lot cagier and didn't like to telegraph how glad they were about the bad "news" or how excited they were to share it with their besties.

CeCe Womax, who'd yelled at Cole and said he was a class-A jerk, had been on a date at a Mexican restaurant in Prairie City during the forty-five-minute window that Trudy's dress was taken.

Two down, one to go. Brianne Johnson, who'd wished Cole well. He didn't know Brianne all that much, but his gut told him the warm, friendly dog trainer wasn't a thief. Though her home *was* right around the corner from Trudy Dunbar's Airbnb. He knocked at Brianne's front door.

He heard a cheery "Coming!" and then footsteps. Brianne opened the door, her elderly grandmother, Delia Johnson, in a hot-pink tracksuit with a white headband around her forehead, behind her.

"Hi, Detective," Brianne said. "Need to make an appointment for one of your brothers' dogs?"

Before he could say a word, he noticed Brianne's grandmother slowly backing away. Nervously.

"Everything okay, ma'am?" he called over.

Brianne turned around. "Gram? What's wrong? You're white as a ghost."

Delia's shoulders slumped, and she held out her arms in front of her, wrists together. "The officer is here for me."

"What?" Brianne asked, confusion in her eyes.

Ah. Suddenly things were making sense.

"Oh, foof, I couldn't help myself," Delia said. "I saw her leave with that dog—the kind I always wanted—and I just thought, humph. It's not fair."

Brianne stared at her grandmother. "Gram, what on earth are you talking about?"

Delia sighed. "Follow me," she said, turning and heading down the hall.

Brianne glanced at him, and they both followed her grandmother into what appeared to be her bedroom. She went to the closet, reached into a big black bag and pulled out a plastic-sheathed white lace dress with a ruffled hem.

Sometimes Ford's job did itself.

"What is that?" Brianne asked.

"It's Cole Harmon's fiancée's wedding dress," Delia said. "I snuck into her house once she left with her dog and I took it."

Brianne gasped. "What on earth for?"

"I thought the two of you were getting serious," Delia said. "Then he just tosses you aside and proposes to someone else? Who does he think he is?"

"Gram, you stole someone's property? A *wedding gown*?"

"I'm not proud of it, but yes. Sorry, Detective," she said. She held out her wrists again. "You can read me my rights now. I know them from watching decades of *Law and Order*. My favorite program."

Brianne dropped her head in her hands, then looked at Ford. "Are you going to arrest my eighty-four-year-old grandmother?"

"Tell you what," Ford said. "Give me the stolen property and a little time, and we'll take it from there."

"My grandmother is very sorry," Brianne said. "And I'm very embarrassed. Please let Cole's fiancée know how sorry we are." She handed him the dress.

"I'll be in touch," he said, heading for the door.

"Aren't you going to tell me not to leave town?" Delia asked.

He almost smiled. "Don't leave town."

Her eyes widened and she nodded.

"We'll be right here when you're ready to talk

about next steps," Brianne said, shooting her grandmother a chastising glance.

Once he was back in his vehicle, the dress folded in its plastic wrap on the seat beside him, he called Trudy Dunbar and said he had news. She told him to come right over and that she was now staying at Cole's house, soon to be their house.

When he exited his car at Cole's, the garment over his arm, Trudy came rushing out and called, "The detective has the dress!"

Danica, who was holding a crying baby, emerged from the house. She was accompanied by another woman, who looked a lot like her. As always, his heart skipped at the sight of Danica. She was dressed for work in a pale pink suit jacket and miniskirt, lots of jewelry, four-inch shiny heels and glossy lips. Her long blond hair was in a low, wavy ponytail over one shoulder.

"You found it!" Trudy exclaimed as Ford handed it to her. Trudy held out the dress to examine it. "Not a mark on it."

"Wow, that's great," Danica said, stepping down off the porch and bouncing the baby in her arms. "There, there," she said to the tiny girl. "Aunt Danica's got you. Everything's okay."

The baby cried harder, reaching out her hands for the other woman.

Danica sighed and handed over the baby. "Detective Ford Dawson, this is my sister, Candace, and her daughter, Brandy."

Ford nodded at Candace. "Nice to meet you. Adorable baby," he added, making a quick peek-aboo at the little Brandy. The baby perked up, so Ford did it again.

Danica grimaced. "Does this child like everyone but me?" She smiled and shook her head.

"Brandy loves her aunt Danica," Candace said, smoothing the baby's curls. "I think when she sees you, she thinks you're me because we look so much alike, then realizes you're *not* and gets fussy."

"Huh," Danica said. "So it's not me. She just wants her mama."

Ford could tell Danica wanted to believe it but didn't.

Candace nodded, then turned to Ford. "Nice to meet you, too. I'm so relieved you found my aunt's dress. Where did you find it?"

"I think I'd better speak to Trudy privately about that," Ford said.

Danica and Candace eyed each other.

He gestured for Trudy to join him over by the tree. But before he could get a word out, a car came up the gravel drive to the house. Two women got out—Brianne and, more slowly, her grandmother.

The eighty-four-year old ambled up to Trudy. "I'm Delia Johnson, Brianne's grandmother. I'm very sorry I took your dress."

There were three sets of gasps.

"*You* stole my dress?" Trudy asked the elderly woman.

"You know I'm always watching everything in the neighborhood, and I saw when you came home yesterday with a dress bag from Bridal Dreams—just a couple weeks after Cole told my granddaughter it was over between them. I started stewing and when I saw you leave with that dog I sneaked right in the side door, looked for the dress and then sneaked back out with it folded under my arm. I hid it in my closet."

"I'm so sorry, Trudy," Brianne added. "And mortified. I have absolutely no hard feelings toward Cole or you." She sent her grandmother another chastising glance.

"Well, I do!" Delia said. "But it was wrong to take the dress and I deserve whatever happens. I fully expect to do some time in prison."

"Prison!" Trudy repeated. "Of course you're not going to prison. I'm willing to forget about this whole thing—if you promise on a stack of

Bibles never to break into my home again, Delia Johnson."

Delia's eyes widened. "Promise," she said. "You heard me swear it, Detective."

"I did, indeed," Ford said.

Danica stepped forward. "We have back the dress, so all's well that ends well." She turned to Ford. Thank you for everything."

"Yes, thank you, Detective," Trudy added.

There was a flurry of "I'm sorry" and "good-bye," and then Brianne and her dress-stealing grandmother were gone.

"Never saw that coming," Danica said. "Life never stops being one big surprise."

"Speaking of surprises," Candace said, "guess who I saw in the grocery store a little while ago when I went to get diapers? A guy I dated a few times in middle school. He asked me out for to-morrow night, and I was so caught off guard I said yes."

"Ooh, interested?" Trudy asked.

Candace shrugged. "I don't know. I'd really rather be matched the way Danica is doing it—based on what I'm looking for and all that. I'm done with making mistakes."

Ford noticed Danica's gaze slide over to him. Was that what he was? A mistake?

"Oh," Candace said, brightening. "He's a cowboy at your family's ranch," she added, turning to Ford. "Know him? Jasper Fields?"

Ford nodded. "Jasper's a great guy. Dependable, always offers to help out even when it's quitting time."

"That's some reference," Danica said.

Candace brightened. "Sure is. I'm kind of excited about the date now." She bit her lip, then looked from her aunt to her sister. "I'll need a sitter, though. I hate asking so last-minute. By any chance, are either of you available?"

Ford caught Danica's face slightly pale, saw the way she took a slight step back. Didn't take a detective to see that she was uncomfortable with the idea of babysitting her niece. Maybe because of how the infant had been bawling in her arms earlier?"

"I would, honey," Trudy said, "but I've got a big night tomorrow. I'm actually meeting Cole's whole family for the first time. His parents are throwing a big dinner party for us."

"That's so nice," Candace said.

"I'll babysit," Danica said. "I don't have much experience with babies, but I love my little niece, so that's something, right?"

"I'll help," Ford blurted out before he could

think about it. "I have too many tiny nieces and nephews to count, and have been on babysitting duty many times in the couple months since I moved back to Bear Ridge."

"My sister *and* an officer of the law babysitting my daughter," Candace said. She gave the baby's head a nuzzle. "You could not be in safer hands, darling."

Danica seemed about to say something and then clamped her lips shut. Ford had a feeling she didn't like the idea of babysitting with him, but she liked the idea of the *help*—and the help won out.

The plan was for him to arrive at Danica's at 7:15 p.m., a bit after the cowboy arrived to pick up Candace.

Well, this should be interesting.

Ford almost stopped to buy flowers for Danica, then remembered with an ice-cold poke in the gut that this wasn't a date. And that he really shouldn't have steamrolled his way into babysitting with her. But he wanted an explanation so that he could get past her, move on, fill out one of those matchmaking forms and see what happened. Besides, if Danica really hated the idea of him joining her tonight, she would have made some fast excuse and he would have backed off. She hadn't.

As he walked up the front steps to her house with the bag from Bear Ridge Toys—just a little something for her niece—he could hear a baby screaming bloody murder. He could see Danica through the big front window, pacing back and forth, rubbing the baby's back and looking exasperated. She was still in her work clothes, that sexy pink suit and high heels. He rang the bell and kept his eyes on her in the window. She glanced out and he waved, and the relief that crossed her features made him feel better about being here.

He heard the click of her heels on the floor, and then the door opened. She shifted the baby into her other arm and bounced her up and down.

"Look, sweet pea, it's Detective Dawson," Danica said with a mix of hope and exasperation.

Brandy kept sobbing. Sure was loud for a tiny person.

Ford smiled and reached into the little bag from Bear Ridge Toys. He pulled out the orange teether with rattling rings and twirly bits. He held it up to the baby girl. "This is for you, Brandy. Matches your pj's."

Brandy stopped crying and reached for the teether.

Danica bit her lip. "I tried three different toys and nothing worked."

"Probably the novelty of something new," he said.

"It was nice of you to bring her something," Danica said. She held the door open and he stepped in.

"Just get home from work?" he asked, wondering why she was still in her fancy little pink tweed suit and four-inch heels.

"Just fifteen minutes ago, right before the honorable cowboy arrived to pick up Candace," Danica said.

Brandy grabbed on to Danica's long swirly ponytail, which cascaded over one shoulder.

"Ooh, this little one's got some grip," she said, wincing and trying to get the baby's hand from her hair.

Brandy held on tight.

Ford distracted the baby and held out his arms. With what looked like clear relief, Danica handed her over. He held her against his chest, giving her back a rub. "Hey, there, cutie."

Brandy stared up at him with enormous blue eyes just like her mother and aunt.

"I should really go put up my hair and change," Danica said. "A client called just as I was about to head home and was dying to see a particular house, so I showed it but got here just before Candace's date arrived. I didn't have a chance to change."

"I've got Brandy. Go ahead."

She looked at him and then dashed up the stairs as quickly as was possible in those shoes. Halfway there, she stopped and took them off, then continued.

He moved into the living room, which was elegant, like Danica. The couch and love seat were white. "You know what doesn't mix, Brandy?" he said to the little one in his arms. "Babies and white couches. Let's head into the kitchen."

Ah. The kitchen showed evidence that someone actually lived in this house. A slew of baby bottles were lined up by the sink. A coffeemaker with about a cup left in the carafe. A big bowl of apples and bananas. The round table by the window was almost completely covered by papers—forms of some kind—and a legal pad.

"Much more comfortable," came Danica's voice.

He turned around—and swallowed. Danica wore a tiny white V-necked T-shirt and close-fitting pink sweatpants with a drawstring tied in a bow. One pull… Her hair was in a loose bun. She looked incredibly sexy. He'd only ever seen her all dressed up to the nines…or naked.

Her gaze moved to the table. "Mayor Abbott bamboozled me into taking over the matchmaking since I've been in town forever and know just about everybody, even the newcomers, since most of them came into the realty to see about vacation rentals."

"And as a bonus you can save the best ones for yourself," he said without thinking.

She shook her head. "Oh, I'm done with dating. I should have figured I'd have a tough time."

He stared at her. "Tough time? Why?"

Her face flushed for a second as if she hadn't realized what she'd said. "Oh, um, you know, dating is hard."

Was she talking about them? In general? "Yes, it sure is."

Brandy put little fists to her eyes and rubbed, then let out a yawn.

"Looks like it's someone's bedtime," he said.

Danica stepped toward him, reaching out her arms. "I'll take her." Brandy screeched, and Danica held up her hands. "Maybe you'd better carry her up."

Ford gently rubbed the baby's back and followed Danica out of the kitchen.

"We made a nursery of sorts in the spare room," she said as they walked to the stairs. She turned to look at Brandy, whose eyes were drooping, her cheek against Ford's chest. "I wish I had the touch with her, but I definitely don't," she said, hurrying up the steps and into the first room on the left.

A bassinet was between the windows in the dimly lit room. Danica took the baby and laid her down on the pad on the dresser and changed her, Brandy yelling her head off the entire time. Then Danica picked her back up and paced the room, singing under her breath what sounded like "Hush Little Baby."

Brandy cried harder, and Danica looked like she herself might burst out sobbing any second.

"I can try to settle her down," he said. "I babysat my twin niece and nephew a couple nights ago and got Chance to stop screaming in two seconds by making funny faces at him."

She handed the baby over, and Ford sat down in the rocker by the window.

"How about a story?" he asked the baby. "Once upon a time there was a llama named Dolly. Dolly was really funny looking with teeth that stuck out in weird directions. But she was a favorite at the Dawson Family Guest Ranch back when I was a kid." Brandy's eyes were drooping again. He smiled up at Danica, and the smile she sent him back was so warm and tender that he felt his heart move in his chest. He gave his throat a low clear. "Well, one day Dolly fell in love with a mean brown goat with a white spot on his head. And guess what happened? The mean goat fell in love, too, and was sweet to everyone, most of all Dolly, from then on. And they both lived happily ever after."

"Is that a true story?" Danica whispered.

"Every word," he whispered back. "And look— success. I'll just lay her down in the bassinet and cross my fingers." He stood up. Brandy quirked her tiny lips, but her eyes remained closed. He walked over to the bassinet and put her in, her arm shooting up by her head, her pink-and-purple-covered chest rising and falling with each sleeping breath.

"I'm not going to tell my siblings about this," he whispered as they left the makeshift nursery. "They'd make me babysit every night."

She didn't laugh. The smile wasn't back. She just headed down the hall, eyes on the Persian runner, then paused at the top of the stairs. "No one would ever ask me to babysit unless they were desperate, like my sister. If you hadn't come to the rescue, Brandy would probably still be crying her eyes out. Like I said, I just don't have the touch. Never have. Even when I babysat some as a teen-ager, I was bad at it."

"Well, then, lucky for you I was here," he said,

not sure exactly what to say, and whether he should probe or keep it light. It made him realize how little he actually knew Danica, how little of herself she'd revealed during their night together.

"You said you wanted six kids. At least four." She turned away. "I'm not sure I want kids at all. Even one."

He stared at her, then reached for her hand, which she allowed him to hold. "Is that why you left on me?"

She nodded. "Everything in me froze up, Ford."

"Yeah, I know what that's like. Before I felt ready for marriage, whenever a woman I was seeing would bring up commitment or getting engaged, everything in me would freeze up, too."

She tilted her head. "So you understand. That's a relief. I'm sorry I didn't just say something at the time. The subject always makes me feel so inadequate. Like I don't want something I'm supposed to want."

"You're not supposed to want anything," he said. "How you feel is how you feel."

He could see her shoulders relax. She seemed to take that in, nodded and then headed into the kitchen. "Coffee?"

"I'd love a cup," he said.

She washed out the carafe and made a fresh

pot, then pointed at the papers all over the table. "Maybe we'll find you a match in here."

So that was it? No discussion?

Then again, what was there to discuss? He did want a big family. She wasn't sure she wanted even one child. The smart thing would be to walk away from each other, as she had. Because if they started a relationship, a few years down the road, when he was itching to see toddlers trying to climb on the tire swing hanging on the big oak in the front yard of his farmhouse, she would be shaking her head. She'd say, *You knew I was up-front.* He'd say, *That's true, but.* And there'd be a stalemate. Ford knew how stalemates usually went. Resentment. Anger. Slammed doors. Then barely a goodbye.

She poured two mugs of coffee and they sat at the table. "I woke up early this morning to see if I could make a few matches before work, and I have five successes." Her smile lit up her face. "My ability to date might be complicated, but I can bring others together, right?"

He was about to say that he was sure there were plenty of men in town who didn't want kids. He used to be one of them. Same with all his brothers, all four of whom were now doting dads. But the thought of her with someone else? Made his stomach twist. He mentally shook his head, knowing he was in for something here. Trouble.

"I haven't found a match for you yet," she said, sipping her coffee and picking up a form.

"Me?" He glanced at the paper in her hand. Wait a minute. Was that his photo in the upper right-hand corner?

She waved it. "Ford Dawson. Age 35. Never married. Dedicated detective on the Bear Ridge P.D."

He frowned. "I did *not* fill out a matchmaking request! Let me see that."

"That *is* you," she said, tapping the photo and handing him the form.

Ford scanned the page, which had been submitted online. He shook his head. "This has my sister, Daisy, all over it. 'What I'm looking for,'" he read. "'Just someone I connect with. She can be anything or anyone, but she likes dogs and wants or has children.'" He glanced at Danica. "Tell me you don't like dogs. That'll make it easier for me to put you out of my head."

Her almost-smile got him in the gut. "I love dogs."

"So there's just that one big, fundamental thing standing in our way," he said.

"It destroyed my marriage," she said. "There's

no point in starting something," she added on a whisper.

So why was he finding it impossible to think of her only as a friend?

"I'll find someone for you and you can find someone for me," she said with definitely too cheery a smile. Too forced. She was trying to get him out of her head.

What he should do was leave. The baby was asleep. All was well on that front. He should walk out the door and let Danica Dunbar get on with her life, find someone compatible.

"I'll need a lot more caffeine for that," he said, instead of getting up and running for the hills.

This time her smile was genuine and went straight to his heart.

## Chapter Four

Danica slowly picked up a profile she'd noted earlier would be a match for Ford. She glanced at him, sitting beside her at the kitchen table, wondering if he had any idea how hard this was for her. There had been so much between them the night they'd shared, but their relationship couldn't go anywhere and that had to be that. *Let it go. Let him go, as you have for the past two months.*

"'Lily Mallard, thirty-four, single, social justice warrior lawyer now ready to meet her match and start a family,'" Danica read, biting her lip as she stared at the three photos Lily had attached to her form. In one, she wore a power suit and killer heels on the steps of city hall in Brewer, and was kneeling beside an adorable cinnamon-colored shepherd mix, matching red-and-white bandannas around both their necks; another featured Lily in jogging clothes. And the third showed her in a pretty summer dress with the Bear Ridge River behind her. Dammit. She sounded kind of perfect for Ford.

She held up the photos, and Ford barely glanced at them.

"No can do," he said. "Conflict of interest. I issued her a speeding ticket three weeks ago coming off the service road."

Danica tried to hide her relief and smile. But this was wrong. She had to find the man someone to fall for so that they could move on. Except she was in a holding pattern, and a man who'd moved on from her would not be here right now helping her babysit.

She held up another profile of an attractive blond with an amazing body. "'Lexie Parks. Thirty-three. Divorced. Newcomer to town from Cheyenne. Loves hiking, Mexican food and watching Wyoming Wildcats games.'"

"Nope," he said. "A couple weeks ago she called in a complaint about her neighbor's dog, fourteen years old with cancer, blocking the sidewalk when the dog clearly needed to rest."

Danica grimaced. "Ugh. I don't think she'll match with anyone."

"Oh, trust me. She will. You don't want to know an eighth of what I've seen from humanity."

She regarded him for a moment. "I'm glad you're here in Bear Ridge. I know there's crime everywhere, even tiny towns like ours, but it's got to be a little easier on you here, right?"

"It is. Yesterday, a wedding dress stolen by an eighty-four-year-old perp and a spurned lover who wouldn't stop serenading a woman outside her house were the only two reported crimes."

Danica grinned. "Mayor Abbott said there was a lid for every pot. Do you agree?"

"Yup. Just have to find each other."

"Well, that's where we come in for each other. Matchmaking buddies!" she added, aware she'd put on her fake cheery smile.

"This is awkward as hell, Danica."

She put down the next profile she'd set aside as a possible match. "Yeah, but we're friends now. And I like that. I'd rather have you as a friend than the big fat nothing we had for the past couple of months."

He held her gaze for a moment, then finally said, "Oh hell, me, too. So let's see if I can find someone for you in here." He picked up a stack of male profiles and scanned a few. "No," he said, putting the top one down. "Definitely not. Nope. Yeah, right." He shook his head. "I give that last guy credit for taking a shirtless selfie with that beer belly. He is who he is. But he's not right for you."

"Why not? Or that guy. Or that one. Or that one?" She gripped her coffee cup to have something to do with the hands that itched to touch Ford. His shoulder. His back. All that thick, silky dark hair. She glanced down, face flushed, as memories of their night together came over her. Ford unzipping the back of her dress. His gasp at the sight of her in just her bra and underwear. Danica liked sexy underthings and always wore lacy, satiny, pretty bras and matching undies. Her ex had stopped responding to her physically years ago, his interest having waned, and it had taken a terrible toll, doing a number on her self-esteem. Ford's reaction had made her so damned happy.

"One's been divorced four times," he said. "Another gets arrested at least twice a month for drunk and disorderly. And that one," he added, pointing, "says any woman he dates would have to deal with weekly dinners with his mother, who he describes as hell on wheels."

Danica smiled and picked up one of the forms.

"And what's wrong with this one? 'Looking for a kind, funny, interesting woman who's been through a thing or two and is still standing, like me. She should probably love movies, sharing popcorn, and the idea of growing old together on our porch with three dogs.'"

Ford tried to hold back his scowl. "He doesn't say anything about kids either way. So you'd have to meet, and the subject would have to come up. I mean, why put in the investment at all?"

The man did *not* want her to date. The goose bumps that traveled up her spine at the thrill of that were soon replaced by little chills. They could like each other, be attracted to each other all they wanted. It wasn't going to make them want the same things.

A cry came from upstairs.

They both shot up, and it was clear he also needed the break from how personal things were getting.

"Hope your sister's date is going well," he said as they went upstairs.

"You should have seen them when he picked her up. Both of them all smiles, stealing peeks at each other." She bit her lip. "I'm just so glad Candace is here. Our family has never been close, not even when Candace and I were young, and now she's staying with me and I'm babysitting my niece. I can't tell you how happy that makes me."

The warmth in his blue eyes almost undid her. She was already exposing too much of herself. "I'm glad for you. Your sister and niece are here. Your aunt is here. I know how important it is to be close to family. For a long time, I lived hours away because I felt close to my siblings no matter what," he said. "But after a while, I needed them in my daily life."

She held his gaze for a moment on the top step and nodded. He seemed about to say something, but another shrill cry came from the nursery and they headed in. Danica rushed over to the crib and leaned in to pick up the baby. Brandy started screeching like crazy, and Danica took a step back.

"You've got this," he said. "If you want to be close to Brandy, you've got to develop a relationship with her. So go show her who Aunt Danica is and what she's made of."

"Not very strong stuff," she said with a frown. "I always think I'm strong and independent, and then something will happen that makes me feel like porcelain."

"Yup, ditto."

His kindness rallied her, and she reached into the crib and picked up her screeching little niece.

Brandy looked at her and scrunched up her face. Danica held her straight against her chest, letting her legs dangle some in case she had a gas bubble. In anticipation of babysitting, she'd spent a good hour this morning with her phone, researching all kinds of baby-related facts. She rubbed Brandy's back, and the baby quieted down and yawned.

Danica looked at Ford and smiled, something tiny fluttering in her chest and stomach. "Better now, sweet pea?" she whispered to the baby, whose eyes were drooping. She gently rocked Brandy, humming an old lullaby she'd never forgotten, and now Brandy seemed to be asleep. Danica set her down in the crib, and she and Ford tiptoed out.

"That felt good," she said. "Maybe I can learn how to be an auntie yet. Thanks, Ford. I owe you."

"I'll call it even for a slice of whatever that was on the counter. Cheesecake?"

"Raspberry cheesecake. I could use another cup of coffee, too."

For the next fifteen minutes they had their treat and coffee, Ford telling her funny stories about babysitting his baby nieces and nephews, who the shriekers and spitter-uppers and unfussy ones were. They talked too easily. Laughed too hard. And this felt too right.

But then a car turned in the driveway, and a

door slammed and heels could be heard clicking on the walk. Ford brought their plates to the sink, and before they could turn around Candace was stalking into the kitchen, her hands balled into fists at her sides as she paced, steam coming out of her ears.

"Uh-oh," Ford said.

"You okay?" Danica asked her sister.

"How is possible for someone to be that arrogant?" Candace asked. "That much of a know-it-all? How dare he!"

The problem with not knowing her own sister well was that Danica wasn't sure how badly the night had gone. Had the cowboy from Dawson's Family Guest Ranch been a jerk? Or had they just not been a match?

"I'm surprised to hear this," Ford said.

"He's impossible!" Candace said, throwing up her hands. "We didn't agree on a single thing all night. We're total opposites. The date ended before the poor waiter could even ask if we wanted dessert. No, thank you!"

"But he was a gentleman..." Danica prodded.

"Well, yes. And do you believe he had the nerve to walk me to the door and not even ask if he could kiss me good-night? I mean, if he had, I would have said no, but still!" Candace stalked up the stairs, then turned. "I'm sorry I'm full of complaints. Thank you both for babysitting. Just a peek at Brandy will make me feel better about my awful night." She hurried the rest of the way up the stairs.

Danica looked at Ford. "Guess I'd better find someone new for my sister to get her spirits up."

Ford shook his head. "I'd hold off. Sounds like she and Jasper are about to fall madly in love."

Had he lost his mind? "What? Did you hear a word she said?"

"Yup. Remember when we met at your office for the first time and I argued with you about everything? We couldn't discuss square footage without it getting heated."

She'd forgotten that she hadn't liked him at all at first, that he'd been an arrogant know-it-all hiding under a polite demeanor. Because when she did start liking him, the feeling had gone from zero to sixty in a hot second. "I said black, you said white. You said up, I said down. I guess at the house-warming party, I started looking at you in a different way. Suddenly, you were in the midst of your big family, and I saw how close you all were and how doting you were to your little nieces and nephews. You won my heart that day, Ford Dawson."

Oh, God. Why had she said that? Yes, he'd won her heart, and she'd had to take it back.

"Ditto," he whispered, staring at her, and if this was any other guy, there'd be an amazing kiss. But it was Ford and so he took his leather jacket and Stetson off the coatrack.

"Well, let me know if I'm right about your sister and Jasper."

"I will," she said. "And thanks again for helping me out tonight."

"Anytime, Danica." He shrugged his incredible arms and shoulders into the jacket, put on the cowboy hat, tipped it at her and left.

She let out a breath and closed her eyes.

"Ooh, I might have a bad night, but you definitely had a good one," Candace said, coming down the stairs, eyebrows raised.

"Brandy still asleep?" Danica asked.

Candace nodded. "I stood by her crib watching her sleep, and everything went right with the world again. So, what's the deal with you and the hot detective?"

Danica felt tears sting her eyes.

"Oh, man, sorry," Candace said, taking her hand. "How about we have some ice cream? I need a few scoops of something decadent."

"We just had cheesecake, but hey, what's another five hundred calories?" Especially when this was her sister, someone Danica had wanted to be closer to for so long. She'd eat five bowls of ice cream if it meant the two of them sitting down and really talking.

Danica got out the Ben & Jerry's, and Candace brought two bowls to the table, shoving aside the matchmaking forms.

Candace stuck her tongue out at the forms. "Ugh, I'm done with romance."

"Yup, that's what I said after Ford." She scooped out their ice cream—Phish Food with its gooey marshmallow and chocolate wonders—and they dug in.

"So what happened?" Candace asked.

"He wants six kids. I'm not even sure I want one."

"Yeah, I felt the way you do until I was suddenly pregnant," Candace said. "The idea of a child, of my own family, seemed so alien. I mean, we didn't exactly have a close family."

Danica nodded. "The idea just seems so foreign. Like something I wouldn't really know how to do." She shook her head. "That's really sad."

"I was scared to death when I found out I was pregnant. But you know, you figure it out. I love Brandy. I actually love being her mother. And I'm good at it. I'm bad at just about everything else, it turns out."

"Oh, come on, Candace. You are not."

"I failed at even getting one-line commercials," her sister said, digging her spoon into her ice cream. "And I managed to fall for the biggest jerk in LA, who told me Brandy wasn't his and that I was a liar. I have to get motherhood right, Danica. I *have* to."

Danica put down her spoon, reached for her sister's hand and squeezed it. "You will. I know you will. And I'm here for you. So is Aunt Trudy."

Candace squeezed her hand back. "So should I stop dating or look for a good father for Brandy? Should I be working on myself? I don't know. I want to find a partner, someone to love, someone to love me. I want to feel *safe*. But I sure don't want to have more dates like tonight. I just want something easy. Something that feels *right*."

"I know what you mean. I think you just have to follow your instincts. And sleep on it. You'll feel better about everything in the morning."

Candace already seemed in better spirits from their talk and the ice cream. Danica felt her heart give another little leap of happiness. Here the Dunbar sisters were, sitting together, opening up, really talking. That they could grow close meant so much to Danica.

Candace finished the last of her ice cream. "This is just too good," she said, licking her lips.

"Amazingly good," Danica agreed, finishing her own bowl.

"Maybe you and Ford will find a way to work it out," Candace said, getting up to wash out the bowls and spoons.

Danica glanced at the stack of matchmaking forms. She thought about Ford's—filled out by his sister: *Just someone I connect with. She can be anything or anyone, but she likes dogs and wants or has children…*

Now she was going to lie in bed, tossing and turning because she'd be unable to stop thinking about him. When she had to. Maybe she would try to find someone for herself in the fresh stack coming her way tomorrow. But who was going to outdo Ford Dawson?

The next morning, Ford got up way too early— Danica Dunbar on the brain. He had two cups of coffee. He ran four miles. He oiled a creaky hinge on a door and did two loads of laundry. Nothing got Danica off his mind. He couldn't stop thinking about how she'd opened up to him, how vulnerably honest she'd been. Then his mind traveled back to February, in his bed. And to last night, sharing cheesecake, funny stories.

That he had strong feelings for her wasn't in doubt. But he did want a big family, just like the one he'd grown up in. He wanted children catapulting themselves on him to wake him up on Sunday mornings, when he'd make sixty pancakes and a hundred strips of bacon. If only he'd met Danica a year ago, when he'd still been in his "not ready" stage, which had lasted years. Not ready to commit to anyone, to anything, other than his work. But he wasn't about to think that if he, of all people, could change his mind about wanting a family, anyone could. He had no right to *want* Danica to change her mind or imagine she would; how she felt was valid and that had to be respected.

So she was right. They weren't a match, and he had to start thinking of her as a friend.

A *friend* might stop by her house this morning with coffee and muffins from the great Bear Ridge Bakery, but there had already been blurred lines last night. He'd almost reached for her, yearning to have her in his arms, against him, to kiss her, touch her. But he hadn't, of course. Thankfully, her sister had come home just when he'd been bursting with insane levels of desire for her, so he'd left.

And still couldn't shake her from his thoughts.

It was just before eight, and he had two hours before he had to be at the PD, so he texted his siblings to see if anyone wanted to meet him by the main barn at the Dawson ranch, where they all lived, to help him look for the bane of his existence: the diary. The diary he was beginning to think he'd never find. And maybe it was better that way.

By eight thirty, Ford and his middle brothers, as he'd always thought of Axel, Zeke and Rex, from his father's second marriage, were down by the river on the ranch, about a half mile down from the main barn. Ford had a shovel, Axel and Zeke had metal detectors, and Rex had a pitchfork. Once a week or so, Ford came out here with the hand-drawn—definitely *drunkenly* drawn—map his father had bequeathed him when he'd died a year and a half ago. Bo Dawson hadn't had much to his name, but he'd left all six of his children either letters or something personal tucked into an envelope. His sister, Daisy, had finally gotten her mother's wedding rings that she'd been asking for since she was eleven; they were all surprised their father hadn't sold them long ago for booze or a horse race. Ford's envelope had contained the map, scrawled in marker.

Apparently, when Ford was very young, his father had found his wife's diary, didn't like what he'd read, stuck it in a metal fishing tackle box and buried it somewhere on the property. Ford had overheard his mother talking to a friend about that, and every day he'd go outside at five years old, trying to find it to make his mother less upset. He never found it. Neither had his mother, and Ford remembered her looking with her own metal detector and shovels, poking into the earth. When he'd inherited the map, Ford had gone to visit that friend of his mother's to ask for more information, but the woman had been cagey, telling him only that Ellen Dawson hadn't ever found it, got madder and madder, had finally had it, and packed up and left her husband, taking Ford with her and resettling across town.

Bo had remarried, had three more kids, then divorced again and married his third wife. They had two more kids—Noah and Daisy, both of whom would be helping right now, but Noah, the manager of the Dawson Family Guest Ranch, was at a cattle auction and Daisy, the ranch's guest relations manager, had a guest emergency.

For a long time, Ford hadn't wanted to find the diary. God knew what it said. Bo's drunken exploits, including with other women? His mother's anguish? Something had driven Bo to get rid of the diary. Was it documentation of something he'd done, or that Ellen Dawson had done? The wondering had made Ford tired. It wasn't his business. But it was *unfinished* business. And unfinished business had a way of poking into raw spots until it was dealt with.

So whenever he visited his siblings for a birthday or holiday, he'd come out here with the map and a pitchfork and stab at the ground, trying to hit the metal box that the diary was buried in. Since he'd moved back to Bear Ridge, he'd been trying to find it in earnest. Something told him he'd make peace with his father, with his parents' marriage, with how little he really knew, if he read it. He'd lost his mother when he was twenty-one and in the police academy, but she'd never liked talking about her first husband when Ford had been growing up.

His siblings had found that peace through dealing with what Bo had left them in their bequest envelopes. Ford was 99 percent sure it was the final step on this strange transformation of his. From city cop to small-town detective. From saying buffalos would fly across Wyoming before he'd ever move back to Bear Ridge. Now he was living here, serving the community. To being so confirmed a bachelor that he'd never committed to any woman, even when he was aware he did have feelings, to finally giving in to his heart. He'd gotten slammed for it; the woman he'd been involved with back in Casper had left him for someone else who was more this and more that; apparently, she felt she'd waited too long for him to come around, and by then it was anticlimactic instead of the start of something beautiful.

He'd spent a fitful few months stalking around Casper until he realized it was time to go home. To face who he was, who he'd been and how those two meshed. Time to find the damned diary and settle things in his chest with his father. Here he was. And his siblings, who he could always count on, even at eight thirty on a cold April morning, were right here with him. The three who could be, anyway.

"Dad's drawing might be that cluster of trees," Zeke said, gesturing at the maples. He peered over at the map, under Ford's foot at the moment so they could see it without it blowing away in the light wind. "I mean, the drawing looks nothing like those trees, but the cluster does. And remember how Gram and Gramps used to tap these trees for syrup? Maybe Dad was drawn here for that reason."

Huh. Bo Dawson had been surprisingly sentimental for someone whose actions said he didn't give a damn about anything, so that was possible. And Ford was pretty sure he'd dug into just about every inch of ground leading away from the barns. But he hadn't been down here. Axel and Zeke started going over the area with their metal detectors while Ford and Rex stabbed at the grass, still hard patches this early in the spring, with their tools.

Ford watched them for a moment, sometimes unable to believe they were really all here. All three of his middle siblings had fallen for single mothers of babies when all three had sworn off dating single mothers for pretty much the same reason Ford had: not ready, would never be ready, for family life, for commitment. Love had conked his younger brothers over the head one after another. Zeke, the businessman of the family, who'd opened a consultancy on Main Street and found love with his administrative assistant, who'd loved him since middle school. Zeke had actually had a long-time crush on Danica from high school, but when Zeke had moved back to town a couple months ago, he quickly discovered that he only had eyes for Danica's best friend, Molly Orton. Now they were engaged, and Zeke doted on her year-old daughter.

Then there was Axel, the director of safety for the ranch and a wilderness guide for guests. A former search and rescue worker and lone wolf, Axel had found a missing toddler on a mountain, reunited mother and son, and found himself unexpectedly joining a family.

Rex, who'd left the US Marshals and was now a cop at the Bear Ridge PD with Ford, had found an old bottle in the Bear Ridge River with an old letter to Santa inside from a foster child with a Christmas wish: to be adopted. He'd felt compelled to find Maisey Clark and make sure her wish had come true. He ended up marrying the single mom of a baby girl.

And rebuilding the ranch had brought his brother Noah together with Sara, his first love, and her twin babies. Sister Daisy, who'd been pregnant and alone when she'd come home, had fallen for a man—very reluctantly at first—who'd come to claim the Dawson Family Guest Ranch as belonging to his family, but had surprised everyone by falling madly in love with Daisy.

And here was Ford, the oldest at thirty-five. Unable to let go of a woman he couldn't have. He'd just have to. Ford was nothing if not disciplined.

"So have you been matched with anyone yet?" Rex asked with a grin, his blue eyes—the same blue eyes all the Dawson siblings had—lighting up. He shot a glance at their brothers, whose grins gave them away.

"So it was you guys who filled out that form for me," he said. "I was about to go yell at Daisy for that."

"Nope, it was us," Zeke said. "We've noticed you haven't been going out much the past couple months, so we took matters into our own hands now that there are a ton of women in town. So how'd we do? Go on any dates yet?"

"Nope," he said, stabbing at the ground. "I'm on hiatus."

"Because of Danica?" Rex asked. "We were all at your housewarming party. We all saw you two lip-locked—more than once."

Slam. He suddenly remembered giving Danica a tour of the house well into the party, and suddenly they were kissing in a dark corner, and he couldn't wait for the party to end and everyone to leave so they could explore each other more. Which they had.

"Not meant to be," Ford said. And clearly glumly, because his brothers all stopped metal detecting and poking at the ground and stared at him.

"Gotcha," Zeke said, clapping him on the back.

"Well, when you want to start dating again, just

let us know and we'll exaggerate on your match-making form so you sound like a catch," Rex said with a grin.

"You can count on us," Axel added, pretend socking Ford with a one-two punch in the stomach.

Ford rolled his eyes, but he was touched. His brothers had his back. Noah and Daisy did, too. He was lucky and he knew it.

They spent the next hour trying to find the diary but came up empty. No surprise there. And then they'd all had to get going: Zeke, mind like a ledger, reminding them all that the twins' birth-day party was this weekend. Little Annabel and Chance—Noah and Sara's children—were turn-ing a year old.

Ford was heading through the gates of the ranch when he noticed Jasper Fields, the ranch hand who'd gone out with Candace last night, about to pass him in his pickup on his way in to work. Jas-per waved and slowed, and Ford stopped and rolled down his window.

"I'm not going to get fired for that fiasco of a date with your friend's sister, am I?" Jasper asked. Ford could see that the guy was serious. He truly looked worried.

"Of course not," Ford assured him. "Date disasters go hand in hand with dating. Sometimes a couple just doesn't mesh."

"That's the thing," Jasper said, running a hand through his tousled blond hair. "I thought we did. Candace Dunbar has to be the prettiest woman I've ever seen in my life. But then we started arguing about country versus city life and then whether babies should be picked up immediately when they cry in the middle of the night or not, and suddenly, she's telling me I don't know everything and asking for the check. I was hoping to take her dancing, but the night ended way too early."

"Know much about the sleeping habits of babies, do you?" Ford asked.

He shrugged. "I was just trying to act like I knew what I was talking about. I knew when I asked her out that she had a baby, so I went home and googled some facts. I was trying to get across that I was interested in what she was saying."

Ford smiled. The guy tried so hard it had backfired. "Well, maybe you could ask for a do-over. See how it goes."

Jasper brightened. "A do-over. Yeah... I will. Hey, thanks, Ford."

As he watched Jasper's truck head through the gates and up the road that would lead to the main barn, he chuckled. He'd called that one. There would definitely be a second date, a second chance.

And maybe he could help Danica babysit again. Of course there could be no second chance for them. But he sure liked the idea of spending time with her.

## Chapter Five

Danica rarely used her vacation time, but she asked for the week off so that she and her sister and niece could spend time together and also help with Aunt Trudy's wedding preparations. Thanks to a cancellation, Trudy and Cole had managed to snag one of the small ballrooms in the lodge at the Dawson Family Guest Ranch lodge, a beautiful white building with a steeply pitched roof that overlooked Clover Mountain and had a spectacular view. The three of them were in the ballroom now and had been for the past hour, Trudy deciding on the color of the runner and guest chairs for the ceremony, the arrangement of the tables for the reception and, of course, the flowers. Danica had been drawn to the windows, imagining Ford, who'd grown up here, running up and down the halls of this level of the lodge with his sister and brothers as a young boy, climbing the mountain in the near distance.

On the drive over she'd wondered if she'd run into him, then realized of course she wouldn't. She'd been his Realtor, after all, and knew exactly where he lived—in a renovated farmhouse right in town. But he could be visiting his family, and if she happened to catch a glimpse of him she wouldn't mind one bit. Just being here on the property made her feel connected to him, a feeling she wasn't used to. But he'd shared some of his family history with her, the story of the ranch, how his grandparents had started the original guest ranch over fifty years ago, how his father had inherited it and quickly destroyed it, how the siblings had banded together to reclaim their legacy and rebuild.

Danica loved this room with its polished dark wood floor, warm white walls and the huge arched windows, three along the back wall. Somehow, the space managed to be both rustic and elegant at the same time. Neither Trudy nor Cole had big families, and they weren't expecting more than forty people.

"How many people were at your wedding?" Candace asked Danica. "Over two hundred? Maybe even three hundred?"

"Two eighty-four," Danica said, and she'd barely known half of them. Her ex-husband had a huge family and they'd run the show, including the guest list, particularly once they'd learned that Danica's mother didn't intend to help plan the wedding at all. Danica's former mother-in-law had been thrilled not to have to deal with the mother of the bride.

Danica had had misgivings about marrying Troy, but she'd been twenty-one, they'd been a couple since middle school, and he was a golden boy whose big family, very involved in Troy's life, drew her. She wanted to be a part of the family, in attendance at loud, huge family dinners. And in the early years, his mother and grandmother and aunts had welcomed her with open arms, their "Dani" that they'd known forever—until she was about twenty-five and a grandchild wasn't forthcoming. With each passing year, they got colder and colder, pushier and pushier, demanding she see a doctor to find out why she wasn't getting pregnant. She'd finally burst out with the fact that she was on birth control and wasn't sure she wanted a child. Her mother-in-law had stopped speaking to her. Troy had started his affair soon after or maybe even before. But he used it to excuse the affair.

She'd been disappointed by the Dunbars' lack of warmth and disinterest in family connection, family ties. Then she'd been dumped by in-laws for not being what they wanted. Somewhere along the way, her confusion over what she wanted got stronger and stronger, and keeping her distance from people became the new normal. She let out a sigh, hating all this muck. Right here, right now, was a new beginning with the women in this ballroom: Aunt Trudy, Candace, herself, and baby Brandy. Brandy would not grow up without a strong, supportive family.

"I think Trudy's wedding sounds absolutely perfect," Danica said. "Forty people, small and intimate, close friends and family. The people you love and care about with you on the happiest day of your life."

Her aunt beamed. Danica loved seeing Trudy, who'd been through the wringer, so happy. Trudy's phone pinged with a text and she pulled it from her purse. "Oh, what a surprise," she muttered, shaking her head. She dumped her phone back in her bag with quite a frown.

"What's wrong?" Danica asked.

"Guess who's sorry but unable to make it to the wedding and sends best wishes for a lovely event," Trudy said, looking from Danica to Candace.

Danica knew instantly the text was from her parents, and she felt the usual clench in her chest. Her parents weren't exactly cold, just standoffish and extreme introverts. And now they had the excuse of living hours away and "you know we don't travel well."

Candace's expression said she knew it, too. "I just don't get it. I mean, I do. I've been like them, too. For too long. But I see where that's gotten me. Feeling alone. *Being* alone."

"I guess they have each other and that's always been enough for them," Danica said.

"I'm a witch, but I'll tell you," Trudy said, "your mother steers that ship. My brother was more family oriented until he married your mother. No offense."

"None taken," the sisters said in unison, then both gave dry laughs.

"But it's been what, thirty-five years they've been together," Trudy said, "and they are who they are. I accepted it long ago. To the point that I let my husband steer our ship and keep me from reaching out to you two more. I was just so used to being basically estranged, and he wanted no part of family obligations." She let out a breath. "Awful."

Danica nodded. "Well, we're together now and it's a fresh start. Especially for this little beauty," she added, kneeling down in front of Brandy's stroller to gently cup the baby's chin.

"To fresh starts," Trudy said, holding out her hand.

Danica smiled and put her hand on Trudy's, and Candace put her hand on Danica's.

Then they bent down and put their hands under one of Brandy's tiny ones.

Just as the door opened, they heard a familiar voice. "Oh, sorry, I didn't realize this room was occupied."

Danica turned just as her best friend, Molly, was hurrying out, her long, wildly curly brown hair bouncing behind her. "Molly, wait! It's fine!"

Molly turned, her baby daughter, Lucy, in a carrier on her chest, and her mouth dropped open. "Danica? I didn't even register that was you."

Danica glanced down at herself. She usually didn't leave her house without being dressed to the nines, even on Saturday morning runs to the coffee shop—and that included full makeup, hair flat ironed and curling ironed to beachy wave perfection. Her skin care regimen alone took thirty minutes and had nine steps. But since she'd morphed into full-time Aunt Danica, she rolled out of bed, took a fast shower, twisted her hair into a bun so that tiny fists couldn't yank the long strands, and wore comfortable jeans and tops that didn't require dry-cleaning from baby-spit up. Right now, Danica was in a simple T-shirt dress with a jean jacket and ballet flats, something she'd normally wear to a baseball game. And had she even put on makeup this morning? She'd gotten up early with Brandy, and honestly, she couldn't remember if she'd bothered with even mascara. And Danica was usually a five-coat gal. This new her took so much less effort, and now she wondered if she'd been hiding behind all that gloss and veneer. She'd never looked at it that way before; she'd just taken herself for a girly girl who liked glamming it up.

"Guess who's visiting and hopefully moving to Bear Ridge permanently with this little darling," Danica said to Molly. "My sister, Candace. You guys remember each other, right? Molly's been my best friend since second grade."

"I definitely remember you, Molly," Candace said. "And wow, I don't even think I have any friends from school anymore. That's impressive."

"Danica and I are forever," Molly said, giving

Danica a quick hug, taking care not to squish the baby between them.

"And hello to you, my sweet goddaughter," Danica said, gently caressing Lucy's pretty brown hair. She adored the baby girl but all the baby-sitting and outtings with Molly and Lucy hadn't sparked baby fever for Danica.

Molly turned to Danica's aunt. "Nice to see you again, Trudy, and congrats on your engagement. Omigosh, are you having the ceremony here?"

Trudy nodded. "I love this room."

"Me, too," Molly said. "I've been looking at lots of venues, but I keep coming back to this particular one. Just look at those windows and that view."

Molly was engaged to Zeke Dawson, Ford's brother, who owned a consulting business in town. He and Molly were now full partners, even though she'd started as his administrative assistant. They didn't have a wedding date yet but were working on it.

"That's what we all said when we walked in," Candace noted, nodding and looking around the lovely space.

"Aw, the babies like each other," Candace said, pointing.

They all turned to see Brandy and Lucy staring at each other with big grins, batting their little hands in the air. Candace and Molly exchanged numbers so they could arrange a playdate for the girls, talking a mile a minute about the babies' schedules and habits and milestones, and Danica could feel herself stepping back, shrinking, not part of any of this. She'd picked up a lot in just a couple days of having a baby in her house, but she was the aunt, not the mom, and as she'd watched her sister take care of Brandy, really saw what went into motherhood on so many levels, she'd found herself feeling kind of scared. But if Candace had taken to being a mother, couldn't Danica, too? They'd been raised in the same home, the same way.

She was so lost in her thoughts that she'd barely heard Molly saying goodbye, and then it was again just the four of them in the ballroom. Trudy had her list of everything she needed to take care of for the wedding as did Danica and Candace, so they headed out.

"Oh, God, there he is," Candace said, eyes narrowed on a tall, muscular blond man in jeans and a cowboy hat, a saddle in his arms near the barn. "Jasper from last night."

Jasper noticed them, lifting his hand in a wave, then jogged over to a nearby pasture and knelt down. He shot up with a bouquet of wildflowers in his hand and jogged over. "Morning, Candace. These are for you," he added, extending his hand.

Candace eyed the flowers without a smile but took them. "Thank you."

"This beautiful baby girl must be Brandy," he said, making peekaboo faces at her. "Aren't you the spitting image of your mother."

Candace tilted her head. "Well, we don't want to keep you from your work."

He glanced a bit bashfully at Danica and Trudy, who took a step back to give the guy some privacy. "I'm hoping you'll give us a second chance, Candace. I think last night, we just had so much to talk about, so much in common, that we just both really got truthful instead of holding back and being all polite with each other. I think that's a good thing. I'd like to get to know you better."

"As long as you admit right this second that I know more about babies than you because I'm the one who has a baby," Candace said.

The handsome cowboy grinned. "You absolutely do. I was trying to show I related and that I like babies."

Candace smiled. "Well, then, I'm looking forward to that second date."

He pumped his fist in the air. "Hope you're

free tonight. I wanted to get started on our second chance right away."

"I'm happy to babysit," Danica said. "And, hi, I'm Candace's sister, Danica. We didn't have the chance to meet last night. And this is our aunt Trudy."

They shook hands and a time was set, and the cowboy loped away with another fist pump.

"Aw," Trudy said. "I like him."

Danica smiled. "Me, too."

"Me three," Candace said, "but I'm gonna be cautious. I can't afford to make mistakes with someone I might bring into Brandy's life."

Danica stared at her sister, struck by what she'd said. The mother bear protectiveness. Their own mother hadn't been that way. Not that there had been divorce and boyfriends coming in and out of the home, but careless sitters—a teen down the street who ignored them completely, a woman who brought over her boyfriend and sent the girls outside and locked the door for an hour. *I've been afraid of motherhood because of what I grew up with*, she realized. *Not necessarily because of who I am, how I am.* Huh, she thought.

Tonight she'd try looking at Brandy in a different light, imagining herself as a mom and the type of mother she might be. Maybe her maternal instincts would rise up and baby fever would come calling. Of course she'd tried that countless times during her marriage, and the feeling that other women seemed to have so effortlessly never even pricked the skin. But she wasn't that same Danica anymore, in a terrible, lonely marriage, made to feel that there was something wrong with her, something deficient.

This is *my* second chance, she realized. At this new person I've become—*am* becoming.

The thought sent goose bumps up her spine—in a good way.

Ford and his brother Rex were returning to the police station after lunch at the diner when a woman, midthirties, marched up to them. She wore floral scrubs and a name pin that showed she worked at the nursing home. She didn't look happy, that was for sure.

"I'd like to file a complaint about a breach of expectation," she said.

Rex glanced at him, then at the furious woman. "What was this breach of expectation about, ma'am?"

"I really don't like being called 'ma'am' but that's neither here nor there right now," she muttered. "Two nights out, I went on a date with a man

who told me he'd like to get together again and
then never called or texted. Not five minutes ago,
I saw him through the diner window sitting with a
blonde and having pancakes. And you *know* they
spent the night together if they're having breakfast at the diner! What are my rights in terms of
lodging a complaint?"

Did he have time for this? Ford understood that
dating was a killer, but the petty complaints were
blowing up the BRPD lines, and he was constantly
being asked questions like this. "I'm very sorry,
but he didn't break a law," Ford said.

"I don't care about him," the woman said. "I'm
talking about the *town*. Bear Ridge and the mayor
and the town council are in breach of expectation! Obviously, they bit off more than they could
chew with their matchmaking request forms, and
they're just putting any old couples together based
on age. I had absolutely nothing in common with
that man!"

"But then why does it bother you that he didn't
call?" Rex asked.

The woman scowled. "Because he said he
would. I was raised to do what I say I will." She
lifted her chin and folded her arms across her
chest. "It was my first date since my divorce,"
she added. A moment later, everything she'd

said seemed to weigh on her shoulders and they slumped in defeat.

That was dating for you. Hell.

Ford nodded. He felt for the woman. "It's unsettling when someone doesn't do what they say they will." But really, Ford was used to that. He'd grown up with a father who'd said whatever it took to get through the moment. *I'm running out to the store to get you kids something for dinner.* Then not returning until the middle of the night—and drunk. Promising to drink less while chugging a tall can of beer before the start of the school day. Reminders of his children's birthdays and then forgetting. Ford knew he could count on his siblings and his fellow officers. The rest of humankind? He didn't have any expectations *to* breach.

The tension in her face softened. "That's exactly it. I don't like it. Don't say you'll call when you don't intend to."

"I hear you," Ford said with a compassionate nod.

Rex also nodded. "Dating is rough."

"Not for the faint of heart," the woman said, brightening at her fortitude to be out there on the singles scene.

Ford leaned a bit closer. "I have an idea. Why don't you head over to the town hall or the coffee shop and pick up another matchmaking form—you can also find one online. Start from scratch now that you've got experience under your belt. You can include exactly what you're looking for and *not* looking for. *Honorable* is a good trait."

She lifted her chin, much cheerier than she'd been two minutes ago. "I'll do exactly that. Thank you, officers. You've been very helpful." She turned and left, headed right for the coffee shop across the street.

Ford and Rex resumed walking, waiting for the light to change at the corner of Main Street.

"I sure as hell wouldn't want to be out there," Rex said with a mock shiver.

Got that right. *Nothing* about love was for the faint of heart.

"Yoo-hoo, officers!" trilled a voice.

Ford turned to see Mayor Pauline Abbott hurrying their way with a thick packet in her hands.

The mayor pushed her square silver glasses up on her nose. "Ford," she began, "At least twenty women have complained to me—and members of the town council—that they've heard you're not partaking in the matchmaking despite being single, and so I'm wondering if you might do our dear community a big favor."

Ford raised an eyebrow. He supposed *those* complaints could be considered flattering, but it was also scary as all get-out. When the social media blast and articles in the local and county papers went viral about the town seeking single women for its lonesome bachelors, he'd had newcomers—from the very attractive to the pushiest of the pushy— sidle up to him, eye his left hand and then start flirting like mad. He'd had to explain he wasn't on the market, which got him blank stares, protests, lectures and even anger—*jeez, just say outright that I'm not your type instead of making excuses!* His sister, Daisy, had called it the Bo Dawson curse. Women had always been drawn to their tall, good-looking father with his Clint Eastwood blue eyes and thick, tousled dark hair. His sons were dead ringers for him.

Out of the corner of his eye he could see Rex smirking.

"Lots of breakups and disappointing dates the past week," Mayor Abbott continued, "and now I have sixty-two new matchmaking request forms, even more in-depth as to what they're looking for and not looking for. You know Danica Dunbar, right? She's our matchmaking angel, and I wonder if you might partner up with her to work on these. As a team, you'll speed right through them. Oh, and we should really set up another speed dating event, and between the two of you, you'll get it all good to go in no time."

This sounded like a full-time job. Ford already had one of those. "Anything else?" he asked in a politely sarcastic tone, but she didn't seem to catch it.

"Oh, this will keep you busy in your spare time, so I don't think so. Thank you so much, Detective. You already give so much to Bear Ridge, so we really appreciate this."

Ford held back his sigh of resignation. "Happy to help," he said, though he wasn't sure he was.

"Now, Officer Dawson," she said, turning to Rex. "I know you've got a toddler, and a baby on the way, so you have your hands full."

Rex smiled. "I sure do."

Ford sent a surreptitious scowl to his brother as Pauline handed Ford the stuffed packet and ran off after someone else. God only knew what she was about to make them do.

"You, a matchmaker?" Rex said, laughing as they resumed walking toward the police station. "Now I've heard everything."

"Right," Ford said, shaking his head. "How'd I get roped into this?"

"Hey, get married and get busy with kids, and

you'll be instantly exempt from a lot of torturous volunteerism."

He'd been willing to settle down, hadn't he? Ford had come home fully intending to find his wife, have those six kids, make all those pancakes and strips of bacon on Sunday mornings. And then the one woman he wanted was the one who didn't want to turn that fantasy in his head into reality.

No kids. *Could* he commit to that? If he were deeply in love? If Danica Dunbar was the only woman for him?

He mulled that over, not getting anywhere, half-listening to Rex talking about the first birthday presents he'd gotten Noah's twins, something about a chair in the shape of a tiger and a bear.

At the PD, Rex got pulled away by the rookie who was shadowing him for the rest of the day, and Ford went to his desk. He took out his phone and opened up his message app, tapping on Danica's lovely photo.

Mayor Abbott just got me to agree to be your matchmaking partner and to arrange a speed dating event, he texted. Apparently, some in town are throwing fits on their bad matches and want their new loves ASAP. Got some free time tonight?

Echoing in his head was to say no so they didn't get in any deeper. One of them had to be gatekeeper here, and despite his badge, it wasn't going to be him. He had to be near Danica, had to see her. Even if they could just be friends.

He froze for a second. Wasn't that getting close to the "only woman for him" category?

His phone pinged with a text. Danica.

I'm on babysitting duty tonight—you were right about Jasper and Candace!—if you don't mind helping out again.

He smiled. See you at seven?

Perfect, she texted back.

I'll grill, if you'd like, he typed without thinking.

Even more perfect, was her response.

Far from perfect, actually, he thought. But spending time with Danica was just what he needed right now.

## Chapter Six

Turned out there was something unsettling about being in her backyard with a man grilling steaks and asparagus, a baby in her playpen on the patio making adorable gurgling sounds. All that was missing was a family dog, maybe a snoozing cat.

It was too much. And it was magic. All at the same time.

Danica's ex-husband had grilled all the time, but immediately afterward he'd settle down in his chaise, filled plate on a small table beside him, tablet turned to a baseball game, and they'd eat in silence—well, except for the announcer and the crowd cheering or her ex yelling at the screen when his team didn't do well. It had always been like that, and they'd been together for so long—class couple from seventh grade—that there had never been a honeymoon phase.

When Ford had arrived, she'd immediately noticed his very quick and appreciative perusal of her. He'd actually done a double take, and the goose bumps had broken out all over her body. Once again, Danica of the four-inch stilettos and sexy pastel-colored suits, long blond hair always coiffed to stylized perfection, had on no makeup, her hair was in a loose bun at her nape, and she wore a comfortable pair of skinny jeans and a long pale yellow cardigan with a white cami underneath. And slip-on sneakers that felt like heavenly slippers. Babysitting wear. Danica's new look.

Oh, and she'd had an eyeful of him, too. Dark jeans. Black leather jacket. Green Henley shirt, rolled up on his forearms. She couldn't look at him—ever—without remembering that first kiss against the wall in his house. The kiss that had lasted at least thirty seconds before they'd come up for air and only because they heard someone whisper, "Get a room." And then, of course, being alone with him once all the partygoers had left. How he'd held her gaze while he'd unzipped her dress. The sight of his bare chest had made her knees truly wobble.

Their attraction was palpable, that was just a fact, so when he'd immediately asked her to lead him to the grill, she'd understood why. Distraction had been necessary. He'd grilled and she'd made a salad, watching him from the window, and she'd loved every peek he'd sneaked at her. They ate outside, conversation nonstop but light, avoiding talk of them. It was such a gorgeous night that Ford had suggested they pack the stroller and head into town so he could buy presents for his twin niece and nephew, who were turning one this Saturday.

Now they were in Bear Ridge Toys on Main Street, standing barely an inch apart by a huge display of stuffed animals, Brandy in her stroller in front of them.

That felt even weirder—and more magical. Again at the same time.

Her phone pinged with a text. Aunt Trudy. Danica read the text, not sure how she felt about it.

"Everything okay?" For asked.

Danica shrugged. "Aunt Trudy and Cole decided to elope. Instead of getting married at the lodge on Saturday, they're flying to Las Vegas to a fancy hotel, having the ceremony at a quickie wedding chapel, and then staying there for a week's honeymoon."

"You sound disappointed," Ford said.

"Well, it would be nice to attend her wedding, help her with the finishing touches. Being a part of the wedding planning made me feel like we were really on our way to becoming close. But I get it. They couldn't shake the bad vibes with the dress being stolen, and Trudy's still getting looks from one of the women, so they just want to fly off where nothing can touch them."

"That's the kind of wedding I figured I'd have if I ever got married. Vegas. Just me and my bride."

That got her attention. "So you did think about marriage at some point? As a possibility for yourself?"

"I've had mostly short-term relationships, but a few of my exes talked about marriage, and when I tried to imagine myself getting married, I couldn't. Or at least not some big wedding. Vegas seemed special in itself, just the two of us."

"I guess that's how Trudy sees it." She sighed. "I just want to be closer to my family. Now I won't even be going to my aunt's wedding."

"Sounds like she's planning to come back to Bear Ridge and settle down with Cole in his house. You two could work on building bonds then. You just keep inviting her, reaching out, opening up, and she will, too."

Danica nodded, about to thank Ford for, once again, not only understanding what she was trying to say but being supportive and compassionate.

"What a beautiful family!" said an elderly woman holding the hand of a young boy. "The baby looks just like both of you!" She smiled and the group moved on.

"Who wants to tell her?" Ford quipped. "Although Brandy does look a lot like you. You and your sister could be twins. And I suppose I do have blue eyes, just like you and our baby here." The moment the words were out, he choked to the point that he had to use his fist against his chest.

"We do look like a family out shopping for toys for our baby daughter," she said.

"Make you want to run for the hills?" he asked.

She glanced down for a moment, then back at Ford. "You know, to make pleasant conversation, clients, prospective clients, house sellers always ask if I have kids, and when I say no, they look so surprised. Then there's that moment of 'oh, maybe I shouldn't have asked because she probably can't have kids.' I always read that on faces. Then there's a brief awkward silence before I quickly fill it. So, when that woman mistook us for a family, all

I felt was…normal, Ford. For just a moment, like everyone else." She turned toward a huge stuffed panda holding a shiny satin heart, realizing she'd exposed too much of herself, not unusual when she was with Ford Dawson. He had a way of making her talk. Had to be a detective trait.

He squeezed her hand. "I've always admired people who march to their own drum."

She liked that, but she wasn't so sure that applied to her. "I married my ex-husband knowing something wasn't quite right. I went along. But with a baby, bringing a new life into the world? That was a firm no, not ready, not sure."

"Interesting," he said. "So maybe it's not that you don't want a child, Danica. Maybe you just knew you didn't have the right husband. The right family setup. Maybe you just recognized that and refused to 'go along anymore.'"

"Maybe. I don't know."

"You don't have to be sure of anything except that I shouldn't buy these giant pandas, right?" he said, gesturing behind them at the display. "Noah and Sara live in the foreman's cabin on the ranch. Despite it being small, it has history for both of them, so they want to stay there even though they're running out of room as the twins get bigger."

"Yeah, no giant pandas," she said, wanting to reach up a hand to his handsome face. She was so touched by how he was able to talk to her about the child issue, how he seemed to support her without saying too much. She appreciated it.

And instead of keeping him safely in the friend zone, she was falling further and deeper for him every time they were together.

Instead of the giant pandas, Ford bought two colorful play tables with lots to squeeze, press and bat at. Ford was a sucker for personalization, so when the owner offered to stencil the twins' names on their tables, he said yes, and then he and Danica and Brandy went to the coffee shop to kill the half hour it would take. They made it back to the shop just before closing at eight o'clock. Most of Bear Ridge's Main Street stores extended their hours with the warmer weather and since daylight saving time was keeping dusk later and later.

Now they were at Danica's house, the yawning, eye-rubbing Brandy easily put to bed. Ford and Danica were on the sofa, the matchmaking forms on the coffee table.

Ford picked up the first one in his stack. "'Lonesome cowboy seeks his one and only,'" he read.

"Aw, that's sweet," Danica said.

"Do you think there's a real 'one and only' for everyone?" Ford asked, reaching for the tall iced mocha he'd brought back from the coffee shop.

"I don't know. I think some people find theirs, and they're really, really lucky. And others may have to kiss a few frogs or frogettes. You can think you found your person and then discover they're not that anymore. Things can change."

"Yeah," he said. "Exactly that."

"Did you ever think you'd found yours?" she asked.

"You'd think by my age the answer would be yes, but if she came along I didn't recognize her. I think that may be another issue for people. Wrong timing. The perfect person might be right there, but you can't see it for whatever reason."

Were *they* perfect for each other—with the exception of that one big fundamental issue? All Ford knew was that until she'd left in a hurry in the middle of the night, he'd felt Danica Dunbar dead center in his chest, and he'd never experienced that before. He'd always heard people say "you'll just know." He *knew* that night back in February.

He was aware he was staring at her, wanting to touch her so badly he squeezed his drink cup too hard, so he glanced down at the matchmaking profile. "Thomas Whittaker, forty-two. Divorced.

Twin seven-year-old boys. Senior accountant. 'I'm looking for a hilarious, life-of-the-party type with a big laugh because that's me. Sure my job sounds dry, but numbers can be funny, too. Except when it comes to the number one. It's the loneliest number, right? Oh yeah, must love attending all rodeo championships and enjoy really boisterous children who will drive you insane in ten minutes.'"

Danica laughed. "He sounds great. And I know just the woman for him! A Realtor in my office—Carrie. Biggest laugh in Bear Ridge and loves the rodeo. He described her to a T. And she's very open about the fact that she wants to meet a single dad because she can't have kids." She rummaged through her stack until she found Carrie's form, holding it up. She peered over at the photo of Thomas. "Hey, they even kind of look alike! I have a good feeling about this!"

"That one was easy," he said, using a paper clip to attach the two profiles together. According to Danica, the protocol to pair matches involved one of the matches getting in contact with the other. One of the first boxes to check off on the form was whether you wanted to be the caller or the called or either. "Callers" wanted to see the forms they matched with and decide if they wanted to call the match. "The Called" wanted to be called by their matches if they passed muster. Thomas had checked off "The Called" and Carrie had checked off "Caller" which gave her the leg up in deciding if she wanted to match with him or not. The Callers would then receive an email with the matched profiles attached. The system was wonky, in Ford's mind—what if both checked off the same box— but it seemed to be working.

They went through five more forms, making five matches, and found more than one for a few, which required scanning the profile and attaching it to the matched request.

Danica sipped her iced coffee and set it back down, picking up another profile. "Okay, now we have Jolie Parkwell, thirty, single, high school social studies teacher, grew up on a ranch, hoping to meet marriage-minded man of character and integrity who wants a big family. 'I have a thing for a man in uniform, whether serving his community or country…'" She glanced up at him. "Well, I guess we'll just clip this one to your form. She sounds just right for you. Or a coffee to start, anyway."

He shook his head. "No way. I told you—I didn't fill out that form. And it turns out my sister, who lives for matchmaking, didn't either. My brothers did."

"That's even sweeter," she said. "They want you to have what they have."

"Still. I'm not in the mix here."

"Form says you are and she does sound just right, Ford. No reason not to meet her."'

*Except I have a thing for someone else, so what's the point?*

That was the point, actually. That he had to let go of his feelings for Danica.

"Fine, I'll meet her. Now let's find someone for you." The idea made him sick to his stomach, but he poked through the profiles. Staring back at him was an old rival from high school who'd beaten him out for captain of the lacrosse team even though he was a couple grades behind. Good-looking guy. Real Estate Developer. *Hoping to meet a lovely woman, inside and out, who's looking for commitment. I should add, I like kids, have a bunch of cute nieces and nephews, but I'm meant to be an uncle and not a dad.* Damn—it was almost too perfect. He stared daggers at the guy's photo as he handed her the profile. "And this one is for you."

She took the form and smiled. "I remember him! He was a very popular senior when I was a freshman." He watched her read the form, her smile fading when she got to the part about what he was looking for. She put his profile on the coffee table and picked up her coffee. "I don't know, Ford. I'm not so sure I should date someone who's sure he's an uncle and not a dad. I mean, what if I'm struck by baby fever next year?"

He gave a slow nod, not realizing she was more ambivalent about the subject than resolute. Maybe they didn't have cross each other off their lists, after all. "But doesn't that knock out every guy?"

"Yes," she said, biting her lip. "I've been thinking about this, and until I know what I want in that department, I should probably just concentrate on myself. No dating. At all."

Huh. Of course, she could decide her ambivalence had always been for good reason: because she didn't want children, end of story. Or not. But the bottom line was that she was *not* available.

"Well," he added, wishing she didn't smell so good, that she wasn't sitting so close, that he didn't want to kiss her so badly. "Let's try to get through ten more."

Over the next hour, they did, making lots of matches. There was a growing pile of "difficult to match" forms, though, and they were determined to find at least one match for each of those. One man was triggered by redheads and petite women, and would prefer potential in-laws who lived more than three hundred miles away from the area. A hard-to-match woman wanted a fellow devout Christian who looked like "that hot actor who plays Thor."

"Got him!" Danica said, holding up a profile in triumph. "I mean, he's not Chris Hemsworth, but he's a blond rancher with serious muscles."

An hour later, they'd found at least one match for twenty profiles, and Ford couldn't bear to look at another request. They moved on to planning the speed dating event, deciding on the Saturday night after next. Ford insisted on charging a twenty-five-dollar fee because a nominal charge meant those who paid would take the event seriously; twenty-five bucks would get them appetizers and refreshments at "get to know you even better" stations. That idea led to Danica suggesting they hold the event in one of the lodge ballrooms at the Dawson Family Guest Ranch to make the setting more exciting and festive. The town hall had two large meeting rooms, but nothing about those rooms was romantic. Sara, Noah's wife, responded to Danica's text about setting things up. She and Maisey, his brother Rex's wife, were going to town on the decor, nothing too cheesy, she promised. They watched some YouTube videos on speed dating events to get the gist on how to set up theirs.

Some elements clearly didn't work, which had them both cringing and laughing.

"I like the idea of card tables for two, set a few inches apart for privacy. We can assign every entrant a number to be ID'd by, and they'll also be given either the letter *A* or *B*. *A*'s will stay seated at the tables. *B*'s will move every two minutes."

Ford nodded. "Sounds good."

"So from what we watched, how about if we give each entrant an index card to jot down those people they wish to be matched with. Once the speed dating time ends, we'll call for mingling. Then we'll go through the cards and match those who selected each other, and write down the registration numbers of each entrant's choices. The chosen can see photos and descriptions and decide if they want to match with who selected them, then they'll leave their cards with us and we'll go through those and—"

"Or I could ask my rookie, who likes creating apps, if he could develop something simple to streamline all this. Entrants could download the app and make their choices right there at the moment, and then the app does all the work."

"I'm for that," she said. "And completely zonked."

"Romance is hard work, but we knew that," he said.

Their exhaustion came at the right time because a car pulled into the driveway. Candace. Danica popped up, anticipation on her face. Even Ford was curious how the date had gone.

They waited. And waited. And waited. Finally Danica walked over to the window overlooking the yard and pulled aside the curtain.

"They're kissing," she said with a smile. "Now they're talking. Now they're kissing again." She dropped the curtain and darted back to the sofa. "He's walking her to the door."

They waited. And waited. Ford figured there was one hell of a good-night kiss happening on the porch.

Five minutes later, Candace walked in, a moony expression on her face. "Omigosh," she said. "I'm so glad I gave Jasper a second chance. He's wonderful in every way. And guess who's taking me and Brandy to the zoo tomorrow?"

Ford smiled. Tomorrow was Saturday and supposed to be a gorgeous spring day, low sixties and sunny. He'd be at his niece and nephew's birthday party at the ranch, which was going to be held outside behind the main house, where his sister Daisy lived with her husband and son.

"Thanks for babysitting, Danica *and* Ford," she added with a sly smile and a glance at her sister. "I'll just go get changed," she said to Danica. "Back soon."

"We got a lot accomplished," Danica said, collecting the matched forms. "I'll scan in the profiles that were on paper and email all the 'Callers' in the morning."

He didn't want to leave. "Thanks for helping me pick out the birthday presents for my niece and nephew."

"Anytime," she said.

They headed to the door, Ford walking as slowly as possible. Dammit.

"Well," he said.

"Well," she whispered back.

And what was supposed to be a friendly, quick peck on the cheek turned into something else because she clearly hadn't been expecting it and turned slightly at just the moment his lips made contact with hers. He felt that kiss everywhere, memories of their night together hitting him left and right. Danica kissing every inch of his body.

She stepped back, face flushed, eyes smoldering.

"I was aiming for a chaste peck on the cheek. Sorry about that," he said.

"Oh, trust me, I liked it."

"Yeah, me, too," he said, holding her gaze.

Footsteps on the stairs had them turning. Candace was coming down.

"We should probably get together tomorrow night," he said, "to get through the rest of the matches."

"Your house or mine?" she asked.

"How about mine? Seven?"

"Sounds good," she said.

He peered around her. "Bye, Candace. Glad tonight went better than last time."

"Me, too!" Candace said, her eyes lit up.

He finally opened the door and walked outside, and when he turned for a last time, he knew he was in big trouble here. Danica Dunbar had his heart.

## Chapter Seven

On Saturday morning, Danica and her sister sat outside on the back patio, sipping their coffee and eating bagels with veggie cream cheese. Every now and then, Danica would stare at Candace, unable to believe she was really here, the older sister she'd longed to be closer to her entire life. Last night they'd been about to talk about their love lives, or lack thereof for Danica, when Jasper had called. Candace had disappeared into the guest room with her phone, and by the time Danica had heard Candace's door open almost two hours later, she had been practically asleep in bed.

Hey, she got it. Falling in love was magical.

Danica should know. She was going through it herself.

About an hour ago, they'd stopped at Cole's house to see Aunt Trudy and surprise her with her wedding gifts. They were covering the newlyweds' hotel room in Vegas and had gone a little overboard in a boutique in Prairie City, buying Trudy some sexy lingerie. Their aunt had been thrilled, and cried and hugged them both, and Danica had been left with a good feeling about the future of their family.

Once she and Candace had settled down with their breakfast outside, Brandy in a playpen with her favorite toys, Candace had told her all about her night with Jasper. He'd planned a mega date— a fancy dinner in Prairie City, followed by dancing at a country and western club because Candace loved country music. After, they'd parked at Harmony Overlook with a view of the mountains and stars and had talked, so easily, about everything for over an hour before they'd kissed, and then they'd kissed for hours. Jasper was in the process of buying a small but prosperous cattle ranch from a rancher ready to retire, and Candace liked how sturdy he seemed on all levels. Apparently, Candace had a new dream of her own poking at her, to open up a makeover shop in town, transforming women. With all the newcomers and focus on matchmaking and dating, Candace thought she'd have a steady stream of customers. Apparently, Jasper had been so positive and supportive that all the walls Candace had up came crashing down.

While she'd been waiting for the coffee to brew and the bagels to toast, Danica had demonstrated her real estate chops and called storefronts that were either empty or about to be, negotiated a rent that Candace could afford based on the last of her savings, and now Candace had appointments to check out the spaces tomorrow. Her sister would be putting down roots in Bear Ridge, and nothing made Danica happier.

"Okay, so tell me what's going on between you and Ford," Candace said, taking a bite of her bagel. "And something clearly is."

Danica looked at Candace, then took a sip of her coffee. "Something is. The strange thing is, we're just friends, we've kissed just once since our night together, but every time we get together it feels so romantic and sensual. Is that crazy?"

"Not at all. I think you and Ford are in love and have been since February, and you're both forcing yourselves to ignore how you really feel."

"We have to, though," Danica said. "I can't start something with a man who wants a big family when I don't know if I want even one child. So we decided to be friends, but it's hard."

"Can you imagine having a family with Ford?" Candace asked.

"I have thought about it. Last night we went into town with Brandy to pick up toys for Ford's niece and nephew's birthday party, and someone mistook us for a family. I liked it. I felt like I was part of something special."

Candace glanced at Brandy. "Yup, I know exactly what you mean. One minute it was just me, not really connected to anything except scattered relatives I wasn't close to, and suddenly I was someone's mother. The instantaneous bond and connection I felt with Brandy the moment she was born and placed in my arms was the most amazing thing I've ever felt."

"But you didn't necessarily want kids before?" she asked.

"Not really. I didn't think about it. I was focused on trying to get work and trying to find a great guy. I found neither. Like I said, until I was pregnant I had no idea I *wanted* to be."

"It's definitely not coincidence that we both felt the same on the subject," Danica said. "Both not struck by baby fever, I mean."

"Yeah, not coincidence. We were raised in a

pretty cold family with a lot of stupid estrangements. Family has never meant for us what it
seems to for other people."

That struck Danica as so sad that she just sat
glumly staring at her bagel.

"Remember how you wanted *eight* kids when
you were little?" Candace asked on a laugh.

Danica stared at her. "What? I wanted eight
kids?"

"You don't remember? You were seven, I think.
You had lists of name possibilities for all eight
kids. Their names would all start with the letter M, after your best friend, Molly. You had this
black-and-white notebook that you labeled 'Danica's Dreams.' I used to think that was so barfy,
but now it seems really sweet. I think you were
in second grade. I can't believe I remember this
and you don't."

Danica tried to latch on to a memory fighting
to surface, but she couldn't recall saying anything
like that. Her memory of a lot of her childhood was
pretty spotty; the mind had a way of repressing the
bad. She could definitely see planning to name her
children all after Molly, her first real friend. They
were best friends to this day.

"You should look in your old keepsake chest,"

Candace said. "Mom made one for each of us, and she'd put the usual milestone stuff in it."

"Maybe Mom was warmer and fuzzier than I remember? A keepsake chest seems sentimental and sweet."

Candace sipped her coffee and then nodded. "Grandma Eliza bought the chests for her when each of us was born, so it's not like she went out and got them herself. She'd put in old report cards, school stuff, clothing we outgrew but that she liked. I think you have my chest, too."

"I'll look through it later," Danica said. "But I'm sure Mom wouldn't have kept that notebook."

"You never know what you'll find in that old stuff," Candace said.

Old stuff. A chill ran up her spine at the idea of riffling through the past. Danica had always thought it better to follow the old adage to leave well enough alone, but if she wanted to understand herself better, pawing through her past just might be a way.

"Candace?"

Her sister tilted her head.

"Do you think it's the bond with Brandy that's made you so open to finding your Mr. Right after you've been through the wringer?"

"Definitely. I used to date jerks. Now, I want a

good father for Brandy. Someone who'll love us both with everything he is, put us first. But I think that deep down, I really do believe in love and the fairy tale even though I know, from firsthand experience, that there aren't always happy endings. I think it's possible. It's possible for you, too, Dani."

The use of the nickname she'd given up long ago had her all wistful.

"Good," she said. Because she might not know what she wanted, but she wanted to know that love just might conquer all. Even her deepest fears.

In the huge backyard of the main house at the Dawson Family Guest Ranch, full of family, friends and a lot of kids, Ford played soccer with his two-year-old nephew, Danny. The adorable little boy kicked the foam ball right in the goal Ford had declared between his wide spread legs, earning cheers from the crowd. Ford scooped up his nephew, who held his ever-present lovey—a stuffed cape-draped lion named Zul, and ran with him around the yard, chanting "goal, goal, goal."

"Goal!" Danny repeated, flying Zul high over his head.

Ford hugged his nephew tight and set him down, his chest overflowing with love for the little guy. Danny had named the superhero stuffed animal after his own hero, Ford's brother, Axel, before he could actually pronounce Axel. These days, Danny called him Daddy. Axel had married Danny's mother, Sadie, after rescuing Danny, who'd gone missing on a family hike up a mountain. Sadie was expecting their second child soon.

Ford watched as Danny raced over to his father, who hugged him and set him on his shoulders as they both watched the birthday party unfold.

*I want that*, he thought. *I want my toddler up on my shoulders. Another one pulling at the leg of my pants. Another one in my wife's arms. I want a backyard of littles.*

As he glanced around the party, catching sight of his five siblings with their babies, that feeling was stronger and stronger. He loved this. For so long he'd run from it—from family, from kiddie birthday parties, from the Dawson name here in Bear Ridge. Since he'd been back in town, Bear Ridge didn't remind him of his father or haunting memories that for years had woken him up in the middle of the night, frantic with worry that as the eldest Dawson kid, he'd forgotten one outside, responsible for them all while their father was drunk and out of it. Now, his hometown was only about what he saw in this yard—his siblings, future generations of Dawsons that would grow up proud of who they were. By the buffet table, filled with burgers and hot dogs and fruit and beverages and an incredible assortment of cookies, his brother Noah stood with his wife, Sara, each holding a twin—the birthday duo—and chatting with their sister, Daisy, and her husband, Harrison, who held their baby son, Tony. Sitting down and chomping on burgers piled high with the works were his brothers Rex and Axel, chatting with their nearest neighbors to the west, who had a longtime ranch and had known their grandparents. And over by the huge pile of presents was his brother Zeke and his girlfriend, Molly—

And beside Molly, kneeling down in front of baby Lucy's stroller, was Danica Dunbar.

He did a double take, the sight of her at his family party so unexpected. He wound his way through the crowd. "This is a surprise."

"I got an SOS from Molly," Danica said. "Emergency babysitting pickup."

Zeke leaned close. "One of Molly's cousins is having an emergency appendectomy. We thought we'd just leave Lucy with someone here, but she's been so cranky the past half hour that we figured she'd be better off away from the action. This party just might go on till tomorrow."

Ford smiled. "Probably."

Lucy started shrieking and banging her fists on her little stroller table, her curly hair bouncing in every direction. Ford knelt down, undid her harness and took her out, standing as he cradled her against his chest and rubbed her back. The baby stared at him for a long moment with huge green eyes, then rested her head against his chest and grabbed his ear, her eyes drooping.

"Um, ow," he whispered, smiling at Molly.

"Oh, I forgot to tell you she does that," Zeke said with a grin. "Champion ear grabber. She's never letting go. Sorry."

Ford grinned. "Annabel threw up on me the other day. Trust me, that was worse. Look, you two go ahead. We've got this."

"Oh, we do, do we?" Zeke said, eyebrow raised.

"Danica and I are partners on a town initiative," he said, "so we needed to get together tonight anyway. Everyone knows I'm the baby whisperer of Wyoming."

"I'm definitely not, so I appreciate that he is," Danica said with a smile. "Yeah, you two—go. We'll take good care of Lucy. Good luck to your cousin, Molly."

After explaining what was where in the stroller and diaper bag, the two of them left, and since Lucy started screeching again, Ford said his goodbyes to his family, kissed the birthday twins and he and Danica headed out. They'd both parked at the main gate just down the road, so they got Lucy settled in her stroller with a new stuffed animal to clutch, and like magic, she fell asleep by the time they made the walk to the gate.

Ford eyed their cars. "Why don't we take yours? I'll have the rookie drive me over tomorrow morning so I can get my truck."

"Sounds good. Oh, no—Molly and Zeke were going to put one of their car seats in my car, but it slipped our minds."

"No worries—I've got three different car seats in the back of my truck for any little relative or pint-size citizen who might need a lift. I've got it covered."

"I'll just text Molly that so they won't worry," Danica said.

As he lifted the rear-facing seat out of his truck and carried it over to her car, he stopped short and stared just beyond the gates to the wide grassy area on both sides, trees lining the road out of the ranch.

Wait a minute.

Yes.

"You okay?" Danica asked, eyeing him. "You look like you saw a ghost or something."

"I think I did," he said, staring out at the sides of

the road just past the gate. "My dad died two De-
cembers ago. He left me a hand-scrawled map that
he made when he was clearly drunk, and it showed
an area about a half mile out from the barns near
a certain cluster of trees. All this time, my siblings and I have been digging like idiots looking
for what he buried. But I just got socked with this
intense feeling that he buried it out there, just beyond the gates, as if he wanted whatever offended
him in the diary off ranch property."

"What was it he buried?" Danica asked.

"My mother's diary."

"Oh boy," she said. She glanced at Lucy in her
stroller, the baby fast asleep. "Let's take advantage
of her deep sleep and try to find it."

"Yeah?" he asked. "I can come back tomorrow.
We've got Lucy and a pile of matchmaking forms
to go through."

"We're here, and there are two of us. One for
each side of the gate."

He appreciated that. As Danica wheeled the
stroller over to a shady spot under a tree, he tried
to think like his dad. Bo Dawson had found the
diary in the middle of the night, read it, got upset,
got caught with it and had run out of the house
with it, hiding somewhere in the dark until his
wife had given up and gone back inside. Ford could

imagine his father going just past the gate, to the left, where the grassy area was wider and led to the woods. If a car came or his wife's footsteps sounded, he could easily hide between one of the huge tree trunks.

But he would have been drunk, so he wouldn't have gone far. Ford looked over to two big trees just to the left and walked behind them.

"I might be completely off, as I have been for a year and a half. But something tells me this might be the spot. Something feels right."

And wrong. Like maybe he wasn't meant to find the diary. Sometimes he thought his father did such a bad job with the map on purpose. Maybe he wanted to make it impossible for Ford to find the diary to save him from whatever had set Bo off, while at the same time scoring points for at least trying to give Ford something of his mother's history, her thoughts, the truth behind his early childhood.

Ford had no idea what it could be. It had to be something bad.

"As long as I don't find out I'm not really a Dawson, I think I can handle whatever's in there," Ford said, explaining about the night his father buried the book.

Danica grimaced. "Ugh, Ford, maybe you should just leave it buried."

He shrugged, stuffing his hands in his pockets. "My dad wanted me to have it. Sort of. So he was trusting the truth. Maybe. I don't know what the hell I'm talking about."

"Well, if you want to try to find it, I'm your gal. Got a shovel?"

He held up a finger and jogged over to the gatehouse, which was staffed during working hours. There were always a few tools and a first-aid kit in there. He found a shovel—you never could predict April weather in Wyoming—and rushed back over to where Danica stood.

"Here," he said, poking the shovel down into the grassy dirt. "Behind these two trees. Hidden from view of the road both ways."

He poked at the ground for a good ten minutes, every thirty seconds glancing over at Lucy to make sure he hadn't woken her or that she wasn't awake and about to shriek.

"Don't worry about Lucy," Danica said. "If she wakes up, I've got her."

He also appreciated that. Which was funny because he'd actually horned in on her babysitting session.

He struck the ground again and the shovel sank

in. Ford froze, his breath catching. "Oh, man. I just a hit a hole." He looked at Danica, who stared at him wide-eyed, then down at the ground. He shoved out some dirt and dropped to his knees, scooping out more dirt, his knuckles grazing something hard.

Like a metal box.

He reached in and grabbed the edge of it, tilting it until he could finagle it out of the hole on its side. "I can't believe it. I actually found the thing." He stared down at the old fishing tackle box and popped the latch. "Better make sure the diary is actually in here."

Danica wheeled the stroller closer and knelt beside him. He opened the lid. And there in the box was a dark red leather diary, imprinted in gold lettering with the word *Diary* and the year: thirty years ago. Beside it was a bunch of tiny pieces of paper, kind of a pale yellow. Maybe that had been a page Bo Dawson *really* hadn't liked.

Ford closed the lid and shoveled the dirt back in the hole, trying to fill it best he could and then packing it all down hard. They walked back to the gate, Ford returning the shovel to the gatehouse and then meeting Danica by her car. He finally did the transfer of the car seat, got Lucy settled with only the slightest stir, and they both got in.

"Wow," she said.

"Yeah."

"Look, if you want some privacy right now, I can drop you home. We don't need to work on the matchmaking forms tonight."

He wasn't sure if he wanted to be alone with the thing, frankly. "I know it seems crazy, but it took me a long time to come around to even look for the thing. Kept me away from Bear Ridge knowing it was here. I don't know that I'm ready to jump in and actually read it. For now it's enough to know I have it."

"I totally understand that," she said, covering his hand with hers.

He wanted to reach for her so badly, just wrap his arms around her and hold on. But instead he buckled his seat belt.

"Ready?" she asked, turning the ignition.

He really didn't know.

## Chapter Eight

Danica glanced at Ford as they arrived at his farmhouse just a few blocks past the center of the town. He'd been quiet on the ride over—understandable—and though he'd shut off the ignition, he didn't otherwise move.

Danica turned toward him. "Like you said, you don't have to read the diary. Right away, anyway. Or ever. You have it, at least."

He nodded, but stared out the window. "For the past year and a half I think I was relieved every time I didn't find it. Who knows what that thing says? My father wasn't easy to offend, so it had to be something bad."

She put her hand on his forearm, and he turned to look at her. She'd never seen him like this. Vulnerable. Unsure. Off balance. If only she could put her arms around him. A *friend* could do that, but there was just too much in the air between them to pretend they were just friends.

"Well, let's get this very cute baby to bed," he said. "I made a nursery in one of the bedrooms so I'd always have space for my little relatives. Oh, wait, you know that. You were at my housewarming party." He glanced at her, and clearly even the thought of their day and night together couldn't lift his heavy heart. He cleared his throat. "Anyway, Lucy will want for nothing."

He turned to smile at Lucy, but she was rear-facing, and all they both got was a view of the back of the car seat. His shoulders slumped.

*I want to give you everything*, she thought out of nowhere. *You're so thoughtful and good. So damned gorgeous. I want you to have everything you want.*

She suddenly pictured herself giving a gentle push to that tire swing hanging off the oak tree in the front yard, their little one belly down, arms and legs dangling, happy squeals and shouts of "higher, faster" called at her. Ford was right there, too, giving a monster push, then he scooped their child from the swing and put him on his shoulders—ah, it was a boy—and they took a walk down to the creek in the backyard to look for frogs.

The images filled her heart instead of freezing it. Made her feel…tingly.

*It's probably the right husband who'll turn your head and heart around about the idea of having children*, she remembered Molly saying when Danica had finally opened up to her about her ambivalence about having kids. *Of course, it's totally possible that you just don't want kids and that's absolutely fine. But your Mr. Right will be the one who makes everything feel right, Danica. Kids in your future or no kids.*

Anyway, the feeling and those images of herself as a mother and Ford as the father were brand-new and tentative, and she'd keep it to herself while it blossomed…or didn't. Maybe she was reacting to Ford being all vulnerable in front of her. Or maybe something inside her was beginning to shift. Because of Ford. Because of Candace being home. Because of helping care for her baby niece.

Ford took Lucy from her car seat and handed her to Danica, the baby stirring slightly. Danica gently caressed her back and slightly rocked her, and she immediately settled down. *Stop trying to make this easy for me*, she thought with a smile.

*I'm still scared to death about the idea of being a mother. But I can imagine it.* And that was something she'd never experienced before. With her ex-husband, she *hadn't* been able to imagine it.

As they headed up the blue stone walkway, they passed the tire swing and she felt the tiniest thrill. Danica had a secret; for once, a secret that was hers alone and felt good to have and keep.

The moment Danica came through the door, she was hit by memories. She'd loved this house from the moment it had come on the market, and when she'd met Ford and heard what he was looking for in a home, she knew this was the one. The three acres of land, the pristine white farmhouse with its wraparound porch, managing to seem ancient and modern at the same time, the woods and creek at the far end of the backyard. Inside was gorgeous, too. A big country kitchen with state-of-the-art appliances, a huge living room with a dark-wood-beamed ceiling and a river rock fireplace that practically took up an entire wall. When she'd been his Realtor, he'd only mentioned that he was single now but wanted a house in case he "ever did get himself married," and she'd been charmed by that. She'd felt included, crazy as that sounded, as if someone felt the same way she did—single, but you never knew what the future held. But then the night of his housewarming party, he seemed to know exactly what he wanted his future to hold. He'd only been back in Bear Ridge a short time then, but maybe the town and his family had worked their magic on him.

Maybe he'd work his magic on her and she'd want the unexpected, too. That little picture she'd had just a little while ago in his car certainly made it seem possible.

He took the car seat from her to carry Lucy upstairs, and she trailed behind him. In the nursery, he held the carrier up for her to unclick the harness, and she took out the baby, then set her down gently. She stirred again, her arm quivering a bit before shooting up near her head. Success.

"Hey, I'm getting pretty good at this," she said with a smile. She stared down at beautiful Lucy, all those curls like her mommy's, and the slightest pitter-patter thrummed in her chest. "My sister told me that when I was little, like sevenish, she remembered me saying I was going to have eight kids and give them all names starting with *M* after my new best friend Molly. I can't remember that at all. Isn't that strange?"

He tilted his head. "Not strange, actually. There's a lot of my childhood I've forgotten. Noah and Daisy will start up a 'remember when' and I don't—even though I say I was definitely there. From the innocuous to the rough."

She bit her lip and nodded. "Well, when I was seven, I also wanted to be a princess and an astronaut and a puppy, so I won't put too much stock in saying I wanted eight kids." She tried to add a laugh, but it wouldn't come out. If that want had been in her once, maybe her upbringing, the coldness, the estrangement of aunts and grandfathers who'd simply walked out decades ago had seeped into her bones and cells, and the whole concept of family had felt like something scary instead of warm and comforting. Maybe that was why she couldn't remember about the eight kids. Candace probably didn't remember some old childhood dreams of her own, either.

"Lucy is one lucky little girl," Danica whispered. "Best mom in the world. And since Molly and your brother are so hot and heavy, it looks like she might soon get an amazing stepdaddy too."

"They do seem very serious," Ford said. "It's wild how the family you end up with can dictate your whole life. Or try to. Mine had a hold over me for far too long."

Did hers? How could she be sure her upbringing was the reason behind her disinterest in having kids? Didn't some women just not want children?

Not everything had to be rooted in how a person was raised.

"I think mine has, too," she said. "I don't know. Big questions that I don't love thinking about."

"I know how that goes. Story of my life. It's why I'm gonna keep that diary in the box forever probably. Does that sound nuts?"

"It's hard to say whether you should read it or not. On one hand, it's your mother's private journal. Her thoughts. It was wrong of your father to read it, let alone hide it from her. But both your parents are gone and you do have questions about what broke up their marriage, what got your dad upset enough to bury the diary. Maybe you're right that reading it will bring some closure."

"If not exactly peace," he said.

She nodded. "Or maybe…"

"Or maybe I'll get the opposite of peace and therefore no closure."

She let out a sigh. "Easier question is—are you hungry? I can root around your kitchen, which I still know like the back of my hand, and whip us up something."

"I had two burgers and a hot dog and a ton of pasta salad. I'm done eating for days."

"I'm pretty full, too," she said. "How about coffee?"

He nodded. "I'm on it. And let's make some matches. I need to clear my head, think about something other than the diary." He got up and headed into the kitchen. She grabbed her folder of matchmaking request forms that she'd brought in from the car and sat back down on the couch.

By the time he returned with two cups of coffee on a tray with cream and sugar, she'd found two matches for Stella Winkler, who worked in the bakery, one for a rancher named Henry Cowler, and three for Ethan Gawlings, a sixty-four-year-old retired widower looking for a movie companion.

"I'm on a roll," she said, looking up at Ford as he set down the tray. "Sixty-three-year-old Lila Gomez has been widowed for five years and is finally ready to go on a first date since she was twenty and married her first love. I found her one match, and I'm hoping for a second in case Ethan Gawlings doesn't work out."

Ford sat down and slid the tray over to her. "Hey, I know Ethan. He started an animal sanctuary that his son and daughter-in-law now run. He took in injured or unwanted farm animals and let them live out their golden years in peace."

"That's very sweet," Danica said, adding cream and sugar to her mug.

Ford added cream to his own mug and took a

long sip. "Let's get to it." He opened his folder and got busy, but Danica would catch him staring out the window time and again. He did manage to find four matches in an hour—Danica had found matches, and multiples in many cases, for fifteen. By the time Molly and Zeke arrived to pick up Lucy, who had slept like a champ the entire time, Ford seemed weary, like the weight of Wyoming was on his shoulders.

After Molly and Zeke left with Lucy, Danica packed up her folder, including the matches Ford had made, and headed to the door.

"If you need an ear, mine's available," she said.

"I appreciate that." He opened the door, the pink-and-orange setting sun so beautiful in the distance.

She didn't want to go. She wanted to give him privacy with his thoughts, to mull over what he wanted to do about the diary, but she would have to force herself out the door. "Well, bye."

"I'll text you about another matchmaking night," he said, and then suddenly reached out his hand.

She took it and wrapped her arms around him, and he pulled her close.

Danica closed her eyes, reveling in the feel of him against her, his strong chest, the scent of his soap and shampoo. She glanced up at him, and he touched her face, and then suddenly they were kissing, his arms tightening around her, one hand winding its way in her hair. Her legs were all wobbly.

"I didn't intend on that," he said. But he didn't step back.

"Me neither." *And I want more.*

But suddenly the wobbly got to her head, and she was so unsure of what was going on with them, whether this was playing with fire. It felt like it.

"I'd better get going," she said. "See you soon."

"Night, Danica."

She stepped out into the sunset, knowing she was leaving her heart behind.

If Danica hadn't left when she had, Ford would have picked her up, kicked the door shut with his foot and carried her upstairs to his bed. Good thing she was thinking straight because he sure wasn't. The combination of her nearness, how understanding she'd been of his mood, that she'd been there when he'd found the diary, and how damned attracted he was to her had had a powerful grip on him. What he would give for a repeat of two months ago, though this time without any conversation to send her fleeing, so he could be with her, lose himself, forget. But she *had* left, wisely.

After a long, hot shower, he headed down to the kitchen for yet another mug of strong coffee, the tackle box in front of him on the table, lid open, the diary and its ripped-up page right there. "What the hell do you say?" He asked it aloud, then realized he was losing it and grabbed his phone to punch in a group text to his siblings.

Found the diary when I was leaving the ranch today. Had a lightbulb moment that Dad might have buried it right outside the gates to "rid the property of it." I was right. Haven't cracked it open. Might not.

*Ping.* Daisy: Holy cannoli, Ford. You okay? I can come over with the really good Hungarian mushroom soup I just made.

*Ping.* Rex: Damn. You gonna read it? I don't know if I would.

*Ping.* Axel: What Rex said.

*Ping.* Zeke: Read the first couple of lines, then decide if you can KEEP reading. Good luck, bro.

*Ping.* Daisy: I like Zeke's advice.

*Ping.* Noah: What Daisy said. Otherwise it'll eat you alive and you won't be able to think of anything else.

*Ping.* Rex: Let us know when you want to talk.

He texted back: Will do. Thanks, guys. I'll take a rain check on that soup, Daisy.

He put down the phone, took another slug of coffee and picked up the diary. It didn't burn his hands or make him explode like he almost thought it would.

He *could* read the first few lines. Just to see.

Thirty years old. He shook his head, trying to remember back to being four, but everything was a jumble. He flipped through the diary without actually reading anything. He could see his mother's handwriting, sometimes blue ink, sometimes black, pencil now and again. Toward the end there was a page ripped out jaggedly. He glanced in the box and the matching ripped-up pieces. Whatever had been on that page had sent Bo Dawson into a tailspin.

*Okay*, he thought, finishing the coffee. *Here goes everything.* He opened the diary to the first page. It wasn't January 1, as most diaries began; the page was dated May 2. His mother wrote about confiding her troubles to a friend, who'd suggested she get it out in a journal. Ellen Dawson had never kept a diary and wanted one, the old-fashioned kind with a lock and key, but she'd only found this one in three colors at the drugstore and so had bought it.

Maybe she'd go on about the different colors available. What else she'd bought in the drugstore. If she'd run into a neighbor. He'd like to read all that everyday stuff. Not what was surely about to follow.

Ford was pretty sure he knew what his mother's troubles had been. An alcoholic husband with a wandering eye who was slowly destroying the ranch. That was common knowledge. The next paragraph was about two of the cows going missing, and Bo saying they'd gone off in the direction of Clover Mountain. *He's drunk right now. Though when is he not?* she'd written. *How could the cows have wandered off out of sight without either the foreman or their two last ranch hands noticing? I have a terrible feeling that Bo is sneaking the animals off the ranch for drinking and gambling money. I hate thinking this way—this ranch is our future, our son's future, and Bo's family legacy. But come on. Last week, two goats mysteriously disappeared. Now two huge cows.*

There were pages of this kind of thing. Ford sat at the table, his shoulders relaxing a bit. This wasn't anything new or unexpected. He could deal

with this. Zeke's advice, siblings-approved, to read
the first page and see if he could go on was solid.

Of course he wasn't anywhere near the ripped-
out page. If things were starting to get bad for his
mother on page one, things had to be plenty bad
that close to the nearly full diary.

He didn't have to read far.

*May 8. I saw Bo kissing a woman—and I'm
talking tongue down the throat, hand in the
bleached blond curls—just down the little alley
between the pizza place and the office building.
For all that bastard knew I could have been driving past with our son. He knows I like to go into
town at least once a day. Thank God I was alone.
I pulled over to the side of the road and cried hard
for a good fifteen minutes. What am I going to do?
This isn't how it was supposed to be. I want better
for myself, and I want everything for Ford. What
the hell am I gonna do?*

Ford's shoulders were back to tense, bunched-
up rocks again.

*Oh, Mom*, he thought, his heart breaking for
her. She'd been a good mother, kind, loving, nur-
turing. But as a divorced parent with an ex who
drank and gambled his depleting income away,
she'd had to work long hours to make ends meet.
She'd been a typist for two lawyers in town, and

they'd encouraged her to get her paralegal certificate, which meant reluctantly dropping him at his negligent dad's for her night classes three times a week. But Bo had remarried the minute the ink had dried on their divorce papers, a baby already on the way—Axel. Ford had liked his stepmother, but his mother had tried to warn her, and Diana Dawson, who was apparently madly in love with her husband, didn't want to hear it. The two women barely got along. Once his mother had become a paralegal, Bo had only seen his dad every other weekend for a while.

He'd admired his mother. And to read of her heartbreak at the hands of his father...

He shut the diary, dumped it in the box and closed the lid, stalking around the kitchen. Maybe he'd read enough. Drinking, gambling, cheating, his mother sobbing on the side of the road in her car. Broke, with a young son to raise.

Every reason he'd ever had for not wanting to marry or have kids came surging back into his cells. Danica had the right idea. He'd had the right idea until so much time away from his old memories had made him forget, made him soft.

Six kids? No. He was just fine on his own,

where no one got hurt, no one got disappointed, and no one cried on the side of the road because of him.

## Chapter Nine

On Sunday morning, 5:07 a.m., Danica yawned and hurried into Brandy's nursery so that the little screecher wouldn't wake up her mother. Candace had come home late, and Danica had poked her head out of her room to check in. Her sister's moony smile told her she'd had a wonderful time on her long date with Jasper.

Danica dashed over to the crib, Brandy letting out sharp little cries and waving her fists. She lifted the baby out, Brandy liking that and immediately piping down, her big blue eyes on Danica. "You are such a marvel," Danica whispered. "Look at you. A tiny human, the entire world open before you, everything to learn, everything to know."

She held Brandy against her for a moment, relishing the warm, solid weight of her in her arms. She loved the baby shampoo scent, her soft fleece yellow-and-white footie pj's with the little brown buffalos charging across the yellow stripes. "Let's get you changed and into a cute little outfit, then we'll go have breakfast. Sound good?"

Brandy reached up and grabbed the side of Danica's jaw.

Danica laughed. "Guess it does!"

After getting Brandy changed, Danica held the baby while she poked through the baby's clothes. She gasped happily at the sight of a white fleece shirt, "Awesome Niece" embroidered with tiny blue stars across the front. Beneath it were the matching little fleece stretchy pants. And in the drawer with the diapers and socks, Danica found the collection of socks and baby booties she'd sent, a package arriving for her sister just about every month since Brandy was born. Candace might not have been open to her sister visiting, but that didn't mean Danica couldn't show she cared, that she was thinking of her sister and niece. She changed Brandy into the cute outfit, then snuggled her against her chest and kissed the top of her head.

"Let's go have breakfast, cutie. And then I need at least two cups of coffee."

As she gave Brandy's soft cheek a gentle caress, she was gripped by *I want*.

There it was again. I want.

A baby? A Brandy of her own?

She grinned and gave a little spin, holding Brandy in the air. "What have you done to me, baby girl? Suddenly I'm thinking I want my own little one?"

A warm burst of gooey something spread in her chest, and she cuddled Brandy against her and then headed downstairs, wondering if the feeling would follow her around. It did.

Maybe it's Ford, she thought. Like Molly said— maybe when you fall for someone for all the right reasons, you stop being scared for the wrong reasons.

She really had no idea and wasn't interested in analyzing it too closely. For now, that these pops of feeling, of want, of what seemed to be maternal urges were happening inside her was enough. She thought back to picturing herself and Ford swinging their toddler on the tire in his yard.

*Maybe I'm changing, Brandy,* she thought as she put the baby in the playpen in the kitchen while she made up a bottle. A few minutes later, she sat down at the kitchen table with the beautiful view of spring flowers she'd spent a fortune on for the porch, Brandy nestled in her arms as she took her bottle. *Maybe everything that's had a grip on me the past year since my divorce is finally letting go.*

All she knew for sure was that it felt good. And that she couldn't wait to see Ford again.

Maybe they could be a perfect match, after all.

Ford knelt in front of the Lexus's slashed rear tires and took some photos with his phone, zooming in on the note that was stabbed into the slashed area with a long nail: LOL. It was almost five in the afternoon on Sunday, and Ford was on his sixth revenge-crime of the day. Dating and breakups were bringing out the worst in residents of Bear Ridge. His brother Rex had taken the rookie up and down the block and across the street to look for evidence, whether fast getaway tire tracks, a receipt that had dropped out of a pocket, chewed gum, a cigarette butt, even a wallet or cell phone. Some bad guys weren't very bright and dropped their IDs.

"I want whoever did this prosecuted to the full extent of the law!" Ethan Stutley all but shouted, pointing at the tires. Tall and imposing, but neither taller nor more imposing than Ford at six-two and solid muscle, Ethan was in his early forties with white-blond hair and ice-blue eyes. He wore square silver-framed glasses and a business suit. Ethan was a CPA with his own shingle on Main Street. Ford knew him from the town basketball league. Ethan got many fouls.

"Understood," Ford said. "Given that your and your neighbor's video camera didn't pick up the perpetrator's face or any identifying details, this won't be an easy case to solve. My rookie has dusted for prints, so we'll see if anything pops up there. But I'll tell you, Ethan. People who pull this kind of crap will likely make themselves known. Brag about it to someone who gossips, or he or she will try to do something else and be caught in the act. They'll think they've gotten away with this and it won't be enough."

Ethan nodded, calming down some. "I'm installing another camera from the front yard, so hopefully that'll catch the scumbucket." He extended his hand. "Thanks for coming out, Ford. Appreciate it."

Ford shook his hand. "I'll let you know if the fingerprints are a match."

Unfortunately for Ethan, he wasn't very well liked around town. He was a complainer, called the cops on dogs that barked too long or about teens congregating near his house. He told loud talkers on cell phones to shut the hell up already, though some people appreciated that he did that. He was divorced and had filled out a matchmaking profile—before Ford had joined the team—and had been doing a lot of dating. For the past week he'd been seeing one woman, and Ford wouldn't be surprised if someone didn't like that, for reasons myriad and varied.

As Ethan headed inside his house, Rex and the rookie were back. The rookie carried an evidence bag containing a gross wad of gum.

"We found only this," Dylan said.

Ford nodded. "Like I told Ethan, the perp will probably make another move and mess up and get caught. We'll get him eventually."

"These revenge calls are driving me nuts," Rex said, taking off his officer's hat and running a hand through his dark hair. "The relationship didn't work out. Move on, people."

"Yoo-hoo, officers!"

Ford turned to see Mayor Abbott calling out her open car window as she was driving toward them. She pulled against the curb and came rushing over, a flurry of fast activity, as always.

"A favor, if I may?" she asked, looking at all three of them but focusing on Ford. Uh-oh.

"What can we do for you, Pauline?" Ford asked,

"Well, I heard about Ethan Stutley's slashed tires," she said, then leaned closer and added, "though that might not be matchmaking-dating related at all. I mean, the man makes enemies while waiting for his coffee order at Java Joe's." She shook her head. "And there were two other incidents this morning, weren't there? Can you believe someone untied Jennifer Sabu's French bulldog from the post in front of the bakery and just left the leash on the sidewalk? Someone wanted that dog to run away! He could have been hit by a car." She shook her head again.

Luckily, Banjo had stayed put, refusing to budge until he saw his owner walk out of the bakery.

"So I was thinking," the mayor continued. "I'm going to announce that these crimes will not be tolerated and that our matchmaking initiative is being put to an end because of a few bad apples. Our speed dating event will be canceled unless, between now and next week, there is not a single crime related to someone being pissed off about someone dating someone else."

"Sounds good to me," Ford said, Rex and rookie Dylan nodding.

"And about that favor," she said. "I'd like you to give a talk to the entire town. An actual emergency town meeting to discuss what's going on. People like and respect you, Ford. You're the law *and* you're single. You're right out there with the daters, as far as they know. I think you'll have more of an impact than me or the chief."

Ford mulled it over for a second. "I don't know that a lecture on right and wrong is going to get through to the perpetrators, though."

"Agreed. Your uniform will speak to and for the right and wrong. You want to talk about why the revenge crimes should end, why those committing the acts need to shift their mindset. There's someone for everyone in Bear Ridge, and no one needs to get so upset over an ex dating someone new that they unleash someone's dog on a post."

Ah. He got it. She wanted him to come from the human angle. The heart.

"I think it's a great idea," Rex said. "We should probably incentivize people to show up—the ones who need to listen most, I mean."

"Oh, I thought of that," Pauline said. "Trust me, I think of everything."

She wasn't kidding. Pauline Abbott was a one-woman powerhouse, and she'd likely one day be governor of Wyoming.

"We'll advertise through word of mouth and on social media that any Bear Ridge resident who attends the talk will receive free admittance to the speed dating event, which otherwise will be twenty-five dollars. If we're forced to cancel that event, the offer is null and void."

"Smart deal," Ford said. "The perpetrators are most likely still single and will want to attend the speed dating event—and for free." Though, of course, there was one eighty-four-year-old wedding-dress thief who broke that mold.

"This Thursday at seven at the town hall?" she asked. "I think we'll have around two hundred attendees. We'll use the large meeting room."

"I'll be there and prepared," he said.

"Knew I could count on you, Detective," she said, patting his arm. She nodded at Rex and Dylan and then dashed back to her car.

The three drove back to the PD, Dylan rushing in to attend a training session with the chief.

"So did you read any of the diary?" Rex asked, turning to glance at Ford as they both got out of his vehicle.

"I read enough to feel like hell," Ford said. "And I only got two pages in."

"Oh, damn. Sorry. Though I guess that was expected, given that Dad stole the diary and buried it."

Ford nodded. "He tore out the most offending

page and dropped the tiny bits of ripped-up page in the tackle box with the diary. So I won't know what that says. Unless maybe there's some context in the pages leading up to it."

"You gonna bother?" Rex asked. "I don't know if I would. Could just make you more unsettled."

"Well, the worst thing I can find out is that I'm not a Dawson, right? That my mother had an affair and I'm someone else's kid, which would open up another whole stinking can of worms. But I look just like the rest of you—and we all got Dad's strong coloring and features."

"Good point. You do have my same good looks."

Ford gave his brother a playful punch on the arm. "So what then? What could she have written that had him so upset he'd bury the thing? I can't come up with much that seems bad enough. I mean, what could possibly offend Bo Dawson to that degree?"

"Yeah, I know what you mean. He was hard to upset unless you got in the way of his booze or persisted in calling him out on it. He'd take that for a good long time before he'd lash out."

"Well, given that this is all in my head now, I have to deal with it instead of just trying to forget about it."

"I'm with you on dealing, Ford. The ostrich approach always backfires."

Yeah, it did.

His phone pinged with a text, and Rex clapped a hand on his shoulder. "I'll head in. Here if you need me. We all are."

"I know. And thanks."

He watched his brother walk into the PD, grateful for all the Dawsons, then looked down at his phone. Danica.

Team Matchmakers are on hiatus? Just when I was getting the hang of it.

He texted back: Hopefully we'll be back up and running soon. The mayor asked me to give the town a heart to heart to try to get the vengefully scored to change their ways.

If anyone can, it's you. After all, you're helping turn me around...

He stared at that last text, wondering what she meant.

In fact, I'd like to take you out on a date, Ford Dawson. I hear the steaks at the Bear Ridge Inn are incredible...

He swallowed. Oh, hell. By "helping turn me around," was she talking about wanting a family? Why else would she suddenly ask him out on a date when they were not dating because she didn't want kids and he did.

Except now he had no interest in marriage or family.

Again, oh, hell.

How was he going to respond to this?

## Chapter Ten

While her sister poked around Danica's closet for "the perfect dress to wear for her date with the perfect man" that night, Danica kept staring at her phone, waiting for Ford's response.

Nothing.

Five minutes later, still nothing.

By the time Candace had found a dress, shoes, accessories, and had tried everything on, there was still nothing but radio silence from the detective.

Danica's heart dropped. Maybe she'd been too cryptic with the "you're helping turn me around." Was it possible he didn't know what she meant even after asking him out on a date? He knew why they *weren't* dating. So he had to know what she'd been referring to.

She'd felt so vulnerable typing that, putting it out there, especially to the man himself. The thought of her feeling maternal stirrings was such a big deal to Danica and she'd been so sure he'd respond with a "pick you up at 7" or "I'm coming over right now" and a heart emoji—something— but the moments were ticking by and her phone screen was glaringly empty.

She let out a sigh.

"Uh-oh," Candace said, stopping half-turned in the full-length mirror on her closet door. "What's that sigh about? You're not mad about me borrow-ing this incredible dress, are you?"

"No, of course not. And it looks amazing on you. The shoes, too."

Candace tilted her head. "Then what's wrong?"

"I asked Ford out—granted, via text—and he hasn't responded." They weren't even dating and it was hell already.

"Danica, you know that man is crazy about you. I know it and I just got here. If he didn't respond, it's because he's chasing down a suspect or got called into a meeting. Come on."

Maybe. "Or he's not interested in me that way anymore."

"Look at you," Candace said, moving out of the way of the mirror so that Danica could see her reflection from the bed. "You're stunning. Easily the most beautiful woman in this town."

Danica looked at herself. Hair in a messy bun high on her head so her niece's little hands couldn't yank. No makeup. A long-sleeved T-shirt and yoga pants. The old Danica would have looked like this only to go jogging or to deep clean her kitchen. She liked this new Danica, though. Natural. The real her. She'd had no idea she'd been hiding behind two hours of makeup application and hair styling until she went bare. Exposed. Her look had become her identity instead of her personality and character.

Danica shook her head. "Looks might lure someone, but like Mom used to say, pretty is as pretty does. It's far from important. Connecting with someone is about what's in here," she said, touching her chest. "It's about chemistry."

"Ugh, I hated when Mom or Dad would say that to me. They'd both say it with such disdain whenever we made the slightest misstep."

Danica remembered. "I used to be so focused on my appearance. And, yeah, for work I'll still dress up and go in polished because I'm still that woman, too. But I like this natural look. It feels right. It feels like I'm shedding something and becoming who I really am. Does that sound all new agey?"

"No. I get it."

"I used to think all I had was my looks. But between you being here and my getting to bond with Brandy, I've discovered how much family—you guys—really mean to me. I was so afraid of the word *family* for so long. And now I'm not. To the point that I think I can see having a baby of my own, Candace."

Her sister gasped and rushed over to her, squeezing her into a hug. "That's really wonderful. Neither of us is being held to old crud or patterns or beliefs that have nothing to do with who we want to be."

"Yeah!" Danica said. "Team Dunbar—*our* way, *our* version!"

The doorbell rang, and Candace grinned. "There's my hot date. We'll talk tomorrow over breakfast?"

Danica nodded. "Have a great time. You look amazing."

Candace grinned, slipped on Danica's lightweight shiny black trench coat and left in a haze of perfume-scented air.

Danica walked over to the mirror and peered at herself. "Who *we* want to be is right. I decide that. Not my parents or how I was raised or old fears. I decide."

*Ping.*

She eyed her phone on her bed. Forty-five minutes after her text, he'd finally responded?

She grabbed the phone.

He'd texted: Free right now to talk?

Oh, phooey. This didn't sound good.

Sure. Babysitting but Brandy is asleep. Come on over.

She went downstairs to pace. And wait.

Ford pulled into Danica's driveway, cutting the engine but not moving. He didn't want to deal with this at all, didn't want to talk to her about this, didn't want to disappoint her, hurt her. Once again, they were on different pages.

He forced himself out of the car and knocked on the door.

When she opened it, as usual the sight of her stole his breath for a moment.

"So our timing is once again all wrong?" she asked.

He loved this about her. Getting right to it, putting it out there. Asking the question.

He stepped inside, shutting the door behind

him, and followed her into the living room. She sat on the edge of the sofa, so he stood, hands jammed in his pockets. "Yeah," he finally said. "Yesterday, I would have jumped at the chance to take you out for an amazing night. And now. Everything's just…" He trailed off, not sure what the right term was. *Dead inside? Festering?*

She tilted her head and looked at him. "Just…"

"I thought I'd changed, but it turns out I haven't. Marriage, kids—" He shook his head. "Not in my future. I need to just be on my own, like I've always been."

Danica stared at him. "What—" She stopped, understanding dawning in her eyes. "Oh, Ford. You read your mother's diary."

"Just a few pages. And trust me, those were enough to remind me how easy it is to rip apart a family, bring people you supposedly care about to their knees. I don't want any part of that."

He moved over to the windows and stared out. "You know how you said everything in you froze when I said I wanted six kids? That's how I feel now. Like everything in me froze when I read those pages."

He turned to look at her. Her expression killed him. Concern, regret, despair, maybe even horror. "There are some great men out there, Danica.

Men looking for everything you are. Match yourself with someone who deserves you."

She seemed about to say something and then didn't, until he started walking to the door and touched the doorknob.

She sprang up. "Ford, I understand why the diary got to you so deeply. Based on what you've told me about your parents' marriage, it must have been terribly heartbreaking to read her words. But I think this is going to be a process—not easy, maybe long—as you work through how you feel about it. It doesn't have to change your dreams for yourself."

"Well, it did," he said. "I need to get going."

She came up to him, standing just an inch away, and brought her hands up to either side of his face. "I care about you, Ford."

He moved his own hands to her face and kissed her so deeply that her legs shook. "I care about you, too. Which is why I'm going now."

And with that, he turned and left, his heart clenching.

Danica spent the next couple days with Candace and Brandy, special time with her sister and niece helping to keep her mind off Ford Dawson, and babysitting duty reinforcing that these new feelings she was having about being a mother were very real. Ford hadn't been in contact, and she'd wanted so badly to hear his voice that she'd forced herself just to give him space by merely sending him a quick text: I'm here for you as a friend, just know that.

He'd texted back: Appreciate that. And ditto. I mean it.

So they were friends. Again. As if she could possibly look at any other man in this town and think of him romantically when she'd fallen in love with Ford Dawson. And she had, of that there was no doubt.

Now, Thursday morning, she was back at her desk at the realty office with a busy day of showings. As she'd gotten ready for work, she'd found herself toning down her usual routine. Her skin care regimen she'd never veer from, but did she need a foundation primer, liquid foundation, powder to set it, then a setting spray? She'd used a tinted moisturizer, a touch of blush, a little mascara and her favorite lipstick. This would have been her look for visiting a farm or waiting to have the oil changed in her car. Now it was her new work look, and she liked it. Her hair, too, hadn't been flat ironed and then curled into beachy waves, artfully arranged and sprayed. She'd just added a little gel, blown it dry and put it into a low ponytail. Now that she'd gotten used to having her hair out of her way, she liked that, too.

Expecting a young couple at nine, she glanced at her watch. Twentysomething firefighter Matthew McHaul had made an appointment last week, noting he and his fiancée were just starting the process of looking for a home together. When the door jangled, she glanced over and saw a couple coming in. She heard the tall blond man tell the receptionist they were there to meet with Danica.

She walked over, hand extended. "Hello, welcome to Bear Ridge Realty. I'm Danica Dunbar. It's a pleasure to meet you both."

Matthew introduced himself, then his fiancée. "And this is Lauren Anderson. As I mentioned on the phone last week, we're recently engaged and looking for a house. But we're not sure what we want."

Danica fussed over Lauren's gorgeous round diamond ring as she shook her hand. "Well, let's sit down and get started on finding out what that is." Once the couple was seated at Danica's desk, coffee in front of them, she got out her tablet and electronic pen. "Let's start with what type of property you're interested in. Bear Ridge has so many different types, from condo developments right here off Main Street to single family homes."

"We're looking for a cozy single family house." She gave a price range and Danica entered it into their file info. "Small but at least three bedrooms—one for us, one for a nursery, and one for a guest room for our parents to stay over when our little guy is born." She patted her belly.

"Oh!" Danica said. "Are congratulations in order?"

Matthew grinned and nodded. "Due in November."

"Congratulations!" Danica said. *You are so lucky*, she wanted to say.

And that was a first. She'd never gotten envious about someone announcing a pregnancy before. But as Lauren told a sweet story about how every first baby in their family was a girl and that was how they knew they were having a boy, because they both marched to their own drummers, Danica was aware of how happily jealous she was. *I want to be pregnant and planning the rest of my life with the man I love*, she thought. *Buying a house that's just right for us.*

"I know four off the top of my head that you might love," Danica said. "Within your price range. A couple don't have updated kitchens but they do have tons of charm and character. Let's see those four and go from there. Maybe you'll find your dream home today. Or maybe you'll discover you want more this and less that, less this and more that."

"I'm so excited!" Lauren said, standing up.

Matthew grinned at her and took her hand.

*I want what you have*, Danica thought again. And I didn't get all the way to this point so that Ford Dawson could do his own one-eighty—for reasons that had and would continue to make him miserable. He was her dream man and if she wanted a future with him, she'd have to help him see he could have it all—the family he'd discovered he wanted *and* peace with his past.

The thing was, Danica had come to this point organically, and Ford would have to, as well. Talking wasn't the way. *Showing* was. And showing was what Danica Dunbar did best.

# *Chapter Eleven*

Mayor Abbott had been right about the large number of attendees for Ford's talk about the "vengeance crimes" Thursday night at the town hall. Promised free admittance to the speed dating event—if good behavior would allow it to be held—222 singles had crowded into the large conference room. Lemonade and doughnut holes, made by the Bear Ridge Cares Society, in abundance on a back table as people came in, were now almost gone. He didn't love the idea of the perpetrators, particularly of the more serious crimes, enjoying refreshments on his time, but he had a good feeling about this plan working.

Ford stood at the front of the room, microphone in hand, slowly moving from one side to the other and back, making eye contact. He wore his uniform, which was navy blue with silver patches, and his hat, which he'd take off when he got started. He'd spent just about all his spare time the past few days working on what he'd say, going over lines in his head, fine-tuning. It helped keep his mind off the diary, and off Danica and how he'd very likely blindsided her the other day. He felt like hell about that. He'd taken her beautiful, tentative step toward a whole new future and turned his back on her—as a potential partner, anyway. He'd made it clear he would always be her friend. That didn't make him feel better, though.

He glanced at the big analog clock on the wall. A minute till seven o'clock. He'd start on time, knowing that perps either came at the appointed hour or a few minutes late. The door opened and a few people came in. Including Danica. She smiled at him and he found himself giving a tight smile back, which made her smile fade.

Exactly what he didn't want to happen was happening. He was affecting her, causing her grief by just being himself. By being tied in knots over the diary and everything he was, everything his parents had been.

The second hand moved to the twelve. Showtime.

He introduced himself, welcomed the audience, and was about to start talking when the door opened and a few more people came in. He noted Andrew Morton going to the back wall to grab an unfolded chair and make his own last row. A ranch hand. Andrew didn't have a record, but Ford had cited him for "making a disturbance," after a fight almost broke out in front of the one bar in town. Andrew apparently hadn't liked seeing a woman he'd briefly dated leaving with someone else, and they'd had words, but someone had called police before a punch could be thrown. He'd happened to catch Andrew driving a couple times in town and kept an eye on him, but the guy hadn't committed any crimes.

"Dating. Romance. Relationships. Weddings," Ford began. "That's what's supposed to be up in Bear Ridge. Instead, crime is up. Forty-two percent in a month. This is our town. It belongs to all of us. And when someone's tires are slashed, when someone's dog is let loose from a post, when rotten eggs are thrown at someone's car windows, that's against all of us. I'm here to tell you that the revenge crimes have to stop."

He glanced around, taking in the nods and mur-

murings, and a few shouts of "That's right. You tell 'em, Detective Dawson."

"Look, I'm a single guy," he continued. "I know dating can be rough. And I know firsthand that getting dumped hurts. I know how hard it is to see someone you may still have feelings for with someone new. One of the reasons why I left Casper two months ago to move back to my hometown and join the police force was because a relationship fell apart. So, yeah, I know how it feels. But I also know that when you're down-and-out over something not working out, the answer isn't lashing out at either the person who hurt you or a new person in their life. That's about revenge. But that's unfair. How many of you in this room have broken up with someone because it just wasn't working out, didn't feel right, wasn't moving forward, didn't make you happy, or yes, because you met someone else and wanted to pursue a relationship with that person? How many?"

Just about every hand went up. Including Andrew Morton's. Including Ford's. And Danica's.

"Exactly," he said. "We've all been the ones to end a relationship. And we've all had it done to us. So if you're upset, if you're thinking, I know what will make me better—I'm going to throw a brick through my ex's window—I'm asking you not to.

I'm asking you to let it go, let that person go. And use your energy to find the right person. That's what it's about. That's what we all want. It's what this whole matchmaking initiative is about, it's what the speed dating event is about—if we can still hold it. If there's even one revenge crime in the next few days, the event will be canceled. I'm asking for all y'alls' support here. And I'm going to offer up mine. If you're feeling out of sorts over a relationship not working out and you could use a friend, someone to talk to in confidence, come see me at the PD or call me on my cell." He read out the number, hoping he wouldn't regret that with prank texts and calls. "Thank you."

There were cheers and claps and whistles.

Mayor Abbott marched up to him, her hands full of folders and bags, as usual. "Excellent, Detective. I knew I could count on you. Just excellent."

He smiled. "I have a good feeling that the speed dating event will go on."

She squeezed his arm and hurried off. The woman probably had meetings until midnight.

Two men, the Lotter brothers, both mechanics, came up to him. "Great talk, Ford," Harry Lotter said. "I'll tell you, I got—" he leaned closer to whisper "—dumped the other day, and then I saw her walking into the Italian place with someone, hand in hand, and I wanted to punch his lights out. But I air punched instead in my truck. It helped."

"Air punching works," Ford said with a nod, and the two sauntered off in the direction of the refreshment table.

He didn't have to look to the left to know that Danica was heading in his direction. The slight scent of her intoxicating perfume had preceded her. He turned, his heart giving a little flip at the sight of her.

"I'm just going to come out and say it, Ford."

Uh-oh.

"I really need your help with the matchmaking forms. Pauline just dropped fifty more on me!"

He was so relieved that she wasn't talking about them that he would have done anything she asked. "Where and when?" he asked. "Happy to help."

"Oh, phew, thanks. Your house? Right now? Unless you have plans. Candace and Jasper have taken over the living room for a movie night, and I don't want to interrupt their canoodling, you know?"

"Canoodling? I think I last heard that term from my grandmother about the goats. But yes, right now works fine. Follow me home."

Ten minutes later, lots of hands shaken, goodbyes said, pats on the back had, they finally left. There were a few low wolf whistles indicating it had been noticed that Ford and Danica left together. He wanted to announce that they weren't together-together, that dating and romance and love led to nothing but heartache, pain and misery.

But, of course, he couldn't. And he didn't really believe that—not for other people. He hadn't even read more of the diary, and he still felt what he'd read so keenly—like the pages, his mother's despair, had turned into sludge that had formed a hard ball in his chest, in his stomach. How could anyone feel good about love, in any context, after reading that?

"My brother Rex had a baking day with his two-year-old son and made pumpkin cheesecake brownies. Want one? And some coffee?"

Danica smiled as she followed Ford into his kitchen. "Aw, that's incredibly sweet to think of Rex at the counter, toddler standing on a chair, both in aprons, covered in flour." She had a sudden image of Ford doing the same with *their* toddler, Danica snapping photos. Yes, she liked the thought of that. "I definitely have to have some of their baking day results."

She stopped short as she recognized the rectangular metal box on the kitchen table. The diary was in there. The diary that had changed everything. Chills slid up her spine.

Clearly Ford caught her noticing it because he grabbed it, but the latch wasn't on and the contents fell out onto the tile floor—the diary and a ripped-up page.

"Oh, boy," Danica said. "I almost feel afraid of the diary, like it might burst into flames or hex me." Okay, probably not the wisest thing to say. But those chills remained at the sight of it on the floor, the tiny pieces of the torn-up page beside it, its secret—maybe thankfully—gone. Whatever it had said was very likely something Ford did *not* need to know.

"Yup. Every time I pick it up I half expect it to burn my hands," he said. "Diaries are heavy stuff. It's where people write their deepest, darkest truths." He knelt down, and put it and the little pieces of paper back in the box.

"I'm sorry about it," she said. "That something meant as a gift is bringing you so much unhappiness."

He stared at her. "A gift? That's not what my father meant it to be."

"He bequeathed it to you for a reason, though. Certainly not to hurt you."

He seemed to be taking that in, thinking about it. He went to the coffeemaker and got busy on that, then opened a container on the counter and put two of the brownies on plates. "I don't know what his intention was. There was no letter with the map. Just the map. Maybe he meant it more as a gesture of goodwill to my mother and wanted me to know that. That he wished he could have returned it to her."

Danica really had no idea. "That is possible. Then maybe you're *not* meant to read it, Ford. Maybe he just wanted you to have possession of it, for your mother, like you just said."

The coffee was ready, so he got out the mugs and poured, adding cream and sugar to hers just as she liked it. He gestured to the table and they sat down, coffee and a brownie in front of each.

He reached into the box and took out the diary, stared at the front and then handed it to her. "Open any page, any random page, and read it. You'll see why the little I read affected me so much—and so badly."

"I don't think I should—"

"Just so you understand, Danica. It's important to me that you do." He put the diary down beside her plate.

"Why?" she asked, her heart hammering.

"Because I feel like you offered me something beautiful, something of yourself, and I let you down. I hate that."

"I didn't ask you to be the father of my child, Ford," she snapped. "I just asked you out on a date."

He lifted up his hands. "Whoa, I know. I just mean…" He stopped and picked up his mug, wrapping his fingers around it.

"I know what you mean. Sorry." She took a quick sip of her coffee and picked up the diary. She'd seen this type of journal so many times in the drugstore and in the bookstore and gift shop in Prairie City. She let out an inward sigh and flipped through, letting her thumb catch on a page. This was toward the end. Probably not the best place to land. "You sure?" she asked him.

He nodded.

She opened the diary a little wider. *Bo has cheated on me countless times. And every time I say I'm going to leave but I never do. Every time I don't, my self-esteem withers. One day, I won't have any regard for myself and I'll just stay, like I don't deserve better. Like Ford doesn't. And he deserves the world.*

Danica's eyes filled with tears, and she put the diary back on the table. "Oh, God."

He nodded. "That's my mother. My *mom*." He was staring at his coffee, looking as down as she clearly was. Danica stood up and went behind his chair, wrapping her arms around his shoulders, her head against his. She felt him take her hands in his, and then he stood up, too, suddenly facing her.

Again he took her face in both his hands and kissed her. She slid her arms around his neck, kissing him back, leaning into him, needing to get closer. When he tightened his arms around her, she felt herself sag. She'd needed this.

"What am I doing?" he whispered. "I'm trying to explain why I can't get involved with you. How'd we end up like this?"

"Because we have strong feelings for each other, Ford," she said, looking right into his eyes, her arms still around his neck. "And there's no denying that or trying to ignore it."

He closed his eyes for a second and took a half step back so that she had to let go of him. Dammit.

"Half the people in that folder you brought over?" he said, gesturing at the matchmaking requests on the table. "They're going to end up crying and heartbroken and divorced. Just like Ellen Dawson."

"So everyone should just give up? Be cynical about the most beautiful thing there is?"

He moved to the counter, leaning against it. "I just know that since I read what little of the diary I did, everything I thought I wanted changed. I now want nothing to do with dating—let alone marriage and kids. I took down the tire swing in the yard, by the way."

She gasped. "You did not."

"I did. The past few days, I'd drive past it out the driveway and it would make me feel like hell."

"Oh, Ford."

He sat back down and took a long slug of his coffee, leaning back and staring up at the ceiling.

"What do you think was on the page your dad ripped up into tiny pieces?" she asked. "What could it have said?"

"I can't even imagine. Not sure I want to. Had to have been bad. It was the whole reason he buried the thing. I thought about asking her friend just so there'd be no loose ends, but that seems like a bad idea. Like I just said, I'm not sure I want to know."

"What friend?"

"A woman named Junie. She and my mom were close when she was married to my dad. When I first got the envelope with the map, I went to talk to her, and she wouldn't tell me anything and made some excuse to get me to leave."

Danica's eyes widened. "Junie? Junie May-wood?"

"You know her?"

"She's family. Estranged family, but family. My mother's cousin. They stopped talking decades ago. I only met her once, at my grandmother's funeral when I was little."

"See? What the hell is the point? Estrangements. Decades without speaking. First cousins?" He shook his head and drained his coffee mug.

"I won't let it rule my life anymore, Ford. The cold front that runs in my family, the grudge holding, the ability to turn away from close relatives. I'm done with it. I wasn't happy in the slightest when my aunt Trudy decided to elope. In the past, I might have let that bother me, thinking that it means she didn't want me or Candace at her wedding. It doesn't mean that at all. It means she wants to elope. My job is to be happy for her. To support her."

"I know how far you've come, Danica. But I feel how I feel."

This was so frustrating. She understood what he was saying. She understood him. She just wished she could help somehow. And not just so they could finally be together, see if this chemistry, their feelings for each other, were solid. She wanted to help him for *his* sake.

"Well, let me just say this. If you want the ultimate closure on this and want to know what that diary page said—" she pointed at the tackle box "—I will drive us over to my mother's cousin's house and ask her, in the name of family, to tell you. Your dad wanted you to have this book. We can't know exactly why. But I know it wasn't to hurt you. I believe that."

He dropped his head back. "I don't know anything, Danica."

She gave him a gentle smile. "I think we'd better eat this amazing brownie. So you can tell that adorable nephew of yours how good his baking skills are, and then we'll jump into the matchmaking forms—if you're still up for helping with that."

"Absolutely," he said. He glanced at his watch. "No calls from Dispatch yet alerting me to crimes of vengeance. That's a good sign."

His smile lit up his face, and she was so happy to see it she almost hugged him. But she didn't.

She could see his shoulders finally relax, along with a muscle in his neck. They started talking about the speech he'd given at the town hall, and he actually laughed a time or two, and so did she. Right now, she had to let all this personal stuff go and give him some space. He was going to need some time.

Either he'd come for her or he wouldn't, and she'd have to accept the possibility that he'd never be hers. Heartbreaking as that sounded.

Danica couldn't sleep. She glanced at her phone on her bedside table—1:28 a.m. She'd already checked on Brandy, hoping the baby might need a little soothing, but her niece was fast asleep. Candace was, too. She'd had a great night with Jasper; apparently they were now officially exclusive and a couple. Her sister had been beaming when she'd told her about their conversation.

And everything was conspiring to keep Danica awake. Wanting what her sister had. Wanting Ford to revert back to wanting six kids. Not that she did, but *that* Ford, who'd dreamed of a house full of children. Wanting him to be at peace with his past and with himself.

She got out of bed, stuffed her feet in her fleecy slippers, and was about to head downstairs to make some herbal tea when she turned right for the door that led to the attic. Her mother had given her two trunks when her parents retired to Arizona, saying that it was full of old stuff of hers and her sister's, and if Danica didn't want it she'd just hurl the trunks into the Dumpster they'd rented to get rid of stuff. Danica had never been very sentimental or pulled by nostalgia, but she liked the idea of there being childhood trunks in the first place. Who knew what was in there, what her mother had kept and why. The idea that Judith Dunbar had kept anything had been a nice surprise, and it had led to Danica feeling more warmly toward her mother when they drove off for their retirement community. Danica's father was a passive, quiet man who'd always deferred to his wife, so her mother loomed larger in her mind when she thought of her upbringing.

She walked up the steep steps into the big space. Not much up here. Seasonal stuff and boxes of Christmas decorations were along one wall. Another area contained Molly's stuff since Molly's house was small and didn't have an attic. Molly was a sentimental saver—there were old posters she couldn't bear to toss and her childhood desk, white with purple knobs on the drawer. Molly was saving it for Lucy.

Danica knelt in front of a trunk and opened it. Her prom dress, wrapped in plastic, greeted her. Danica stared at the slinky black dress she'd been so proud of, had felt so elegant in. There were accordion folders marked Elementary School,

Middle School, and High School. Danica peered through the high school one, full of clippings from the Bear Ridge Buffaloes Student Newspaper. Danica, cheer team co-captain. Voted Best Looking each year. Danica and Troy, Class Couple, also each year. Prom Queen and Prom King. She had photos in her albums in her bookcase and she hadn't looked at them in a while, but the thought of them had long stopped hurting. Time and self-awareness and a little—a lot—of soul-searching did wonders.

In the elementary school file she found what she was looking for. A black-and-white composition notebook with Danica's Dreams written in pink marker in the little box on the front.

She sat down at Molly's desk and opened the book. It was in diary format, each page dated, the first entry in early September, the eve of the first day of second grade. Apparently Danica wrote faithfully every Sunday night at seven-thirty. The book started with how she hoped she'd make a best friend this year and how girls seemed to like her and include her, but she didn't have a best friend like Zoe Parker or Evie Ramez did. The next entry was all about Molly, and Danica grinned as she read about how she'd been paired with Molly in "science lab" where they discovered what happened when you dropped a penny into a beaker full of water. As she flipped the pages, Danica was touched by the sweet, hopeful, curious girl she'd been, happy that she'd found her best friend, a love of the color yellow and wearing pretty clothes, which her mother had been only too happy to indulge her in because she liked her daughters to look elegant.

And then there it was. *May 18. Candace asked me how many kids I want, two like Mommy and Daddy or more or none. I want eight kids. Four girls and four boys. I'll name them all after Molly because she's so awesome. Madeline, Melody, Mia, and Maisy for girls. The boys I'll name Matthew, Michael, Max, and Mason.*

*I want to have a huge family.* Interesting. She closed the notebook and hugged it to her chest. She definitely couldn't imagine having eight kids. Six kids. Even four. One sounded just right now. But Danica had loved having a sister and she knew she'd want to give her child a sibling. So two.

She stood up and closed her eyes, hardly able to believe how much she'd changed in such little time. She'd broken through her own walls. Ford had done it, too, and he could do it again.

"Dani, you up there?"

Candace.

"I'm coming down," she called.

She put away the notebook and climbed down, turning off the light at the bottom of the stairs.

Candace stood peering at her, looking sleepy. "Brandy was crying, so I helped her work out a little gas, got her back to bed, and then realized the attic door was open and a light was on. What were you doing?"

"I was looking for that notebook you told me about—the one I wrote in about wanting eight kids. You were right."

Candace smiled. "Ha, I knew I wasn't making it up. Mom saved that notebook? That's unexpected."

"Right? Maybe there's more to Judith Dunbar than we both ever realized."

"I think there's more to everyone than most people realize," Candace said. "That's something that's really opened my eyes lately."

Danica nodded. She closed the attic door, hugged her sister good-night, and was pretty sure she'd manage to sleep well tonight after all.

## *Chapter Twelve*

Ford had Friday off, but he'd asked the chief to alert him to any crimes of vengeance. Overnight Thursday: zero. He felt damned good about that. And he'd needed good news. He made coffee and stood at his kitchen counter chomping on a bagel and cream cheese, wishing Danica was still sitting at his table. What he'd give to feel her behind him, her arms around his neck, her perfume enveloping him.

And that kiss. He'd thought about that incredible kiss until he'd finally fallen asleep.

His phone buzzed with a text. His brother Zeke.

Hey, I happen to be on your porch. I got news, bro.

Ford walked over to the door and opened it. Zeke stood there in a brown leather jacket and jeans, a wool hat against April's morning chill. "Why not just ring the bell?"

Zeke peered behind him. "Do I know what you're doing? Or who might be over? I don't want to interrupt anything."

"All alone," Ford said. Not liking how that sounded. "So what's the news?"

Zeke came in and shut the door behind him. "Guess what you are?"

"A detective. Thirty-five. Blue eyed. A great guy."

"Not even warm."

Ford raised an eyebrow. "Your favorite brother?"

"One of them," Zeke said, folding his arms across his chest. "Okay, I'll tell you. Invited to a wedding. Tomorrow night at the lodge."

"Sorry, I have plans," Ford said, then grinned and pulled his brother in a hug. "Congratulations. That's some advance notice."

"The ballrooms have been booked for months, but then there was a cancellation—Cole and Trudy ended up eloping. Molly tried to snag it but even with the family in at the Dawson Family Guest Ranch, she was like five minutes too late and someone had already grabbed it. But then *that* person canceled—apparently an ex came back into the picture. So if we want to marry right here in that perfect room with the deck and view of Clover Mountain, we're saying 'I do' tomorrow. I would have group texted, but Molly said no way. I think she's at your friend Danica's right now."

Even the sound of her name made his heart give a little jump. Which his brother must have picked up on.

"So what's going on with you two?" Zeke asked, sitting on the arm of the sofa.

"We're friends. Bad timing. Once again."

"Oh?" he said, then added, "Oh…yeah, I know about that. And not because Molly tells me anything. Because back in February, when I couldn't decide between buying a house like you did or building on the ranch property, I met with Danica at her office and she told me herself that she wasn't sure she wanted kids. We just got to talking."

February seemed forever ago. Zeke had moved back to town from years away in Cheyenne, having gotten as far as he could from home the moment after high school ended, only to be drawn back because Danica Dunbar had gotten divorced. He'd had a wild crush on her in middle school and thought he'd finally have his chance—only to discover that not only had his long-standing crush not grown up with him, but he was madly in love with Danica's best friend, Molly, Zeke's administrative assistant.

"So Danica doesn't know about kids," Zeke said, "and you want eighteen kids or some crazy number."

Ford dropped down on the sofa, head back against the cushions. "Past tense. Wanted. And six. Like us. But that's done with."

"What's done with? Wanting children?"

Ford sighed. "Yeah. I've been reading my mother's diary and it cured me of all that."

He hadn't planned to read any more of it, but last night, when he'd been unable to think of anything but that kiss and of being in bed with Danica that one and only time, he'd grabbed the diary to reinforce his belief that he was meant to be on his own, the lone wolf he'd always been. No one got crushed that way. He'd read about ten entries, anger and tears warring, and one entry had made him literally sick to his stomach. He'd closed the diary after that and stuffed it in a drawer, done with it. Done with it all.

"Bo broke her heart over and over and was responsible for all her misery," Ford said. "She was trying to take care of their young kid—me—while

he was drunk all over town, flirting and humiliat-
ing her, drinking and gambling away their income
so that she had to get a part-time job in addition
to her ranch duties. She'd had to learn some jobs
on the ranch she had no idea how to do because
the cowboys had left—they weren't getting paid—
and it was down to the two of them. One day—I
was five—my mother got kicked in the ribs by a
wild horse Bo had brought in. She had to go to the
clinic because she was in terrible pain. She told
me she slipped and fell and cracked one of her ribs
but she'd be okay. She didn't want me to blame my
dad for a drunken move like trading one of our last
goats for that horse. *She* didn't want to blame him.
She had to call her friend to pick her up, take her
to the clinic and sit with me in the waiting room
because Bo had been sleeping off a bender."

Zeke shook his head. "Damn. Sorry you're dealing with this. Why the hell did Dad leave you that
damned map in the first place? Why would he
want you to find the diary and know all this? What
was the point?"

Ford shrugged. "I can't figure that out."

It really made no sense. His dad was negligent
and a disaster as a parent, but he'd been loving
in his own way to his children. He wouldn't *try*
to hurt Ford. He'd left him the map because he

wanted him to find the diary and understand something. But what?

His mother's friend would know. Not necessarily what drove Bo to leave Ford the diary but what had been on the page his father had torn up into tiny pieces. Something so terrible it warranted his running out of the house with the diary and burying it just beyond the gate. Weeks later, his mother had left with Ford and their suitcases.

Maybe he'd take up Danica on her offer to connect with Junie, his mom's friend—the same one she'd called for help when the horse had kicked her. Her mom's cousin. But the woman hadn't wanted to talk about her old friend a year and a half ago when he first got the map, and Ford didn't expect her to be any more forthcoming now. He wasn't even sure involving Danica's aunt would help, given that she'd been estranged from Danica's mother for decades.

He looked at his brother, whose eyes reflected his concern for Ford, and he appreciated that. *Family* could be a loaded word, but he could count on his siblings and knew it without a moment's hesitation.

"Let's change this cruddy subject to a better one," Ford said. "Your wedding. I'll be there, of course."

"Yeah, you will. Because you're my best man."

Ford's mouth almost dropped open.

"That's what you get for being the oldest and the one we all went to with everything growing up. If it wasn't for you, things would have been much worse for us, Ford. And that's the truth. You weren't much older, but you were standing between us and Dad."

"That means a lot," Ford said. "I'm honored, Zeke. Thanks for asking me."

Zeke nodded and clapped Ford on the shoulder. "We're having a quick rehearsal in the morning. Meet at the lodge at nine. Come hungry—we're having bagels and coffee. I'll even get cinnamon raisin, your favorite."

"I'll be there."

As Zeke left, Ford realized that after tomorrow he'd be the last single Dawson.

Danica was doing her pre-work yoga video when the doorbell rang. Mayor Abbott with even more matchmaking forms? Ford to say he couldn't live another day without her?

She pulled open the door. It was neither of those two. Molly stood on the porch—and not dressed for work in her usual trademark pantsuit and little scarf. Molly had on jeans, boots and a heavy sweater, her wildly crazy curly brown hair loose past her shoulders. She also didn't have her fourteen-month-old daughter with her.

And she was absolutely beaming. Something was definitely up.

"So," Molly began, her eyes all lit up. "Turns out there was a cancellation at the Dawson ranch lodge ballroom for tomorrow night, and Zeke and I grabbed it. We're getting married tomorrow!"

Danica screamed and wrapped her arms around Molly. They both jumped up and down. "How exciting! What do you need? Everything? I'm supposed to work today, but I can call in and we can head to Prairie City and—"

"I don't need a thing, crazy enough. You know how I always said I wanted to wear my grandmother's wedding gown, which my mother also wore? We had it altered right after Zeke proposed so it's all set. Veil, too. And my grandmother surprised me with the most gorgeous satin heels—not too high, of course. I have 'something old'—my aunt Catherine's diamond stud earrings. 'Something new'—the shoes. 'Something borrowed'—the dress. And something blue is where you come in."

"Ooh, what?"

"Remember the necklace you gave me for my

Sweet Sixteen, the delicate gold chain with the three little sapphire stones in the shape of a heart? I'm wearing that. Gotta represent my bestie."

Danica's eyes misted. "I'm so happy for you, Molly."

"I don't need to ask you if you happen to have a maid of honor gown in that closet of yours. You probably have twenty perfect dresses."

Molly had asked Danica to be her maid of honor the day after she'd gotten engaged. Danica couldn't wait to stand up for her friend.

"Any color scheme?" Danica asked.

"Nope. Any color you want. We're keeping the wedding party tiny. Just the maid of honor and best man."

"Who's doing the honors for Zeke?" Danica asked.

"He's asking Ford as we speak."

Danica swallowed. And of course Molly noticed the gulp and whatever weird thing had happened in her expression.

Her best friend narrowed her eyes. "Exactly what is going on with you two?"

"Absolutely nothing, unfortunately," Danica said. "Well, maybe a little something. But Ford's dealing with some stuff. I really hope we get our chance."

"Hey, if Zeke and I worked things out, you and Ford will, too. It takes the Dawson brothers a while to realize they're actually in charge of their own destiny. But they've had a lot to grapple with. Ford'll come around. I know it, Danica."

"From your mouth…" she said with a nod.

"I'd better get going. My mom's at the coffee shop with Lucy and my aunts and grandmother. We'll be heading over to the ballroom to meet Daisy Dawson and make sure everything's set for tomorrow night. Oh—and rehearsal tomorrow morning at nine—there will be bagels and coffee. Does that work? Sorry for the last-minute notice."

"It works fine. I'll see you then. And congrats again, Molly." She gave her bestie a fierce hug.

And as she watched Molly head to her car from the porch, she was very aware of how badly she wanted to be in her friend's satin shoes, marrying a Dawson brother.

Danica was deciding between two dresses for Molly's wedding—pale yellow halter gown or a very pretty mauve with delicate beading at the waist—when Candace came in, a shopping bag in one hand, baby Brandy in the other. Candace had spent the day in Prairie City with her baby girl, attending a "music for babies" class at the library and window shopping. Her sister put down the bag and dropped into the easy chair between the window and the closet, not looking particularly happy.

"Hey, you okay?" Danica asked, giving her niece's baby curls a little caress.

Candace bit her lip and rested her head atop Brandy's. "I'm fine. Just a little zonked."

Her sister wasn't fine, but she wasn't up for saying why yet.

"What's in the bag?" Danica asked. "Ooh, from Best Dressed?" she added, noting the label.

"Oh, yeah. I was ogling a really pretty dress in the window of that shop when Molly texted me and invited me and a plus-one to her wedding tomorrow night. How sweet was that of her to invite me? I do feel like we all grew up together so I was really touched by her text. I've been trying to conserve money till I get a job, but I had to get the dress in the window for the wedding. It's the prettiest shade of periwinkle."

So why did Candace look like she might burst into tears?

"But now I don't even know if Jasper will be attending the wedding with me. We got into a really bad argument. He might not be the one, after all." Her eyes welled with tears.

Danica sat on the bed. "Honey, what happened?"

"Well, I called him about the wedding and he was excited to go—until I mentioned that I would be bringing Brandy, too. He hesitated for way too long and asked why I wouldn't get a babysitter so we could be assured a great time Saturday night. And it made me really focus on the fact that Jasper hasn't wanted to spend any time with Brandy. Granted, she's five months old and not the most interactive, but she's my child. He's always like, 'Oh, I made reservations for tonight at the steakhouse, your sister can babysit till at least one in the morning so we can go out after, right?' He never suggests the three of us spending time together. In fact, the only reason he agreed to have a movie night here the other day was because we'd had a long day hiking and Brandy was already asleep when I suggested he come over."

"Have you talked about why he's reluctant?" Danica asked.

"He just said we've only been seeing each other for a couple weeks and he wants to get to know *me* first, get to know *us* first as a couple before we get more family oriented. I don't know, Danica. It didn't sit right with me. I told him that since babies were not only welcome but encouraged at the wedding, because Molly has a baby of her own who'll be there, that Brandy would be my plus-one and that he could join us or not. He got quiet after that."

"But he's going, right?" Danica asked, not liking how it this was sounding.

"He said he'd really have to think about it." She held Brandy tight against her, rubbing her little back. "Why didn't I see this before? How could I let myself fall crazy in love with a man who isn't interested in spending time with my daughter? Brandy comes first. That's how it is."

Danica was so impressed by her sister. They hadn't been raised to put children first. "Your priorities are definitely in the right place, Candace. And given how he obviously feels about you, I'm sure he just has to get comfortable with the idea of how serious he's getting with a single mother. Maybe that hadn't hit home for him until now."

"What if now that it has, he walks away?"

"I can't see that happening, but if he does do that, then he's just not your guy. But I think you have to give him a little time. God knows I'm trying to do that with Ford, to not necessarily take him at his word because even though it's important to believe what someone tells you, sometimes they need to do some thinking or soul-searching and come to some new conclusions."

"I hope so. For you and me." Brandy let out a yawn and a little shriek. "Let me go get her to bed and I'll show you the dress."

Danica gave her sister an encouraging smile, her heart pinging as Candace left her room. She'd send up a little prayer tonight for both of them that their fervent wishes would come true. But Danica wasn't so sure that either of them was going to get the happily-ever-after they were hoping for.

## Chapter Thirteen

On Saturday morning, Ford poured himself a cup of coffee from the buffet table in the lodge's small ballroom. In attendance at this rehearsal breakfast were the minister, the bride and groom, the bride's parents, her dad—who was giving everyone a gift certificate for two free tacos from his taco truck, Tim's Tasty Tacos in Prairie City—and Danica and Ford, maid of honor and best man. Molly, her mother and Zeke were making last-minute adjustments to the seating arrangements for tonight. Danica and Ford would be seated at the head table, beside each other, and both would give a short speech.

Ford was going to need a little help with that speech. He wasn't feeling particularly solid on everlasting love. Maybe he could find out what Danica had in store for her speech and go from there.

"We keep getting paired," Danica said as she came to the table and poured herself a mug of coffee.

Ford nodded. "It's like the universe is trying to tell us something."

"It definitely is," she said. "Of course, I might be taken by the time you come around."

She was both kidding and not kidding. He could see the glint of humor in her eyes and also the steely resolve.

He wanted to say that he couldn't see coming around, not with the sludge-like gunk in his chest, in his gut, covering his heart. But as he looked at his beautiful Danica, he wanted to have the faith in himself that she did in him, the faith she'd had in herself.

"I guess I'll just have to dance with Brandy tonight," he quipped.

She smiled. "Well, Brandy will definitely be in attendance. Candace's plus-one, we're not so sure about." She explained what was going on.

"Well, he's not wrong," Ford said. "He should get to know Candace better before getting emotionally involved with her baby. They haven't been dating that long."

"She's a package deal, though. There's no Candace without Brandy when it comes to a man in her life."

Ford downed the rest of his coffee. "Nothing wrong with taking it slow, though."

"It's not about slow or fast. It's about accepting that she's a single mother. If he doesn't want to spend time with the two of them, then maybe he's not the guy for her."

"So he has to be all in right away?"

"I didn't say that. But he should be—"

"Boy, do you two bicker like an old married couple," Molly's mother said, pulling Danica into a hug. "I am getting an invitation to your wedding, I hope."

Ford hoped his cheeks weren't as red as Danica's at the moment. She introduced him to Molly's mother, Abby, then her father, Tim, who he talked tacos with to change the conversation. All the conversations. Ford had met Molly's parents at the engagement party Daisy had thrown a couple months ago, but there had been so many Dawsons there that he was sure Abby and Tim couldn't remember who was who.

Luckily the minister called them up to go over

the ceremony, and Danica gave him a lift of her chin and a turn of her heel.

At the altar, he stood beside his brother, and Danica stood beside Molly as the minister went over the vows. He tried not to look at Danica as the words *love, honor, and cherish* were spoken. But as he heard the words *your bride*, he looked straight at her and knew in his heart that she was his bride, that she was the one, that she'd always be. Danica, on the other hand, seemed to be working hard not to catch his gaze. She kept her eyes on the minister or the floor or the red carpet created as an aisle.

Then it was over, Molly's mother talking a mile a minute about adding more flowers. Danica's phone pinged and he watched her read her text, then kiss everyone but him goodbye and hurry out. He wondered what that was about. Since she probably wasn't talking to him, he likely wouldn't find out.

"You like tummy time," Danica cooed to her niece, who was on her belly on a mat on the rug in Danica's living room.

At the end of the rehearsal breakfast, Candace had texted that Jasper wanted to talk and asked if Danica could babysit for a couple hours. This was one time when the two of them would need to really listen to each other, and Danica was happy to watch Brandy.

Besides, she needed a distraction from her thoughts. Danica had started it—getting all quippy with Ford about the universe throwing them together, which did seem very true—and suddenly there had been some uneasy tension in the air between them. Usually they were on the same page about not being on the same page. But this morning she felt only the discord and she hadn't liked it.

And then she'd felt Ford's eyes on her while the minister had gone over the vows. Danica's heart had felt so bruised and poked. She yearned to say those vows, to hear those vows spoken by her own groom, the man she loved.

And the man she loved was Ford Dawson.

"Why is everything so upside down with me and Ford?" she asked the baby, who turned her little head to look at Danica with a big smile, her tiny hands batting at the mat and rug. Danica was sitting beside her, in lotus position, which had taken her months to achieve.

Wait a minute. Danica leaned forward, her heart thumping. What was that in Brandy's hand? Something shiny and silver. A coin? She couldn't be sure.

Danica gasped and lunged for the baby and whatever she'd grabbed, but Brandy brought her hand to her mouth and suddenly the shiny silver object was gone.

A cold sweat broke out across Danica's neck, and she looked all over the rug around Brandy for the shiny silver thing—a dime? She didn't see anything. Oh, God, had the baby swallowed it?

She scooped up the baby and raced out to her car, buckling Brandy into her rear-facing car seat, her hand on the phone to call 911 if Brandy started choking and turning blue, which she didn't. Was it possible she'd swallowed the dime?

Her heart racing, Danica kept one eye on Brandy as she texted her sister, then Ford. Why she'd alerted him, she wasn't sure, but he was the law, and she was in trouble. Scared trouble. She drove to the Bear Ridge Clinic at the tail end of Main Street, a complete mess of tears and fear.

She explained what she was afraid had happened, and the nurse was just finishing asking if Danica was the baby's mother when Candace rushed in with Jasper.

Candace was freaking out, and the nurse took her and the baby into an exam room, shouting out that an X-ray was needed for a five-month-old baby.

Jasper looked slightly green. Danica sat beside him, neither of them speaking, both staring straight ahead at the pale gray clinic walls, the usual signs posted.

"Everything's okay, right?" Jasper asked.

"I think if Brandy wasn't choking or blue or purple, then she's probably okay. She might have swallowed whatever it was I saw in her hand, but it doesn't seem to have lodged in her airway."

"Okay, phew," he said. He stood up. "I should probably go, then."

"Or you can stay," Danica said gently. "I'm sure Candace will appreciate that you're here, that you care," she added, trying not to emphasize the word.

He bit his lip and sat down, then stood up. "I really should go. I'm supposed to be at work. Will you ask Candace to call me when she knows something?"

Oh, Jasper. Wrong move.

"They'll probably be out in fifteen minutes or so, once the X-ray is taken and the doctors read it. Are you sure you can't wait?"

More lip biting. A bit of pacing. "I really need to get to the ranch. You'll ask Candace to call me. I mean, I'll text her, too."

"I'll tell her," Danica said.

He nodded and rushed out. A few seconds later, Ford came hurrying in.

Danica jumped and threw herself into his arms, sobbing. He wrapped his arms around her, holding her close.

"Is she okay?"

"She seems okay," Danica managed between sobs. "She's being x-rayed."

He nodded. "Let's sit down before your legs give out. If she wasn't choking, her airway must be clear."

Danica breathed out. "I think so, too. I hope so. I'm so scared, Ford. I'm such a neatnik—how would a dime get on my rug anyway?"

"Are you sure it was a dime? Maybe just a bit of silver from the play mat that became dislodged or something?"

"I just don't know. It happened so fast. I saw something shiny and silver in her hand and then in a second her hand was against her mouth and the silver thing was gone."

"You did the right thing rushing her here." He had his arm around her, and if he even attempted to move it she'd grab it right back. That arm was keeping her going right now.

"Thank you for coming, Ford. I've never needed anyone more."

"I'm here," he whispered, and tightened his arm around her. She leaned her head against his arm and let out another breath.

Time ticked by so slowly. A few people came in, someone left, and every time there was movement, Danica practically jumped.

Finally, around a half hour later, Candace came into the waiting room with Brandy, holding a rattle in the shape of an elephant, in her arms. Her sister seemed relieved—a good sign.

"She's okay!" Candace shouted. "There was nothing in her esophagus or stomach. Whatever it was you saw, she must have dropped it and not eaten it."

"I'm so sorry I worried you," Danica said, shaking her head. She could not feel more awful.

"No, I'm glad you rushed Brandy here." Candace glanced around. "Where's Jasper? Restroom?"

"Actually he left about a half hour ago. He asked me to tell you to call him when you knew something. He said he had to get to work at the ranch."

Candace's face fell. "Oh." She shook her head, then lifted her chin. "I'd better get Brandy home. She seems tired and the X-ray freaked me out to the point that *I* need a nap."

Ugh. Danica had tried with Jasper, she really

had, but he wouldn't have it. And that really was a bad sign. Or maybe she was being too hard on him, like Ford seemed to indicate she was? She wasn't sure. He shouldn't have left. That much Danica did know. He should have stayed out of support for Candace, to be there for Candace. Even if he was inwardly freaking about what it meant to be getting serious with a single mother.

They headed out, past Candace, who was settling Brandy in her car seat in the back seat of her car. "See you at home in a few."

Danica nodded and walked with Ford to her own car. He opened the door for her, and she practically collapsed on her seat.

"I know we're on the outs right now, in more ways than one," Ford said, "but would you like to be my plus-one to a wedding tonight? I know for a fact you happen to be going to the same event."

Danica gave him a wobbly smile. "It's a date. Or not." She shook her head. "You know what I mean."

"I do," he said, and then they both did a double take. It was so ridiculous, they both laughed.

*Oh, Ford. How I love you*, she thought as he closed her car door and put a hand to the window before walking to his SUV.

*How am I going to ever let you go?*

## Chapter Fourteen

The Dawsons cleaned up well, Ford thought, watching his brothers and sister as they entered the ballroom for Zeke and Molly's wedding. His brothers wore dark suits, and Daisy was decked out in a long pale pink gown. Maisey, his brother Rex's wife and the head nanny at the ranch, had hired three of her employees from the lodge's babysitting program to work the wedding so that fussy babies could be quieted in a second and little kids would have supervision while they dashed through and under tables as their parents chatted or danced. The wedding was small, under forty people, and there were babies and kids everywhere.

And couples. Even Andrew Morton, the rancher who Ford had been keeping an eye on before and since his talk on the vengeance crimes, was with a date. Apparently, Andrew and Zeke and Molly and Danica had gone to high school together. Ford counted at least three couples that he and Danica had put together. There hadn't been a single crime of vengeance committed since his talk, and if this continued through the weekend, Mayor Abbott would green-light continuing the matchmaking and holding the speed dating event.

Ford stood at the back of the room behind a row of planters with the groom. Zeke's bride was in the small room to their left, getting ready for the ceremony, which was slated to start in about ten minutes. Danica was in there, along with Molly's parents. When he'd picked up his lovely date a bit earlier, he'd gasped at the sight of her. He hadn't seen Danica Dunbar dressed up in a long time; she usually had her hair in buns to avoid it getting yanked by her niece's grabby hands, and very casual clothes that were meant for spit-up and crawling on the floor.

For tonight, Danica wore a long pinkish red gown that skimmed her body, with delicate straps that curved around her shoulders. Her long, silky blond hair was loose down her back, the dress dipping low. How she walked in those at least four-inch heels he had no idea, but she was exceptionally graceful. He couldn't wait to dance with her, an excuse to touch her, hold her.

With their children being watched by a sitter, the Dawson clan came over for hugs and some ribbing, and then the minister gestured to him that it was time for him and Zeke to take their places, so his siblings darted back to their table. The piano player began a classical piece, and a hush came over the room. He and Zeke walked down the red carpet to the front of the room, where an altar had been set up atop three steps. Zeke stood to the side of the minister, Ford beside him.

As maid of honor Danica came walking down the aisle, carrying a bouquet of red flowers, he couldn't take his eyes off her, even as a pint-size outlaw scooted out of his father's arms in the guest chairs and ran up the aisle, his dad quickly catching him. Danica took her place on the other side of the minister, and then everyone turned as the wedding march began. Just past the row of planters he could see Molly's parents and a flash of white, and then they began their procession with Molly being walked down by both Abby and Tim.

He glanced at Danica, who had tears in her eyes, then watched as Molly's parents both lifted her veil and took their seats. The ceremony began, and the minister's words echoed in his head. *Love. Forever. Blessed union.* Ford's tie began to squeeze his neck, and he forced himself not to gnarl a finger in to loosen it. He'd come home to Bear Ridge because he thought he'd changed, thought he was ready for everything the minister was talking about, everything his brother Zeke was about to embark on, and now Ford stood here, that sludge still sitting in his gut, having too much power over him.

And then the bride and groom were kissing to cheers and claps and whistles, and Danica had her arm wrapped around Ford's as they walked back up the aisle together.

"That was such a beautiful ceremony," she whispered. "I tried hard not to cry. My best friend since second grade is now married to the man of her dreams."

"They both looked so happy," he said as they rounded the planters.

The bride and groom were beaming as they joined them behind the planters. The guests were led out onto the huge deck overlooking Clover Mountain, white lights twinkling from overhead as waiters intermingled with trays of champagne.

A waiter came over with a tray, but Zeke and

Molly had started their first dance. Ford and Danica, staring into each other's eyes, took two glasses of champagne each. What was between the bride and groom was so romantic, so intimate, that Ford glanced away, hoping he wouldn't drop his or Zeke's champagne.

"They really do," Danica whispered, her voice full of emotion.

He had that tie-strangling sensation again, but this time it was rivaled by an overpowering urge to take her in his arms and slow dance, too, to look into her eyes and hope to see his future and not the front cover of his mother's diary and the torn-up page, which always quickly replaced any image of possible happiness when it came to thinking about marriage and a life with Danica.

And then the music changed and the guests began coming back in, moving over to their elegant tables. Ford and Danica handed the happy couple their champagne, had a quick toast, and then reached their seats just as the band leader began to announce the bride and the groom.

Ford was sitting between Danica and Molly's dad, who was wiping away tears. The first course was served, a delicious-looking butternut squash soup. The table got busy digging in and sipping their wine.

"Oh my," Danica whispered, peering to the left at Table 4. "Looks like Candace was placed at a singles table."

Ford glanced over. Candace sat chatting with the man beside her, a squirmy two-year-old on his lap. Ford couldn't recall the guy's name, just that he was divorced and an old friend of Zeke's. He'd been in one of Ford's pile of matches and hadn't been easy to pair up. Candace laughed; the guy beaming.

That neck tightening was back. Because this was how it was going to go with Danica and some new guy. She'd be laughing at something funny he'd said, they'd lock eyes and off they'd go into their new happy romance, Ford left standing alone in the cold, like Jasper with Candace. Forever. His decision, right? He was picking this over the woman he couldn't get enough of.

He turned his attention back to his table. Danica was telling Molly's dad that she'd tried one of his special tacos at the food truck he parked in Prairie City and that it was so delicious she got back in line and ordered another. Ford had to agree that Tim's Tasty Tacos were the best in the area. But there was something bigger on his mind than tacos. He knew that when the first course started to be cleared away, he'd be called up, as best man, to give his speech.

The band leader gestured to him, and as he stood, Danica whispered, "I know you'll inspire and touch everyone." Her smile was so genuine that he wanted to pull her into his arms and kiss her.

He went onstage, cleared his throat and kept his gaze on Zeke and Molly. "I'm Zeke's eldest brother, Ford Dawson, so I've known the guy his whole life. Zeke is one of the best people I know. Need a friend at three in the morning—he's there. Need a hand with something hard and annoying when he just got off work—he's there. Need the shirt off his back—it's yours. Zeke came home to Bear Ridge to seek a fresh start in his hometown, and what did he find? The love of his life, a woman he'd known since middle school. Now, Zeke will be a doting and loving father to Molly's baby daughter, Lucy. He'll be a loving, supportive, stand-by-his-woman husband to Molly. I wish all three of them a lifetime of love and happiness."

He handed the mike back to the band leader, cheers and whistles as he left the stage.

Danica passed him on the way up to give her speech as maid of honor, her perfume wrapping around him.

"I've been best friends with Molly since second grade, when we were paired as science lab partners to do an experiment about dropping coins into water. She was my first best friend, and she's been my first throughout my life—the first I share everything with. I've been so lucky to know Molly and have her friendship. An amazing mother, a true friend, a warm bright light to anyone who needs her, Molly is just the best. Zeke, I've heard you say many times the past couple of months that you're the luckiest guy in Wyoming. Yup, you are. And so is Molly. It turns out that she's been waiting for Zeke Dawson since seventh grade—and she's finally got her man. I wish the two of them all the happiness in the world."

More cheers, more claps. Danica barely got to the table before Molly ran over and hugged her tight, then her parents did the same thing.

"Beautiful toast," he said when she sat down beside him.

"Yours, too," he said.

"I love how everything tonight is about promise," she said, smiling at the waiter as he set her petit filet mignon with its side of rosemary roasted potatoes in front of her. "The promise of happiness, of partnership, you know?"

"I believe everything I said about Zeke and Molly. And I believe everything you said."

"That's a very good sign, Ford. You might be very cynical right now, but somewhere, whether on the surface or deep down, you believe love and forever are possible."

"It feels surface. Like it'll all blow away any second. The goodwill, I mean."

"Don't let it," she said.

He turned and looked at her, taking her hand. "Do you think my mother's friend Junie—your mother's cousin—will be more likely to talk to me about my mom if you're there?"

She almost gasped. "I'm so glad you want to talk to her. I think it's the right move. But I have to be honest—I really don't know if I'll have any impact. I haven't seen Junie since I was little. I don't know if I mean anything to her at all. But we should try, Ford. That's what it's about. Trying."

She held his gaze and, dammit, of course she was right, and that was what he was doing. Trying.

"I'll call her in the morning and I'll call you right after," she said. Was it his imagination or had she moved a bit closer to him, her entire demeanor slightly less wary?

He wanted to warn her that *trying* and *accomplishing* were two very different things, but maybe trying was all he needed to do in this case. He had no idea what he'd learn from Junie, if anything, or if it would help or hurt, but if it meant a second chance with Danica Dunbar, he had to try damned hard.

At the moment, seated in Ford's car as he pulled into her driveway after the wedding, all Danica could think about was the good-night kiss that had better be coming. All those hours of romance in the air, toasts about love and permanence, the slow dancing in Ford's arms where she'd melted against him... She wanted much more than a good-night kiss, but she knew they'd have to take things slowly right now.

Just a half hour ago, they'd been wrapped around each other on the dance floor as the band played Etta James's "At Last," and Danica kept thinking, *yes, yes, yes*, her love had come along. She'd been afraid to look at Ford during the romantic, sultry song, thinking it might do him in when he *was* clearly trying, hard, so she just kept her cheek against his, the length of her snuggled up against him. Those moments were absolute heaven.

Candace had left about halfway through; the single dad at her table kept asking her to dance

even though she'd explained she was seeing someone. The guy kept reminding her that her boyfriend wasn't there and that he was, and Candace
had told him that he was a classic mansplainer
and to have a nice life, packed up her baby and
let Danica know she needed to get Brandy to bed.
Danica had walked her out and heard the whole
story of the pushy, smarmy single guy. Her sister
had looked so hurt over what was going on with
Jasper, but when Danica offered to leave with her,
assuring her that Molly would understand, Candace insisted she stay, that she'd go home, put the
baby down and do some moonlit yoga on the back
deck since it was such an unusually warm night
for April in Wyoming, high fifties.

A light was on in Candace's room, and Danica
was glad she was still awake so that they could
talk—and so Danica couldn't get any not-smart
ideas of inviting Ford in. Not yet.

Ford cut the ignition and turned to her, clearly
noticing her peering up at the window. "Is Candace okay?"

"Wish I knew the answer to that, too," she said.
"It's a blow. The first guy she's fallen for and he's
afraid of a fifteen-pound baby with huge blue eyes.
I've never known Brandy not be able to wrap anyone around her grabby little finger."

He smiled. "She is pretty cute. But she's also very real."

"Meaning?" she prompted, not liking the sound of this.

"Meaning that it doesn't make Jasper a bad guy or necessarily wrong for Candace because he's struggling a bit with the fact that she has a baby. It seems natural that he would. He has no experience with babies. He's single. He fell for Candace, and now he needs a little time to get used to the idea of getting serious with a woman who has a child. A very young child."

Ford certainly wasn't wrong about any of that. "He shouldn't have left the clinic, though," she said.

"He's going to get stuff wrong. That's how people grow."

"Answer for everything," she said, sliding a bit of a smile at him.

"It's practically my job."

She laughed, then looked up at Candace's window again, and her smile faded. "She's so hurt. He did leave the clinic when she needed him, needed his support. And instead of coming to the wedding, he told her they needed a little break to both really think about what they wanted."

"I'm not saying it's easy or fun to go through.

But not every relationship is sunshine and roses even in the very beginning. There's a complication between them, and now they're dealing with it. If Candace wants to be with him, she needs to give it some time. If his actions are a deal breaker, then they're not right for each other."

"I guess," she said on a hard sigh. "I do want her life to be sunshine and roses right now. She's come home disappointed in life, in herself. I just want her to be happy."

"Because you're a loving, caring sister. You're the best, Danica."

She grabbed his face and kissed him. And he kissed her back.

"I wanted to do that all night," he said. "You beat me to it."

She smiled and rested her head on his shoulder for a moment, then sat up. "I don't know what's going on with us, if there is an us, if there'll be an us. I just know that we're got something very special."

"Agreed," he said.

"At *least* we're on the same page on that."

He smiled and squeezed her hand.

She squeezed back. "I'll call Junie in the morning, around nine, and I'll call you right after."

He nodded and she got out of the car, leaning

down to blow him a kiss. She hadn't intended to do that, but Ford brought out a spontaneous side of her.

He caught the kiss in his fist and pressed it against his chest in the region of his heart. And that was it, Danica Dunbar was deeply in love.

## Chapter Fifteen

Candace had been crying in her room when Danica came upstairs last night, and the two had talked for a good hour. Candace was exhausted, emotionally and physically. She'd broken up with Jasper when she'd gotten home from the wedding, as much as it pained her. She wanted a man in her life who accepted her as a package deal from the get-go, who wanted a baby in his life, who wanted to be her baby's father. She'd told him she needed a man who'd have stayed at the clinic, that it had been a deal breaker. Jasper had been full of "this is all so new, can't we just…" and Candace had felt she had to walk away.

Danica's heart ached for her sister, but this morning Candace seemed stronger and was full of purpose. She and Brandy were dressed and set for a day in Prairie City, where they'd attend a baby event at the library and do some shopping, and tomorrow Candace had two interviews in town at day care centers and was thinking of getting her associate's degree in early childhood education. Danica was so proud of her.

With the house empty and the clock chiming nine, it was time to make The Call, and she was hesitant. She had picked up her phone and put it down on the counter twice already, fortifying herself with a cup of coffee and a bowl of raisin bran. Nine twenty. She knew Ford was counting on her, so she entered June Maywood's name and Bear Ridge in the search engine and up popped her telephone and address. She still lived in the same house she had when Danica had last seen her, about ten minutes away in a more rural stretch of town. No surprise. Junie didn't like close neighbors or trespassers on her property, like in-town dogs or kids waiting for the school bus.

Danica pressed in the number and held her breath, then slowly let it go.

"Who's this?" Junie said by way of hello.

"Junie, this is Danica Dunbar, Judith's daughter," she said, and mentally crossed her fingers that Junie didn't hang up.

"The pretty Realtor with the long blond hair," Junie said.

Huh. Junie had kept tabs on her? That was unexpected. "I've worked at Blue Ridge Realty for ten years now. I definitely found my calling."

"Are you calling because your mother's gone?" Junie asked.

Danica felt herself frown. "No. My parents are alive and well and retired to Arizona. They have several orange trees in their yard." She bit her lip and thought she'd better get to the point. "Junie, I'm calling because someone I care about... Oh, I'm just going to say this outright. The man I'm in love with is looking for some missing pieces of his past. And it turns out you were close to his mother. We're hoping you can shed some light—"

"Are you talking about Ford Dawson?"

"Yes, Ford. He's—"

"I know what he wants to know. He came around about a year and a half ago after that rat bastard father of his died. I'm surprised it took Bo that long to meet his maker."

"Well, you know then that his dad left him a map to where he buried his mother's diary. Ford tried to find it for the past year and a half and had no luck until just recently. He found it buried just beyond the gate of the Dawson Family Guest Ranch."

"Figures. Ellen never thought to look outside the ranch gates. Drove her nuts not to have her diary."

"Will you talk to him, Junie? He read some of the diary and it has him all tied up in knots. It's made him feel like pursuing a family for himself is a bad idea, that it'll only bring despair like it did for his mother."

"Well, he's not wrong. Ellen ended up alone, a single mother. I've been divorced for almost twelve years. But I have dogs so I'm set."

*Say you'll talk to him. Say you'll bring him the peace he needs.*

"I'll make you a deal, Danica. I don't get around well these days because I have a bad hip. You bring me a cheesecake from the bakery, and I'll talk to Ford."

Danica almost pumped her fist in the air. "You have a deal. What time should we come over? If today works for you?"

"How about noon? If you could also pick me up a sandwich or something, that would be nice."

"Sure thing, Junie. Any particular kind? BLT? Chicken salad?"

"I do love chicken salad on a good rye," June said.

Danica smiled. "Got it. See you then."

Instead of a "see you then" or a goodbye she got a click in the ear, but Danica had a good feeling about this. About Ford getting his information—and a longtime estrangement coming to an end. Junie had a bad hip? Didn't get around easily? Danica could be a help. Her mother's cousin had opened the door, even if just a sliver, and Danica was going to walk right through.

Ford picked up Danica at ten forty-five and now they were en route to Junie Maywood's home, with two cheesecakes—one plain, one raspberry—and a chicken salad sandwich with a side of homemade potato chips from the Bear Ridge Diner, which had won Best Chicken Salad in Converse County for the past five years.

"So this really does sound promising on two levels," Ford said. "If I'm reading her right, she sounds open to talking to me about my mother, and she sounds open to developing a relationship with you—if *you're* open to it, that is."

Not that he wasn't nervous as hell about what Junie would reveal to him and to Danica. For all he knew, his mother had done something god-awful that had led to that torn-up diary page. And maybe Danica's mother had done something god-awful that had led to her and her cousin's estrangement. Something neither he nor Danica would want to know.

"I am. I barely remember her from childhood, but I know she's my mother's first cousin, and if they had a falling-out that lasted decades, that's not about me—it's about them and foolishness. I'll take all the family I can get."

Such was the problem of jumping into the unknown willingly. You never knew what you'd get.

"Speaking of family," he said as he turned onto the service road that led to Junie's house, "how's your sister?" Danica had told him about the breakup with Jasper, and how sad Candace was. Knowing Jasper—though granted, not well beyond the basics—the guy was likely miserable, too. Ford understood where they were both coming from and didn't think either of them was wrong. But that wasn't going to bring them back together, either.

"She's very sad but she's focusing on her future— she has interviews lined up tomorrow and she's thinking of going for her degree in early childhood education. I think she's going to be okay. She just needs some time."

He nodded. "And she's lucky to have such a supportive sister."

"You know, when I was going through my divorce and I didn't have any family support because we just weren't close enough to warrant it—emotionally or distance-wise—I didn't even really lament it because I didn't know otherwise. It never would have occurred to me that my sister might rush to my side or that my aunt Trudy would call every night to check on me. Now, if one of them was hurting, I would do just that. And I think they would for me. So much has changed."

"Good," he said. He knew she had Molly and her friends at the realty, but family brought a special comfort.

"How much farther to Junie's, would you say?" Danica asked, glancing out the window. "I want to mentally brace myself."

"You think she'll be difficult? Withholding?"

"I'm thinking no. Wanting cheesecake and a chicken salad sandwich—she struck a very easy deal to meet with you. I sensed a warmth under the prickly. But we'll see. I've learned not to get my hopes up about anything. Expectations can be easily squashed."

He glanced at her, but she kept her eyes on the windshield. She was talking about him, he figured. And once again, the sludgy feeling that was starting to dislodge wedged back in some. He hated hurting her. But that was what he'd been doing lately.

"Actually, we're here," he said, turning onto Rural Route 22. "Her house should be just down this road, two miles or so."

They were quiet as they approached the small farmhouse on acres of property. The place was a bit run-down. Two dogs, a shepherd mutt and a tiny yapper, came barreling off the porch as Ford pulled into the gravel driveway.

The front door opened and out came Junie May-wood. She was tall and slender, like Danica, with very straight ash-blond hair to her collarbone. She wore jeans and a fisherman's sweater and felt clogs. Ford wasn't sure of her age, but since his mother and Junie had been friends from school, he figured she'd be around fifty-five or so.

"I don't remember her," Danica said. "How sad. My mother's first cousin, who I definitely know I met, and she doesn't look at all familiar."

"Her coloring and features are similar to yours and Candace's," he noted.

"And my mother's."

Junie stood on the porch, arms crossed against her chest.

"Well, here goes everything," Ford said, un-buckling his seat belt.

He got out and held up a hand in greeting, and Junie did, too, a good sign. Danica carried the bags with the cheesecake and the sandwich, glanced at him, and then started toward the porch.

"Oh, wonderful," Junie said with a little clap. "The Bear Ridge Diner has the best chicken salad sandwiches in the entire county."

"I know it," Danica said. "I just love their food." She walked up the porch steps, the dogs at her heels, sniffing the air.

"Good golly, you're pretty. Of course, you were as a little kid. Everyone said you and your sister would grow up to be supermodels."

Danica smiled. "You look so much like my mother."

Junie's face fell, and Ford could tell from Danica's expression that she instantly regretted saying it.

"Your mother was some piece of work," Junie said. "Has she changed at all? Or is she still a cold fish?"

Danica seemed taken aback. "Well, my mother was never very warm and fuzzy, but I don't feel comfortable talking about her that way. She is my mom, no matter what."

*Good for you for speaking your mind*, he thought. Just as Junie was.

Junie shook her head. "You and your sister were both such respectful little girls even at five, six years old. Guess there's worse things to be."

"Trust me, there are," Ford said. "I'm a cop, remember?"

Junie laughed. "I remember. Well, come in. I'd like to try that sandwich. Like I told Danica, I don't get into town much, so I make my own chicken salad, and it's good, but I love getting takeout."

"Me, too," Ford said. "I pretty much keep the Bear Ridge Diner in business." He glanced at Danica, hoping she didn't mind the rapport he was trying to build with Junie. She'd already slighted Danica's mother, and it was clear that hadn't sat well with Danica.

They went inside. The house was small and cozy. They went into the living room, and Danica set the bags on the coffee table.

Junie poked her head in the bag. "Ooh, you brought me an iced tea. I love iced tea." Junie unpacked and brought over a standing tray, on which she set the container from the diner. "Can I get you two anything?"

Ford could tell she was hoping the answer would be no so that she could drop down in the chair and dig in. "I'm fine, but thank you."

"Ditto," Danica said. "You go ahead and eat. I love the diner's homemade potato chips."

"Scrumptious," Junie said, popping one into her mouth, the dogs sitting patiently by her side, clearly hoping for a crumb or two tossed their way. Junie did not disappoint them.

"Junie, why did you and my mother stop speaking? I wasn't going to ask—I was planning to wait to see if you wanted to bring it up, but I have to know. What happened?"

"Your mother told me I could do better than Jim Peffernel. That's what happened. He dared to be on the short side for a man, for one. And he worked as a ranch hand so she thought he wouldn't amount to much."

"Jim Peffernel?" Ford said. "He owns one of the biggest ranches in town."

Junie nodded. "Yup, he sure proved your mother wrong. It's why he got so successful."

"Wait, what do you mean?"

"Well, my dear cousin Judith was over at my house one day, baking something with her aunt, my mother, and she was telling my mother how awful it would be if I ended up marrying Jim since he'd never earn much and I'd be poor and so would my kids. I remember my mother telling Judith that he was just starting out and everyone began at the bottom, and he was very cute, and Judith said but he's short. My mother just shook her head, but apparently Judith took it upon herself to tell Jim that he was beneath our family and should find a girlfriend more suited to his station."

Danica gasped loudly. "No she did not."

"Oh yes, she did," Junie said, putting down her sandwich. "Because Jim told me so and I confronted her, and I told her I was done with her, and she said fine with her. And we never spoke again. We weren't particularly close before that, kind of competitive with each other, so both of us liked not having to deal with the other. We were in our late teens and since our parents weren't very close, they didn't push the issue."

"What happened between you and Jim Peffernel?" Danica asked.

"Oh, we kept dating for a few months but it fizzled out. He had such a great sense of humor, but we didn't have much in common. We stayed friendly, though. A couple years later, I ran into him and he said he'd never forgotten my cousin's nasty words and that it propelled him to keep striving and that he'd saved up enough to buy his own small ranch. His little empire grew from there."

"Good for him," Ford said.

Danica nodded. "Yeah, good for Jim Peffernel."

"And that's the stupid reason why your mother and I have been estranged for almost thirty years. I had my good friend Ellen Dawson, so I didn't miss Judith much."

"You and my mother were close till the day she passed when I was in the police academy," Ford said, his chest tightening. "I miss her every day."

"Yeah, me, too," Junie said. She took a big bite of her sandwich, then popped another chip into her mouth. "Wow, this is really good. I appreciate you two bringing this over. And the cheesecakes. Boy, am I looking forward to a slice."

Danica smiled. "We brought you two kinds. We couldn't choose between plain and raspberry."

"You're my kind of people," Junie said, then bit into the second half of her sandwich.

Danica glanced at Ford, and he thought she seemed pleased or more settled, perhaps. She'd learned the story behind the estrangement, and it wasn't something that would keep her up at night. Junie didn't strike Ford as particularly easygoing, but he had a feeling Danica would actually enjoy bringing her aunt chicken salad sandwiches and spending time with her.

"So there's the thing," Ford said. "I'm going to be very honest here. I have very strong feelings for Danica. She's an amazing person. But this diary has me all messed up. Entries about my mother sobbing and praying her husband would change his ways. Seeing him kissing other women in alleyways off Main Street in broad daylight. Needing to go grocery shopping but finding his paycheck spent on gambling and liquor." He shook his head. "I moved back to Bear Ridge to start fresh, settle down. Then I read some of the diary and everything inside me seized up and went cold."

Junie nodded and took a sip of her iced tea. "I get it. Your father was a disaster as a husband and father. Good-looking, but a real mess."

"Yeah, he was," Ford agreed.

"But he got one thing right. Somehow he made six terrific kids with three different women. And he tried to save your mother from himself. I told Ellen she should leave your dad over and over, but my words fell on deaf ears. But boy, when she gave up, when she wrote that she'd lost any self-esteem or sense of self that would make her pick herself up and take her son and leave her rat bastard husband, guess what your father did?"

Ford leaned forward, pinpricks breaking out along the nape of his neck. "What?"

"Well, he'd found her diary and was reading it. That's how he knew she was giving up on life, on herself—because it was the final entry. He read that page and freaked out. He tore it out and ripped it to shreds and told her she had to leave him for her own good. She was furious that he'd read the diary and tried to get it out of his hands but he grabbed some old box, shoved in the diary and the torn-up pieces, and ran out of the house with it. She chased after him but lost track of him. He kept telling her to leave him, that she deserved better, but she was so out of steam in every way that she couldn't see it anymore."

"But she did leave," Ford said. "She packed our suitcases and we left."

Junie nodded. "Because one day your father was drunk and she came home from her part-time job, scared as she was to leave you alone with him, and he'd passed out across you so that you couldn't move. When she got him off you, you were all sweaty and practically blue. Your father could have suffocated you, Ford. She packed that day and left."

Ford stood up and went to the windows, tears stinging his eyes. Hell, he wanted to know, hadn't he?

"So your father wanted to save your mother from him, and she finally saved you from him, and that's what happened."

"Junie," Danica said. "Why do you think his

dad left him the map to the diary? Why do you think Bo wanted Ford to read it?"

"To show he cared about Ellen and his little son. That he couldn't bear what he'd read, that his long-suffering wife had given up and was planning to stay with a cheating alcoholic who'd destroyed his family legacy—the Dawson Family Guest Ranch. He wanted her to have better. He loved her, much as he could love anyone, and he wanted her to find happiness, a better life."

Ford dropped his head in his hands, then finally looked up. "Well, I appreciate you telling me. I'm not sure I want to know any of this. It's so damned…sad."

Junie nodded. "Yeah. But it's life. And life isn't a bucket of clams or a chicken salad sandwich from the diner. It's messy."

"Messy is right," Ford said. "But you know this story from my mom. We really can't be sure what Bo thought or intended."

"Can, too," Junie said. "Because Bo Dawson himself came to see me the day after she'd left him. Wanted me to relay that message loud and clear to Ellen next time I saw her and to say he was sorry. And that he loved you, more than either of you would ever know, but he had a problem and he didn't want to deal with it, and leaving him was the right thing."

Suddenly everything was flipped but still felt so heavy. The sludge was less inside him than sitting on his shoulders now. He had a lot to think about.

"Family can be great or full of hardship and sometimes both," Junie added. "It's why I'm happy with my dogs. No arguing. Just unconditional love. They're all I need."

"Well, I'd like us to get closer, Junie," Danica said. "If you want. Besides me, there's my sister, Candace, and her five-month-old baby, Brandy. And our aunt Trudy, our dad's sister. She's in Vegas on her honeymoon right now. I'll bet they'd love for us all to get reacquainted."

"Oh, I remember Trudy," Junie said. "I liked her."

Danica smiled. "Maybe I can bring Candace and Brandy over soon?"

"How about tomorrow?" Junie asked. "I love babies. As long as they don't throw up on me or pee on me."

Danica laughed, and then she glanced at Ford; he could feel her eyes on him, and he moved back over to the window, looking out, the little dog sniffing his foot.

"We'll come over with breakfast," Danica said. "Eight o'clock?"

Junie nodded. "Perfect. I love the bagels at the bakery, particularly sesame. And bacon scallion cream cheese."

"Gotcha," Danica said with a smile. "Well," she added, standing up. "We'd better get going. I'm so glad we connected."

Ford turned. "Thank you, Junie. If it weren't for you, the story would have stayed buried with my parents, and I needed to know, regardless of how awful it is."

"Yup," Junie said. "The truth matters."

They petted the dogs goodbye and left, and Ford wasn't sure who let out the biggest sigh of relief to be back in the car—him or Danica.

"God, that was intense," she said.

"Yeah. Good word for it."

"You all right?" she asked. "That was a lot to take in."

"I don't know, honestly. I feel like hell."

A montage played in his head—leaving the Dawson Family Guest Ranch main house with his mom and their suitcases, visiting his dad on weekends and finding him passed out drunk often, getting a kind new stepmother, Bo getting divorced from his second wife, and Ford being a "father figure" to his not much younger half siblings, Zeke, Rex and Axel...paying for groceries and Christmas and birthday gifts when his dad drank and gambled money, watching him destroy the guest ranch after his grandparents died. The heartbreak of Bo's third wife dying from cancer, leaving two kids, his brother and sister, Noah and Daisy... Bo destroying the guest ranch and himself. And then his father's funeral, the six Dawson kids holding hands, barely able to speak through their complicated grief. The scattering—and then coming back together where they'd all begun. The ranch.

Danica leaned over and put her arms around him. They sat like that in the gravel driveway until Ford said he had to get out of there.

Then he drove into the nature preserve and parked by the river, and he opened his arms and she fell into them. They stayed like that for a good long time, neither of them saying a word.

## Chapter Sixteen

After dropping Danica off at her house with promises to check in by text or phone that night, Ford didn't want to go home and be alone with his gloomy thoughts, but he didn't want to talk to anyone, either, even his brothers or sister. His dad was their dad, yes, but he was the lone Dawson who didn't share a mother with any of his siblings. He drove around town for a while, pulling over when he noticed a guy, maybe late thirties, receding hairline, ducking between cars in the diagonal spaces along Main Street. *What are you up to, buddy?* He got out of his SUV and kept a surreptitious eye on the man. Ford glanced up ahead; a young couple—

they looked like high school kids—were walking hand in hand and reading the menus on the doors of Bear Ridge's few restaurants.

Ah. Perhaps a crime of vengeance was about to ruin the run of good behavior among the daters. The young woman couldn't be older than eighteen. *Way too young for you, dirtbag*, Ford thought, watching the skulker dip in along the next car, rush two cars up, and then reach for something in his pocket. Ford was about to call out to distract him from whatever awful thing he was about to do when he saw a small heart-shaped box of chocolates in the guy's hand.

"Psst, psst!" the skulker called out. The guy walking with the young woman looked over and the other man, kneeling down to avoid being seen, gestured him near. "You forgot this. I didn't want to embarrass you by having your date see your old dad chasing after you."

The young guy smiled. "Thanks, Dad." He pocketed the little heart-shaped box and rejoined his date, the dad slipping away.

So this was what he'd come to. Seeing negativity in everything. Not who he wanted to be.

He got back in his car and drove around awhile longer, finding himself on the road to the Dawson Family Guest Ranch. Maybe he just needed to be there, to let everything Junie Maywood had told him earlier gel in his head while he was right where it had happened.

Once he'd arrived at the ranch, he drove up to the main house where the argument had taken place and then turned around, parking by the gatehouse and walking over to the creek. He knew the spots the guests wouldn't go; what looked like heavy brush actually hid a winding path that led to the water's edge, where he could just sit and think. Or not think. The sky was lit up with stars, the moon casting its glow over the water. He sat back against a big rock, watching a brown frog hop at the edge of the creek and disappear between the little rocks nestled there.

What was he supposed to do with everything he'd heard? The whole story was nuts. His father had drunk and gambled and cheated the life force out of his young wife, to the point that she'd given up on expecting anything and had been planning to stay with her husband. Said husband read this in her diary and felt so bad that he wanted her to leave him. Great. Ford was supposed to feel better about any of this? The truth Junie had mentioned only made his heart hurt.

His father had been an addict, yes. And somewhere in that tall, lanky body of his, he'd loved his first wife and maybe that was how he'd shown it. He had saved Ellen Dawson, perhaps, by driving her out. Hell, maybe he'd collapsed drunk on his five-year-old son on the sofa knowing it would be the last straw, that she'd be home at six and would push him off his little son, then pack and leave.

The only thing Ford knew with absolutely certainty was that he wished Danica was here right now. They'd sat in his car for over a half hour, silent, just taking comfort in each other's company, presence, the shared knowledge of some hard stuff to bear between them. Maybe he needed a good night's sleep and things would be clearer in the morning.

He stood up and walked back through the brush to his vehicle, the car lights on an old Jeep almost blinding him.

"Oh hey, Ford," someone called out the window.

He peered closer, shielding his eyes. Jasper, Candace Dunbar's ex-boyfriend.

"Hi, Jasper. You all right?" he called over as he walked up to the Jeep.

Jasper looked away for a moment, then back at Ford and burst into tears, covering his face with his hands. "No, I'm not okay." He shook his head, swiping under his eyes with the back of his hands. "Oh, God. Am I really crying in front of you?"

"It's okay. Trust me, I know what's it like to be in a different mindset or place than the woman you care about and have it screw up everything. I'm right there, Jasper."

"Yeah? You gonna fix it?" he asked.

*Hey, I'll ask the questions here,* he thought, his collar feeling tight again. "Let me ask you, Jasper. This thing with you and the fact that Candace has a baby. What is it exactly that scares the hell out of you?"

"I'm scared enough of how I feel about her," he said. "I've never felt this way about anyone and I've had a lot of relationships, mostly short ones. But being a father? I don't know anything about that. I didn't exactly have a role model in that department, let's leave it at that."

"Yeah, me neither," Ford said. Although maybe in his own way, his father had tried. In some twisted way. As June had said, life was messy. "But it sounds like losing Candace is worse than your fears about fatherhood."

"It is. But every time I think about rushing over to see her and tell her I love her and I'll be a good father to Brandy, that I need to develop some actual confidence in that department, I think about how Brandy is just five months old. If I marry Candace, I'll be in that baby's life from the start.

I'll be all she knows as a dad. And what the hell do I know about being a father? I barely know mine. I could screw up, you know?"

"I don't see why you would if you love Candace and care about the baby," Ford pointed out. "I mean it's your feelings that dictate how you act. Your sense of responsibility toward them. If you have both of those things, you're golden."

Jasper brightened considerably. "I never thought of it like that. It's kind of like my mom always telling me if you think you can, you can. She was always trying to get me to believe more in myself."

"She sounds wonderful," Ford said. "And she's right. If you think you can, you can."

How many times had Ford read *The Little Engine That Could* to his two-year-old nephew? Ten times in the last two months? Danny loved that book. Why hadn't such a simple lesson knocked into his head before now?

And why the hell couldn't he apply that to himself? His situation was different from Jasper's, though it didn't sound all that different. Maybe Jasper didn't have a harrowing diary and history and story lurking in his parents' past, but he'd had his own troubles when it came to his father.

"What if I'm too late?" Jasper asked. "She broke up with me."

"Tell her how you feel. Tell her the truth. Kick fear to the curb. Let how you feel about Candace make your decisions for you."

*Ah*, he thought. That was the difference between him and Jasper. Ford wasn't scared; fear wasn't what was ruling him. No, it was more like horror that had Ford all turned around—upside down.

"I'm going to see her right now," Jasper said. "Thanks, man."

Ford nodded and watched the red taillights until they disappeared. He'd go home, sleep on it all and hope his own words came back to him in the morning. Maybe he'd find some peace for himself.

He pulled out his phone and texted Danica: Drove around, stared at the creek, had an unexpected conversation. Headed home now to try and sleep on everything. If I can.

She texted back right away: I think you need to do something with the diary, Ford. Something ceremonial to let it go, to say goodbye. You know what you know and maybe honoring that, in whatever way feels right, is the way to go. Oh my gosh, Jasper is at the door to see Candace! Crossing my fingers.

He looked up at the stars, glad about that. At least one couple would be reunited tonight.

\* \* \*

Ford sat at his kitchen table with a beer and a slice of the pie his brother Rex had dropped off from another baking day with his toddler. He kept thinking about what Danica had said.

*I think you need to do something with the diary, Ford. Something ceremonial to let it go, to say goodbye.*

Maybe. But what? He wanted to honor his mother in some way, but also acknowledge what his father had tried to do to roust Ellen Dawson from her terrible rut.

He thought about where his parents had met, at a park in town where his mother used to walk her little dog. Bo had been stood up on a blind date there by a woman who'd heard about his reputation, or so his father had said, and then Ellen's wire terrier had peed right on Bo's pant leg. They'd had a good laugh about it, and Ford always remembered his mother saying that it was either a wonderful way to meet someone or an ominous way that foretold of not great things to come. Life is a mix, she'd always said.

She'd loved Bo Dawson and he'd loved her. There had been some very hard times, but in the end, Ford decided that all he needed to know was that he'd been conceived in love. Not everything worked out. Some things did. Some things you had to fight for. Seemed to him that his mother had fought for her marriage and she'd lost, but she'd tried. In the end, her husband had loved her enough to save her, force her to start fresh. Ellen Dawson had gone back to school, she'd painted in her spare time, and she'd doted on her only child. She'd been so proud of him when he'd joined the police academy; her father had been a police officer.

He smiled as he remembered his mother, her favorite phrases. He was ready to put the diary to rest where it belonged, where the two people who were the star of it had tried in their own way to be together—and then not. Theirs had not been a magical love story blessed by the stars. If his dad had been a different person, he and Ellen Dawson might have been more like Ford's grandparents, married decades, solid. Instead, his father was who he was and had had three wives, breaking their hearts, breaking his kids' hearts. He shook his head, picked up the damned tackle box and headed back out.

A half hour later, he pulled into the Bear Ridge Park, a huge recreation area with trails and picnic tables and footbridges over the creek. He imagined his parents meeting here, the dog peeing on his father's leg, Bo laughing. He would find that very funny.

At the park, Ford found a good spot off the beaten path, where no one would likely notice the disturbed earth; soon enough it would be covered by wind-blown brush and the diary would have a forever resting place. He knelt down and dug a hole, then put the box in, diary and the torn-up page inside, and covered it with the dirt, packing the top layer tightly and adding some leaves and twigs.

There. It was at peace, even if he still wasn't. He'd work on that, try to understand both his parents—or maybe just accept what he'd just been thinking about: that they were who they were and it wasn't his place to judge either of them, especially now that they were gone. Judging would only leave him his own wounds to fester, his memories to be sour.

He pulled out his phone: Meet me at the park? I'm on the footbridge near the wishing well. I want to show you something.

She texted back immediately: Be there in three minutes.

He'd let the diary go. Now he'd let Danica go.

This was it, Danica thought. Ford was finally free and now they could be together. He would put the tire swing back in his front yard. The image of that tire on the big oak filled her mind, her heart leaping, butterflies zipping around in her stomach—in a good way.

If Jasper had surprised and shocked her sister with a change of heart, anything was possible, and Danica knew that Ford had already been there, been ready, until the diary had changed things for him. Maybe he was going to tell her that he was taking her advice to do something ceremonial with the diary and wanted her opinion on what, exactly. She wasn't sure where the park fit in, but it must have some significance.

As she hurried from her car to the bridge where Ford had said to meet him, she thought about all Candace had told her about her talk with Jasper a little while ago. Apparently, he'd come over, expression and voice clogged with emotion, and apologized profusely for blowing it at the clinic and assuring her that would never happen again. How he'd be there for her, through good times and bad, and that he'd step up even if he had no idea what the hell he was doing. He'd figure it out, he'd said, because he was madly in love with her. And he wanted to learn how to be the father he'd never had. He wanted to start tomorrow afternoon, showing Brandy the petting zoo at the Dawson Family Guest Ranch, then hitting up the toy store to buy her something special that she'd have forever.

Turns out he'd had an inspiring talk with Ford when he'd run into him earlier tonight after his shift at the ranch. That had almost made Danica cry. Ford had been throwing around lines from *The Little Engine That Could*? A child's book that he'd clearly read his nieces and nephews. The man was so ready, so there, and unless Danica was reading this all wrong, Ford was going to tell her that he'd taken his own words to heart.

As she arrived at the wishing well, she could see him on the footbridge, looking down at the creek. Her Ford. He turned at the sound of her footsteps.

"My parents met in this park. My mom was walking her dog and it peed on my dad's leg. The most auspicious beginning. That should have clued them in."

A chill slid up Danica's spine. He did not sound remotely at peace.

"Their love story and what it turned into isn't your story, Ford. It's theirs. You came out of that union, but you're your own person. Your father had some good traits and you have those. Your mother had some beautiful traits and you have those. Take the good and let the sadness go with that diary. What did you decide to do with it?"

"That's what I wanted to show you." She followed him to some brush, which he held aside for her to walk through, and there was a small clearing near a cluster of trees. "I buried it here. I put their story to rest. I feel like I returned the diary to my mother, letting her have her truth. My father's truth is also out there now because I know what happened. I let it go, Danica. And that's thanks to you."

"I'm glad to hear it." But… She felt a hard *but* coming, a heartbreaking one. She tried to gear up for it, to brace herself, but she was looking at the man she loved.

"Everything I came back to Bear Ridge for? Settling down, having six kids… That's just not who I am anymore or what I want. I know you were hoping I'd come around, revert back. But I've changed, Danica. And it feels irrevocable."

Tears stung her eyes. "Do you love me?" she asked.

"It's not about that."

"Oh yes, it is. Do you love me?"

"Danica, this is about *me*—not us. I think you just need to accept where I am and find yourself the future you want. It's not with me."

He'd turned away as he'd said that, and she knew it had cost him to say that, that it would bother him, even if that was how he'd felt. Ford wasn't one to shoot arrows in a broken heart. And he just had.

"I'm just trying to be very clear," he said.

"No, Ford. You're not *trying* at all." She turned and ran back to the path, then to her car, wanting to sit and cry but she had to get out of there. The park where she'd left her heart behind.

## Chapter Seventeen

In the morning, Danica just wanted to stay in bed, her quilt pulled up to her neck, a box of tissues under the covers with her for easy access. But she was supposed to be at Junie's at eight o'clock—with her sister and the baby, and Candace was excited to meet a long-estranged member of the family whom she barely remembered.

*Everything about her family will be different for Brandy*, Candace had said last night.

Danica wished Ford could look at it that way. Why couldn't he see that he could be the change? His siblings had done it. Why was he so stubborn about this? She couldn't understand it.

When she'd gotten back from the park last night, Candace was looking at the old photo album she'd found in her trunk. There were pictures of Junie and Judith, and their expressions alone told a story. First cousins who could not stand each other. Danica had told Candace only a little about what happened with Ford, that the timing just wasn't right and she was going to have to move on. Candace had been so touched and moved by the family photo albums, which she hadn't seen since she'd left home at eighteen, that Danica hadn't wanted to inject her misery.

She'd saved bursting into tears for her own bedroom and had slept like hell.

Now she threw off the covers and took a long, hot shower, then had a strong cup of coffee. Her phone pinged, and Danica grabbed it, her heart hoping it would be Ford, but it was Aunt Trudy, sending photos from her honeymoon. Danica called Candace down and they smiled at the pictures, Trudy and Cole looking so happy.

One day, she'd find happiness for herself, once she was good and over Ford Dawson, which was going to take a while. In the meantime, she'd continue bringing couples together in Bear Ridge. Always a matchmaker, never a match.

The family photo album was on the kitchen

table, and Danica took her coffee over and sat down, flipping through it. She stared at photos of her mother, never quite smiling, even in pictures with her husband. Her mother was who she was, but Danica was who she was. And she wasn't someone who ignored or avoided family.

She picked up her phone and pushed the button on her mom's contact page.

"Danica? Something wrong?"

Danica shook her head. "No, nothing at all. I just wanted to say hi and hear your voice. It's been a while."

"Oh, how thoughtful of you. Well, I'm just here with your father, sitting on the patio admiring the orange trees. We're having fresh squeezed orange juice from our own backyard. Isn't that something?"

"Nothing beats it," Danica agreed. They talked about oranges and the weather, and then Danica mentioned that Candace and Brandy had moved back to Bear Ridge and were staying with her. Her mother asked how they were but said nothing about visiting. *People are who they are*, she thought again. *You can't change them just because you want to. They have to want to change.*

Like Ford.

Danica decided not to mention that she'd reconnected with Junie or that she and Candace and the baby were going over for breakfast. That would sit weird in her mother's head, and Danica knew it. She'd save it for another time, maybe. Or maybe she'd just keep it to herself. Judith and Junie were the past, and Danica's relationship with Junie was the future. Her mom said she had to run, that she and Danica's father were heading out to buy a new patio set, and Danica didn't feel the usual emptiness when the call ended. She'd develop a relationship with her mother on her terms, not her mother's. If it made Danica feel good to speak to her mom once a week, then her mother was just going to have to get used to being called often.

"Okay, we're ready," Candace said. Brandy was in her arms, wearing another of the outfits Danica had sent recently when her sister still lived in LA, an adorable sparkly purple tutu over tights. "I figure we'll be back by tenish, and my first interview is at noon. You're still okay to babysit?"

"Absolutely."

"You're the best, Danica. Coming home was the smartest thing I ever did."

Danica beamed and gave her sister a hug, and they headed out.

"Oh, and Danica? I know you may not believe it

right now, but Ford will be back. I know that like I know you. And I've gotten to know you very well."

"Well, I won't hope too hard on that one. But since I'm not gonna get over him for a long, long time, I might as well fantasize that he'll come bursting through the door to tell me he's been an idiot."

Candace smiled. "He will. Want to know how I know? Ford is not an idiot. That's very clear. So how long can he act like one before coming to his senses?"

Danica laughed, but she was a second away from crying. She wished she had her sister's faith, but after last night, she was out of hope where Ford Dawson was concerned.

Ford was back in his private spot at the Dawson Family Guest Ranch, through the brush and on the short path that led to the river, where he was sure there would be no guests. He'd gotten up way too early, jogged his miles, drank too much coffee, did two loads of laundry and he still had two hours before he had to be at work. He'd barely slept, waking up constantly, thinking about what he'd said to Danica, hating himself for hurting her but unable to move past this point he was stuck in.

Stuck. He'd thought moving home was going to

be about a fresh start, and instead he'd been pulled back into a time warp.

He heard footsteps and scowled, wondering how a guest had unearthed this perfect patch of solitude. The footsteps were coming closer. Dammit. Ford shot up, preparing to leave, but the face that greeted him was his brother, Zeke, a baby carrier on his chest, a pink-capped baby's head visible.

"Hey, this is our secret getaway," Zeke said with a grin.

"It *was* mine."

"Did you used to come here when we were kids? It was the best place to hide. No one ever found me during hide-and-seek."

Ford laughed. "I wouldn't even have thought to look here because I was under the false impression that no one knew it existed but me. That brush at the start looks really thick and wild."

"I have no doubt we all come here and have for decades," Zeke said.

"Lucy asleep?" he asked, gesturing at the baby.

"Yup. We're supposed to be spending the day together but here she is, dead to the world. Some father-daughter day," he said on a laugh.

"How'd you get to this point?" Ford asked. "How did any of you become so comfortable with fatherhood?"

"Well, to be honest, most of us fell for women with babies. So we had to or else."

Ford thought about that. "That damned diary really did a number on me. I can't shake it. I can know all I want that I can be a great dad and husband, but every time I think about either, I think about my mother's entries, and I just can't get past it. It's made me not want any part of a future with anyone. Particularly children."

"So you're just going to let Danica move on to someone else? The love of your life?"

"I already told her to move on. For all I know she's matched herself on a date with someone who's ready to get married and have kids."

"You know, Ford, it took me a while to get Dad and everything we went through out of my head and away from my relationship with Molly. I also thought I didn't want kids. But there comes a point where something forces the issue. And choosing nothing over everything is really dumb, bro. Dad is gone. Your mother is gone. The past is gone. You want to spend the next five years alone, stewing over a bad marriage that had nothing to do with you?"

"No, I don't. But I can't seem to get past it. That's the problem."

"But that problem is you, Ford. You've always

been our hero. We know where those little match-
box cars came from on our birthdays every year,
supposedly from Dad. We know where the bagged
lunches came from when he told us to scram from
the house for the days we were visiting. The kid,
the teenager, who looked out for his five younger
siblings isn't looking out for himself? That's hard
to swallow."

Ford gave something of a shrug. "You know
why I left Bear Ridge, Zeke. I have the same feeling of dread."

"I do know why you left. Because you were
afraid you'd have to arrest your own father. And
he baited you to do it at least twice—I was there
one time, so I know. But Ford, like I just said, Dad
is gone. The past is over. And Danica is here. A
happy future is here. The five of us did it and if
any of us could, it's you."

"Great, now I feel like I'm falling down in my
siblings' estimation." He leaned his head back and
let out a harsh breath.

"Never, Ford. Never. I get it. I'm just saying
you're stronger than this."

Ford looked at Zeke, and he would have pulled
him in for a hug if the baby wasn't in the way. He
didn't feel stronger than the swirl of leaves moving in the April breeze.

"Don't give up happiness for bad memories," Zeke said. "That would be the worst thing you could do."

"I'd better get to the PD," Ford said.

"Ah, classic deflection. A business tactic I'm well used to."

"Nah, I really am due there. But I'll promise you that I'll think about what you said. You had some pretty intense points."

"But more importantly, I'm *right*."

Ford grinned and headed through the brush, his mind echoing with all his brother had said.

Breakfast with Junie had been wonderful. She'd been terrific with baby Brandy, and she and Candace had connected easily. They hadn't talked about their mom or the rest of the family; they were forging their own bonds, their own relationships. Junie had made an excuse for them to leave after an hour, and Danica knew her cousin needed to go slowly, that too much too soon would feel invasive after decades of nothing. They made a plan to get together every week, and Junie was looking forward to getting to know Trudy, who was close to her age. Now, as Danica got ready for work in her bedroom, she felt so hopeful about the future where her family was concerned.

She was slipping into her favorite four-inch tweed pumps when Candace burst into her room, waving what looked like a matchmaking form.

"I know you probably don't want to even think about dating, but I got curious about the matchmaking requests so was nosing through and I think I found the perfect guy for you." She held up the profile, and Danica recognized a dentist she'd dated already, back before she met Ford.

"Yup, we went out already. He talked nonstop about his ex-girlfriend and asked if I'd ever considered breast implants. The date lasted twelve minutes before I feigned a headache. No, wait, I didn't even have to fake it—he gave me one."

Candace offered a gentle smile. "That's the problem—so many people sound great on paper, but a list of traits mean nothing till you meet."

"Anyway, like you said, I won't be dating for a while. I'm content to just put couples together. Mayor Abbot told me I'm responsible for three engagements."

Her sister sat on the edge of her bed. "You look so sad, Dani. Is there anything I can do? I thought I'd try cheer and possibilities, but what you really need is time and hugs and old movies. Don't think I'm one of those women who ditches her sister for her boyfriend, either. If you want a movie night or to go to Prairie City and shop and just get away from Bear Ridge, I'm there. Anytime."

Danica leaned over and pulled Candace into a hug. "I love you."

"I love you, too." She looked at Danica, biting her lip. "What can I do for you today? I've got my interview at noon but after we can go for the soup and sandwich combo at the diner for lunch and then mani-pedis?"

"Lunch today is a work birthday party, but I appreciate it, Candace. And I will definitely take you up on those movie nights. You must be so excited for this afternoon's fun outing with Jasper and Brandy."

Her sister's eyes lit up. "I feel really hopeful about everything. I'm pretty crazy about Jasper Fields."

Danica smiled. "It's the best feeling in the world. To be in love." Even if hurts like hell, she added silently.

Her sister seemed to pick that up. "I didn't think Ford Dawson was an idiot, but he must be," Candace said. "Just a matter of time before the right guy makes his way into your life. And then it'll be too late for Ford."

"Yeah," Danica agreed, but she could hardly believe that. Who could top Ford? Who could she love more than she loved him? She was never sure about the concept of a soul mate, that there was one person who was *your person*. But Ford was that for her. And she believed she was that for him.

"Sorry, this is hardly making you feel better. Want me to bring you some coffee?"

"Yes, actually. Thanks, Candace."

Candace gave Danica a gentle pat on her arm and then left the room.

She might not have the man she loved, but she did have her sister.

Ford had just gotten back in his car at the ranch gatehouse when his cell phone rang. Junie Maywood. He'd programmed it in a year and half ago when he'd first gone to see her about the map and the diary.

"Hi, Junie," he said, wondering what this could be about.

"I can't talk long because I'm about to do major spring cleaning of my house now that I'll be having company on a regular basis. I never have people over, and now I'm suddenly a hostess with company yesterday and this morning."

He could hear the happiness in her voice. "I know Danica was looking forward to coming over with her sister and the baby for breakfast," he said.

He'd learned long ago not to rush people in talking; they would when they were ready and then they'd really let loose. In his line of work, he needed motor mouths.

"Listen, I couldn't say anything with Danica over since I don't know what's between you two," she said, "but I wanted to tell you something your mother said. A few years after she left your father and you two were more settled."

He took a deep breath, not sure what he was about to hear.

"She was over helping me weed, and you were running around with the dog, not the ones I have now, of course. And she looked at you and she said, 'Junie, you know what my deepest wish is for Ford?' And I said, 'No, what?' And she said, 'For him to have a beautiful love story. To find the right person for the right reasons.' Isn't that lovely? And then she added something I'll never forget. She said, 'Bo and I set a terrible example for him, but he's going to steer the family ship in a different direction. To all good things.' She was so happy when she said all that. Like she was setting your course by putting it out there."

He sat down hard on the kitchen chair, his mother's words echoing in his head, entering his heart. He could feel them seeping inside his chest. *Steer the family ship in a different direction.*

His siblings had done that.

*To find the right person for the right reasons.*

He thought about the diary, the torn-up page. His mother had known she'd planned to stay with Bo for the wrong reasons. But she'd come out of that marriage still believing in love, in change— for herself. And she had changed her life.

Why hadn't he realized that before? She'd gone back to school. She'd gotten a decent-paying job, and she'd raised Ford with all the good things she'd wanted instilled in him. She'd stayed in town so that he'd have easy access to his dad, despite how terrible their marriage had been. She'd made him what he was with her strength and her big heart.

Man, had he been an idiot.

"I appreciate you telling me all this, Junie. Now *this* was something I needed to know."

"Well, I'd better get to dusting for the next visit," Junie said. "Bye now."

There was a click, and he smiled. *I owe you one, Junie Maywood*, he thought, mentally adding two things to his to-do list after work.

He just hoped he wouldn't be too late.

## Chapter Eighteen

Danica glanced at her phone—5:32 p.m. She sat on the patio in the backyard, a glass of white wine on the table, a bowl of pistachios beside it. The late afternoon was gorgeous and warm, low sixties, the sun still out, and she stretched out on her zero-gravity chair, taking a sip of her wine. Everything inside hurt like hell, but life around her was good and solid and kept her positive.

Candace was still out with Jasper and Brandy and would be till around seven. They'd gone to the petting zoo and then to Prairie City. Candace had texted her photos of the adorable classic teddy bear Jasper had bought for Brandy. Danica immediately envisioned her niece at nine, at fifteen, her teddy bear from Daddy beside her. Yes, she was getting way ahead of herself, but the picture felt true. She could see Candace and Jasper getting married at Christmastime, Brandy toddling down the aisle.

She reached for her folder of matchmaking forms—Mayor Abbott had heaped a new batch on her, now that the crimes-of-vengeance perpetrators had decided to focus on love. The speed dating event was back on for this weekend and she'd need a new partner to help with that and the forms.

A new partner. She didn't want a new anything. She just wanted Ford.

Her phone pinged and she glanced at it, expecting it to be Pauline Abbott to ask if she could drop off more matchmaking requests.

But it was Ford.

He texted: Can we talk face-to-face? Right now?

Don't get your hopes up, she thought. Maybe he's just coming to say he wants to be friends and plans to honor his commitment to the matchmaking and speed dating.

I'm out back, she texted.

He responded: Be there in five.

She took another sip of wine, and suddenly there he was, still in uniform. He looked so gorgeous under the setting sun.

"Junie called me this morning with another story," he said, sitting down on the chair across from hers. "About my mother's hopes for me. That I'd steer the family ship in a new direction—to all good things."

Danica sat up straight. He was not here about matchmaking or speed dating.

"You're all good things, Danica. The diary tore me up, but my mother's words about finding the right person for the right reasons—got right in here," he said, bringing a fist to his chest. "You're the right person for the right reasons. You always were."

Tears stung her eyes and she was too overcome to speak for a moment. She leaned forward and took his hands. "First I ran from you and then you ran from me, and now here we are."

"Here we are." He got down on one knee and took a small velvet box out of his pocket and opened it. A beautiful antique diamond ring twinkled. "I don't want to wait another second to start my life with you, Danica. I love you. Children, no children—all I want is you."

"All I want is you. But I'd like two kids." She stared down at the ring, then at him.

"Will you marry me?" he asked.

She flew into his arms. "Yes. Yes, yes, yes."

He held her tight and kissed her. "We made our own match, after all."

Danica grinned, kissing her fiancé again. Theirs would be a match to last forever.

## *Epilogue*

Just a few days before Christmas, there was a double wedding in the biggest ballroom at the Dawson Family Guest Ranch lodge. Danica and Candace, the two brides, were in the small bridal room putting on finishing touches. They'd covered the something old, the something new and the something blue, but they both realized they'd forgotten "something borrowed."

Danica was about to call Molly to ask for the beautiful gold bangle she wore every day; it had been a gift from Danica for her eighteenth birthday, and Danica liked the idea of borrowing something she'd given her best friend so long ago.

Candace got out her phone to ask Aunt Trudy if she could bring over Brandy's jeweled baby barrette; she planned to put it in her own hair, which sounded very sweet to Danica.

But a knock sounded at the door, and Judith Dunbar came in. The sisters had fully expected their parents to come to the wedding; even Judith couldn't have made an excuse for something so special—the double wedding of her daughters. Over the past several months, Danica and Candace had made weekly calls to their parents, and though it had taken Judith a while to warm up and open up, she had quite a bit. She'd been touched that Danica had asked her to play the wedding march for their trek down the aisle, Judith was a very talented pianist.

Judith was wearing a beautiful pale blue gown, her blond hair in a shiny bob. "I have something for both of you." She reached into her little beaded purse and pulled out two pairs of diamond stud earrings. "These were my mother's and I'd love it if you wore them. Unless you have your heart set on earrings already."

Danica glanced at Candace and smiled.

"Mom, I was about to borrow my baby daughter's rhinestone barrette to have something borrowed, so you saved me from baby wear."

Judith laughed and handed each of her daughters the earrings.

Danica put hers on and admired how they twinkled in the mirror. "I feel like Nana is here with us now."

Judith hugged each of them and then left, her eyes misty.

"Wonders will never cease," Candace said, turning left and right to see her sparkling earlobes. "Was that our mother?"

"Everything is so different. We wanted it to be and so it is."

Candace seemed to think about that for a second. "You're right. We're both marrying the men we love. I'm getting my degree in early childhood education. You're taking classes in interior design. Our mother and her cousin are both actually in the same room at the same time and not killing each other."

Their mother wasn't thrilled that her daughters had gotten close with Junie, but she'd accepted it. The cousins had been forced into the same room twice in the past several months for wedding festivities, and though they got along like oil and water, there they both were—for family. And that was family for you.

Danica smiled. "Here's to us," she said, lifting the two glasses of champagne that Molly had brought in earlier. They each took a sip and then immediately fixed their lipstick.

Danica peered out the door into the ballroom, which was full of guests who were mingling over champagne. All the Dawsons were there—Noah, Sara, and their year-old twins Annabel and Chance; Daisy, Harrison, and their baby Tony; Axel, Sadie, their toddler Danny and their baby Jasmine; Rex, Maisey and one-year-old Chloe; and Zeke, Molly and little Lucy. What no one knew, except for Danica and Ford, was that another little Dawson was about to join the family, helping to steer the family ship into new directions. She was pregnant, just six weeks at this point, and she and Ford were keeping that under wraps until she was out of the first trimester. Danica had never known she could feel this happy, this excited, this full of hope. She was going to have a baby.

As a lovely classical piece of music began—Judith on piano—the guests began moving to their seats and Danica and Candace's father came over in his tuxedo, all smiles. Their dad was a quiet person, but they could both see how touched he was to have been asked to escort his daughters down the aisle.

As she wrapped her arm around her father's, Candace on the other side of him, she looked down the aisle at her waiting groom, and his expression almost made her cry. He looked so happy, so handsome.

She made her way down the red carpet, her gaze on Ford, the two of them the only people who knew that their baby-to-be was attending their parents' wedding. A brand-new family was forming, a new beginning forged.

\* \* \* \* \*

# MILLS & BOON

## Coming next month

### TUSCAN SUMMER WITH THE BILLIONAIRE
Susan Meier

It wasn't right. He was feeling things he wasn't allowed
to feel, definitely mixing business with pleasure, when
he knew better.

He shook his head. "I could virtually run our multi-
billion-dollar conglomerate in my sleep, and your simple
family business is breaking all my rules, making me
crazy."

She shrugged. Her lips turned up into a smile that
stole his breath and made his blood race.

He still held her hand. They stood only a few inches
apart. The full moon smiled down on them while the
vineyard that was at the center of their problems rustled
in the breeze.

But she was smiling. Amused by him.

The humor of it struck him and his own lips rose.
"This is crazy."

"There's that word again. You use crazy a lot...espe-
cially about yourself."

She really was funny. Fun. He felt like he was getting
a glimpse of her as she really was, maybe as she had
been before their employee embezzled.

With their gazes locked, everything inside him
slowed to a crawl. Warmth suffused him, along with a
yearning so pure he couldn't fight it. He inched closer.

The connection between them rose, swelling around him, urging him even closer.

"I think I'm going to kiss you."

Her eyes didn't even flicker with surprise. And why would they? They'd been attracted since the second they'd laid eyes on each other.

"You shouldn't."

Her voice was a soft whisper that skipped along his spine, but she didn't move. Didn't step back. Held his gaze.

Expectantly.

The hum of whatever it was that buzzed between them drowned out his common sense and reasoning. Simple curiosity filled him, as desire surged in his blood and temptation promised fulfillment, pleasure enough to make it worth the risk.

He lowered his head and kissed her.

*Continue reading*
**TUSCAN SUMMER WITH THE BILLIONAIRE**
Susan Meier

*Available next month*
www.millsandboon.co.uk

# COMING SOON!

We really hope you enjoyed reading this book.
If you're looking for more romance, be sure to
head to the shops when new books are
available on

# Thursday 29th April

# LET'S TALK
## *Romance*

For exclusive extracts, competitions
and special offers, find us online:

**f** facebook.com/millsandboon

**𝕏** @MillsandBoon

**◉** @MillsandBoonUK

**Get in touch on 01413 063232**

For all the latest titles coming soon, visit
## millsandboon.co.uk/nextmonth

# MILLS & BOON

## THE HEART OF ROMANCE

---

## A ROMANCE FOR EVERY READER

---

**MODERN**

Prepare to be swept off your feet by sophisticated, sexy and seductive heroes, in some of the world's most glamourous and romanti locations, where power and passion collide.

**HISTORICAL**

Escape with historical heroes from time gone by. Whether your passion for wicked Regency Rakes, muscled Vikings or rugged Highlanders, awa the romance of the past.

**MEDICAL**

Set your pulse racing with dedicated, delectable doctors in the high-pres sure world of medicine, where emotions run high and passion, comfort love are the best medicine.

*True Love*

Celebrate true love with tender stories of heartfelt romance, from the rush of falling in love to the joy a new baby can bring, and a focus on t emotional heart of a relationship.

*Desire*

Indulge in secrets and scandal, intense drama and plenty of sizzling hot action with powerful and passionate heroes who have it all: wealth, statu good looks…everything but the right woman.

**HEROES**

Experience all the excitement of a gripping thriller, with an intense romance at its heart. Resourceful, true-to-life women and strong, fearless face danger and desire - a killer combination!

---

To see which titles are coming soon, please visit

## millsandboon.co.uk/nextmonth

*t might just be true love...*

# MILLS & BOON
## HISTORICAL

### Awaken the romance of the past

Escape with historical heroes from time
gone by. Whether your passion is for
wicked Regency Rakes, muscled Viking
warriors or rugged Highlanders, indulge
your fantasies and awaken the
romance of the past.